KU-675-671

SPECIAL MESSAGE TO READERS

THE ULVERSCROFT FOUNDATION
(registered UK charity number 264873)
was established in 1972 to provide funds for research, diagnosis and treatment of eye diseases. Examples of major projects funded by the Ulverscroft Foundation are:-

- The Children's Eye Unit at Moorfields Eye Hospital, London
- The Ulverscroft Children's Eye Unit at Great Ormond Street Hospital for Sick Children
- Funding research into eye diseases and treatment at the Department of Ophthalmology, University of Leicester
- The Ulverscroft Vision Research Group, Institute of Child Health
- Twin operating theatres at the Western Ophthalmic Hospital, London
- The Chair of Ophthalmology at the Royal Australian College of Ophthalmologists

You can help further the work of the Foundation by making a donation or leaving a legacy. Every contribution is gratefully received. If you would like to help support the Foundation or require further information, please contact:

THE ULVERSCROFT FOUNDATION
The Green, Bradgate Road, Anstey
Leicester LE7 7FU, England
Tel: (0116) 236 4325

website: www.foundation.ulverscroft.com

As the fourth of six children, Debby Holt discovered at an early age the joys of losing herself in a brilliant book. After graduating from the University of Exeter with a history degree, she taught in a boys' comprehensive school, then gave up full-time teaching when her twin sons were born, and started writing when her fifth child began primary school. She has had over 65 short stories published at home and abroad, and has written seven novels in eleven years. She lives in Bath.

You can discover more about the author at www.debbyholt.co.uk

THE DANGERS OF FAMILY SECRETS

Family secrets are like moths in cash-mere. They dig themselves in and eat their way out . . . Genealogist Freya Cameron has the perfect life. A devoted husband of nearly thirty years and career-driven, successful twin daughters. But what if it's all a lie? So skilled at excavating her clients' family histories, Freya has no idea why her own family are so cold towards her. They know something she doesn't. But some secrets are better not left untold as the years pass, attitudes harden, and assumptions become accepted reality. Freya's family don't speak about what happened. They are determined to make her pay for what she did. But when the truth finally emerges, their lives will be shaken to the core . . .

Books by *Debby Holt*
Published by *Ulverscroft:*

THE EX-WIFE'S SURVIVAL GUIDE
THE TROUBLE WITH MARRIAGE
THE SOULMATE

DEBBY HOLT

THE DANGERS OF FAMILY SECRETS

Complete and Unabridged

CHARNWOOD
Leicester

First published in Great Britain in 2017 by
Accent Press Ltd
London

First Charnwood Edition
published 2019
by arrangement with
Accent Press Ltd
London

The moral right of the author has been asserted

The story contained within this book is a work of fiction. Names and characters are the product of the author's imagination and any resemblance to actual persons, living or dead, is entirely coincidental.

Copyright © 2017 by Debby Holt
All rights reserved

A catalogue record for this book is available from the British Library.

ISBN 978–1–4448–4122–0

Published by
F. A. Thorpe (Publishing)
Anstey, Leicestershire

Set by Words & Graphics Ltd.
Anstey, Leicestershire
Printed and bound in Great Britain by
T. J. International Ltd., Padstow, Cornwall

This book is printed on acid-free paper

For my friend Simon Lansdown.

Acknowledgements

Thanks to Doctors May Erskine, Audrey Ryan, and Nina Anderson for their advice and expertise. Also, thanks to brilliant holiday companions and fellow researchers, Fiona and Richard Mottram. And last but not least, thanks to Gina and Richard Pelham for introducing me to the Scottish Borders.

'The worst families are those in which the members never really speak their minds to one another; they maintain an atmosphere of unreality, and everyone always lives in an atmosphere of suppressed ill-feeling.'

Walter Bagehot

1

Something happened at the balloon debate. Freya had no idea what it was, but over the next four months, she was increasingly convinced that whatever it was that *had* happened, started there.

She hadn't even wanted to take part. Vanity had been her downfall. When she turned down the invitation, Dulcie Makepeace had lowered her voice to a confidential whisper. 'We need some star quality on the panel,' she explained, 'and I immediately thought of you.'

Later, Freya grumbled to Felix that the only reason Dulcie approached her was because she needed a token woman.

'In that case,' Felix said, 'make a virtue of it. Choose someone who can make a rousing feminist argument for staying in the balloon.'

It was a good idea and there were any number of admirable role models. She could be Florence Nightingale or Boudicca or that woman who pioneered birth control whose name she could never remember. But they were predictable choices. They were precisely the sort of women her audience would expect her to choose.

Freya did not want to be predictable. She was queuing at the post office when the idea came to her. It would be difficult, it would be unexpected, and it would be more high-brow than Dulcie anticipated or wanted. So much the better, Freya thought. She still smarted from the ease with which Dulcie had persuaded her to perform.

She decided not to tell Felix beforehand. It would be hard to explain what she was trying to do; Felix would offer a number of sensible suggestions as to why she shouldn't do it; she would be discouraged and she didn't *want* to be. She felt she was creating something difficult and fragile and fascinating. The slightest criticism would blow it all away.

On the evening of the event she left Felix eating chicken salad — she was far too nervous to eat a thing — and went upstairs to change. She put on what she called her Glamour Outfit — a figure-hugging black dress and a matching bolero jacket with a fake-fur collar. She made up her face, sprayed her neck liberally with perfume and stared at herself in the mirror. At her age there was a fine line between dressing to make an impression and looking like a Joan Collins wannabe. She had forgotten how short the dress was.

She applied a final coating of lip gloss to her mouth and went back down to the kitchen where Felix was loading the dishwasher. She put her hands on her hips, extended one leg in front of the other and adopted her Lauren Bacall look, a stance she had frequently plagiarised in her modelling days. 'What do you think?' she asked.

Felix straightened his back and scrutinised her. 'I think,' he said thoughtfully, 'that every man in the room will want to take you home tonight. I know I will.'

'Seriously. You don't think I'm mutton dressed as lamb?'

'If you are,' Felix said, 'then you're very sexy mutton. You look beautiful.'

'Oh Felix!' Freya smiled. She *had*, long ago, been beautiful. Now that she was middle-aged she could see that. When she looked at old photos, she admired the tiny waist, the long legs, the blonde hair and the cheekbones. The waist had long since thickened, the legs were defaced by gristle-like knees and thin blue veins, and the blonde hair posed a constant dilemma: should any woman over fifty have long hair?

The miracle was that Felix saw none of this. When they first got together, he described them as Beauty and the Beast. He had had tiny green eyes, a large if indeterminate nose, untidy short hair and a small scruffy beard and moustache. All of these features, apart from the beard and moustache, were still in evidence. The addition of laughter lines around the eyes, broadened shoulders and a bulkier chest provoked an irresistible comparison with a rumpled teddy bear. If Felix was a Beast, he was an endearingly attractive one.

In the car, Freya checked she had her notes in her bag, took a few deep breaths and gazed out of the window. She loved the woods at this time of year. The green leaves on the trees continued to be a novelty and, even though it was almost June, there was a still-flourishing carpet of bluebells and pale primroses.

The first time Felix had brought her to see the cottage, she had been taken aback by its rural solitude. Now she couldn't imagine living in London again. Here, their nearest neighbours

3

were a quarter of a mile down the lane and, as they passed Pam's house, Freya noticed that her red Renault Clio was gone. Freya felt a slight easing of tension. Pam was one of the best by-products of moving here. She was loyal, kind, and utterly reliable.

'She must have left already,' Freya said. 'I asked her to sit near the front. I need a friendly face to look at.'

'I'm a friendly face,' Felix said.

'You're *too* friendly. You'll be nervous for me and that'll make *me* nervous.'

'Rubbish. You're brilliant at these things.'

They were coming into Darrowbridge now. Felix drove past the railway station and then the garage. Freya stared into her bag to check she had her phone. 'I told the twins I was dreading this,' she said. 'I thought they might have rung.' She felt a little hollow-chested. She should have eaten something earlier.

Her phone gave two little bleats and Freya took it out of her bag and studied it.

'Let me guess,' Felix said. 'It's from one of the girls?'

' "Off to Scotland tomorrow! Hurrah! Good luck tonight, love Tess." Now I feel bad.'

'Oh, ye of little faith,' Felix murmured.

Freya sighed. 'Tess does love Scotland. She'd move there like a shot if a job came up.'

'I rang Ma to wish her happy birthday the other night. She's so excited about Tess's visit.'

'They've always been close. I hope I'll be close to *my* grandchildren. If I ever get any.'

'Of course you will. People take longer to

4

settle down these days, that's all.'

'Most twenty-seven-year-old women have at least had a *few* long-term relationships.' Freya swallowed hard as Felix turned into the town hall car park. 'Oh God, it's almost full.' She watched him slide the car into one of the few remaining places. 'I wish it was all over.' She opened her door. 'Dulcie told me to go in by the side entrance. Wish me luck.'

'You don't need it,' Felix told her. 'You'll be terrific. You look terrific.' He switched off the engine and reached across to kiss her mouth. 'I'm very proud of you.'

'Tell me that when it's finished,' she said. She climbed out of the car, straightened her dress, hoisted her bag over her shoulder and went through the side door into a room with walls covered in alphabet posters. Her four fellow-panellists were there and, as she accepted a glass of wine from Dulcie, one of them, an ex-editor of the *Darrowbridge Gazette*, came over and kissed her cheek.

'Freya, my darling, you look good enough to eat!'

If the girls were here they would roll their eyes but Freya could never resist a compliment.

'Thank you, Roland, I hope I've not overdone the party look.'

'I love your party look,' he assured her. He enjoyed his reputation as a ladies' man and took great care of his teeth, which were now fully in evidence, in all their radiant regularity.

Dulcie's phone let out a shrill screech and she clapped her hands together. 'That's my alarm.

5

It's time we went in.'

And so, in they went. Freya felt a flutter of apprehension as she took her seat and noted with gratitude that Pam sat right in the middle of the front row. The hall was almost full, a testament to the formidable organizational powers of Dulcie, who stood up and waited for the excited chatter to subside.

'Tonight,' she proclaimed, 'we have five local celebrities who have given up their time to bring you this entertainment. Each of them will take on the role of someone they admire. Each will give a brief talk in which he or she will try to persuade you to keep him or her in the balloon. Your job is to vote one of them off. The remaining four will then speak again, you will vote another one off and so it goes on until only the victor remains. So, without further ado, we will begin the proceedings with our first celebrity. Most of you will know her as Freya Eliza Cameron, one of *Darrowbridge Life*'s favourite columnists. Every month, she gives us regular insights into the complexities of ancestral research. An experienced genealogist, her website, *RevealingFamilies.co.uk* is extremely popular and I would recommend it to you all. Ladies and gentlemen, I give you Freya Eliza Cameron!'

Freya stood up and acknowledged the applause with a modest smile. She was aware of the adrenalin charging round her brain, firing up synapses and sharpening her memory. This happened every time she spoke in public. Beforehand, she would feel nervous and unwell, but as soon as she started to perform she'd put aside her notes and enjoy herself.

'Before I start,' she said, 'I have an admission to make.' She shut her eyes for a few seconds. 'I am . . . ' she paused for dramatic effect ' . . . an unfaithful wife.'

There was a slight, nervous rattle of laughter, a reaction Freya had anticipated. 'I am Madame Bovary,' she continued, 'and I want you to keep me in the balloon despite my reputation as a fallen woman. Some of you may have read my story as told by Gustave Flaubert. He is famous for his insights into the female mind and for his compassion towards me. I can tell you now: his reputation is undeserved. I am the victim of a stitch-up!'

A mobile in the front row exploded into action. Its ringtone, the first few chords of 'Under My Thumb', provoked a ripple of laughter in the audience. The owner, a middle-aged man with a limp ponytail, muttered an apology and turned off his phone. Freya threw him an understanding smile, an Oscar-winning performance in itself, and took a deep breath.

'Flaubert begins the story — my story — with a description of my husband as a little boy, jeered at by his schoolmates because he has been given a ridiculous hat to wear by his mother.' She stopped to glance around the room. 'Do you see what Flaubert does? Despite the fact that Charles grows up to be a dangerously inadequate doctor and an oafish husband and lover, he remains a figure of sympathy because of that first childish episode. The odds are stacked against me from the start!'

Freya's idea had seemed so clever when she'd planned it. Now she was aware of a big, shimmering question mark hovering over the heads of the audience and, worse, it was hovering over her head too. She had wanted to reclaim Madame Bovary as a victim, a woman trapped in a loveless marriage and starved of romance. She knew as she stood on the stage that she'd lost her audience with the story of little Charles in his ridiculous hat. Everyone felt sorry for children who were bullied. *She* felt sorry for children who were bullied. Felix was right. She should have gone for an obvious heroine, someone like Florence Nightingale or Boudicca or the woman who pioneered birth control.

She struggled on, trying to paint Madame Bovary as a universal symbol of downtrodden women, but when she finally finished she knew she was as confused as everyone else. She had wanted to portray Flaubert as a misogynist and instead, she had ended up supporting his silly, self-absorbed creation. She felt she could weep.

The applause was polite. Freya attached a calm smile to her face and let her eyes wander over the audience, her expression only faltering when they settled on her husband. Felix was not clapping, he was not even looking at her. He was staring down at his phone, his attention fully engaged on the small screen in his hands. Freya wanted to wave her arms and shout out, 'Felix, what are you doing? I'm here! I'm humiliated! I need your support!'

The rest of the evening was a gruelling ordeal.

Freya listened to a wise-cracking Casanova, a sing-along Walt Disney, an unlikely Sir Winston Churchill and a hip-swerving Elvis Presley. Freya was the first to get voted off by a large majority. Elvis Presley won. Freya knew she had entirely misjudged the nature of the evening. She had come across as humourless, inarticulate and, worst of all, dull.

When the event finished at last, Freya made her excuses, found Felix and murmured that she had to go *now*. In the car, as he negotiated his way out of the car park, she broke the silence with a loud groan. 'I was a disaster,' she said.

She waited for Felix to do what he did so well: reassure her, make her laugh, put things into some sort of perspective. When he didn't respond, she glanced across at him. 'Was I really terrible?'

He kept his eyes fixed on the road. 'Perhaps your speech was a little too subtle. I couldn't understand what you were trying to say.'

She waved a hand in the air. 'Oh I can't bear to think about it. I totally failed to get my point across.' The truth was, Freya could no longer remember what her point was supposed to be. She folded her arms together. 'And *you* were looking at your phone. You hate people looking at their phones!'

'I'd forgotten to turn it off,' Felix said. 'I had a text and I was trying to switch it off.'

'Did you even listen to my speech?'

'Yes. Yes, of course I did.'

'I feel so stupid,' Freya raged. 'That's the last time I will ever take part in one of Dulcie's

9

fundraising evenings. Not that she'll ask me again after this.'

In her bag, her phone made itself heard. Freya read out the message. ' "Good luck, Mum, love Anna." ' She shuddered. 'At least the girls weren't here to witness my humiliation.'

'Freya,' Felix protested. 'You're being melodramatic. You weren't *that* bad.'

'Thank you,' Freya said. 'That's very encouraging.'

Back at home, she stood in the hall and made a face at her reflection in the mirror. She turned in time to catch Felix staring at her with an expression of almost clinical disinterest, as if he wasn't sure who she was. It disconcerted her. It was unnerving. She said, uncertainly, 'I can see what you're thinking.'

'Can you?' He seemed surprised, almost guilty.

'I could see it in your face. *How could Freya get it so wrong?*'

'Don't be silly.' He took off his jacket and hung it on the coat-stand. 'I think I'll watch the news. Do you want some tea?'

'Only if you're making some. I shall go to bed and read my book.'

When she woke in the morning, Felix had already left. She couldn't remember a time when he'd set off to Bristol without first saying goodbye to her. She presumed he must be preoccupied by something at work.

She had planned to spend the morning at her laptop but it was impossible to study dusty old census records when she felt so frazzled. She had made a fool of herself last night and she had no one to blame but herself. She should try to stop thinking about it. She was aware that, these days, her emotions were dangerously incontinent. A brief, bland call from Anna could reduce her to tears followed by an afternoon's soul-search as to how she had failed her children. A new liver spot on her hand plunged her into a gloom accompanied by sinister presentiments of mortality. Middle age was a frightening place for anyone cursed with the sin of vanity.

Vanity, she thought suddenly, had been responsible for Felix. How could she resist a man whose first glance was one of startled adoration, particularly since his shyness had forced *her* to do the running? She remembered the odd way he'd looked at her last night, and then rolled her eyes. She would get nothing done if she carried on like this.

Freya opened her top left-hand drawer and pulled out her perfect displacement-activity project. In just over three months, she and Felix would celebrate their thirtieth wedding anniversary. Six weeks ago, demoralised by an inconclusive trip to the National Archives in Kew, she had brought out a new pink folder and labelled it 'Anniversary Stuff'. She had selected a possible date for a party, one close to Christmas when Felix's mother would be with them. This morning she would spend a half-hour composing a speech.

She pushed her laptop away, reached for her pad of A4 paper and picked up her pen. She imagined the sitting room, full of family and

11

friends all staring expectantly at her . . .

Thank you for coming here tonight. Thank you for helping Felix and me to celebrate our anniversary. And forgive me for making a speech. I know it's self-indulgent but you are a captive audience and I'd like to say a few words about marriage.

First of all, I like it, obviously. Otherwise, we wouldn't be having this party. But actually, now I'm so old, I do find it odd that I went into marriage and motherhood with such blithe optimism.

Motherhood is easier to understand. You feel broody. You have a baby — in my case you have two at once — and you love them. They love you. And then they're teenagers and they want nothing to do with you. Even when they're adults, you're still low on their list of priorities.

Marriage seems equally straightforward at first. You fall in love with a man, he falls for you and you marry. Then you discover there are times when he irritates you. Even more outrageous, you know there are times when you irritate him. You can catch him staring at you like you're a stranger and . . .

Oh dear God! What a load of self-pitying, pompous rubbish! Freya wrote in big capitals 'DO NOT TRY TO WRITE SOMETHING POSITIVE WHEN YOU FEEL NEGATIVE!' Then, reaching for her felt-tip pen, she drew thick lines over everything she'd written. She tore out the piece of paper and put it in the folder which she returned at once to her drawer. What was wrong with her today?

Action was imperative. No to census records; no to anniversary speeches; and double no to Madame Bovary. She glanced at the window. The weather was lovely. She would go into the garden, which at this time of year had exploded into its usual overwhelming fecundity. She would arm herself with her trowel and her fork and she would decimate the weeds. On her return to the house, she would go back to her census records in the happy knowledge that the balloon debate would soon be forgotten. And as for Felix's odd expression last night, it was ridiculous to dwell on something so silly. He was probably just tired and fed up. She couldn't blame him for that.

2

'We need 2 talk.'

When had Richard learnt to *text?*

Tess Cameron sat on the steps of the stone Mercat Cross, the hood of her anorak tied tightly under her chin, her hands already cold without their gloves. She stared intently at the small screen as if it would provide an answer. Richard was the only man she knew who didn't have a smartphone or a tablet. She wasn't even sure he knew about Facebook. The text was so incongruous, like Prince Charles wearing leather trousers.

'We need 2 talk,' he said, but no, they absolutely didn't. They — *he* — had talked for England. He had been devastated, apologetic and awkward, and then defensive, angry and outraged. The words had kept coming and she'd tried to apologise — it was *her* fault, she'd been taken by surprise, she'd lashed out in panic when he lunged at her. He *had* lunged — she would always think of him now as Richard the Lunger — but she hadn't meant to hit him; his chin had got in the way of her fist and she was *sorry.* He hadn't tried to listen, his words kept crushing her like a steamroller: *violent, disproportionate, extraordinary, psychotic, aberration.*

And yes, she supposed, her reaction had been disproportionate. She was sufficiently aware of her oddness only ever to have confided in three

14

people, two of whom she no longer saw. Rachel, the first, had been her flatmate and a close friend since university days in Durham. At first, Rachel had compared Tess's problem to a fear of death. Her sister, she said, had been obsessed with her own mortality since early childhood but could now go for at least three days without dwelling on it. Rachel's conclusion was that Tess would grow out of her fear of sex. In the months after that first conversation, Rachel would occasionally ask, 'How's the fear of sex coming along?' and Tess would say, 'It's still there, thanks for asking.'

Rachel, ever the optimist, assured Tess that one day she'd meet a man who would be so right that Tess would *want* to have sex. This seemed highly unlikely. She was extremely fond of Richard, but when he lunged at her on Thursday evening, she'd felt nothing but terror. And now, as a result, she had lost a good friend.

Her long-planned trip to Scotland could not have come at a better time. Tess had cherished for some years a secret fantasy, a glorious scenario that, in her more positive moments, she really believed might come true. She would finish her PhD in London, turn it into a biography of Sir Walter Scott which, for reasons currently unclear, the whole world would wish to buy. Every university in the country would clamour for her services and she would graciously bestow them on Edinburgh. She would move up to Scotland, buy a small terraced cottage in Melrose and commute to Edinburgh in her new little car — a Mini or a convertible

Golf, either would be more than acceptable.

The cottage was so real she could see it. It was on a short cobbled lane that led nowhere. It had one of those front doors that were horizontally partitioned across the middle, and the top part would be fully opened in order to let in the streaming sunlight. On dark winter days, she would sit by her fire, sipping cocoa — a dubious detail since she didn't even *like* cocoa but it was a word that evoked warmth and safety and comfort. On the long summer evenings, she would roam across the hills, absorbing the peace and the beauty of the place, so at odds with its history of battles and massacres. London would soon be a memory and the Border country would be her home.

In the meantime, she had to make do with the occasional visit. It had taken her nine hours and ten minutes to travel up on the coach from Victoria Station to Melrose and as far as she was concerned it was worth every minute. At nine o'clock that morning she had left London with its chaotic traffic, its anxious commuters, its grimy buildings and its billboards promoting the increasingly unreachable rewards of financial success. And now here she was, in her black jeans, her polo-neck jumper and her red anorak, sitting on the steps of the ancient stone cross in the wide market square at Melrose. She dropped her phone in her bag, put on her gloves, and watched two elderly women chatting with great animation while their pets — identical white poodles — circled busily in impotent attempts to sniff each other's rear end.

Melrose was as different from London as Heaven was from Hell. Melrose was a small town with no traffic jams and no taxi drivers hooting angrily at wayward cyclists and lumbering buses. Melrose had no tower blocks or huge, anonymous offices with sad, anonymous employees. Melrose had slow, sedate cars that stopped unquestioningly to let the women with their poodles cross the road. It had the soft sandstone ruins of Melrose Abbey with its seemingly random foundation stones scattered on the lawn around it. It had a friendly high street that opened into the generous square where Tess now waited. It had rugby fields and trees and quiet streets with terraced houses, and bungalows with fenced gardens. It had, on every horizon, undulating green hills dappled with purple heather and darker green copses and, best of all, it had pure Scottish air. Tess could almost feel it purging her pores of the last vestiges of London.

Her phone went and, pulling off her gloves again, she took it out of her bag.

'Hi, Tess.' Her sister's voice sounded breathless. 'Is it today you're in Scotland?'

Anna's voice always sounded breathless on the phone. She was not the sort of person who liked long, chatty calls — at least, she didn't like them with Tess — and therefore tended to ring while on the move: going into or out of her hospital, in which case her words competed with the sound of ambulance sirens; or walking from one part of the building to another, in which case there would be constant interruptions while she exchanged information with other members of staff.

17

'I arrived a few minutes ago,' Tess told her. 'It's very cold. I'm sitting in the square waiting for Grandma.'

'That's why I rang. I forgot her birthday was on Wednesday. Will you tell her I'm sorry?'

'Can't you tell her yourself?'

'Have you called the Commune lately? I've tried three times this week and it just rings and rings. Give her my love and tell her as soon as I can get hold of a car, I'll come up and see her.'

'I'm sure she'll be impressed.'

'Don't be sarcastic, Tess, it doesn't suit you. You know coaches make me sick and train fares are exorbitant. It's Grandma's fault for living somewhere that's insanely inaccessible. I must go. Have a good holiday.'

'I'm not here for a holiday. I'm here to do research.'

'Yeah, right. Have a good time and kiss Sir Walter for me.'

Tess put her phone back in her bag. She could imagine Anna scurrying after a patient or hailing colleagues and engaging them in earnest conversation about some diagnosis. Anna had phenomenal energy. Tess supposed it must be an essential requirement for a doctor.

The fact that she and Anna were twins was a never-ending mystery to Tess. She knew the science. They were the result of two different eggs and two different sperm. It was therefore no surprise that Anna should have big breasts, blue eyes and straight blonde hair while she had what might be politely described as an androgynous figure with green eyes and auburn curls. To be honest, Tess thought, they had little in common apart from once sharing a womb.

At school, Tess excelled in English and History and Art while Anna came top in Science. They were extraordinarily different, no more so than in their attitude to the Borders. For Anna, the place was cold and dull and, 'It doesn't even have a proper cinema!' Tess must ask her sometime what an improper one might look like.

She saw Grandma approaching the square in her antique Ford Escort, sitting bolt upright with her face a little too close to the windscreen. Tess stood up and waved.

Grandma was out of her car in a moment. No one would think she was now eighty-three.

'Darling girl, I'm so sorry I'm late, there was a stupid sheep in the middle of the road and I hooted and hooted and it just stared at me! I had to get out and virtually push it back into the field. You must have thought I'd forgotten you . . .'

'I wasn't worried for a moment . . .'

'That's sweet of you to say so, you must be freezing. I can't believe we're in June next week. Let's get you home. Katherine's made one of her casseroles in your honour.'

Tess put her case in the boot and climbed into the car. As always, Grandma had to turn the key in the ignition twice before the engine started, and, as always, she swore under her breath as she did so. Her short wiry hair still had the rogue lock at the back that refused to lie flat. She wore her corduroy trousers, her puffa jacket and one of her Guernsey jumpers. They were almost a uniform.

Tess stretched her arms in front of her. 'Oh Grandma,' she said, 'it is so good to be here again! I wish I could get here more often!'

'Felix rang me on my birthday. He and Freya are definitely coming in October. You should cadge a lift up with them.'

'I will, if it's during my autumn break. I'll talk to Dad. What about this week? Am I all right to borrow your car?'

'Of course. Will you have to go to Edinburgh every day?'

'I might be able to take Friday off. How are all the Communards?'

'They're fine. Sheila had another story published two weeks ago.'

'That's great. What's it about?'

'Two lonely people are brought together by their love of a homeless kitten.' Grandma spoke without expression.

'Oh.' Tess thought for a moment. 'I read that one at Easter.'

'No,' Grandma said. 'In that one, two lonely people are united by their love for a bird with a broken wing. Sheila is a great believer in recycling.' She braked as they reached the crossroads and then turned left out of the town centre. 'You might notice a change in Linda. She has problems with her memory. It's not easy for her or for Derek.'

'I'm so sorry,' Tess said.

'Well.' Grandma shrugged. 'It's one of the perils of getting older.'

Her tone and her body language indicated that the subject was closed. Forthright in so many ways, she had never been a woman to welcome sympathy over matters that truly upset her. Grandpa Philip's great idea had never fully addressed this problem, Tess thought. It was all very well for a group of old friends and relatives to set up house together, but what was to happen when members began to grow frail and die?

Grandpa Philip had been so confident. Retirement had made him restless, he was bored with Surrey and he began to pine for his homeland. On a visit to his brother and sister-in-law in Scotland, he introduced the idea of a commune.

Four years later, the plan came to fruition and nine Communards moved into a house outside Melrose. Grandpa Philip and Grandma brought with them Grandma's oldest friend, Sheila, and their neighbours from Surrey, Linda and Derek. Great-uncle Andrew and Great-aunt Katherine arrived with their friends, the Knoxes. On their first evening in their new home, Grandpa Philip, apparently hale and hearty, celebrated his seventy-fourth birthday.

Three years later, Grandpa Philip was buried in the nearby churchyard. Two years after that, Great-uncle Andrew and Mrs Knox died within four months of each other. For a time, it looked as if the Commune would fall apart. Great-aunt Katherine accepted an invitation to move in with her daughter and son-in-law. Doctor Knox toyed with the idea of renting a small bungalow in Melrose. After a bracing discussion with Grandma, Doctor Knox decided to stay put. Great-aunt Katherine spent two months with her daughter and came to the conclusion that she preferred the company of her peers to that of her son-in-law. No one was told what the son-in-law thought.

And so, like a dignified old ship, battered and buffeted by storms, the Commune slowly righted itself. These days, the six remaining pensioners employed a gardener and a cleaner, and at least three of them continued to drive regularly. But every day they grew older. Tess couldn't bear to think that Linda, who was always so sensible and kind, could be brought down by dementia.

Grandma, clearly determined to change the subject, said, 'I hope you remembered to bring a dress with you.'

'Of course I did. You didn't tell me why I needed to bring one.'

'Our friend, Flora, is having an eighty-fifth birthday party next Friday. Her late husband was a great pal of your grandpa's. I told her it was your last night with us and she said she'd be delighted if you came along too.'

'That's very kind but quite unnecessary. I'm more than happy to stay behind.'

'That's what your great-aunt said.' Grandma paused in order to let the full significance of that statement sink in. 'Of course if you don't want to go, there is no pressure on you to accompany us. Katherine has assured me you'd find the event very dull.'

'I see.' Tess knew what was expected of her. 'Well, I'll be delighted to prove Great-aunt Katherine wrong.'

Grandma released a small, satisfied smile.

'Good girl! Now tell me: how's the PhD coming along?'

This was one of many reasons why Tess loved her grandmother. There were never any coy enquiries about possible boyfriends. Grandma, in her time a probation officer and then a JP, had always believed that it was work that defined a life. The Communard women had all had careers. Great-aunt Katherine had been a teacher; Sheila had been the indispensable secretary to a brilliant but highly strung businessman. Linda had been a highly regarded crossword compiler. Grandma always said she was the cleverest person she knew.

In many ways, Tess thought, their generation had been truer to feminist principles than her own. They'd lived through tough times and valued their independence. Certainly, they never viewed romantic love as an excuse to sidestep careers.

Tess was fond of all of them. She had a number of good friends in London, most of whom discussed their love lives with her. She did sometimes feel like the sole vegetarian in a burger restaurant. The Communards might be vegetarians due to age and circumstance rather than by choice, but at least they proved it was possible to get by without meat.

3

Anna's consultant was small and slight with smooth brown hair neatly tied in a chignon. There were many stories about Miss Diamond, the latest only two months old. She had looked into the labour ward before going out to a dinner party. In a matter of seconds, she took in the distinctive aroma of panic, pulled off her diamond bracelet, calmly called a crash team and performed a Caesarean section before the husband returned from the vending machine. She was a genuine star. Her cool rational tones could often be heard on the *Today* programme and *Woman's Hour*. Her book, *How to Love Your Labour*, was invariably recommended to mothers and midwives.

Miss Diamond was easily the most terrifying person Anna had ever encountered. Her smile could freeze a desert. The first time it was directed at Anna was after Anna's suggestions concerning a pregnant patient's diabetes. Miss Diamond had exposed her pearly white teeth and gazed at Anna with apparent amusement before falling on the diagnosis like a lion feasting on an antelope. After months of continuous put-downs, Anna was beginning to wonder if she was deliberately singled out for regular doses of vitriol.

Today, Miss Diamond, surrounded by her disciples, stood beside the bed of a grossly obese patient whose layers of fat made a palpation of the foetus almost impossible. She gave a little sigh and requested Anna's opinion. Anna took a deep breath and ran through the systematic procedure, to no avail. The baby's cushion was, unsurprisingly, of the extra-large variety.

When she finished, Miss Diamond proceeded, in her quiet, gentle voice, to demolish entirely the medical technique that Anna had set out. 'I wonder, Dr Cameron,' she concluded, 'if you are sure this is where you want to be.'

If this was a film, possibly one starring Kristen Wiig — Anna would *love* to be played by Kristen Wiig — Anna would respond with a scathing, 'What do *you* think, Miss Diamond?' She would turn on her heel and stride out of the hospital, backed by the awestruck, if silent, respect of her peers. Unfortunately, it wasn't a film, Anna wanted to keep her job, and Miss Diamond held all the aces.

It was possible that Miss Diamond genuinely thought Anna was a hopeless, ignorant, misguided and potentially dangerous doctor. It was also possible that within Miss Diamond's sylph-like body, there existed the corrosive soul of a bully who sought out potential victims and tried to reduce them to gibbering wrecks. On balance, Anna was inclined to believe the second hypothesis was the correct one.

Fortunately, her timetable left little time for self-pity, however justified it might be. As she hurried along the corridor, she caught sight of William Niarchos, her good friend and true confidant.

25

'I'm off at five,' he called out. 'Do you fancy seeing the new X-Men film?'

She had only time to nod before speeding on to her destination. Just the thought of recounting Miss Diamond's latest put-down helped to lessen its poison.

At the gynaecology outpatient clinic, she attended to patients with menstrual disorders, utero-vaginal prolapses and stress incontinence, all of which helped to put her problems with her consultant into some sort of perspective. In the afternoon, stopping only to have a leathery sandwich, she made her way to the maternity ward.

The visitors' hour was coming to a close when she arrived. She exchanged notes at the desk with Andrea Arnold, the specialist nurse, and watched the usual procession of shell-shocked young fathers and overexcited new grandparents file out through the doors. Then her eyes focused on a man in denim jeans and a red and green checked shirt.

She hadn't seen Patrick for fourteen years but she recognised him at once. There were some people whose good looks made them permanently memorable. In Patrick's case, ash-blond hair, dark eyebrows and eyelashes, along with perfect bone structure, ensured his inclusion in this tiny elite.

'Patrick?' she said.

'That's me.' He stared back at her, his demeanour expressing surprise at being accosted by a strange doctor. His eyes hovered over her hospital ID badge and then widened with disbelief. 'Anna? Anna Cameron! Is it really you?

I don't believe it!' He reached for her hand and shook it vigorously with both of his. 'After all this time! You look so different. You've got short hair and you're . . . '

'Slimmer? I hope I'm slimmer. You look exactly the same.'

'How long is it since . . . ? It must be at least fifteen years.'

'It's fourteen. Not that I've been counting.' She laughed and he grinned back at her with no hint of awkwardness or embarrassment. He was genuinely delighted to see her. She wondered if he'd forgotten the circumstances of their last meeting. It *was* fourteen years ago. She said briskly, 'I must get on. Do give my regards to your parents.' She put a hand to her forehead and nodded towards the new mothers in the ward. 'Oh Lord, I'm sorry, I didn't think. Presumably, I should be congratulating you . . . '

'What? Oh I see . . . No, I've been visiting a friend. Look, this is ridiculous. You can't just walk away.' He reached into the pocket of his jeans and pulled out a card. 'We have so much to talk about. Are you working next weekend? Can you come over to lunch? Where do you live?'

'I have a flat in Deptford. But I'm afraid I will be working.'

'This is so weird! We're virtually neighbours. You *have* to come round. What about the weekend after? Come to lunch. I'll introduce you to Fizz and Lola.' He scribbled a few words on the back of his card and kissed her cheek before handing it to her. His skin smelt of wood-shavings. 'It is so amazing to see you! And you

27

look . . . you look fantastic!' He gave her a final smile. She restrained herself — with difficulty — from staring at him as he left.

A rather less attractive smell of well-worn scrubs heralded the close proximity of Andrea Arnold.

'Well,' Andrea said, '*he's* very easy on the eye.'

'He's quite beautiful, isn't he? We were at school together. I haven't seen him in years.'

The last time she'd seen him she was thirteen. Thirteen! It seemed like a lifetime ago. She couldn't resist looking at his card. The words *Furniture Repairs and Fine Upholstery* were emblazoned in red. There was a phone number and a business address in Blackheath. His parents had had an upholstery business in Wimbledon. Perhaps they'd moved it to Blackheath or perhaps Patrick had set up on his own. At school, everyone, including Patrick, had assumed he'd become an actor.

Anna turned the card over and noted a Lewisham address he'd written for her. He *was* almost a neighbour. He certainly only lived a short bus ride away. She wondered who Fizz and Lola might be. They could be flatmates or a wife and daughter. They could be cats or dogs. Patrick had always liked dogs. She hoped they were dogs.

She finished at five and breathed a sigh of relief. It had been a long, long day and if she was sensible she would probably go home and have an early night. But the X-Men film would help to exorcise the most recent memory of Miss Diamond and, if that didn't work, William was the perfect friend for the situation. He rarely allowed himself to be upset by scathing superiors. When a senior doctor once threw his stethoscope at him, William simply assumed he was having problems at home. (In fact he'd been right on that occasion. The doctor had apologised to him the following morning and confessed that his daughter had recently announced her engagement to a very unpleasant boyfriend.)

They both enjoyed the film. Afterwards, she and William sat in a pizza place, united by a mutual adoration of Jennifer Lawrence, while disagreeing about the charms of James McAvoy. They had an interesting conversation about the strange alchemy of charisma which reminded her of Patrick. She told William about their meeting.

'I was in the maternity ward and I bumped into him. He was my first boyfriend. I haven't seen him since I was thirteen. He hasn't changed at all.'

'He looks like he's thirteen still?'

'No, stupid, I mean he's as beautiful as he always was. He's asked me to lunch. He wants to introduce me to Fizz and Lola. Do you think they're his wife and daughter?'

'They could be dogs.'

'That's what I thought. They *sound* like dogs.'

'They sound like lapdogs. If they *are*, he's probably gay.'

'Trust me, William, Patrick isn't gay.'

'My first girlfriend found me through Facebook last year,' William said. 'We went for a drink. It didn't end well.'

'What happened?'

'She wanted to tell me why she broke up with me. We were both thirteen too. She said she watched me dancing with a girl and saw me stroke the girl's bottom.'

'Did you?'

'I have no idea. Who can remember what happened fourteen years ago?'

Anna could. Anna remembered everything: the excitement and passion of first love; the fury she'd felt towards her mother; the despair when they moved to Darrowbridge; and, with a sudden ray of clarity, the fact that at thirteen she had stopped liking herself.

William had been finishing the remains of her pizza. He hated waste. 'I'd better go,' he said. 'I'm on at seven tomorrow.'

Anna could picture him as a thirteen-year-old, with the same untidy dark curls and wicked grin. She bet he *had* stroked that girl's bottom. 'William,' she said, 'do you think it's unhealthy to dwell on the past?'

William wiped his hands with his paper napkin and downed the last of his wine. He gave the question some thought before pushing back his chair and putting on his jacket. 'Only,' he said, 'if it makes you fall in love with a man who has lapdogs.'

★ ★ ★

Freya did wonder, at first, if Felix had succumbed to one of his depressions. The first of them occurred fourteen years ago, a month after

30

they moved to Darrowbridge. Felix described it as a mental migraine and, when Freya said she didn't understand, he said he didn't either. It had lasted three days. He continued to go to work but each evening he came home late and then took off on his bike for a couple of hours. At night he retired to the spare room because he claimed he slept fitfully and didn't want to keep Freya awake. That first time, Freya had been bewildered and alarmed by the change in Felix. After it was over, he apologised, blamed stresses at work and assured her it would never happen again.

Freya had her own theory. She suspected he missed his London colleagues and felt guilty about dragging his reluctant family down to Somerset. In the circumstances, he would find it difficult to confess he'd made a mistake.

In fact, Cameron & West Financial Services soon began to flourish as Felix collected a loyal team around him. Yet the 'sessions', as he came to call them, continued to recur once or twice a year. Felix didn't like talking about them and neither did Freya. The fact that her devoted husband could, if only sporadically, metamorphose into an aloof individual who barely noticed her was a frightening reminder that one could never take security for granted. As a child, Freya had grown up with this knowledge but ever since she'd met Felix she'd done her best to forget it.

This time, she wasn't even sure he *was* depressed. He didn't go for long bike rides or retreat into silence. He came home from the office and chatted to Freya while she cooked their supper. He expressed interest in her caseloads and . . . That was it, she thought, he *expressed interest*. He was polite in the same way that Anna was polite on her fortnightly calls. Surely, it wasn't right for a man to be polite to his wife? She had had to accept the formality of her relationship with Anna, but Felix was a different matter.

Possibly, she was imagining all this. She was fifty-three, an age that was invariably tricky for women. She wasn't sure it was particularly healthy to hope she was physiologically unstable or at least unstable enough to conjure up problems where none existed. But it was far easier to have concerns about herself than to have concerns about Felix.

In the meantime, she had work to do. On Monday, she drove down to Dorset in her canary-coloured Beetle — a best-ever present from Felix on her fiftieth birthday. A client — Henry Riley — had commissioned her to explore his family's history as a surprise for his father's seventy-fifth birthday in the autumn. It was the sort of assignment Freya loved: a generous amount of time in which to collect and collate information, and a specific geographic location that wasn't too far away. None of the Rileys had ventured far beyond the south-west of the country.

At midday she stood in an overgrown churchyard in a tiny Dorset village, looking down at the gravestone of Henry Riley's three times great-grandmother. Freya knelt down to brush aside the cow parsley before taking a photograph. On the gravestone was written *Mary Riley, aged 32, wife of Samuel Riley*. So far, so expected. Underneath these words there were more: *Also Martin Riley, aged 8 and Edward Riley aged 8*.

This was strange. Freya knew that Mary had a son called James. He was a direct ancestor of her client. Until now she'd known nothing of any other children. The fact that Mary and her twins died in the same year seemed to indicate that they'd fallen victim to one of the many infectious diseases that plagued society before the advent of penicillin and a national health service. But why was there no mention of twins on any of the documents she had read? It was a mystery and Freya loved mysteries.

On Tuesday, she cancelled her hair appointment and drove to Taunton to examine the Register of Burials. It was here that she unearthed one of those rare discoveries that made her job so enthralling. She found the names of Mary and her twin sons. Next to the name *Mary Jane Riley* the vicar had inserted in brackets '*suicide after murder*'. And then, underneath, next to the names of Edward and Martin, he had added '*murdered by the above*'.

Freya felt a little giddy. In her imagination she had visualised Mary and her small sons gently fading away together. Now, Mary was a child killer. Why? She had brought up her older son, James, who was eighteen when she died. There was no documentary evidence of maternal mistreatment.

It seemed to Freya that Henry Riley might soon come to regret his choice of birthday gift for his father. Freya had already discovered that the grandson of Mary's oldest son had gone to prison for a year after killing someone in a fight. But then, no one was exempt from bad impulses or errors of judgement. As Freya often said, every family had its secrets.

4

On Tess's last full day in Scotland, she treated herself to a trip to Abbotsford. The walled garden was as beautiful as ever, its wide herbaceous borders a profusion of pastel colours. She walked down to the river and felt the peace steal over her. Sunlight scudded across the water, illuminating trailing ribbons of greenery and shiny black pebbles below the surface. She turned and let her eyes travel across the lawn, up the steep bank and along the formal terrace, before settling on the vast, sprawling house that, with its towers and turrets and gables, was the ultimate embodiment of Sir Walter Scott's romantic vision.

Grandma had brought her here six years ago. It was while gazing at a marble bust of the great writer that Tess had been smitten. He looked so approachable: a sense of warmth and kindness and humour seemed to emanate from his eyes. A sketch of him in the house endorsed her first impression. He held a walking stick at a jaunty angle and had a scarf tied a little untidily round his neck. Were he to come to life, Tess could imagine him saying to her: *How very nice to meet you! Do tell me what you are thinking.*

Tess could not remember her state of mind on that afternoon. She suspected she'd been preoccupied with her personal failings. She'd spent far too much time at university dwelling on this topic. How she managed to make any friends was a mystery.

She still didn't quite understand what had happened to her on that first visit. She and Grandma had returned to the Commune and, over supper, Tess had talked hesitantly at first and then with gathering enthusiasm about Sir Walter. Doctor Knox, still mourning the loss of his wife, had risen abruptly from his chair and left the room, causing the other residents to cast worried glances at the open door. A few minutes later, he'd returned with a well-thumbed copy of *Waverley*.

'Start with this,' he'd said. 'Let me know what you think.'

Everything had followed on from that. Tess had arrived at the Commune as a dejected, self-absorbed streak of misery and left it as an eager student who knew exactly what she wanted to do. And now, six years later, here she was, a fully fledged academic armed with a first-class degree, a teaching post at a good university in London and well on her way to finishing a PhD on the lasting legacy of Sir Walter Scott. These days, she felt quite at home when she walked through the entrance hall with its suits of armour and relics from Waterloo, its armoury stuffed with swords and guns, including Rob Roy's very own pistol. Sir Walter had been an avid collector of historical paraphernalia and he also loved spending money, a weakness that would cost him dearly in the last years of his life.

Each time she entered the rose-coloured dining room she remembered it was here that he died while listening to the sound of the River Tweed outside. In the drawing room, there was a painting of Sir Walter with his dogs. One of them stared longingly up at him and Tess knew just how he felt.

She checked her watch and hastily pulled her car keys from her pocket. It was time to return to the Commune and get ready for the party. Three of the inmates were going and all of them were sticklers for punctuality. Tess drove back along the narrow roads as fast as she dared. Arriving at the house, she raced up the wide staircase, clutching her anorak in her arms.

Twenty minutes later, she walked down the stairs in her black dress. She could hear laughter coming from the kitchen and went through to find Sheila and Linda chopping vegetables at the table while Derek stood, rolling pastry.

'Hi, Tess.' Sheila smiled up at her. 'We're making a mushroom quiche for the three of us. Derek, show Tess your pastry!'

'I don't know why they find it so funny,' Derek said. He held up a vast thin circle of pastry for Tess's inspection. 'I think it looks rather good.'

'Derek,' Sheila said, 'it's just for the three of us!'

As she and Linda started laughing again, Tess kissed Derek's cheek and said, 'It looks very professional. If there's any left over, I'll eat it later!' She hastened through to the hall and found Grandma, Doctor Knox and her great-aunt waiting for her.

Doctor Knox wore a tartan tie with his tweed suit. Grandma's short figure was well served by the brown velvet dress she always wore to parties. Great-aunt Katherine, her short grey hair newly permed for the occasion, wore a long black skirt and a silk shirt, its material festooned with purple flowers. She cast a meaningful glance at the grandfather clock. 'We should go right away. It's a long way to Kelso.'

'It's half an hour,' Grandma protested. 'And we don't want to be the first to arrive.' She smiled at Tess. 'You look lovely, darling. I'm so glad you're coming with us. Robert has something exciting to tell you.'

'I do,' Doctor Knox said, 'but let's get going first.'

In fact, most of the journey was taken up by Grandma's discovery that they had left their hostess's birthday present behind. Doctor Knox was happy to turn round but Great-aunt Katherine wouldn't hear of it, arguing that it was better to be punctual and present-less than to be late with a gift, particularly as the gift was a nondescript scarf. Since Grandma had chosen it, a heated altercation between the sisters-in-law ensued and was only terminated by Doctor Knox's timely reminder that he had news for Tess.

'I met an old friend for lunch yesterday,' he said. 'His wife has a clothes shop in Gaster-lethen.'

'I don't think I know it,' Tess said.

'Not many people do,' Great-aunt Katherine said. 'Gasterlethen is very unmemorable.'

'I don't think that's fair,' Doctor Knox said. 'It has a quiet sort of charm . . . '

Great-aunt Katherine sniffed. '*Very* quiet.'

'It is a small village,' Doctor Knox conceded. 'It's on the road between Galashiels and Peebles. My friend wants his wife to take on some help over the summer. And I thought of you, Tess.'

'Me?' Tess leant forward. 'That's very kind of you but I'm already sorted. I'll be working at a restaurant and . . .'

'You don't *have* to do that, do you?' Grandma asked. 'You could come here instead, borrow my car, do your research on days off. Of course you might prefer to spend the summer in London. You might think Gasterlethen would be extremely dull.'

'Grandma,' Tess said, 'you're as subtle as a sledgehammer.'

'Well,' Grandma said, 'I've never had much time for subtlety.'

Great-aunt Katherine grunted. 'That's true.'

'It's not just the restaurant,' Tess said. 'I'll be doing tutoring work too.'

'I quite understand,' Great-aunt Katherine said. 'You can't let people down.' She breathed a sigh of relief. 'Here we are in Kelso at last!'

Unlike most of the Border towns, Kelso was rather grand. It possessed not just a ruined abbey and a river but also a racecourse and a genuine fairy-tale castle, occupied by the current Duke and Duchess of Roxburghe. Doctor Knox parked in the impressive cobbled square and nodded across at one of the elegant Georgian houses. 'Let's go,' he said.

The pale blue door was opened by a cheerful mop-haired teenager who took their coats and suggested they help themselves to drinks from the trestle table behind him. Doctor Knox took an orange juice for himself and poured wine for the ladies.

Tess followed her companions upstairs to a long drawing room with two high windows, framed by heavy, maroon-coloured drapes. On the walls there were paintings of men and women in silks and satins who stared down at the festivities with grim distaste. At one end of the room, a group of people stood chatting to a regal old lady who sat in a high-backed chair in a long grey skirt and a lilac-coloured jersey.

Tess was aware that two young men were following her entrance with interest. She glanced fleetingly at them. One was dark-haired and wore a suit. The other had red hair and wore a kilt and stared so blatantly at her that she turned away quickly. There had to be about thirty people here, all talking in hushed voices as if in church. The few teenagers in evidence were busy taking round canapés. This was a very well-behaved party.

In the next half-hour Tess was introduced to a variety of guests, most of them seemingly related to Flora Macdonald, the eighty-five-year-old birthday girl in her high-backed chair. The old lady patted Tess's hand and told her she *must* meet her grand-daughter, Susan. She beckoned to Susan and told her to take Tess off for a chat.

Susan was a red-faced woman of indeterminate age, with a very short neck and two thick plaits fixed together on top of her head like an old-fashioned German hausfrau. As soon as

40

Susan heard Tess's English vowels, her eyes narrowed with scorn and she settled her arms on her well-endowed chest.

'We attract foreigners like flies, particularly in this part of the country. I suppose you're here for a holiday?' The last word was spoken with a contemptuous flourish.

'I'm here for work,' Tess assured her. 'I'm writing a PhD on Sir Walter Scott.'

'Are you indeed?' Susan gave a mirthless smile. 'He's certainly an appropriate subject for an English girl, particularly one who is conservative by inclination which I presume you must be, given your choice of subject.'

'Actually,' Tess said, 'my grandfather was Scottish and I'm sure many Scots are impressed by the author of *Ivanhoe* and *Waverley*.'

Susan's small eyes narrowed into dangerous slits. 'Most Scots would rather read a Latin dictionary than plough through a novel by Sir Walter Scott. Have you ever tried to read one?'

'Well, of course I have and . . . '

'They are unreadable. The man himself was an abomination. He was a Tory who did his best to turn Scotland into a playground for the English aristocracy. He rewrote our history and invited to Edinburgh one of your most dissolute kings . . . '

'In fact,' Tess told her, 'George the Fourth probably inherited his dissolute habits from his *Scottish* ancestor, James the Sixth of Scotland, who unfortunately became James the First of England.' She made an effort to rein in her indignation. 'I know that Scott romanticised

41

elements of Scottish history but . . . '

'Romanticised?' Susan's florid complexion had taken on the colour of a tomato. 'The man *fabricated*, he didn't romanticise! He made up a false history to please his posh English friends and he thought the pernicious Act of Union was a good and noble law. Well . . . ' Susan's head nodded violently ' . . . our time has come. This year is *our year* and you and your Sir Walter will have to accept Scotland's independence . . . '

'*I* support independence . . . '

'And I'll tell you something else about your precious Sir Walter! He encouraged the royal family to wear kilts! To this day they wear kilts! They are German, they don't have an ounce of Scottish blood in their veins . . . '

'Well, actually,' Tess said, 'as I think I pointed out, that's not quite true. George the First was the great-great-grandson of James the First on his mother's side . . . '

'He was German! He never spoke a word of English!'

'Yes, but he did have Scottish blood in him and I don't think you can condemn Scott for persuading the royal family to appreciate his homeland. A lot of people accept that if it weren't for him, Scotland would have no tourist industry and . . . '

'I'm supposed to be grateful for that? I'm supposed to be grateful for your caravan parks and your holiday homes?'

'They aren't *my* caravan parks . . . '

'Let me tell you about Sir Walterrrr.' Susan's accent was becoming ever more pronounced.

'He built a preposterous house at Abbotsford which was his idea of what a great Scottish house should be despite the fact that it bore no resemblance to any other great house in the country. He wrote ridiculous novels . . . '

'He was the first *ever* international bestseller who influenced the great writers of his day! Byron, Goethe, Hugo and Austen all thought he was brilliant. And even today there are people like A. N. Wilson and Alan Massie who revere him . . . '

Susan gave a laugh that sounded like a steam engine in full throttle. 'In England, you had a hideous programme called *Big Brother* that had more viewers than any other. That doesn't mean it was commendable. In England, your most famous celebrity is an anorexic airhead called Victoria Beckham. That doesn't mean she's commendable . . . '

'She *is* commendable. She's a very successful businesswoman and a widely respected clothes designer.'

Susan dismissed this with a wave of her hand. 'In England you have a plastic-breasted woman called Katie Price who changes her men and her body every few months and whose books sell in their thousands. Just because the English are obsessed with the base and the vulgar, should *we* have to follow your lamentable example?'

'Who has plastic breasts?'

Both women turned to register the newcomer. He seemed to have appeared from nowhere. Tess recognised him at once as the friend of the red-haired man. Susan gave a loud sniff. 'I was talking,' she said coldly, 'about Katie Price.'

'I can't say I know her,' the man said. He looked expectantly at Susan and then turned to Tess. 'I don't think she's going to introduce us. I'm Susan's cousin: Jamie Lockhart.'

'I'm Tess Cameron,' Tess said, 'and . . . '

'And *you*, Jamie Lockhart, are my *second* cousin,' Susan said, 'and since I'm aware you didn't come over here to talk to *me*, I shall leave the two of you together. I'm sure you will find you have similar views.'

Susan turned and, moving like a stately battleship, set off in search of more congenial company. 'I think you should know,' Jamie murmured, 'that her last comment was not a compliment.'

Susan's voice resembled a hard-bristled broom being dragged across a stone floor. Jamie's soft Scottish tones were far more melodic. Tess had never seen anyone quite like him. He wore an unexceptional black suit and a white shirt. He was of average height and slim build. It was his colouring that was so unusual. He had jet black hair that was pushed back from his forehead and his skin was pale as alabaster. It reminded her of Sir Walter's marble bust at Abbotsford and there was something statue-like about him. He didn't fidget or glance round the room. He kept his hands on his empty wine glass and his eyes fixed on Tess. His face was remarkably inexpressive. The immobility of his features together with the quiet tone of his voice suggested a certain gravity of mind. On the other hand, Tess had a strong suspicion that he had enjoyed baiting his cousin.

'Susan doesn't seem to like you very much.'

'She doesn't seem to like *you* either. What did you do to upset such a sweet, unassuming woman?'

Tess smiled. 'I told her I was doing a PhD on Sir Walter Scott.'

'He's not very fashionable these days. Are you looking to restore his popularity?'

'That's the idea.'

'Trust me, you'll need to add some salacious details.'

'He was a faithful husband, a loyal friend and an honourable businessman. There are no salacious details.'

'Make them up.'

'I happen to believe in academic integrity.'

'The problem with academic integrity,' Jamie said, 'is that it doesn't sell. Are you doing your work in Edinburgh?'

'No. I live in London. I'm staying with my grandmother. I go home tomorrow.'

'Ah.' Jamie opened his mouth and then shut it again.

'You were about to say something?'

Jamie nodded. 'I didn't want to be rude.'

'Please,' Tess said politely, 'feel free.'

'Well then. You choose to focus on a Scottish writer and you decide to study him in *London*. It's odd.'

'Now you sound like your cousin.'

'She's my *second* cousin and I do not. Susan is a bigoted, bad-tempered nationalist who refuses to believe there's any merit in the world outside Scotland. She's also a closet psychopath.'

'A moment ago you said she was sweet and unassuming.'

'I have a tendency to change my mind quite quickly. If I'm honest, it may be unfair to call her a psychopath. As far as I know she hasn't killed anyone yet.' He caught the eye of the mop-haired teenager who was currently refilling glasses a few feet away. 'Hey, Rollo! Come here.'

The boy sauntered over. 'Do you want another drink?'

'We do indeed. And then I want you to do something for me.'

'I might,' Rollo said. 'You may remember, Jamie, I asked you three weeks ago about a holiday job in the summer? You said you'd get back to me?' He attended to the empty glasses and then stood and waited.

'You strike a hard bargain, Rollo,' Jamie said. '*If* — and only if — you do it properly, I'll see what I can do. You notice Andy over there talking to Susan?' He nodded towards the red-haired man. 'Your mission — if you choose to accept it — is to go across and engage him in conversation.'

'What about?'

'Rollo, you are a resourceful young man. You can talk for Scotland. Look, he's poised to come over. Off you go.'

Tess watched Rollo hurry off. 'Why don't you want your friend to join us?'

Jamie shrugged. 'Where women are concerned, Andy is not to be trusted. He is in point of fact unscrupulous. Susan will have told him about Sir Walter and you. He'll pretend he loves

46

Scott's books when I happen to know he's never read a novel in his life. I am trying to protect you.'

'That's very considerate of you.'

Across the room, Rollo had made contact with Andy and was making animated gestures with his bottle of wine. It was clear that Rollo was very keen to get a holiday job with Jamie. Tess's mouth twitched. She was enjoying herself. It was impossible not to be amused by Jamie. He was an attractive man, who was flirting with her. She could enjoy such attentions in the happy knowledge that there would be no complications.

'I'm sorry you leave tomorrow,' Jamie said. 'I would have liked to invite you to my castle. Sir Walter was a regular visitor.'

'You have a castle? Scott went there?'

'Well, he visited once, in 1801. At least we think he did. We think he went with his friend William Wordsworth so that counts for something.'

Tess eyed him suspiciously. 'Are you telling me the truth? Do you really own a castle?'

Jamie reached into the inside pocket of his jacket, took out his wallet and extracted a business card which he gave to Tess.

On one side there was a photo of a genuine castle. On the other were the words: *Jamie Lockhart, custodian of Reidfern Castle*. Underneath there were his contact details. She tried to return the card to him but he shook his head. 'Keep it. Next time you're in Scotland, get in touch. I'll show you around.'

'Is it a real castle or is it just a ruin?'

'It is very real,' Jamie assured her. 'We have weddings and business functions there.'

Tess looked down at the card. 'Sir Walter's son-in-law was called Sir John Lockhart. They were the greatest of friends. I wonder if your family is related to him.'

Jamie gave an authoritative nod of his head. 'I'm pretty sure we are.'

Tess smiled. 'You'd never heard of him until this moment!'

'That might be true but I feel in my bones we must be. My grandfather's name was John.'

'We should have my mother here. She's a genealogist. She reads family trees like other people read newspapers. It would be quite something to be descended from the son-in-law of Sir Walter Scott.'

'It would,' Jamie said gravely. 'I must tell my father. He's been saying for years that he means to explore our family history.'

'Tell him to google Freya Eliza Cameron. Her website will tell him how to go about it.'

'I'll do that.' The red-haired man had extricated himself from Rollo and was now bearing down on them. 'Andy,' Jamie said, 'I was about to tell Tess here I ought to introduce you.'

Andy ignored Jamie. 'It's a pleasure to meet you. Susan has told me you're a fan of Sir Walter Scott. I have to tell you I *love* his books.'

For a brief moment, Jamie's eyes met those of Tess. 'That's very interesting, Andy. I never knew that. Tell us: which is your favourite novel and why?'

On the journey home, the hot gossip was that Susan was walking out with her local SNP agent.

'I found Susan rather difficult,' Tess confessed. 'She's such an *angry* person.'

'She's not easy,' her great-aunt agreed. 'As far as I could see, you spent most of the evening with Jamie Lockhart. He couldn't keep his eyes off you.'

'He was just being friendly,' Tess said.

'We have a saying in the family,' Great-aunt Katherine said. 'When a Lockhart befriends a woman, she should pack her case and run.'

'That's not a saying *I've* ever heard,' Grandma retorted. 'I think Jamie's charming.'

'The Lockharts are always charming,' Great-aunt Katherine intoned. 'You don't know them, Maggie. I was at school with Flora when her sister married into the family. Flora told me her mother cried all night.'

'Her mother sounds very silly,' Grandma said.

'She had her reasons,' Great-aunt Katherine said. 'I will only say that John Lockhart had a *reputation*. And his son is no better. He's left behind a long trail of broken marriages.'

'I don't know about that,' Grandma said, 'but . . . '

Doctor Knox made one of his rare interventions. 'I do. The Lockharts were patients of mine. Jamie's father was a delightful young man. I remember visiting him when he was almost beside himself with pain from an acute ear infection. He still took the time to thank me for calling on him. As far as I know he's only on his third wife and I'm told they're very happy.'

''*He's only on his third wife*',' Great-Aunt Katherine repeated with heavy sarcasm. 'That says it all.'

'I'm glad to hear it,' Grandma responded, 'because you've said quite enough already.'

5

Eliza Sample kissed her friend and agreed they must meet again soon, though, as she walked out into Piccadilly, she decided it wouldn't be as soon as all *that*. She was fond of Jean but she did have a tendency to go on about her aches and pains and, really, what was the *point?* Aches and pains were an essential part of the ageing process and a pretty reasonable price for survival when one thought of all the friends and acquaintances who had succumbed to fatal illnesses and falls.

And to be perfectly honest — and while Eliza might sometimes be a little *veiled* in her dealing with others, she believed in being stringently honest with herself — it was not terribly fascinating to listen to Jean's gossip about her family when *she* had no family of her own with which to contribute and compare. It wasn't as if Jean's family were particularly interesting anyway. Her daughters seemed to live tiresomely exemplary lives with useful careers in the civil service and education, husbands who remained their husbands, and children who were good at sports and exams and joined youth orchestras and ran marathons.

There had been one special moment. Jean's daughter-in-law was trying to unearth the mystery of her great-grandfather, a man who had disappeared one day, never to be seen again. Eliza had said, 'There's a very good website I've found. It's called *Revealing Families.co.uk*. It's run by a woman called Freya Eliza Cameron. You should tell your daughter-in-law about it.' Eliza had enjoyed passing that on.

She was glad she'd chosen to have coffee with Jean rather than afternoon tea because now she could look forward to her twice-weekly treat, knowing she had performed her social duty. The weather, while not exactly warm, was at least dry and she enjoyed walking along Piccadilly and down Regent Street into Pall Mall. It wasn't just the shops and the architecture, it was the people. She couldn't understand why so many of them felt compelled to talk into their phones as they walked; it meant they missed out on so many fascinating little scenes and conversations. Only last week she had heard one snippet of dialogue that kept her happily occupied for days. A couple were walking together and, as they passed by her, the man said, 'So we tell our spouses at six and we meet at seven. All right?'

Eliza had been enthralled. Were they going to announce their departure to their unfortunate spouses and, if so, weren't they allowing rather too little time to break such traumatic news? And how would they broach the subject? Would they suddenly, on the hour of six, break into a robot-like delivery of execution? Fascinating, absolutely fascinating.

And now, two stunning girls in short white dresses were walking towards her in the company of a less stunning young man. 'I hate Megan,' one of the girls said as they walked past her. 'She's such a whore.'

Was Megan a whore? It was an unusually censorious term to issue from the mouth of one who didn't look particularly virginal herself, despite the white dress. Was the word a routine insult these days and, if so, what had happened to feminine solidarity? What had happened to feminism? Eliza often wondered what had happened to feminism. Why did so many girls spend so many boring hours every day counting their calories? Why did so many women spend so much money having unnecessary, dangerous operations in order to attain a mythical approximation of contemporary beauty? In her thirties, Eliza had read books extolling the liberation of women and now, all these years later, the daughters and granddaughters of those thoughtful writers shaved their pubic hair and called each other whores. It was a little depressing.

Her spirits lifted as she reached the National Gallery. As long as she could keep coming here, life was worth living. Eliza knew only too well that in order to sustain a heady love affair one must restrict exposure to the object of one's passion. She never visited the gallery more than twice a week, even though she was often tempted. And with each visit she would only look at one room, or occasionally two. Sometimes she would only look at one painting. She knew what she wanted to do today. She had just finished reading Hilary Mantel's *Wolf Hall* and had been delighted by the appearance of Hans Holbein in the story. Today, she intended to look at some of his paintings and she might as well start with the biggest.

The Ambassadors dominated the room in which it was hung, taking up the whole of the end wall. Eliza sat on the bench opposite it with a little sigh of pleasure. She put her bag down beside her and adjusted her skirt.

The two diplomats in the painting were dressed sumptuously and stood on either side of a table packed with artefacts — a globe, books, scientific instruments. The man on the left was quite handsome in an arrogant sort of way. He wore a black cap, black hose and black undercoat, all of which emphasised the dazzling pinkness of his satin doublet. He stood with his coat deliberately exposed to reveal an extravagant ermine lining. He had a long gold chain round his neck that would be the envy of any of those rappers Eliza occasionally glimpsed on television. He also carried a gold dagger with a ridiculous green tassel.

His friend was *not* attractive. His costume, while less flashy, showed signs of opulence, since his coat was lined with fur. Both men looked out at Eliza — or rather, she supposed, they looked out at Holbein — with expressions of serene confidence in their position in the world.

But what excited Eliza was the fact that amid the conventional portrait of two powerful men there was something so surreal, so contemporary in its deliberate attempt to shock it made her want to laugh. In the foreground of the painting was a sprawling, diagonal shape. It looked like a UFO that had crash-landed onto the rich carpet. On further examination, it turned out to be a skull. Did the two men know that in front of all the pomp and wealth so lovingly reproduced by the artist, a crazy skull would intrude, a V-sign to all that they presumably held so dear?

This was why Eliza loved the National Gallery. How could one be lonely when one visited this place? At the age of eighty-one she no longer had many friends. She rarely left London now. There was only her sister-in-law in Bath who continued to invite her to stay. Yet here, across the centuries, she had made a connection. She was, she felt, talking to an artist who felt as she did about life: that it was a game in which money and position were mere diversions in the face of inevitable death. Life was fragile, death was random, and the best way to live was to regard one's continued existence with sceptical amusement and plenty of gratitude.

A voice said, 'Do you mind if I join you?'

Eliza looked up into possibly the ugliest face she had ever encountered. The man was like an ape. The gap between his nose and his protuberant mouth was excessive and it didn't help that his chin had apparently collapsed into his neck. He was bald, apart from a crescent-shaped rim of grey stringy hair round the back of his head, and he wore a baggy, shabby, brown suit that would have been loose on a man twice his size. She refrained from pointing out that he had already joined her and instead said coldly, 'This bench is public property.'

He sat down and, taking out an enormous handkerchief, blew his nose noisily. 'I love this painting,' he said, pointing his walking stick at Holbein's picture. 'Do you see the ambassador on the left has a badge on his cap? If you look at it carefully, you can see there's the image of a skull on it.'

Eliza nodded but said nothing since she had no wish to let the little man know she hadn't noticed the badge.

'And if you look on the top left corner, you can see a crucifix, almost hidden in the folds of those curtains. Why is it there? The painting is full of clues and puzzles. Look at the table for a start.' He carried on pontificating about the symbolism of each object on the table and she rather grudgingly conceded — if only to herself — that he knew far more than she did. When he eventually stood up, however, she remained stubbornly seated. He glanced at his watch. 'I'm afraid I have to go. Do you often come here?'

'I do,' Eliza said. 'It is,' she added with some deliberation, 'very peaceful.'

'It is, it is,' the man agreed, failing to notice the implied rebuke. 'I'll be here next Thursday. I thought I'd look at the Impressionists. Come along at midday and we'll look at them together. I'll wait for you by Pissarro's *The Avenue, Sydenham*. Goodbye now.'

The little man nodded and walked away without giving time for her to respond, which was just as well since he'd irritated her so much she'd been tempted to forget her manners. Why would she care if he were here next Thursday? Why would he think she would want to look at paintings with him? And why would he assume, as she was sure that he *did*, that he knew far more than she did about art? She had no intention of waiting for him by the Pissarro next week, in fact she would go out of her way *not* to be waiting by the Pissarro.

She gave a slow and careful glance round the room and, having assured herself that he had well and truly gone, rose and walked up to the painting. She felt an almost reluctant surge of interest. There was the badge on the ambassador's cap with what indeed looked like a skull engraved on it. And there was the small crucifix on the top left-hand corner. Her eyes flickered over to the face of the ambassador on the left. It seemed to her that he stared at her with a rather mocking expression. But that was just fancy.

6

Anna supposed that Patrick must be doing well. Lewisham Hill was a pleasant tree-lined road with substantial Victorian houses on either side. Genteel Blackheath was a little further up the hill and Lewisham Station was conveniently situated down at the bottom. His housing block, more or less midway between them, had a big communal lawn, and there was no sign of litter anywhere.

His maisonette was on the first floor and when she spoke into the machine, his voice shot out with unabashed warmth. 'Anna! Come on up!' He was waiting for her on the landing. When he kissed her cheek, he smelt of basil. 'Come in, come in,' he said. 'Meet Fizz and Lola.'

Fizz and Lola were not dogs. Fizz was an attractive woman in leggings and a lumberjack shirt, with a wide mouth and glossy brown hair. Lola was a grave-faced toddler with enormous blue eyes and shoulder-length blonde hair. The child stretched out her arms towards her father and he gathered her up in his arms with practised ease. 'Take Anna through to the sitting room, Fizz. Lola can help me finish the cooking.'

The sitting room was modest in size but full of light, with green walls and a pink carpet. There was a two-seater sofa, a floor cushion and a simple wooden chair. Behind the sofa was a short table with a laptop, a tray with glasses and a bottle in an ice bucket. Underneath the table was a red plastic box stuffed with toys.

Having settled Anna on the sofa with a large glass of wine, Fizz took the floor cushion and said, 'I've heard all about you, you know. Don't you love being called Dr Cameron?'

It was impossible not to like her and indeed, Anna thought, why should she not? Fizz had a low husky voice and a throaty laugh. She was self-deprecatory to a fault — 'I don't want to talk about my job. If you want to freeze a conversation instantly, just try saying you're an industrial land lawyer.' She confessed she was not a natural mother — 'I adore Lola but if I'm on my own with her for more than a few hours I start climbing up the wall.' She admitted she'd find motherhood impossible without a partner like Patrick. 'When I met him he was an actor and thank God he was unsuccessful because he was quite happy to give it up when Lola came along. His parents had bought larger premises in Blackheath and then they bought a house there. That's why we came to Lewisham. Patrick's joined the family upholstery business. He looks after Lola and takes her to work with him. He has ten times more patience with her than I do and his parents are brilliant too. I'm very lucky.'

Fizz *was* lucky. When Patrick called them into lunch, there was a tomato tart along with a Niçoise salad awaiting them. While Fizz helped him serve out, Anna took a seat next to Lola and gave her an uncertain smile. She had no idea how to address such a small and solemn infant.

Lola pointed to her feet. 'I have purple shoes,' she said.

Anna studied Lola's purple trainers. 'They're very nice,' she said.

Lola nodded and gave a little sigh. 'Do you like purple?' she asked.

The child was making polite conversation. Anna had no idea that small children could even begin to do that. 'I quite like purple,' she said, 'though I have to say it's not my favourite colour.'

Lola regarded Anna with a hint of disappointment in her eyes. '*I* like purple. Purple is my favourite colour. I like alpacas too.'

Anna was even more impressed. 'I don't think I've ever *seen* an alpaca.'

Lola's face dissolved into laughter. '*I* have. I see them all the time. I *love* alpacas.'

Lola was lovely, if a little frustrating. Anna doubted she would ever have the patience to cope with small children. Having conversations in their presence was like driving in a traffic jam. Over lunch, Fizz told Anna that she tried to learn something new every six months which meant that on Wednesday evenings she now went straight from work to something called dynamic yoga. Dynamic yoga sounded like a contradiction in terms. How could yoga — all deep breathing and slow motion movements — ever be dynamic? Anna was intrigued but the subject was terminally derailed by Lola who wanted Anna to know that her friend Jonah liked eating buttons from his shirt. And then when Patrick mentioned that Anna's childhood tormentor, Felicity Eggins, was already on her second marriage, Lola said she didn't like tomatoes now and that was the end of Felicity Eggins. Fizz and Patrick were fascinated by Lola's revelation. Anna couldn't imagine a time when she would be more interested in a child's dislike of tomatoes than in Felicity Eggins' love life.

When she said goodbye, she walked down the stairs and turned when Lola called her name. There were the three of them, Fizz, and Patrick, and Lola blowing a kiss at her. She blew one back and went on her way. On the bus back to Deptford, she rang William to tell him Fizz and Lola weren't lapdogs.

'I like Fizz,' she told William. 'You would too.'

'You sound a bit down,' William said.

'Oh well . . . You know . . . ' Anna's voice tailed off. She knew William would understand.

'Who was it who said the past is another country?' William asked.

'I haven't a clue. I expect Tess would know.'

'Well, it's true,' William said. 'And if I were you I'd keep well away from it.'

Anna laughed and said goodbye. Almost immediately she had a text from Olivia. 'I'm back!'

Anna's spirits lifted at once. Olivia was back!

Fourteen years ago, Anna and her family moved from London to Somerset. Their mother had dropped her and Tess off on their first day at their new school. 'You'll be fine,' she said brightly. 'After all you have each other.' Which only went to show that her mother knew nothing about anything since Tess was no help at all. Tess's passive acquiescence towards the move had remained as incomprehensible as it was infuriating.

They found themselves in a class united by old allegiances and shared primary-school experiences. There was only one pupil there who interested Anna and by the end of the day she knew why. She and Olivia were both exiles who were consumed with rage.

Olivia, half Ghanaian and half Italian, had spent all her life in Shoreditch where she had a tight-knit group of friends. Now her parents — just like Anna's — had made an arbitrary decision to move their family away from all that was familiar. Olivia found herself in a class where she was the only black pupil in a room of white teenagers who had never even heard of Shoreditch.

Meanwhile Anna had been forcibly uprooted from Wimbledon, her friends, and Patrick. Her new home was a rural cottage that was nearly half a mile from anywhere of interest. Not that Darrowbridge *was* interesting but at least it offered more than fields and trees and the faint smells of the pig farm down the road.

By the end of that first week, Anna and Olivia were best friends and had remained so ever since. These days the two of them shared a small flat in Deptford. For the last two weeks Olivia had been away in Manchester, working on a programme about a family called the Balderstones whose domestic life was impeded by a ghost in their sitting room. Thus far, the ghost had failed to materialise and the team was forced to rely on ever more lurid accounts from Mrs Balderstone, who relished her moment in the spotlight. The only breath of sanity came from a local builder called Jim who assured Olivia that the entire story was a load of old rubbish. Such lucid common sense meant that Jim had to be discounted as a witness, which was a pity since Olivia said he was extremely easy on the eye which was more than could be said for Mrs Balderstone.

Olivia's job often took her away from home. Each time she went away, Anna expected to enjoy the chance to tidy the flat and have the place to herself and each time she soon remembered that she hated being alone. Anna's sister had once voiced the hope of, some day, buying a small cottage of her own in the country. Tess's dream was Anna's nightmare. She couldn't imagine anything worse than living on her own.

In the flat there were the welcome signs of Olivia's return: the open rucksack on the sofa, the carrier bags on the rug and the signs of culinary debris on the kitchen bar. Anna could hear her on the phone in her bedroom, having what sounded like a heated discussion.

Anna filled the kettle with water and had just located the box of teabags when Olivia came in, looking effortlessly cool in a sludge-green boiler suit that on anyone else would look horrendous.

'Welcome home,' Anna said. 'We can share the last teabag.'

'Just what I need,' Olivia breathed. 'I am *so* pissed off. My brother and his wife have invited us all to Cambridge for Christmas.'

'It's the middle of June. They're making plans for *Christmas*?'

'I know. That's what they do. I can't believe Mum's even considering it. I've just reminded her, 'Do you remember what we said last time? *Never again!*''

'I thought you adored your nephews.'

'I do. I adore them all through the day but there should be a cast-iron rule that children under six should be in bed by six. And meanwhile we have to eat my sister-in-law's disgusting veggie food and, if we don't praise it to the skies, my brother looks anxiously at *her* and then gazes desperately at us and I am *not* going there and . . . Oh, let's not talk about it. It only makes me cross. Shall I tell you the latest about the Balderstones' ghost?'

'You didn't *see* it?'

'Oh, we saw it all right. We saw it yesterday. We'd packed everything away so we could make an early start this morning. We were about to go to the pub when Mrs Balderstone rang and told us to come over at once. We dashed over, she let us in and we tiptoed towards the sitting room. We all heard the noises. Steve and Tom set up the equipment in the hall. I opened the door and felt something furry brush past my leg and I screamed. And then we saw him leap up the stairs. It was a squirrel. I nearly had a heart attack over a frigging squirrel.'

'I can't believe you screamed. How can you make a documentary about a ghost that turned out to be a squirrel?'

'Easy. It will become a witty exposé of human gullibility. I suspect Mrs Balderstone will not be amused. Anyway, I'm already thinking about the next project.'

'Do you have any ideas?' A silly question. Olivia always had ideas.

'I bought a stack of magazines the other day and I've identified two possible subjects. One is a woman whose husband walked out on her and their three children. He went on to marry again and had another child. His new wife died and now the first one's taken him back and is bringing up the new baby.'

'That is depressing on so many levels.'

'The other's a very dishy bloke who runs a holistic garden-design business. He's bringing a book out and he has a great name too: Xander Bullen . . . Why are you staring at me like that? Anna?'

Anna was aware she had the kettle in her hand. She put it down. 'Do you still have the magazine? Can I see it?'

Olivia stood up and went across to one of the carrier bags. She pulled out a folder and brought it back to Anna. 'I tore it out this morning. He's very photogenic, don't you think?'

Anna stared down at the photograph and swallowed hard. 'Olivia,' she said, 'if you make a programme about this man I will never speak to you again.'

7

Felix was about to leave the office when he had a call from Freya.

'I need some Parmesan,' she said, 'and *good* red wine! We are *celebrating*!'

He bought a bottle of Fleurie near Bristol Temple Meads and had to run to get the train. He was lucky: five more seconds and he'd have missed it. He was even luckier to find a seat. The young woman beside him was engrossed in a magazine. The words *SALLY CHEATS ON RICK!* were emblazoned above a photo of — presumably — soap-opera Sally on the phone in a quite ridiculously furtive pose; behind her, a man — presumably Rick — sat reading a paper in blissful ignorance.

He would buy the Parmesan at Darrowbridge. He wondered what it was they were celebrating. Oh God, he thought, it couldn't be the anniversary yet? But, of course, it couldn't. They'd married in September. At some point in July, it would be thirty-one years since he'd first met Freya. He couldn't recall the exact date but he could picture the occasion as if it were yesterday.

He'd gone to a friend's wedding. He had sat in the church, keeping a place for his sister who, as usual, was late. And then this beautiful girl had walked down the aisle in a little pink suit which showed off her tiny waist and hips and her long slender legs to perfection. She stopped by his pew, pushed back her blonde hair and asked, 'Is this seat taken?'

'I was saving it for you,' he'd said, which was totally out of character and quite absurd but he felt as if it was true.

At the reception he stood talking to the bride and glanced across the room. The girl was surrounded by a trio of male guests vying for her attention and she smiled suddenly at him. At the time he couldn't believe he had been the intended recipient. She was way out of his league. But then, later still, she came up to him and asked, 'Shall we see each other again?' and that was it. He was done for.

Alighting from the train, he put the Fleurie in his car and walked on towards the small supermarket. He bought the Parmesan and was about to head back to the station car park when he saw Pam's next-door neighbour, Percy Jenner, along with his small pug, Serge. They made an incongruous pair and the sight of them together always made Felix smile. Percy, a skilled plasterer before his retirement, was a thin, wiry man with curly grey hair. His pet was a tiny, dainty little animal who looked like the perfect lapdog. Percy's wife, Elaine, had acquired him four years ago and — mistaking him for a French bulldog — given him a suitably foreign name. Three months later, she died of heart failure while undergoing what was supposed to be a routine operation.

Felix had a lot of time for Percy. After his wife's death, he had taught himself to cook and kept their cottage spotless. He and Elaine were childless and had been devoted to each other. Now Percy was devoted to Serge. Tonight, he told Felix, he and Serge had walked along the river and spotted a heron.

'Do you want a lift back?' Felix asked. 'I have my car at the station.'

Serge looked up at Felix. Serge looked as if he'd very much like a lift.

'We're going to the graveyard,' Percy said, 'but thank you for the offer. It's a good evening for a walk. Will you thank Freya for the broad beans? She dropped them in yesterday. Tell her I had some last night. Your wife's a very kind lady.'

'She is,' Felix said. 'And I'll be sure to pass on the message.'

Percy was right, he thought, it *was* a good evening for a walk. On an impulse he turned and walked on to the path by the river. He didn't see a heron but he spotted a very unusual bird on the water. It was small and black with a bright orange beak and tiny beady eyes.

He sat down on the bench and wondered what it was about water that was so soothing. Perhaps it was the fact that its inhabitants — the ducks, the elusive heron and the funny little black bird — all had such a simple life, paddling along, foraging for food, enjoying the sunlight. Of course, for all he knew, their lives weren't simple at all. Just now, for instance, the funny little black bird was squawked at by two hostile green and white ducks and emitted a surprisingly guttural squawk of his own. For all Felix knew, the funny little black bird was a lonely creature desperate for friends.

He should get back. Freya would be waiting for him. The truth was that Felix didn't want to go home. The truth was that Felix would like to stay here, open the Fleurie, drink the whole bottle and watch the ducks and the poor little black bird.

★   ★   ★

'*What do u think?*'

Tess stared at the hopeful text and knew she was not yet ready to answer it. She should never have left it to Rachel. She had only herself to blame. As she entered her house — her house for another two weeks — she greeted the cats and said, 'Yes, hello, you two, I'll feed you now!'

She went through to the kitchen and gazed at the royal blue tiles, the double sink and the wide breakfast bar. She felt like Eve taking a last look at Eden before being thrown out into the wilderness.

She knew she had been exceptionally lucky to live here. Eight months ago, Rachel's brother, an insanely successful actor, had invited her and Rachel to move in, for a tiny rent, on condition they looked after his cats while he was filming in the States. The small terraced house was a stone's throw from London Fields with its collection of artisan food shops and cool little coffee bars. She and Rachel had felt as if they'd died and gone to Heaven. And now Rachel's brother was coming home and Hell was on its way.

This afternoon Tess had gone to see the flat that would soon be her home. The building was in an unexceptional if noisy street near Fulham Broadway. As soon as Tess unlocked the front door she was hit by the pungent aroma of cat. She liked cats, she enjoyed looking after Rachel's brother's two, but the smell here was something else, this was the smell of a very sick cat, possibly one on the verge of decomposition. She walked up the first lot of stairs and let herself in through the mud-coloured door. Inside there was a narrow corridor with a small, dark kitchen on the left and a small, dark bedroom on the right. A little further along, there was a small, dark bathroom on one side and a tiny bedroom on the right. And that was it.

She couldn't help wondering if Rachel would have seized on this place so readily if it weren't for the fact that she spent a great deal of time with her boyfriend who had a far more salubrious flat in Putney. To be fair to Rachel, given their budget, it was always going to be difficult to find pleasant accommodation in central London. Tess's income was modest and Rachel had had to take a drop in salary since she worked for an events company that had too few events to organise. The rent here was remarkably cheap, though now Tess had seen it, it seemed not remarkable enough.

Less than a fortnight ago, Tess had stood with her back to the River Tweed, gazing at the enormous majesty of Abbotsford. Already, that seemed like another life. Now, sitting in Rachel's brother's kitchen with the cats down at her feet, she made a decision. She took out her phone and called up a number. After what seemed like an eternity a familiar voice said, 'This is Maggie Cameron speaking.'

'Oh, Grandma,' Tess said, 'I'm so glad it's you. I just thought I'd ask: I don't suppose that job's still going in the summer?'

★ ★ ★

Freya opened the door and beamed at Pam. 'What a nice surprise!' she said. 'I thought you were Felix. He should have been here ages ago.'

'I'm sure you're cooking supper. I'm on the scrounge. I need three eggs . . . '

Pam was wearing her green dress today. She had three work dresses: green, grey and black, which she wore in strict rotation, in order to save time otherwise wasted on choosing what to wear. When her beloved Henry died eighteen months ago, she lost a great deal of weight and her dresses looked like tents blowing in the wind. Freya had suggested a belt and gave her a leather one with a brass buckle. It became an essential part of Pam's working wardrobe and these days she looked rather Bohemian.

'Come on through,' Freya said. 'Let's have a drink. Felix is late and I'm dying to tell someone my news.'

'Just half a glass,' Pam said. 'I have a lot of cooking to do tonight.'

Freya sat her down at the table while she sorted out eggs and wine. 'I've been investigating a client's ancestor,' she said. 'Her name was Mary.

She had an eighteen-year-old son and eight-year-old twin boys. And then . . . Are you happy with Chardonnay? . . . I discovered that she murdered her twins and then killed herself. But there seemed to be no motive. Why would a woman who's brought up one strapping great son want to kill her small twins? And, by the way, she doesn't just kill them in a nice, gentle way . . . '

'Can you kill someone in a nice, gentle way? Freya, that's enough. I need to be sober.'

'I suppose you could wait till they're sleeping and put pillows on their faces. That would be quite gentle, don't you think? Whereas Mary poisons her boys with prussic acid and then takes it herself. The question is: Why?'

'She had to be mad.'

Freya shook her head. 'Eight years after Mary died, her husband, Samuel, still employed his long-standing housekeeper, Maud Harries. According to the records I found today, he also had a sixteen-year-old stable boy called Peter Riley Harries. He was born in the same year as the twins. Do you see what I mean?'

'I'm sorry. You've lost me.'

'He had to be the illegitimate son of Samuel. Why else would he be given the name of Riley? I reckon Mary found out and killed herself and her twins in a fit of jealous fury.'

'She had to be mad. No one would do such a thing otherwise.'

'I know. But it fits, you see, it really fits.' She heard the front door slam and called out, 'Felix! We're in here!'

When Felix saw Pam, he beamed. 'Pam! This

is a treat!' He came over and kissed her cheek. 'Are you staying for supper?'

'No, no, I came over to borrow some eggs. I had a call from Simon this afternoon.'

Simon was Pam's only child and could do no wrong. Felix put the Parmesan and the red wine on the table. 'How *is* Simon?' he asked. 'I haven't seen him for months.'

'He's very well. He rang me at work this afternoon and asked if he and Naomi could come down tomorrow night. He says they have something to tell me. It has to be wedding bells, don't you think? So I thought I'd make a special cake tonight and then I saw I had no eggs.'

Felix accepted a glass of wine from Freya and took a seat by Pam. 'You approve of Naomi, don't you?'

'She's perfect for Simon. They climbed Kilimanjaro last year. Naomi got altitude sickness and vomited for hours but she still said she adored every minute of it. I loved Henry with all my heart but if he'd ever asked *me* to climb Mount Kilimanjaro I'd have told him I couldn't do it. Fortunately, he was quite happy with Swanage.'

Felix laughed. 'It *is* good to see you. Won't you stay to supper?'

'There's quite enough,' Freya assured her.

'No, really, I have so much to do.' Pam finished her drink and stood up. 'Thank you for the wine, Freya, and the eggs. I'll let you know what Simon has to tell me.'

'I'll see you out,' Felix said.

Freya heard the two of them chatting in the

hall and then a low rumble of laughter from Felix. When he came back to the kitchen, he reached for his wine and said, 'I'm sorry Pam couldn't stay.'

'I could see that,' Freya said lightly. 'Now you'll have to make do with me.'

'Freya!' Felix protested.

She put the water on for the pasta and then turned. 'I'm not stupid, Felix. I know you're not happy at the moment.'

'No,' he agreed, 'but I'm working on it.'

'Can I help?'

'No, I don't think so.'

She began tearing up pieces of lettuce for the salad. She'd known the answer before she asked the question. He never liked discussing the strange moods that settled on him like ash.

'So tell me,' he said, 'what exactly are we celebrating?'

For a moment she had no idea and then she nodded and told him about Mary Riley and if he wasn't really interested he made an adequate job of appearing to be.

★ ★ ★

Way back in the Surrey days, long before Maggie had even heard the word 'commune', she and Philip lived in a street of solid suburban houses. Each one had a long rectangular garden at the back. One morning Maggie had woken at six. Going across to the window, she spotted Linda next door, dressed in jeans and jumper, digging up a clump of stinging nettles. Two days earlier,

Linda and Derek had welcomed back their pale-faced son from university. Within a few hours he'd been rushed off to hospital with acute peritonitis. Maggie was not overly surprised to see Linda out working at such an early hour. When Linda was troubled, she always found solace in her garden.

Thirty-five years later, she continued to do so. Tonight, Maggie joined her on a slow perambulation round the lawn at the back of their house. Sheila and Derek were cooking tonight and had announced that dinner would be ready within the next half-hour. It had taken Maggie and Linda nearly ten minutes to put on their coats and their gloves but then, as Maggie told Linda, it didn't really matter since Sheila would almost certainly forget to put the greens on until Derek was ready to serve up.

Maggie was in a good mood. 'I had a call from Tess this evening,' she said. 'Robert had found her a holiday job in Gasterlethen and now she's decided to take it. So she'll be up here with us through August.'

'I'm so glad,' Linda said. 'I always enjoy her visits. Are there any men on the . . . the . . . ?'

'On the horizon? No. There never do seem to be any men on Tess's horizon.'

'Perhaps she doesn't like men.'

'I suppose it's possible. I'm not sure she's interested in women either.'

Linda stopped to point her walking stick at the rose bushes. 'They need spraying,' she said. 'We must talk . . . We must talk to the gardener.'

Maggie nodded. 'I'm sure Gordon mentioned

it a few weeks ago. I'll be sure to remind him.'

They set off again. 'How is . . . Tess's sister?' Linda asked.

This was what Linda did these days. Names eluded her and she would use deceptively formal language to refer to individuals she had known for years. All through the Surrey decades, she and Maggie had been in and out of each other's house, sharing children and then grandchildren. Linda had seen almost as much of Tess and Anna as she had of her own grandsons. And now Anna was 'Tess's sister'.

'Anna's fine,' Maggie said. 'She's a very busy doctor. She was always such a funny little girl. Do you remember a time I brought her and Tess to tea with you? It was the day you and Derek had your old beech tree cut down and you told them it had died. Anna looked at you and me with immense gravity and said, 'I expect you'll die soon.' I said something like I very much hoped we wouldn't and she looked at us with great sweetness and said, 'Don't worry. I'm sure it won't hurt.' She was only four and she said that! Do you remember her saying that?'

'No,' Linda said. 'I don't remember. Is Felix coming here soon? I am so fond of Felix. I haven't seen him for a very long time.'

Felix and Freya had been there with Tess only two months ago for Easter. Maggie said, 'He and Freya are coming in October. It's a long drive for them and Felix works so hard.'

Linda nodded. 'This morning,' she said, 'I sat up in bed and I thought: I don't know how to switch on my bedside lamp. Derek was awake and I told him. I said, 'I feel as if all the lights in my head are slowly going out.' And do you know what he said?'

'No.' Maggie reached out for her friend's hand. 'Tell me.'

'He said I shouldn't worry. He said he'd be my torch.'

8

Anna met William Niarchos when they were both at medical school. At the time she was seeing a charming but complicated boy who shared a flat with William. Her friendship with William had lasted far longer than the relationship with his flatmate. She and William both loved the cinema and he was a non-judgemental and easy-going companion; they were impressive characteristics given the peculiarities of his upbringing. His brother was called Trevor and, as he pointed out to Anna, one only had to consider their names to indicate that there was something dysfunctional about the family. Their father was proudly Greek, their mother was stubbornly English and their favourite pastime was to argue ferociously as to whether England or Greece deserved to be known as the cradle of democracy.

The brothers had grown up witnessing dramatic conflagrations on a regular basis. William had once acted out to Anna one particular family breakfast. He and his brother were eating cereal with their mother when his father burst into the kitchen and emptied the contents of a plastic bag over his wife. It transpired he had cut into pieces the dress she had worn to a party the night before at which, so their father told them, their mother had done her best to seduce the host.

'What did you say?' Anna asked. 'What did you do?'

'We carried on eating our cereal,' William said. 'They started rolling about on the floor trying to hit each other and so I threw a jug of water over them.'

Anna was fascinated by these stories. In her own family, she and Tess had always been encouraged to 'respect' the opinions of others, which as far as she could see meant accepting them without complaint. She told an incredulous William that she had never heard her parents raise their voices at each other.

After medical school, Anna had gone on to Bangor and Bristol and now London whereas William had trained at Durham and Sheffield. His stint in Durham overlapped briefly with Tess's time at Durham University and Anna had put them in contact with each other. They'd only seen each other a couple of times but Tess had reported back her approval.

And then William arrived at St Peter's. His parents had divorced three years ago which, he told Anna, had been a source of great relief to their children. Their mother had married a UKIP activist and lived in Margate, while his father remained in the family home in Reigate where he lived in exhausted contentment with a mild-mannered librarian.

For Anna, the return of her old friend was particularly welcome. Any time Miss Diamond was horrendous, she would seek out William and he would be ready with a cinematic comparison. One day, Miss Diamond was like Bette Davis in

All About Eve, desperately insecure about a stunning young doctor with the look of Jean Seberg. 'I doubt if Miss Diamond's ever heard of Jean Seberg,' Anna said. Another time, William would compare the consultant to Julia Roberts in *August: Osage County*, unable to keep the malice from spilling out because that was the way *her* mother talked. Whenever Anna discussed her nemesis with William, he had the great gift of reducing her power to that of a sadly disturbed woman whose dislike of Anna was completely bound up with her own malfunction. Presumably, the years he'd spent listening to his parents' quarrels had immunised him against the sulphurous behaviour of others.

Tonight, they were back eating pizza, discussing their latest cinematic outing, *Edge of Tomorrow*, a film that William dismissed as a *Groundhog Day* remake without the laughs or the brilliance of Bill Murray.

'I know you're right,' Anna said, 'but I still liked it. I like the idea that you can keep going back to refine and improve your life until you get it right.' She took a bite of her pizza and chewed thoughtfully. 'I'm going to have supper with Patrick and Fizz on Friday.'

William blinked. 'I'm sorry? Is that piece of information connected to the film? Do you hope to refine and improve your relationship with Patrick?'

'I just thought you'd be interested.'

'Two weeks ago you had lunch with them and now you're going over to dinner. Patrick must be keen. Perhaps Fizz is too.'

'Sometimes, William, you just have to accept there aren't always hidden motives.'

'Do you still find Patrick outstandingly desirable?'

'Well, I suppose . . . '

'I rest my case. Let's not talk about it now, it's too depressing . . . Are you going to eat that crust?'

'You know I don't like the outside bits.'

William whipped the offending piece from her plate. 'My brother rang me last night. He's got engaged to his girlfriend.'

'Do you like her?'

'She's beautiful and brilliant and she adores Trevor.'

'Lucky Trevor.'

'He knows he is. He's very smug. He's having a small party for her next month. Will you come with me?'

'Do I have to pretend to be your girlfriend?'

'Certainly not. Just look at me occasionally as if you'd *like* to be. There'll be food. And champagne.'

'All right. I'll come.'

'That's very generous of you,' William said. 'It can be our farewell date together.'

She wished William hadn't brought that up. He was moving on to Reading at the beginning of August, a prospect she found depressing.

'Reading's hardly the Outer Hebrides,' she said. Her phone bleeped and she picked it up. 'It's Tess. We're going down for Dad's birthday on Saturday. I don't know why she thinks I'd forget.'

'How *is* Tess?'

'I don't know. I think she's all right.'

'Next time you talk to her, tell her Marnie says hello and thank you.'

'Who's Marnie?'

'She's my cousin. She met Tess in Durham. She thinks Tess is very wise. Which is more than I can say about Tess's sister.'

'For God's sake, William, I'm just going to *supper!*'

'Right,' William said. 'Of course you are.'

★　★　★

There were two other guests besides Anna, a fact she would pass on to William. Cleo was an old actress friend of Patrick and 'Unlike certain people I could mention,' Cleo said, jabbing an accusing finger at their host, 'I have not given up on the dream.' Cleo was tall and slim with a mane of red hair, a thin pointed nose and a mobile mouth. She had not actually done any acting for fourteen months, she told Anna, and was currently working as a receptionist. She had done three auditions in the last six months and had been recalled four times after the last one. The casting director had virtually promised her the part until a young actress from *Hollyoaks* had expressed an interest and 'That was it. I was out. They wanted a name, even if the name had as much talent as a rotten potato. So I went home and cried for an hour or two. Then my flatmate reminded me that Kristin Scott Thomas lost Hugh Grant to Andie MacDowell in *Four*

Weddings and a Funeral and now Kristin's an international film star and Andie does adverts for hairspray. You have to keep going, don't you?'

The other guest was a broad-shouldered man with a slightly pockmarked face and rather cold green eyes. He looked like Richard Burton in *Where Eagles Dare*. It was easy to imagine him in military uniform barking out orders to his terrified subordinates.

'This is Matthew,' Fizz said. 'He's only here because he's a partner in my firm and I'm hoping if I'm nice to him, he'll make me one too.'

'It's so good to feel needed,' Matthew murmured. He smiled at Anna and instantly looked a lot less like Richard Burton because his eyes were no longer icy but simply amused.

Over supper, the abundant white wine, so generously provided by Matthew, produced different reactions. Anna, after a punishing week at St Peter's, was happy to sit back and observe the verbal fireworks around her. Patrick, perhaps equally tired by the production of the meal, was also content to make only the odd interjection. Cleo charged in with instant opinions which confusingly changed when challenged by an increasingly animated Fizz. Occasionally, Patrick would catch Anna's eye and smile across at her.

Matthew, Anna noticed, liked to throw a topic onto the table and then watch while it was grappled with by his companions. Cleo had been telling them all about a photo her ex-boyfriend had sent her in which he lay naked on his bed. Matthew said, 'Do you remember that poor congressman in the States a year or so ago. He did the same sort of thing'

'Excuse me?' Cleo asked incredulously. 'Did you use the word 'poor'? Are you saying you feel sorry for him? The man had a stellar career and decided to derail it by sending lewd photos of himself to women he met online. You feel sorry for him?'

Matthew shrugged. 'He sent an inappropriate photo to a female follower on Twitter. It's hardly a hanging offence.'

'It's why he did it that's interesting,' Fizz said. 'You read about this sort of thing all the time. Why would someone who has a good career and a happy marriage want to risk ruining everything?'

Matthew shrugged again. 'Perhaps his marriage wasn't as happy as he thought.'

'Excuse me?' Cleo said again. 'Are we therefore supposed to make excuses for him? He was a successful politician and therefore . . . '

'Therefore,' Matthew said, 'we are all entitled to have a go at him. We don't like successful people.'

Patrick shook his head. 'It's not that we don't like successful people. It's that we don't like successful people who abuse their position.'

'Quite right,' Anna said. 'My consultant makes my life a misery.'

'That's different,' Matthew said. 'It's quite healthy to wish disaster on bullies.' He nodded sagely at Anna. 'Your consultant will get her comeuppance one day.'

'I doubt it,' Anna said. 'Unfortunately, she's

very good at her job.'

Matthew settled back in his chair and folded his arms. 'Let me tell you a story,' he said. 'My older sister, Tina, was tormented throughout her schooldays by a girl called Jocasta Kale. Tina grew up to be a dentist and last year she had an emergency patient — one Jocasta Kale. So Jocasta comes in and she doesn't recognise Tina, and Tina gets her in the chair and starts probing her mouth and making polite conversation. 'Did you ever see *Marathon Man*?' she asks and Jocasta nods because she can't say anything at the moment. And then Tina says, 'I love that bit where Laurence Olivier starts torturing Dustin Hoffman by extracting Hoffman's teeth.' And she can see Jocasta's eyes widen a bit and then she says, 'It's so funny to see you after all these years. Do you remember filling my lunch box with used tampons? That was *so* funny!' And now sweat is pouring down Jocasta's face and Tina proceeds to do a skilful and gentle job on Jocasta's teeth and afterwards Jocasta rushes out with a face as pale as milk.'

There was a short silence while the company digested Matthew's account. Fizz gave a theatrical shudder. 'Matthew, that's a really horrid story, if a strangely satisfying one.'

Anna left soon after, not because she wasn't enjoying herself, but because the long day had finally caught up with her. On the bus back home, she remembered Patrick smiling across at her. She caught sight of her reflection in the mirror and discovered she was smiling too.

Her good mood was enhanced when she

found a message on her bed from Olivia. 'Back tomorrow. Thought you'd like to know I've managed to bury the Xander Bullen proposal. We're doing Battersea Dogs' Home instead.'

Anna took out her laptop and googled his name. Under *Images of Xander Bullen*, there were four photos. In two of them he gazed at the camera, his forehead slightly furrowed, his eyes exuding thoughtful sincerity. In the other two he smiled out at Anna.

'Back to the drawing board, Xander,' she murmured but even as she said it she knew she was a King Canute trying to hold back the waves. Men such as Xander would always rise effortlessly like scum. He was handsome, he knew how to charm and he was not held back by scruples of any kind.

9

It was wonderful to have the girls with her. Anna was so positive about her work and Tess was thrilled to be going back to Scotland at the end of her term, particularly since she'd moved with Rachel into a dark little flat on a very noisy road.

Best of all was the change in Felix. When he came back from the station with them both, his eyes sparkled and Freya dared to hope he'd returned to his old self. Over lunch, he sat at the head of the table, accepting his daughters' jokes about his age with great good humour, assuring them he'd be leaping around the tennis courts this very afternoon.

'What about you three?' he asked. He cut a large wedge of Brie and transferred it to his plate. 'Are you going off to Ivy straight after lunch?'

'We'll go at half three,' Freya said. 'We don't want to tire her.' She glanced at her daughters. 'I do hope Ivy remembers you.'

'Last time,' Anna said, 'she thought I was you.'

'It's the blonde hair,' Felix said. 'Last time *I* saw her, she thought I was the cook.'

'That was because you kept going on about her chocolate bourbons,' Freya noted. 'You ended up eating all of them.'

Tess put an arm round her father's shoulder. 'I'm sorry you're not coming with us.'

'I would,' Felix said, 'but unfortunately I have to play tennis.'

'Very unfortunate,' Anna murmured.

'It is my birthday after all,' Felix said. 'But I'm glad you girls are going with your mother. She visits Ivy twice a week and it's not easy.'

In fact, Freya felt guilty that she only visited her stepmother twice a week. There wasn't a mother alive who could be as fiercely loyal and loving as Ivy had proved to be.

Freya and her father had been on their own for seven years when he married again. Freya was, for nearly a year, the stepdaughter from Hell. At fourteen, she was accustomed to being the centre of her father's world and had no intention of surrendering her position to an interloper, particularly when that interloper was a mousey young academic whose love for her new husband was as embarrassing as it was irritating. Freya ignored her when her father was around and was devastatingly rude to her when he wasn't.

And then one evening, everything changed.

Ivy and Freya's father went out to a dinner at which her father was speaking. Freya went to the cinema with a boy she'd been seeing for a couple of months. Afterwards, Russell walked her home and, on the way, he laughed at something she said and she realised for the first time that he had a peculiar laugh. When they got home, she invited him in for coffee and noticed for the first time that his fingernails were unpleasantly long. These revelations forced Freya to tell him she was sorry but she no longer wished to go out with him. Freya had already had similar revelations with her first two boyfriends. Graham had walked out of the house in dignified silence which had been bad enough. Paul had started crying which had been worse. This time was a whole new level of awfulness. Russell sat back in his chair, narrowed his eyes and launched into a lacerating attack on her character. He told her she was conceited and selfish and only ever talked about herself. Reflecting in later years, Freya thought he'd probably been right. He said her looks wouldn't last and now that he was used to them they no longer interested him. All that remained was her character and her character was actually pretty boring.

If he wanted to hurt her — which obviously he did — he was brilliantly successful. Freya knew she was pretty and if he'd tried to convince her otherwise, would have known he was lying. When he told her she was boring, she burst into tears.

And then Ivy appeared in the doorway in her red quilted dressing gown and a nose the same colour. A bad cold and blocked sinuses had precipitated her early return. She stepped into the kitchen and told Russell she had heard all he'd said and felt forced to intervene. She knew he was hurt but she couldn't allow him to voice such wicked untruths. He should accept that part of being a teenager was learning how to reject and how to be rejected. It wasn't Freya's fault that she no longer wished to go out with him. These things happened. If he really thought Freya was boring, he wouldn't be upset at the prospect of losing her and he quite clearly *was* upset. And finally, she said, drawing herself up to her full five feet and two inches, she couldn't allow him to talk to her stepdaughter like that and she would like him to leave.

Russell opened his mouth to speak, thought better of it and left without another word. Freya burst into tears again, flung herself at Ivy, cried, 'Oh, Ivy, I'm sorry, I'm sorry, I'm sorry!' and had loved her ever since.

So naturally, she visited her twice a week and even more naturally she felt guilty she didn't visit her every day. But Felix was right: it *wasn't* easy. Ivy's mind had started showing signs of wear and tear two years ago. When Freya's father died, Ivy didn't cry once, even though everyone knew she'd adored him. She neglected the home she'd always kept so neat and so trim and, more dangerously, she neglected her diet and her appearance. Within a few weeks, she was talking obsessively about her friend, Marilyn. It was as if she had bounced herself out of her real life and into another one of her own making. When it became apparent that she was incapable of living on her own, Freya moved her into a nursing home a few miles away. It was a converted manor house, clean and comfortable and set in delightful gardens, but Freya continued to feel she had let Ivy down by putting her there.

Today was one of her good days. She was delighted to see Anna and Tess and received their embraces with enthusiasm. The girls took chairs on either side of her and she beamed at them both and said, 'You two have such hair! You have such beautiful hair!'

'You're looking well, Gran,' Tess said. 'I haven't seen you in that dress before.'

Ivy's voice sank to a conspiratorial whisper.

'Marilyn gave it to me. She keeps on at me to visit her in Hollywood. I tell her, Marilyn, I can't, I'm needed *here*. She's such a sweet girl but has no luck with men.' She gripped Tess's hand. 'Do you have a young man?'

Tess shook her head. 'No, Gran, I don't.'

'I think that's sensible,' Ivy said. 'You never know what will happen.'

On the opposite side of the room, a frail old lady, with skin like parchment, sat gently weeping. Anna went over to see if she could help and returned a minute or so later. 'The poor woman's wet herself,' she murmured. 'She reeks of urine. I'll go and find someone.'

Anna, action woman incarnate in her blue jeans and black leather jacket, marched out of the sitting room. Freya turned back to Ivy and said brightly, 'Tess is studying very hard these days. She's quite in love with Sir Walter Scott.'

Ivy nodded politely. 'I didn't know she had a young man.'

'Walter Scott was a writer,' Freya said. 'He's dead now.'

'That doesn't mean anything,' Ivy said. Which, actually, Freya thought, in relation to Tess, was probably true.

'He wrote some famous novels,' Tess explained. 'He wrote *Ivanhoe*.'

'I saw Ivanhoe,' Ivy said. 'I saw him on television.'

'She did!' Freya cried. She felt absurdly pleased that her stepmother had at last said something that was sane and true. 'It used to be on television every week. The man who played Ivanhoe

91

was an assistant to the very first Doctor Who.'

'Who, dear?' Ivy asked, and smiled when Freya laughed.

Anna came back in a state of high indignation. 'I found a member of staff and he said he'd have to find someone to help him. How difficult can it be to help an old lady to change her clothes?'

'I don't want to change my clothes,' Ivy said.

'You don't need to, Gran,' Anna said, returning to her seat. 'You look so pretty in your dress.'

'Marilyn gave it to me,' Ivy said. 'She's in love with Tony Curtis at the moment.'

Anna nodded. 'I bet that will end in tears.'

'You're right,' Ivy said. 'I said to her, Marilyn, don't do it. Read a book instead.'

'I quite agree,' Anna said. 'Books are better than men any day.'

Three members of staff came in and bore down on the frail old lady who was whimpering quite loudly now. One of the men said, 'Hello, Iris, let's sort you out, shall we?'

What followed was straight out of a horror film. The gentle old lady turned instantly into a snarling, biting dervish. She kicked and scratched and yelled and was eventually carried out by the three now battered and bruised carers.

Freya and her daughters exchanged horrified glances. Ivy gave them all an understanding smile. 'Don't worry about her,' she said. 'She likes to make a fuss.'

Afterwards, they walked out to the car in silence. Anna looked at her mother and said, 'Are you all right, Mum?'

Freya swallowed a large lump in her throat

and said, 'I feel so ashamed that I've put her in a place like that.'

Anna grasped her mother's hand. 'It's clean, the staff are kind and, quite honestly, Gran has no idea how awful it is.'

'I know,' Freya said. 'It just seems so unfair. And I can't understand how a woman who was an expert on Anglo-Saxon literature can spend all her waking hours talking to Marilyn Monroe.'

'It could be worse,' Anna said. 'Imagine if she were talking to Mother Teresa or Margaret Thatcher.'

★ ★ ★

They arrived home at six. Felix took one look at Freya and announced he wanted presents and champagne *now*. Freya protested it was far too early for alcohol but Felix said, too bad, it was *his* birthday.

Later, as they sat outside eating his favourite meal — steak, new potatoes and spinach — Felix told himself he was truly blessed. He did that a lot these days but tonight he almost believed it. It was a perfect summer's evening with no sound other than the distant hum of a plane in the sky. And there around him were the three most important people in his life: Anna, with Freya's heart-stopping eyes and the easy assurance he used to long for, little Tess whose infectious laugh he heard too rarely these days and, lastly, Freya, so beautiful in her floral dress and pale pink cardigan, and so full of energy and a determination to extract every last bit of experience from each and every day. He hated what he was doing to her, he hated that she tried so hard to be calm and understanding. He worried about all of them. Both his daughters were troubled. He had no idea why but he recognised the signs. He'd say nothing to Freya of course. Heaven knew, she had enough on her plate at the moment. But now, tonight, he could almost convince himself that all was well. Perhaps if he tried hard enough, it would be.

He raised his glass and cleared his throat. 'This has been a quite spectacularly satisfactory birthday. Thank you, girls, for making the effort to come here this weekend.'

'We wouldn't miss your birthday,' Tess said.

'I appreciate that,' Felix told her. 'I feel very happy.'

Freya felt happy too, happy and full of love for Felix and their daughters. She beamed at them all.

'We have another celebration soon,' she said. 'On September the sixth, we'll have been married for thirty years.'

'Will you have a party?' Anna asked. 'You'll have to have a party.'

Freya glanced expectantly at Felix and just for a moment he looked back at her. He looked . . . How did he look? Awkward? Defensive? Taken aback? Then he turned away and reached for the wine.

'We don't want a party,' he said. 'There's nothing more smug or sanctimonious than inviting one's friends and family to marvel at one's perfect marriage. A quiet dinner at home will do very well.'

'Sounds dull to me,' Anna said. 'What do you think, Mum?'

So nothing had changed. Or rather, everything had changed. This wasn't one of Felix's sessions, this was something different, something permanent, and she had no idea how to deal with it. Felix didn't want a party, because he didn't want to celebrate his marriage. For the first time, Freya felt scared. She forced a smile to her lips.

'I certainly don't want a party if Felix doesn't. That wouldn't be fun at all.'

10

Eliza had been determined not to meet the ugly little man again. Curiosity was her downfall. She wanted to know if he really would turn up at his self-appointed position in front of the Pissarro in Room 44. She couldn't believe that any man, especially a diminutive monkey-like man, would seriously expect a woman he'd only just met to agree to meet him in a place and time of his choice.

She had intended to slip into Room 44 and slip straight out again. Her plan was immediately derailed. No sooner had she stepped into the room than a surprisingly loud voice rang out from the other end, 'I'm here!'

Everyone looked at her as if it were *her* fault that the cathedral-like calm of the place had been interrupted. In the circumstances she felt duty bound to walk quickly over to the man before he shouted again. She did murmur in a fierce whisper that it was quite unnecessary to yell at her.

'Never mind that,' he said. 'Just look at this painting! Isn't it beautiful?'

Behind him was a picture of a wide country road under a wide blue sky. She had to admit it was special. It was called *The Avenue, Sydenham* and she could almost imagine she was standing by the artist, gazing beside him at the rural lane and the ancient church. It looked singularly enticing, and enticing was not an adjective she would use about most parts of south London.

'Why did he come *here*?' she asked. 'He was a great Impressionist painter. Why come to Sydenham?'

'I presume he thought it was more congenial than eating rats in Paris. He fled to England when the Prussians decided to invade France in 1870. They laid siege to the capital and, within months, people were reduced to eating their household pets. Even the two elephants at the Paris zoo were made into elephant cutlets. I'm sure you know all the stories.'

Eliza gave a neutral sort of nod. She was irritated by his easy assumption that she knew as much as he did. She gazed at the painting. 'It looks so real,' she said.

'Pissarro was one of the first artists to leave his studio and set up his easel in the open air. But you knew that already, I expect.'

'No,' Eliza said. 'I didn't know.' The man's knowledge about everything was one reason why she had vowed she wouldn't see him again. It was also the reason why in fact she returned for more. He was infuriating and interesting in equal measures.

And so now here she was on her way to her fourth assignation with him. Assignation was hardly the right word to use since it implied something furtive and sexually suggestive and there was nothing even remotely sexy about the man at the National Gallery. Eliza supposed it was a sign of her great age that given the choice between a romantic lover and her annoyingly bumptious art expert she would definitely go for the latter.

In fact, there was little sign of bumptiousness today. He was unusually subdued, possibly because the painting they were looking at clearly moved him. It depicted Gainsborough's young daughters chasing a butterfly. For once it was Eliza who did most of the talking. She commented on the discrepancy between the somewhat sinister backdrop of a dark forest and the almost unearthly radiance of the two children. She mused on the title — *The Painter's Daughters chasing a Butterfly* — and wondered if Gainsborough was trying to make a comment on the fleeting nature of childhood and innocence.

Her companion made an effort to rouse himself. 'I don't know. Perhaps it was simply a literal record of an incident he observed. It's interesting though: it's almost as if he knew what lay in store for them.'

'What *did* lie in store for them?'

'Their lives were difficult. They were daughters of one of the most fashionable artists in the eighteenth century. He regularly carried out commissions for the royal family. So the girls had access to high society without being properly accepted by it. Mary married a musician but the marriage broke down and the sisters ended up living together. I believe Mary suffered from prolonged bouts of mental instability.'

'That's so sad.'

'Yes, it is.'

Eliza waited for him to say more but he had

lapsed into silence again. She was worried. It upset her to see him without his usual energy and enthusiasm. She could see she had been wrong to find him conceited and patronising. He was simply a man who loved art and had a wish to share that love with others. Today, that had gone. Something wasn't right. She said hesitantly, 'I know you have to rush off. Please don't . . . '

'I don't have to rush off any more.'

The statement was all the bleaker for being made without expression. She made a sudden decision. 'In that case, will you allow me to buy us both a coffee?'

She took him to the espresso bar and bought coffee and a flapjack. They sat opposite each other and she was at a loss as to how to proceed with the silent, preoccupied stranger in front of her. She cut the flapjack in half and offered him a piece but he shook his head.

'This is our fourth meeting,' she said. 'I really think we should introduce ourselves. My name is Eliza Sample.'

He gave a formal nod of his head. 'I am Dennis Woodward.'

'Now that we are introduced,' Eliza said, 'I hope you won't mind if I say that you seem a little sad today. It's so unlike you.'

Dennis took a sip of his coffee and then set his cup down on its saucer. 'My sister died three days ago. She's been ill for some time. Every Thursday for some months now I've gone to Bromley to visit her after coming here. Of course, at my age, I am used to the deaths of relatives and friends. But Barbara and I were close and today I feel a little lonely as a result of her absence.'

'I'm sorry.'

'I am grieving for me not my sister. She was always frightened of death. Last week she told me she welcomed it. She told me she was impressed by the cleverness of Nature. 'I feel sick all the time,' she said. 'Why should I want to go on living when I feel sick all the time? You don't need to feel sorry for me when I die.' So I don't. I just feel sorry for *me*.'

'That is quite understandable.'

'Thank you. I'm afraid I am not very good company at the moment.'

Eliza nodded. 'Let us talk about next week. I think we need to see something that will rouse your spirits and I know exactly the picture that will do it.'

'If you are thinking of one of the religious paintings, I should tell you . . . '

'Certainly not.' Eliza took one of the flapjack halves and bit into it, aware that she had at last won his complete attention. 'We shall see *The Execution of Lady Jane Grey* by Paul Delaroche. It never fails to lift my spirits.'

'You *like* that painting?'

'I love that painting. Why? Don't *you* like it?'

'No, I do not. Do you want to know why?'

'I would very much like to know why.'

'I'll tell you. Apart from the fact that it's sentimental tosh . . . ' Dennis proceeded to give a withering assessment of the qualities of Delaroche and, as he did so, Eliza observed with great satisfaction that he picked up and ate the other half of the flapjack.

★　★　★

Maggie left Sheila at the surgery after agreeing to meet later for coffee. Sheila had given up driving after a minor collision with a parked car in Galashiels, and Maggie was happy to act as chauffeur this morning. Katherine had offered to come too but had been diverted by a phone call from her sister in Fife.

Maggie always enjoyed coming to Melrose. In their first year in Scotland she had found communal life difficult. She and Philip would escape to Melrose for lunch together. Philip would sit her down with a large glass of red wine and listen while she ranted about Katherine's tactlessness and Derek's tendency to take an hour to load the dishwasher. After Philip's death she had thought she could never face Melrose again. In fact, she discovered it was here she felt closest to him.

Today, she spent a pleasant half-hour perusing knitting patterns in the fabric place and picture frames in the antiques shop before making her way up to the market square.

She saw Jamie Lockhart walk into the bank. The last time she'd seen him was at Flora Macdonald's birthday party in Kelso, almost a month ago. For a moment she thought about calling out to him. By the time she decided she would, it was too late. He had already gone in. She walked on across the wide square, past the

Mercat Cross and entered the distinctive green door of Randall's coffee shop.

Sheila sat at a table by the window, her glasses halfway down her nose, her ever-present notebook in front of her, ready to receive ideas for poems or stories. Maggie had known Sheila for sixty-eight years. They had helped each other through teenage crushes, miscarriage (Maggie), extramarital temptations (Sheila), career disappointments, maternal worries and bereavement. Now they helped each other through their final years.

'I'm sorry I'm late,' Maggie said, sitting down opposite her and unbuttoning her jacket. 'Have you been here long?'

'Only a few minutes. I've ordered coffee and shortbread. You look a little discombobulated.'

'I suppose I am. How was the doctor?'

'I have to stay on the blood pressure pills. Are you going to tell me what's wrong? Were you worried I might keel over in the surgery?'

'I've just seen Jamie Lockhart go into the bank,' she said.

'He's Tess's admirer?'

Maggie nodded. 'I nearly called out to him.'

'Why didn't you?'

'Well . . . ' Maggie hesitated, already aware that Sheila would find her response pathetic. 'It would look so odd.'

'I don't see why.'

'There's a great difference between striking up a friendly conversation on the pavement and yelling from halfway down the street. He must know that I watched him monopolise my grand-daughter at the party. I would hate him to think I wanted to interfere in some way.'

The waitress arrived with their order and made a point of admiring Sheila's earrings. While Sheila began one of her interminable direction speeches — the earrings had been purchased in a small shop in Edinburgh and if the waitress could follow Sheila's instructions she was a brighter woman than Maggie — Maggie glanced across at the bank and berated herself for her indecisive attitude towards the Jamie question.

Once the waitress had gone, Sheila put her elbows on the table and rested her chin on her hands. 'I've often thought that where your family is concerned, you don't interfere *enough*. And besides, in this case you would be intervening rather than interfering. And anyway, why is it so bad to interfere? Why are we so rude about busybodies and do-gooders? They are busy bodies and they do good. If there were more of them we wouldn't need social workers or dating agencies or therapists. Why is it wrong to want to improve someone's life?'

'Because,' said Maggie, 'I'm not sure I *would* improve it. Suppose I encouraged Jamie to see Tess in the summer and suppose she fell in love with him and suppose he broke her heart — I'd never forgive myself.'

'Suppose Jamie is her soulmate and you do nothing to help them? I think you were *meant* to see Jamie this morning. You think about that while I go to the Ladies'.'

Maggie *did* think about it. She cut her piece of shortbread into four neat columns and took a sip of her coffee. Sheila was a great believer in Fate. Fate was a regular participant in her short stories. As far as Fate was concerned, Maggie was an agnostic. She could not believe her meeting with Jamie was written in the stars. She often saw Jamie in Melrose. He lived in Melrose after all. She sighed and looked out onto the Mercat Cross. A woman sat on the octagonal base with a little girl. The little girl reminded Maggie of Tess. She had the same wild auburn curls and thin little legs and was laughing. Tess used to tell Maggie long, involved jokes that she could never finish because she'd start giggling helplessly and Maggie would laugh too and feel quite weak. It had been a long time since Maggie had seen Tess laugh like that.

'Maggie?' Sheila had returned. 'You were miles away.'

Maggie looked up and, as she did so, she caught sight of Jamie Lockhart talking into his phone by the Cross. 'Sheila,' she whispered, 'that's him!'

The two women stared across at him and then, as he met their eyes, they both waved sheepishly in unison.

'Well, that was embarrassing,' Maggie said. 'For God's sake, Sheila, stop staring at him, he'll think we're both completely mad.'

'Perhaps he likes mad people,' Sheila said, 'because I'm pretty sure he's coming over to see us.'

Sheila was right. In a matter of seconds, the young man had entered the café and was telling Maggie how very nice it was to see her again.

'It's very nice to see you too,' Maggie said. 'This is my friend, Sheila. Sheila, this is Jamie Lockhart.'

Jamie reached across to shake Sheila's hand. 'Mrs Cameron and I were at the same party a few weeks ago. I met her grand-daughter there.'

'We're all so fond of Tess,' Sheila said. 'We're so thrilled she'll be up here for the summer.'

'Will she? Is she coming up to do research?'

'She's got a holiday job in Gasterlethen,' Sheila said. 'She's going to work in a clothes shop there. I'm sure she'll fit in some research though.'

'That's nice,' Jamie said. 'I shall try to call in on her. Do you know when she starts her job?'

'I believe,' Maggie said carelessly, 'it's July the twenty-first.'

Sheila smiled. 'Tess does love Scotland.'

'She obviously has excellent taste.' He glanced at his watch. 'I'd better get on. I'm supposed to be in Edinburgh for lunch. It's been very nice to see you both.'

They watched him run across the square. 'That was interesting,' Sheila said. 'He was very keen to say hello.' She looked across at Maggie and frowned. 'You're quiet. Should I not have mentioned Tess's plans for the summer?'

'I'm glad you did,' Maggie said. 'It meant that I didn't have to. If Jamie does call on Tess . . . '

'And he will,' Sheila said. 'I guarantee it.'

'If he does,' Maggie continued, 'and Tess asks how he knew she'd be there, I can look her in the eye and say that *you* mentioned it.'

Sheila sighed. 'Do you ever think it might be a

lot simpler if you just talked to Tess about all this?'

Maggie picked up a piece of shortbread. 'Yes,' she said, 'but I'm rather keen that Tess wants to keep coming up here.'

11

The supermarket was busy today. The schools had broken up and parents were buying extra rations for the long summer holiday. Freya, negotiating her trolley round children and harassed mothers, came to a halt when she reached the magazine aisle. The covers were like siren voices: pick *me* to find out what Tom Cruise thinks about love; choose *me* to discover the secrets of a perfect complexion; buy *me* to learn the ten steps to lasting happiness.

Now her eyes were caught by a children's magazine. It was the price that shocked her: £4.99 for what was essentially a comic. The cover had a picture of an obviously female mouse since it had a pink tutu, a pink ribbon between its ears and big vertical eyelashes. The magazine promised *One hundred stickers inside!* It exhorted children to *Make a cake-stand!* Who would have thought that all these years after *The Female Eunuch* and a female prime minister, there would be girls' comics for sale, busily encouraging their small readers to make a cake-stand?

A little girl and her mother turned into the aisle. The mother was in her mid-thirties, Freya judged, an attractive woman with light brown hair caught up in a ponytail. She wore faded blue jeans and a sleeveless floral tunic. Her daughter had neatly plaited blonde hair; she wore red trousers and a matching T-shirt and her eyes went straight to the mouse magazine.

She picked it up and looked up at her mother with pleading eyes. 'Can I have this?' she asked. 'Please, can I have this?'

Her mother gave it a quick glance. 'No way,' she said, 'it's nearly five pounds!'

'Please!' her daughter begged. 'I want this so much! I really, really want it! I *love* it!'

'I'm sorry, Chloe,' her mother said. 'We can't afford it and anyway it's a lovely day. You don't want to spend it doing sticking and stuff. We'll go to the playground later.'

'I don't want to go to the playground,' the little girl cried. 'I want *this*!'

The woman stared impassively at her. 'No, Chloe,' she said.

'I hate you, Mummy. I really hate you!'

For a moment her mother glanced at Freya and rolled her eyes. Then she looked down at Chloe and said, 'The only way I can afford to buy that magazine is if I don't buy Friday treats this week and if I don't buy them you'll have to explain why to Martha when we pick her up from playgroup, and then Martha will be quite justified in wanting to share the magazine with you . . . '

'I don't want to share it with Martha. She always puts the stickers in the wrong places!'

'Fine. So the choice is clear. You either get to share the magazine with Martha and she gets to put half the stickers wherever she likes, or we don't buy the magazine and you both get your Friday treats. It's quite simple. The choice is yours.'

'That's *so* unfair!'

'No, it isn't. I'm trying very hard to be fair to both of you.'

'Oh all *right*.' Chloe threw out her arms in a gesture of tragic surrender. 'We'll get the Friday treats!'

Freya was impressed. The mother's tactics had been exemplary: calm, rational arguments followed by careful negotiations. The woman should be in the diplomatic service.

It was only when Freya had loaded her boot with her groceries and was sitting in the car with the key in the ignition that the memory arrived in her mind like the ping of an email. She was in the garden making a den underneath the rhododendron bush. She had swept up the leaves and was serving out tea to Lady Arabella who sat on the ground in her beautiful dress with red roses, her stiff legs splayed out diagonally. Freya passed her a plate with three rhododendron flowers on it. Lady Arabella said they were delicious.

Freya heard her mother calling her and she yelled, 'I'm over here!'

She saw her mother's feet first. They were encased in white sandals and her toes were painted with gold nail varnish. 'Freya,' she said, 'it's time for your bath.'

'Lady Arabella and I are having tea,' Freya said. 'You can join us if you like.'

Her mother didn't want to join her. Her mother wanted her to have a bath right away and when Freya demurred she became very cross and told her to stop being naughty. And then Freya got cross and said, 'I hate you! I want

Daddy to bath me!'

And then her mother did something quite extraordinary. She burst into tears and ran away and Freya sat frozen and scared and didn't dare move. A little while later her father came out to collect her and he bathed her and put her to bed. Later still, Freya heard her mother come into her bedroom. Freya pretended to be asleep and when her mother kissed her cheek she could feel the salty tears on her skin. When Freya's mother left the room, all that was left of her was her rose-scented perfume hanging in the air.

And the next morning, she had gone. Her father told her she'd left them, it was just the two of them now and they'd never see or mention her again. And Freya had nodded and said nothing because she knew it was her fault they were on their own.

Freya blinked and, as she did so, saw the mother come out of the supermarket, a basket in one hand and her daughter's hand in the other. The little girl was skipping. The mouse magazine was clearly forgotten.

★   ★   ★

Stepping down from her coach after a long, weary day of travel, Tess sat waiting for Grandma in the centre of Melrose. Two boys — and they *were* boys, they had to be a good five years younger than her — came up and started chatting to her. Tess was impressed by their confidence. One of them had acne and the other had a very unpleasant stye by his left eye. But they seemed quite undaunted by their physical blemishes and began firing questions in fast Scottish voices that were difficult to understand. She was relieved when Grandma showed up in her car.

It was only a ten-minute journey to the Commune by car and at least half of that time was spent in an argument as to whether Tess should pay rent during her stay.

Grandma was adamant. 'Our house has its rules and one is that we share our guests. If any of them are irksome to at least three of the residents, then we ask them to go.'

'I bet *that's* never happened,' Tess said. 'I can't imagine you standing by the door, demanding someone leaves.'

'It happened a few months ago when Robert's brother, Angus, came to stay. He is one of those men who are so sure they know the answer to everything that you almost believe they do but the longer you talk to them — or rather the longer they talk to *you* — you know that they don't. And the reason why Angus knows so little is because he is so keen to air his own views that he never listens to those of anyone else. We could cope with that most of the time, but then we caught him upsetting Linda, telling her she should make more of an effort to exercise her brain. You may recall that Linda has trouble remembering things these days and she's sensitive about that. So we called a special meeting and the first resident to call for the ejection of Angus was his brother.'

'How did you tell him to leave?'

'Robert told him we didn't like the way he treated Linda and he tried to dig his heels in and insist that he'd been cruel-to-be-kind which is always such a dubious argument, I think. And then Sheila told him he had to go as her children were coming up for her seventieth birthday and there would be no room for other guests. That put Sheila in a good mood for weeks because Angus never even questioned the fact that she was nearly seventy when in fact she is fully six months older than I am.' Grandma turned into the drive of the Commune. 'Now here we are!'

'Grandma,' Tess said. 'Before we go in, can I point out I'm up here for well over a month? I can't — I really can't — stay here so long without making some financial contribution.'

Grandma turned off the engine and fixed Tess with steely eyes. 'When we settled here, my main worry was that we would see less of our children and grandchildren. So it is an undiluted joy to have you staying here. It only becomes diluted when you go on about paying rent. Do you understand?'

Tess's father had always been easy-going where his children were concerned. Just occasionally, he would look at them in a way that made them understand there was a line beyond which they could not cross. Grandma had that same look now.

★   ★   ★

On Monday, Tess borrowed a bicycle from the Commune and set off to work. If she were in

112

London, she would be boarding an overcrowded bus now, trying to find an empty seat and avoid breathing in other people's germs and stale sweat. Instead, she was cycling along roads lined by trees, with the company of a buzzard soaring in the sky above her. She'd been given careful instructions by Dr Knox, which were hardly necessary. All she had to do once she joined the main road was cycle in the direction of Peebles until she came to Gasterlethen.

It turned out to be an odd sort of place. Perhaps early American frontier towns had been like this. There was a wide main street, edged on either side by sober grey terraced housing interspersed with the odd shop. It possessed an equally sober church, a grim-looking primary school and very little else. The place seemed to be deserted apart from two elderly men coming out of the newsagent who gazed open-mouthed at her as she cycled past.

It was not difficult to find Mrs Talbot's shop. It had a bright red door, its glass window frames almost obliterated by posters advertising various entertainments: a production of *Oklahoma!* in Peebles, a meeting of the Horticultural Association in Galashiels and an excursion to Scotland's oldest private house in Traquair. Presumably, interesting events and places were few and far between in Gasterlethen.

Mrs Talbot's shop window had a couple of mannequins who looked like they'd been modelled on the young Doris Day. Certainly they wore clothes that might appeal to the old Doris Day: well-cut slacks, sensible skirts and cashmere twinsets. Scattered around their feet were slim packs of fifteen denier stockings. Tess had no idea that women still wore them and wondered if this was an example of the North/South divide. She must ask Grandma.

She parked her bicycle, as instructed, in a little courtyard behind the shop. She took off her mac and put it over the bicycle while she tried to tie her hair back, a task that took some patience since her curls had become more Medusa-like than ever during the ride from the Commune. She wore the black skirt and white shirt she had always worn when working at the Italian restaurant in London and she smoothed them into shape, collected her mac and went round to the front of the shop.

Mrs Talbot was a small, thin, bird-like woman with grey hair and a soft Scottish voice that rose and fell along with the hand gestures that accompanied it. She had just made a pot of tea, and after checking Tess's particular requirements — milk and no sugar — disappeared behind a brown door, giving Tess a chance to inspect the shop.

The wall to the left of the high counter was covered in shelves on which the knitwear was stacked by colour. On the other side, clothes rails on castors were packed with skirts and trousers. There was a small stiff armchair by the changing room which looked hideously uncomfortable. Tess noted with pleasure the high counter with the burnished wooden surface. There was a pleasing smell of wax polish about the place and the wine-coloured carpet had been newly vacuumed.

Mrs Talbot came back with a tray on which sat two cups and saucers. She directed Tess to one of the two stools behind the counter and set the tray of tea in front of her, before pulling out the second stool for herself.

'So,' she said, 'Dr Knox speaks very highly of you and that's more than good enough for me. I should tell you that your employment is a trial, not for you, of course — at least, I'm sure I hope it isn't — but it is a trial for me. My husband retired a year ago and wants to see more of me, which is very nice, but I have to tell you, I'm not completely convinced that *I* would like to spend more time with *him*. Don't get me wrong; he's a very good man. But I've had this shop for nearly nineteen years and I said to Archie — Archie's my husband — 'Archie,' I said, 'I just can't hand it over and say goodbye, I need to feel the water before taking the plunge,' and that's why you're here, Tess. When Doctor Knox told me about you, I thought you would be just what I need and I shall *endeavour* to stay out of your way and see if I like spending more time at home. As regards our customers, Tess, I have *always* believed my job is to be a peaceful presence amongst the bustle of everyday life. I am ready to offer advice if asked, but otherwise I sit and I smile and I do *not* push myself forward. Quiet discretion is what I do, Tess, quiet discretion. Do you have any questions before I continue?'

'Well, I did wonder,' Tess said with a fleeting glance at the empty street, 'how busy you are.'

'You would be surprised,' Mrs Talbot told her, 'how many people beat a path to this door. We have quite a few foreigners stopping off here and I always like to point out that unlike certain neighbouring factory shops, the standard of our cashmere is second to none.' She stopped to take a sip of her tea. 'Now what I suggest is that, after our tea, I show you the ropes as it were and then I'll leave you on your own. If you have any problems, you can reach me at home and if, by any chance, you can't reach me you can always rely on Mr McTavish at the butcher's three doors away.'

Within the next half-hour Tess learnt how to use the till and record sales, how to fold jumpers and lock up the shop. When Mrs Talbot left, it was with visible reluctance and only after she extracted a promise from Tess to ring her in event of even the slightest difficulty.

The next two hours weren't difficult at all. Tess brought out her much fingered copy of Sir Walter Scott's journal and marvelled once more at his stoicism and good sense. Here he was in 1827, mourning the death of his wife and crippled by debts he was determined to pay back: '*Some things of the black dog still hanging about me but I will shake him off. I generally affect good spirits in company of my family whether I am enjoying them or not. It is too severe to sadden the harmless mirth of others by suffering your own causeless melancholy to be seen. And this species of exertion is like virtue its own reward for the good spirits which are at first simulated become at length real.*'

She could imagine him greeting his many illustrious visitors, chatting to his daughter or his gamekeeper, all the time concealing the fact that his health and his business were falling apart. What a man he was!

At midday Tess had her first customer of the day, a middle-aged woman in a deerstalker hat and brown corduroy trousers. She bought two pairs of stockings and seemed most put out that Tess had replaced Mrs Talbot. Mrs Talbot rang shortly after to check on Tess's progress and Tess described the customer.

'That'll be Edna Murdoch,' Mrs Talbot told her. 'She buys the stockings for her mother.'

'She was not at all happy that you weren't here,' Tess confessed.

'I'm sure that's not true,' Mrs Talbot said, but she was obviously pleased.

At two, an American couple came in and within twenty minutes had bought a total of eight cashmere jerseys and three silk scarves. Tess was thrilled, and when Mrs Talbot rang at three, could barely contain her excitement.

'Didn't I tell you?' Mrs Talbot said. 'You never know who'll come popping by.'

Mrs Talbot was right. Half an hour later, Tess raised her head at the sound of the bell and instantly recognised the young man with pale skin and dark black hair. He appeared not to notice her, focusing with great concentration on the packets of stockings in the window. He wore navy jeans and a navy blue jersey over a white T-shirt, all of which emphasised the slightness of his build. Great-aunt Katherine would probably say that he needed feeding up. Though actually, Tess thought, remembering her strictures on the

117

Lockhart family, she would probably tell Tess to have nothing to do with him. The cuffs of his jersey were beginning to unravel. Tess cleared her throat and said, 'Hello there!'

He raised his eyes, took one of the stocking packets and went over to the counter. 'You're here in Scotland!' he said.

She nodded. 'I am. Do you want to buy those?'

He nodded. 'They're for my mother,' he said. 'So you are here and you haven't rung me. I gave you my card.'

She had forgotten this about him, the disparity between what he said and the way he said it. His voice was soft and gentle, there were no expressive gestures and yet his words expressed an outraged indignation that made her want to laugh. She opened the till and took out his change. 'I've only been in Scotland a couple of days. To be fair, it's not easy to ring a man who once randomly suggested that I ring him some time.'

'I don't remember making a *random* suggestion.'

'You might have forgotten me and then . . . '

'I couldn't forget you even if I wanted to. Thanks to you, Rollo began his first shift on Thursday and dropped a tray of glasses within twenty minutes.'

'You *did* give him a job. I'm so glad.'

'Well, that's all right then.'

She folded her arms and stared back at him. 'If you don't mind my saying so, you seem very . . . very truculent.'

118

'I don't mind at all. I like the word truculent. Truculent suits my mood very well. Do you still want to visit my castle?'

'That would be very interesting, but . . . '

'What time do you finish work on Friday?'

'I'm supposed to lock up at five but I have my bike and . . . '

'That's all right. We can put it in the back of my car. I'll pick you up at five fifteen. I have to go now.'

And that was it. He left the shop before she could raise any objections or even have time to work out if she *had* any objections. She noticed too late that he'd left his stockings on the counter. She did run out after him but he'd already gone.

12

On Wednesday evening, Anna was on her way out of St Peter's as William was on his way in. She called out, 'William!' and watched with glowering eyes as he came across to her. 'I heard this morning,' she said, 'that you had a farewell do at the pub last night.'

'That's right,' he said. 'It was good.'

'I'm sure it was. Did you not think to ask me to come along?'

William frowned. 'I did. I asked you last week if you were free and you said you were working.'

'You didn't say what you were planning. I might have been able to change my shift.'

'You didn't need to,' William said, 'I knew I'd see you at Trevor's party. Which reminds me, it's quite a smart do, so wear a dress.'

She stared at him with mounting irritation. 'I do know what to wear to engagement parties.'

'Great. I'll see you Saturday. And by the way, have you given Marnie's message to Tess?'

'Do you mean the message, *Marnie says hello*?'

''*Marnie says hello and thank you.*''

'I haven't seen Tess recently. She's in Scotland now.'

'Can't you call her?'

'The reception is terrible up there. Can't the message keep? Is Tess so important to Marnie?'

'The thing is . . . ' William hesitated. 'Tess was very good to her.'

'In what way?'

He shrugged. 'I can't say.'

'I don't understand. You can't say or you won't say?'

William looked at his pager — which hadn't beeped — and said, 'It's odd you speak to your sister so rarely.' And then he looked at his pager again and said, 'I have to go.'

As Anna cycled home, she felt increasingly indignant. Who was he to stand in judgement on her sisterly responsibilities? Tess was as bad as she was about keeping in touch. And if Marnie's anodyne message was so important, William could at least explain *why*. And actually, a man who was taking a pretend girlfriend to his brother's engagement party was in no state to sit in judgement on the sibling relationships of others. She would tell him that on Saturday.

She arrived home to an empty flat and remembered that Olivia was going out to dinner with a man called Jason. She wished she could haul herself out of her black cloud. Her whole psyche seemed to be soaked in bile and her future looked bleak. Her career, as far as Miss Diamond was concerned, was a joke. So was her social life. In the last ten months she had had two fleeting and dismally unsatisfactory relationships. Here she was, in her youthful prime, on her own, jealous of Olivia and a man called Jason.

Her phone went and, picking it up, she felt instantly better. 'Hello, Patrick,' she said. She went across to the sofa and settled down with her feet tucked under her. 'How nice to hear from you. How are you?'

'In need of sympathy. Lola threw up over me and the carpet. Fizz is at dynamic yoga and I'm sitting here smelling of sick. How about you?'

'Oh, I'm all right. Work wasn't great today. At least I've had no one throw up over me.'

'That's a perk of parenthood. Fizz is going to Glasgow for the weekend. I know it's work but two nights in a hotel beats spending a weekend with a sick child. I hope you're feeling sorry for me.'

'Yes, Patrick, I am.'

'Good, because I want support. Come and join me on Saturday evening. We could talk about Wimbledon days without boring anyone else. I need you to save me from terminal self-pity.'

'I'm supposed to be going to a party with a friend . . . '

'I can't say I'm surprised, I knew you'd probably have plans . . . '

She heard herself say, 'I could probably get out of it.'

'Oh, Anna, could you? Already I feel better. If you come at eight you won't have to help with putting Lola to bed. You're welcome to come earlier of course.'

'I don't know a great deal about putting children to bed. I'll come at eight. See you then.'

She felt quite breathless. She was letting William down, she knew that. He'd asked her to come to Trevor's party over a month ago. *And* he was moving on to Reading. How to explain that as soon as Patrick asked her, she knew it was

122

imperative to go? I'm a case of arrested development, she could say, I need Patrick to kick me forward. She could imagine William's response. He'd say she was mad, but she was used to that.

She rang him before she could change her mind. He sounded as if he were in the middle of a football scrum.

'Where are you?' she asked.

'At a farewell party.' William raised his voice. 'Not my own.'

'It's all right, I'm not angry now.'

'I can't hear you, I'll go to the other end of the bar . . . What did you say?'

'William, I can't come with you to Trevor's party, I'm sorry. Something's come up and I feel I have to go. First time you're back in London, I'll take you out to make up.'

'It's Patrick, isn't it?'

'It's difficult to explain. I'll tell you when I see you.'

Someone called his name and he said, 'I have to go.'

She felt bad about William. She honestly felt she had no choice.

* * *

Jamie was waiting for Tess on Friday, leaning against a battered old Land Rover. He took her bike, lifted it effortlessly into the boot and went round to open the passenger door for her. This was probably the first time that a man had opened a car door for her. Grandma would be impressed by his manners. She watched him climb into the car and start it up. She asked, 'How is your mood today? Are you still feeling truculent?'

'On the contrary,' Jamie said, 'I'm feeling quite benevolent. I'm always benevolent when showing people round my castle.'

This was not the first time he had referred to 'my castle'. The use of the possessive pronoun triggered a distant memory. When they were children, whenever there were visitors, Anna would ask them, 'Would you like to see my guinea pig?' with the same combination of pride and affection.

They drove out of the small town and on into the open countryside, only to be stopped by a farmer crossing the road with his sheep. Jamie spoke for the first time since he'd got into his car. 'It's rush hour,' he murmured.

She laughed. There was only one other car on the road. She was struck again by how still and patient he was. He didn't drum his fingers on the steering wheel, he simply sat and watched the sheep as they made their leisurely way across to the other side. 'You left your stockings behind,' she told him and, encountering a blank look, added, 'You bought them on Monday for your mother. I've got them here. I'll put them on the back seat.'

'Of course,' he said. 'Thank you.'

'Does your mother live round here?'

'No. She re-married some time ago and moved up near Oban. She and her husband run a small country hotel.'

'Do you see her often?'

'They work very hard. I go up when I can.'

'You must miss her.'

'Well,' Jamie murmured, 'I have my castle.'

He was, she suspected, only half joking. 'Tell me about it,' she said. 'Tell me the history.'

'Are you sure?' he asked. 'It might take some time.'

'I want to know. I'm interested.'

'Well then.' Jamie took a deep breath. 'It was built in the fourteenth century and owned by Sir Richard Palmer, a friend of the English king, Edward the First.' The road was finally clear. Jamie drove on. 'There've been many unpleasant English kings but Edward the First was one of the nastiest.'

'You're sounding like your cousin again.'

'She's my *second* cousin and any history book will confirm what I say. He was a very nasty man and he deserved a friend like Sir Richard.'

'Why? What did Richard do?'

'He stole the king's horses and weapons from time to time. When William Wallace began his rebellion, Richard deserted to William's side. He must have been a smooth-talking charmer. Wallace was captured and hung, drawn and quartered but Sir Richard was forgiven until he made the mistake of deserting again, this time to the side of Robert the Bruce. That wasn't a great career move. Richard was captured and Edward had him brought down to London where he was castrated and disembowelled with his entrails burnt before him while he was still alive.'

'That is disgusting.'

'And *then*,' Jamie continued, 'he was hung, drawn, quartered and, finally, despatched into the hereafter. They didn't leave things to chance in those days. Most of the castle was burnt down and a few years later it was taken over by another family and rebuilt and all was peaceful.' He paused. 'Then it was burnt down by the English again after the Battle of Flodden.'

'There is a distinct edge to your voice when you mention 'the English'.

'I'm sorry. I find this quite emotional.'

She smiled. 'I feel for you. So what happened then? Was it rebuilt *again*?'

'It is that sort of castle. It refused to die. It remained more or less intact until the Civil War when Cromwell's forces did their worst. What you are about to see was mostly built in the eighteenth century by a family who converted it into a tower house. They held on to it until 1901. That was when it was sold to my family. They lived there for a while but it finally defeated them. It was leaking everywhere and they had no money for repairs. Look over there.' He pointed to the only sign of human habitation: a solitary grey tower in the distance. 'That's my castle,' he said. 'By the time my grandfather inherited it, it was in a terrible state and he vowed to restore it. I can remember as a child helping to clear rubble from pathways.'

'So the castle was saved?'

'It was. Grandfather built up a successful legal practice in Edinburgh and he even established a branch in London; in fact, he bought a flat there. But every available penny went to the castle and so, thanks to him, it rose like a phoenix from the ashes.'

They turned into a narrow tree-lined lane and Jamie lapsed into silence. Tess had told the Commune on Monday evening of her chance encounter with Jamie, and Great-aunt Katherine had launched once more into a diatribe against his family. She could remember his grandfather, she said, he'd been a very stubborn man. Tess told Jamie this now and he gave a slight smile.

'People often accuse *me* of being stubborn,' he said, 'when what they really mean is that I'm determined.'

'Sometimes,' Tess said, 'they might just mean you're stubborn.'

'To be honest, I can't see the difference.' He pointed to two neat little cottages on the left. 'I lived in the first one for fourteen months while I did them up.'

'They're lovely.'

'They are *now*. I nearly froze to death at the time. I started renting them out last year. They're both occupied at the moment.'

They drove through an imposing stone arch and suddenly they were there and Tess caught her breath. Perched on the edge of a lush, tree-covered valley was Jamie's castle, standing to attention like a grizzled old soldier guarding Paradise. It was an L-shaped tower rather than a castle, albeit one with rounded corners, battlements and a balustraded balcony. To its left, the hill fell steeply down to meet the River Tweed, to the right was dense woodland. The place was like something out of a horror film or a medieval fairy tale. Tess breathed, 'Oh Jamie, I *love* it!'

He gave a careless nod but she could see he was pleased.

'It is rather fine. Come on, I'll show you around.'

For Tess, entering the castle was like walking into one of Scott's novels. She had feared its spirit might be neutered by all the functions that took place there. She needn't have worried: the place was made of sterner stuff. The Great Hall was full of trestle tables laid out for a wedding the next day but the lighting was muted, there were candlesticks on the tables and Tess could easily imagine banquets in years gone by when weary soldiers would meet to discuss the day's fighting. There was so much to take in — the hall with its vaulted ceiling and its walls decorated with ancient shields, the spiral staircase leading to a small room with a pit dungeon which was supposed to be haunted, a bedroom which Jamie assured her had definitely been slept in by Mary Queen of Scots and another that had seen a tragic murder. And everywhere they went, Jamie told stories and anecdotes in his soft level voice, love of his castle showing through with every word.

When they finally climbed up to the battlements, they stood in the open air, the wind brushing Tess's hair against her face. She buttoned up her thin black jacket and gazed about her, taking in the sharp grassy incline, the dark blue river below and beyond it the equally steep hillside with its clusters of trees and grassy spaces. To be here, she thought, was to elevate the soul. She smiled at Jamie with shining eyes. 'It's so dramatic and yet so calm. I've been to Glencoe and one can feel the violence of its past, but here, it's just . . . glorious.'

'It's like the Border Country,' Jamie said, 'grand and wild and very romantic.' He saw her shiver and said, 'It's also rather cold. I'll take you back now.'

On the way home, he talked about his efforts to turn the castle into a profit-making concern and the plans he had to repair the outbuildings if only he could find the money. 'The trouble is, the Borders are awash with castles. We're all vying with each other for tourists.'

'You really ought to read Scott's novels,' Tess told Jamie. 'Your castle is so like the one described in *The Bride of Lammermoor*. That would be a good tourist angle for you. You still haven't told me why it belongs to you. Did your father give it to you?'

'My father left my mother when I was ten and moved down to England. My grandfather was not pleased. When he died he left the London flat to my brother, and the castle to me.'

'It seems a bit hard on your father. Didn't he mind?'

'He's never been a man to worry too much about possessions. And he always thought my grandfather's obsession with the castle was crazy. Now he thinks I'm crazy too. So does my brother.'

'My mother and sister think the same about me. They think I'm obsessed by Sir Walter Scott.'

Jamie shrugged. 'Speaking as one obsessive to another, I'd rather spend my life caring too much about something than caring too little about anything.'

They were approaching Melrose now and Tess gave him the directions to the Commune. She was conscious of the fact that she wished to see him again. She was also concerned that this simple wish might bring with it a trail of possible complications.

Jamie said, 'Tess, can I take you out to dinner next week?' just as if he'd read her mind, and then he said something so outrageous that she almost gasped. 'I will of course expect something in return.' He absolutely *had* read her mind.

Tess kept her voice admirably level. 'Would you like to tell me what it is you expect?'

If he noticed that the atmosphere in the car had dropped to freezing point, he didn't show it. 'It happened at the party,' he said, 'I've been thinking of you ever since.'

She folded her arms. 'Have you?'

'I have. And now, after this evening, I'm more convinced than ever. I can't think why I didn't think about him before. You're right. I should use Scott to sell the castle. So this is the deal: I take you out to supper and *you* tell me how to do it. Is that a fair transaction?' He gave her a fleeting glance and said, 'I'm sorry. It's not the most exciting way to spend an evening. I shouldn't have asked you. I always forget that other people aren't as fascinated by my castle as I am.'

And Tess, ashamed of her unfounded suspicions, found herself in the unusual position of persuading a man that she wanted to go out to dinner with him.

13

Anna kissed Patrick's cheek. 'You smell nice,' she said.

'I've done my best. Lola's still not well. She threw up again tonight. I've showered and slapped the cologne on but I still smell of sick.'

'Seriously, you don't.'

She sat at the table while Patrick cooked, and they drank the Rioja she'd bought. She asked about former schoolmates and was struck by the inability of men to show interest or even mild curiosity about the personal details of people they knew. He could tell her that Felicity Eggins' second husband seemed a nice guy but had no information as to why her first marriage had failed. Richard Graham — a rather sweet loner at school — was earning a fortune in the City but Patrick had no idea where he lived or whether he had friends now. Most extraordinary of all was the fact that Gavin Millar had joined the Army.

'We went to a party in Wimbledon last year,' Patrick said. 'Gavin was there. He'd just got back from a long stint in Afghanistan.' Patrick might have been telling her Gavin was an estate agent for all the excitement he showed. To be fair, he was busy squeezing cooked garlic cloves out of their skins which looked like a difficult operation.

'Gavin was in Afghanistan?' Anna said. 'I don't understand. Gavin loathed sport at school. What

131

happened to him? Did he change after I left?'

Patrick frowned as if this question had only just occurred to him. 'I don't know that he did. He started going to the gym in the sixth form.'

'Did you *ask* why he'd joined up? What did you talk about?'

'I can't remember.' Patrick's face cleared. 'I think we talked about Andy Murray. He'd been there for the final game.'

Anna sat back in her chair and folded her arms. 'You're a great disappointment. You see Gavin Millar and he tells you he's in the Army and you don't ask him *why*! How could he change so much?'

Patrick set his chicken dish on the table and handed Anna a serving spoon. 'People do change. I wasn't interested in cooking when I was a boy. Now I love it.'

'I don't think people do change that much. Most people learn how to cook when they leave home. I must say this does look amazing.' She took a small helping. She had no appetite tonight.

Patrick topped up their glasses. 'To old friends,' he said.

'To old friends.' Anna clicked her glass against his.

'Tell me about Tess. What's she doing now?'

'She's a university lecturer in London. She teaches English Literature.'

'That doesn't surprise me. She always understood things before the rest of us did. I remember her talking about *Tom's Midnight Garden* in class. She was like you. She had great confidence.'

'I don't remember that. I don't recall Tess

being unusually confident.'

'Well, she was.' Patrick shook his head. 'I can't believe you didn't notice that.'

Anna put down her knife and fork. 'I know what you're doing,' she said. 'I've exposed your indifference to the lives of old friends. So now you accuse me of not knowing my own sister . . . '

'If the cap fits . . . ' Patrick murmured.

'I'll tell you something,' she said. 'You really haven't changed. Do you remember suggesting we meet for a walk on the common after rehearsal? I rushed home to get ready and was there at four, and you were half an hour late and . . . '

'That was entirely your fault. I'd expected you to wait while I did my scene with Mercutio.'

'Why would I wait? I wanted to get changed and look nice.'

'You already *did* look nice. I was blameless.'

'You were very lucky I waited.'

'I was. Do you remember that walk? It was the first time I kissed you.'

Anna picked up her glass. 'Of course I remember. It was the first time *anyone* kissed me.'

'Was it? I wish I'd known. I'd have been less nervous.'

'I'm sorry, you were *not* nervous.'

'You have no idea. You were so lovely. You still are.'

Their eyes met for a moment. She looked away first and he asked after her parents. She talked about her mother's website for a bit and then asked after *his* parents. They were happy, he said, they liked living in Blackheath. 'I'm sure they'd like to see you again. I know Mum was fond of you.'

She nearly choked on her wine. 'I can't believe you said that! Do you *remember* the last time I saw her?'

'Anna, that was fifteen years ago . . . '

'It was fourteen. I still shudder at the memory. The way she burst into your room and saw me half-undressed and then she drove me home and I couldn't stop crying. Oh, it was terrible . . . Patrick, stop grinning! It was one of the worst moments of my life!'

'I know,' Patrick said, 'but it was so like a farce. Mum comes into my room and her mouth drops and then *she* starts shrieking and *you* start apologising while I try desperately to cover my rapidly shrinking erection . . . It *was* funny!'

'You didn't have to share a car with her afterwards.'

'No, but I faced a full-scale grilling when she got back. And the next morning we all drove off to France for a happy family holiday and she would hardly look at me. What happened when she dropped you back home? Did your mother say anything?'

'I was lucky. She came home a few minutes after me. She'd been given a farewell party at her shop and was far too merry to notice I'd been crying. And then later Dad came back with blood all over his shirt.'

'Why? What happened?'

'Someone tried to mug him and he put up a

134

fight. It was all very dramatic and rather lucky for me. I looked like a tragedy queen and no one noticed.'

'It was a rotten way to break up. When we got back from France, you'd moved down to Somerset. I walked over to your house and imagined you were there. I did miss you.' He grinned again. 'You and I were the Romeo and Juliet of Wimbledon.'

'Possibly. I never wanted to kill myself. I wanted to kill *Mum*. It was her fault we moved away.'

'I always liked your mum. She was very nice to me.'

'She's always nice to handsome young men.' Anna put her knife and fork together. 'That was lovely.'

'You haven't eaten much. Can I offer you cheese or fruit?'

'I couldn't eat another thing.'

'Then let's take our glasses through to the sitting room. I have something to show you.'

It turned out to be the sofa. 'It was my first proper effort at upholstery. Sit down. See how it feels.'

She sat down. 'It is quite extraordinarily comfortable.'

'Now you're making fun of me.'

She laughed. 'It *is* nice to see you again.'

He watched her finish her wine. 'Would you like another glass? I have a bottle in the fridge.'

'Thanks, but I'd like to be able to walk back to the bus stop without falling over.'

Patrick joined her on the sofa. 'Do you ever

wonder,' he asked, 'what we'd have done if Mum hadn't burst in on us that evening?'

'We'd have been sensible and stopped. At least, *I'd* have been sensible. At least I think I would.'

'I was crazy about you. You do know that?'

'Well,' Anna said. 'I was crazy about *you*.'

'It still seems unfair. One minute you were there and then you weren't. It always felt unfinished. You know what people say? You never get over your first love.' He leant forward and kissed her lightly on the mouth. 'You make me feel like I'm thirteen again.'

They both knew what would happen next. This time, his kiss was long and easy like the resumption of a long-delayed conversation between old friends. She felt she'd been waiting for this forever. She let her head fall back against the cushions, then arched her back as his hand moved up to unhook her bra.

And then Lola started crying.

Patrick was a good father. 'I won't be long,' he promised. She watched him go upstairs and she heard his voice, soft and gentle as he reassured his child.

So, she thought, first his mother and now his daughter. Someone was trying to tell her something. She stood up and fastened her bra. For a few moments she hesitated and then she picked up her bag and left.

On the journey home she had a text from him. '*Sorry. Sorry about me. Mostly, sorry about Lola.*'

She sent back a jaunty text. '*Just as well!*

136

Thanks for supper!' Already she knew she wouldn't see him again. All she'd wanted, she told herself, was closure. She remembered something William had said a long time ago concerning a difficult relationship from which he was trying to extract himself. 'She says she wants closure,' he'd cried. 'I never trust people who say they want closure.'

And now William was on his own at his brother's engagement party and he'd been right all along. She should have kept away from Patrick. She'd told herself she needed to lay old ghosts and actually all she wanted was to get laid. Patrick was struggling with a sick child and open to temptation. She'd rolled up to his flat like a present waiting to be opened. And the worst of it was she had no one to blame but herself.

★ ★ ★

Freya was at the dentist and feeling quite cheerful. August was turning out to be rather good. Felix's colleague, Ted Davies, had had a heart attack and of course that was *not* good but at least he'd survived and was now taking a well-earned rest. His misfortune had galvanised Felix. He was working all hours but when he did come home he talked to Freya about the pressures on Ted and problems at work. And meanwhile she'd had lovely phone calls from both the girls. Anna had rung last week and been unusually forthcoming, talking about Olivia's new boyfriend, and a dinner date she was about to have with some gorgeous doctor. And Tess sounded so happy in Scotland. She enjoyed her holiday job and was helping some friend of Maggie to promote his tourist business. All in all, life seemed more hopeful than it had for some time.

Freya's eyes drifted towards the magazines on the table and she reached abruptly for one of them. A stunning flower arrangement was displayed on the cover. On either side of it there were allusions to the delights within: *How to get the best out of your allotment! . . . See our sensational herbaceous borders . . .* And then the extraordinary words: *Meet gardener Xander Bullen: dishy and different!*

There couldn't be another Xander Bullen. She rifled impatiently through the pages and there he was. His shoulder-length hair was now short but it was most definitely Xander, in faded jeans and a white T-shirt, one foot poised ready to push his spade into the soil. Fourteen years had actually improved his looks. He'd been a little too thin before, whereas now his T-shirt displayed to flattering effect his rather more solid chest. He looked more confident, too, his eyes staring out at the camera with a hint of amusement. She turned the page and gazed at another photo of him on a bench with a baby on his lap and a pretty girl beside him. The caption below said, *Xander in his garden with his wife, Poppy, and his daughter, Georgie.*

Poopy looked very young. Freya started reading the interview. *''There is nothing airy-fairy about holistic gardening,' Xander told* me. There is nothing airy-fairy about Xander full stop. Forget the gym, boys. If you want a six-pack like his, maintain a successful garden . . . 'Holistic gardening,' Xander says, 'is simply an understanding that everything is a question of balance. So, for example, if you plant horseradish near new potatoes, you'll be doing your bit to deter potato bugs. If you grow thyme near your cabbages, you'll reduce the number of cabbage worm and whitefly. You know how some people bring out the best in you? It's the same for plants. Respect your garden and your garden will respect you.' '

Apparently, he had a book out this month. Who would have thought it? The dentist came through and told Freya he was ready for her. She put the magazine down and resolved to buy a copy for herself as soon as possible.

★ ★ ★

Eliza had invited Dennis to tea.

Such an invitation was quite out of character and Eliza still wasn't certain why she had made it. She had moved into her present flat twelve years ago and had never welcomed guests. If she wished to see friends, she went out to meet them for coffee or lunch or tea. She neither accepted nor proffered dinner invitations on the grounds that she went early to bed.

The fact that she never invited guests to her flat only occurred to her after she extended the invitation to Dennis. She assumed it was because she was lazy, and there was an element of truth in that. It wasn't that she was ashamed of her home. It was very pleasant and ideally situated, being just a stone's throw from Harrods. It had no garden, of course, but it was on the ground floor so there were no wearisome stairs. She kept all her books in the spare room and her living quarters were cool and uncluttered. In fact, should anyone ask her to describe her home in one word, 'uncluttered' would be the word she would choose.

It was also the reason why she had never entertained here. She was, she could see now, a little embarrassed and possibly even ashamed by this aspect of the place. There were no photographs, no family portraits of husbands or gap-toothed children or lanky teenagers. Anyone could see that Eliza Sample was a woman who had left no mark on the world in which she lived. It was not that Eliza regretted the absence of children or grandchildren. She had made her choices and, having made them, saw no point in indulging in pointless hypothetical fantasies about what might have been. She knew she was lucky. She lived in comfort, she had her health and her mental faculties — touch wood — and she had no reason to feel sorry for herself. What she found difficult to tolerate was the idea that others *might* feel sorry for her. She liked her cool, uncluttered flat. She kept people away from it because she didn't want to see it through their eyes.

But Dennis was different. Dennis had never once asked her for any personal details. He had never asked about husbands or children or grandchildren. He was motivated by a passion for art. At first, she had mistaken his passion for an arrogant, pushy desire to show off his knowledge and his erudition, but it wasn't that at all. He wanted her to share his enthusiasm and his excitement. He wanted her to share the fascination he felt when he looked at a painting and the secrets it revealed about individuals who were long dead but not forgotten. He showed her that a passion shared and discussed was ten times more powerful and satisfying than one digested in solitude. Dennis made her happy and that was why she invited him to tea.

She had suggested he come at half past three. She had thought about producing scones but she hadn't made them for years and decided it was safer to prepare egg sandwiches. She did make a cake — a simple sponge, sandwiched with jam and fresh cream — and she was glad she had done so because its aroma filled the flat with a welcoming warmth.

At twenty past three she went into her bedroom and checked her appearance. She wore grey trousers and a crisp pale pink shirt with her usual pearl necklace. Her white hair, cut in a smooth, sleek bob, was as disciplined as ever. She applied a little perfume and smiled at her vanity because she knew her visitor would almost certainly appear in his same, badly fitted brown suit.

Checking her watch, she went through to the kitchen to boil the kettle and warm the teapot. She took out from her cupboard two porcelain cups and saucers and a small matching jug which she filled with milk. At a quarter to four she moved to the sitting room and glanced round at the small desk in the corner with her laptop and her brass lamp, the two-seater sofa with its abundance of cushions, and the coffee table on which sat her latest acquisition, a book about Velasquez's paintings. She was looking forward to showing it to Dennis. She went over to the window and stared out into the street.

An hour later she knew he wouldn't come. She went into her kitchen and considered the food on the table. She wasn't sure what to do about the cake. If she put it in a tin, the cream would go off. She put it in the fridge and turned her attention to the egg sandwiches. She could have some of them for her supper. The rest would keep till tomorrow.

★ ★ ★

It was more than a fortnight since the evening with Patrick. Anna had done her best to rouse herself from her pit of self-loathing. She had been ultra-kind to her patients, she had accepted a dinner invitation from a doctor acquaintance, she had rung her mother and made an effort to be nice. She'd even told her about the dinner date, a big mistake since the evening revealed they had nothing in common except a mild mutual attraction.

Still her dark mood persisted and she knew the reason why. William — kind, easy-going, best pal William — had expunged her from his life with a ruthlessness that shocked her. When she rang, he wouldn't pick up. He responded to none of her texts or voicemail messages. For the time being she'd stopped trying. There was nothing more she could add to the apologies she'd made. Of course she'd been wrong to cancel Trevor's party but if he'd been so upset about it, he should have told her at the time. It wasn't like William to sulk and she felt stunned by his silence. Now she was beginning to be angry with him. If all their years of friendship meant so little to him then, fine, she'd be fine. Eventually.

14

The job of castle custodian was far more complex than Tess had realised. For a start, there were a fair number of castles in the area and Jamie did not have the monopoly in romantic wedding locations. In fact, he told her, weddings provided only a small part of the castle's income. In the last year alone, there'd been a Burns supper for fifty, a marmalade festival, office parties, business lunches, school tours and the hiring of the castle for a four-minute scene in a BBC serial drama.

Tess was convinced that Sir Walter Scott could be a huge draw. She had discovered that he and Wordsworth had indeed visited the place. 'The timing is perfect,' she said. 'There's this huge debate about Scotland's relationship with England. We have the referendum in September. Scott was a huge supporter of the Union but he was also fiercely proud of being Scottish. He was the great reconciler. He couldn't *be* more contemporary.'

'To be honest,' Jamie said, 'his only connection with the castle is that he once spent an afternoon here.'

'There's your name,' Tess said.

'To be honest again,' Jamie said, 'I'm not absolutely sure that I *am* related to his son-in-law.'

Tess frowned. 'You don't need to say you are. You can just talk in your literature about Scott and his great friend and son-in-law, John

Lockhart. People will see your name and make the obvious assumption.'

'Tess,' Jamie murmured, 'I'm worried I'm corrupting you. Whatever happened to academic integrity?'

Tess wasn't sure. In the last few weeks she had spent so much time with Jamie that it was impossible not to share his enthusiasm. As an academic, she did sometimes feel she led a rarefied existence; it was exhilarating to find she could apply her skills and knowledge in the development of a sound business project. She and Jamie had spent evenings in pubs poring over competitors' brochures. She agreed with him that Reidfern Castle was superior to all of them.

Tonight, for the first time, she was driving over to his house in Melrose. Intent on following his instructions, she turned into a small lane near the famous Melrose ruins and parked the car by the green litter bin on the bank. She reached for her bag, climbed out of Grandma's car and locked it before turning round to check that she was indeed opposite Number Two.

For a moment she stared blankly at the small terraced cottage opposite her. She took a sharp intake of breath, felt quite light-headed, and let her back slump against the car. It was her house. It was *her house*. She gazed down at her feet. Here was the cobbled lane and, as she looked up to the left, she could see that it ended in a small clearing a few yards further on. She swallowed and fixed her eyes on the white door with its horizontal partition. She shut her eyes and put her hand to her forehead.

A voice said, 'Tess?' and she opened her eyes. Jamie was there, looking anxiously at her. 'Are you all right?' he asked. 'Is something wrong?'

'It's just that . . . ' Her throat felt dry, it was difficult to speak. 'I know this place. I've seen it. I don't understand.'

He put an arm round her waist and guided her across the lane, through the door and into a small sitting room. He took her to the sofa and sat her down. 'I'll get you some water,' he said. 'Don't move.'

As soon as he left, she sat back, her eyes travelling round the room. A small pine table by the window carried Jamie's laptop and printer. The walls were painted in a soft chalky colour; they were empty of pictures apart from a large black and white print of Reidfern Castle on the wall to the right of the fireplace. On the mantelpiece above the wood-burning stove there were a couple of framed photos. The grey carpet looked like it might once have been white or cream. The sofa on which Tess sat was comfortable though the material was worn, particularly on its arms. Only the curtains, resplendent tartan green and red, looked new. It was easy for Tess to imagine herself sitting here, reading her book and sipping her cocoa.

'Here we are.' Jamie was back with a tray containing a tumbler of water and two glasses of red wine. He put them down on the pine table. 'I prescribe water first and then wine. You do look pale.'

'I'm fine. It was rather a shock seeing your house. I know it sounds weird but I feel I know

146

it. I must have walked here once with Grandma or something. It's a lovely place. If you could see my horrible, poky little flat in London . . . Seriously, you have no idea how lucky you are. Have you been here long?'

'I moved in two years ago. I'd been camping out in the castle cottages while I did them up. It was a great pleasure to move into a place with a working bathroom and kitchen.'

'I can imagine it would be.'

'Are you sure you're . . . ?'

'I'm fine. Tell me about the photos on the mantelpiece.'

Jamie brought them over to her and put them on the table. He nodded towards the first one, a black and white picture of a fierce-looking man with a strong jaw and piercing eyes. 'That's my grandfather. You'd have liked him. He was a great fan of Scott. Every time he drank a little too much whisky he would declaim Scott's words: *Breathes there a man with a soul so dead, Who never to himself hath said This is my own, my native land!* He drank a little too much whisky quite often so that's how I know those words by heart.'

'And what about the other one? They must be your parents. The man looks so like you.'

'Now he would tell you I look like *him*.' He took his wine and joined her on the sofa. 'You're not going to faint on me, are you? When I saw you out by the car, I was convinced you were going to faint. We had a wedding at the castle three months ago and the bride's mother did just that . . . '

It was a pleasure to sit listening to Jamie's soft, lilting voice. She was aware that her first stunned amazement was settling into a sort of dazed acceptance that there was something almost magical about this evening.

When Jamie suggested it was time to eat, she followed him through to the kitchen and again, it was as she'd imagined: a small, immaculate galley kitchen. Either Jamie had impressively high standards of cleanliness or he had made a huge effort. On the table there was a bowl of salad, with places for two and napkins to the side. Tess watched Jamie take the lasagne out of the oven. 'You've gone to so much trouble,' she said.

'I owe you,' he told her. 'I think we make an excellent team and I'm very grateful for all your help.'

'I'm enjoying myself. I think I might be getting slightly obsessive. I woke up this morning with ideas for castle worksheets for schools. You could find out what people ate and wore, you could bring in the Battle of Flodden and Mary, Queen of Scots. The possibilities are endless.'

'I know,' Jamie said, 'but I need someone who knows about that sort of thing to organise it. I need someone who's good at research and academic work. I'd pay her, of course, and I'd be happy to give her free board and lodging here. I'd even cook her lasagne from time to time.'

Tess smiled. 'That sounds nice.'

'I hoped you'd think so.' Jamie began to serve out the lasagne. 'I'm serious by the way.'

'I'm sure you are.' She took the plate from

him. 'This smells good.'

'Help yourself to salad. Would you like dressing?'

'Please.'

He placed a small jug on the table. He sat down beside her and then stood up again. 'Do you want salt and pepper?'

'Jamie, I'm fine. Please. Sit down. You're making me nervous.'

'I'm sorry. I *am* nervous.'

She stared at him. 'Why? Is there something wrong?'

'I don't know. That's the problem. I have absolutely no idea.' His voice was as level as ever but his eyes never left her face.

Tess wasn't naïve. She had suspected his interest in her was not just professional. She had even been ready to politely deflect any advances tonight. But the sight of his house — *her* house — had thrown her. She had a queer impression that she was in some parallel universe in which she could contemplate with a degree of curiosity the idea of kissing the man sitting next to her at the table.

She had a sudden conviction that she was at a crossroads. Tonight — this moment — she was ready to be kissed. She leant forward. 'Do you want to explain?'

'The thing is . . . ' Jamie murmured, and now, very slowly, he brought his face towards her own. She felt a wave of panic but she didn't turn away.

And that was when the doorbell rang.

★ ★ ★

149

Freya should have been preparing supper. Instead, she was re-reading an intriguing email.

'Dear Mrs Cameron,

I heard about your website from my son, Jamie, who lives in the Borders and has been seeing quite a lot of your daughter. For some time now, I have had the idea of researching my family tree. We're quite an interesting bunch. One of my ancestors on my mother's side was Lord Chancellor. I have a picture of him in our library. My mother maintained that we're descended from the half-brother of Mary, Queen of Scots. By all accounts, he was not a very nice man so perhaps I shouldn't boast of the connection.

Having studied your website, I would love to engage your services. I also have a rather cheeky suggestion. On 6 September, my wife and I are throwing a party to celebrate our tenth wedding anniversary. I've been trying, so far without success, to persuade Jamie to come down for it. I have a strong suspicion that if he knew Tess and her parents were invited, he'd make the effort to do so. Would you and your husband and Tess care to join us? I quite understand if you can't but I'd be delighted to meet you all. Yours, very sincerely, Neil Lockhart.

His son had been seeing 'a lot' of Tess! Freya felt a surge of excitement. Was it possible that Tess had at last found a man who appealed to her? The fact that Jamie had told his father about her seemed to indicate a level of confidence on his part. Neil Lockhart obviously believed there was a serious romance. Why else would he want to meet Tess and her parents? Freya read through the email again. The man had a library! She picked up the phone.

The trouble with ringing the Commune was that one had no control over who answered. At the moment it looked as if no one would. She couldn't believe that all of the inmates were currently out on the town. She drummed her fingers on her desk and then stopped as she heard sounds of life from the receiver.

'Hello?' The voice was tentative.

'Linda? Linda!' Freya's voice increased in volume and enthusiasm. 'Hello there! It's Freya!'

'Oh.' There was a pause followed by a cautious 'Hello.'

'It's Freya,' Freya said again, 'Felix's wife.'

'Felix!' Linda said, with more enthusiasm. 'How is he?'

'He's very well! We're both looking forward to seeing you all in October. Linda, could I have a word with Tess . . . or with Maggie?'

'Right,' Linda said, 'I'll go and see.'

'Thank you,' Freya said. If she ever ended up in a commune she would make sure that each of the residents had mobiles. It was ridiculous for all of them to share just one house phone. She glanced at her watch: half past seven. She had no idea it was so late. Keeping her phone clamped to her left ear, she went through to the kitchen and poured a large glass of Sauvignon. The fact that Tess had at the very least a *possible* boyfriend was definitely a cause for celebration. Felix might say — Felix *often* said — that Tess would find a partner in her own good time but

151

there was no denying that it was odd for a pretty young woman to be resigned to celibacy at twenty-seven and Freya was as sure as she could be that Tess *was* resigned. Freya used to believe that all she wanted for her daughters was that they were happy. But actually, she wanted them to be normal as well. She didn't mind if Tess proved to be gay. She just wanted to know that she was capable of loving *someone*, because if she wasn't, Freya felt that somehow *she* must be to blame.

She went back to the study with her wine in one hand and her phone in the other. She took her place in front of the computer. Linda was taking a very long time. Freya shouted, 'Hello,' into the silence. Linda was clearly losing the plot and sooner or later so would the others and eventually no one would answer the phone, and concerned relatives would be left hurling out greetings into the ether.

And now at last a voice responded. 'Hello? Is anyone there?'

'Aunt Katherine! Hello there! It's Freya.'

'The receiver was lying on the hall table.' Aunt Katherine sounded quite aggrieved as if this was Freya's fault.

'I spoke to Linda. She said she'd go and find Tess and Maggie for me. I've been waiting some time.'

'Tess is out, I'm afraid. She's very rarely *in*. How is Felix?'

'He's very well.'

'I'm glad to hear it. We're about to have supper. I'll go and get Maggie for you.'

'Thank you, that's very kind. I'm sorry to ring now. I only want . . . ' But Aunt Katherine had gone. It was interesting that both she and Linda had asked after Felix and had shown no interest in *her* at all. She had another sip of wine and hoped Aunt Katherine's attention span was sharper than Linda's.

It was. A familiar voice came to the phone and said, 'Freya, how nice! We were having our sherry in the garden. It's the most beautiful evening up here.'

'It's lovely down here too. Maggie, I'm ringing about an email I've received. It's from a man called Neil Lockhart.'

'Oh.'

There was a rather odd intonation in her mother-in-law's voice. Freya asked, 'Do you know him?'

'I know his *son*.'

'I gather Tess does too. According to the email, they've been spending a great deal of time together.'

'That's true. Jamie owns a castle. He hires it out for functions and weddings. He wants to expand the tourist side. I gather Sir Walter Scott went there and . . . '

'How *fascinating*! Tess told me she was helping one of your friends promote his business and I imagined some sweet old gentleman and instead he's a young man with a castle! Are he and Tess close?'

'I have no idea. Why did his father write to you?'

'He seems to think there might be a romance.

153

He's invited Felix and me and Tess to a party in London.'

'Has he? How extraordinary.'

'Jamie has told him about my website and he wants me to research his roots.'

'His what?'

'His roots, Maggie. He wants me to look into his roots. Could you ask Tess to ring me sometime soon? I've tried her mobile once or twice but there doesn't seem to be a signal.'

'That doesn't surprise me. It's not easy ringing people up here.'

'So I've discovered,' Freya said with feeling.

'Now tell me, Freya, how is Felix?'

'He's very well.' Freya could hear Aunt Katherine calling Maggie to supper and added quickly, 'I must let you go. We'll speak soon.' She put the phone down and wondered, not for the first time, why Tess had to be so secretive. Why had she said so little about the mysterious man? A man with a castle known to Walter Scott had to be perfect for her. She was aware she was being watched and saw her husband in the doorway.

'You were miles away,' he said, 'staring up at the ceiling like it was about to fall down on you.'

Freya pointed at the computer screen. 'Read that,' she said.

His face looked increasingly bewildered as his eyes scanned the text. 'Has Tess talked to you about this man?'

'She said he was a friend of Maggie. I rang Maggie just now and she says she knows him but . . . you know what Maggie's like. She's not very forthcoming.'

'Well . . . I don't know what to say. I suppose you and Tess might find it fun.'

'Don't be silly, Felix. September the sixth is our *own* wedding anniversary.'

'I know.' Felix pushed back his chair. 'I'm afraid I'll be in Spain for it.' He rose to his feet and put his hands in his pockets. 'It's because of Ted. We're opening up a new office in Madrid. Ted was in charge and of course now he can't go . . . '

'And so *you* have to go?'

'There's no one else. I'm sorry. I only found out today. It'll be fine. We'll celebrate when I get back. I know it's an important anniversary . . . '

'I thought it was.' Freya turned off the laptop. 'I suppose if I'm not having my own, it might be fun to go to someone else's.'

'Freya, I've told you I'm . . . '

'It's all right, Felix, I'll have fun in London. I'd like to go to the party. The truth is I'm curious. We've been worried about Tess for years . . . '

'*You've* been worried. I'm not.'

'Well, of course, it suits you very well to have Tess all to yourself without any annoying boyfriends in tow.'

'What does *that* mean?'

'Oh I don't know.' She picked up her wine glass. 'I suppose I'm fed up with the fact that we keep pedalling along as if everything's great and now I have an email from a man who seems to think that our younger daughter might at last be interested in a flesh and blood male and you're saying we're fine and I don't think we are, Felix, really I don't.' She stared at him, almost out of breath. If he laughed at her she would cry.

Felix didn't laugh. He looked down at the floor and then back up at her. 'Go to the party. Stay at a hotel and buy a new dress. You'll be the belle of the ball. You always are.'

★ ★ ★

Fortunately, there was more than enough lasagne for the three of them.

Jamie's brother was every inch the actor. Rory was very good-looking, he *knew* he was good-looking, he loved to be centre stage and he took it for granted his audience was thrilled to see him.

'I cannot believe,' he said, helping himself to more lasagne, 'that my big brother would *forget* that I was coming to stay with him. Do you want to know something, Tess? The last time I saw Jamie was at Christmas — *Christmas*! That was over half a year ago. A couple of months ago, anxious to pay my fraternal respects, I went out of my way to suggest a fortnight when we could see each other and now, I wend my weary way to his house and . . . '

'Rory, you are such a bullshitter,' Jamie said. 'The only reason you're here is because you've been performing at the Edinburgh Festival and you wanted an easy, inexpensive holiday afterwards. How *was* your play?'

'Thank you for asking, Jamie, particularly since you failed to turn up even though I got you a ticket. There I was on stage, peering out into the audience, trying in vain to spot my brother and all I saw was an empty seat. The play, I have

156

to tell you, was a dog's breakfast. Mona — and never was a name more aptly given — Mona wrote it herself and if I'd known what an appalling director she'd be, I'd have turned it down at once. The rehearsals were a joke. And then, when we get to Edinburgh, it's clear she's shagging Bernie Root. If I tell you that Bernie is the most repulsive actor in the world, you should know that I am being kind to him. At the first rehearsal in Edinburgh, Bernie has to rape Ruthie and Bernie gets carried away and throws her down so hard that we have to call an ambulance and she has to have an X-ray on her head or her neck, I can't remember which, and then, just before we start again, without poor Ruthie of course, we see Mona bend over for something — and you have to know that Mona has started wearing very short skirts — and Mona bends down and we all see Bernie push his hand up her legs and we all try our hardest not to puke. Trust me, if you could see Bernie, you would puke. He refuses to wear shoes on his feet and they are quite disgusting; he doesn't approve of alcohol and he sits around eating revolting food. His favourite snack is bread smeared with vinegar. He and Mona both have partners but they spend their time slipping, very subtly, into the conversation that they don't believe in monogamy. And none of this would matter if the play had been any good but it was supposed to be sexy and meaningful and it was about as sexy as a fart in a lavatory.'

'In that case,' Jamie said, 'it was just as well I didn't see it.'

'I'm sorry, but that is no excuse.' Rory turned to Tess. 'The trouble with Jamie is he's a workaholic. He lives and breathes his stupid castle. He can talk about nothing else. He can *do* nothing else. He is, I'm afraid, a complete bore about it.'

'It's quite a beautiful castle,' Tess said. 'It's easy to be obsessed by it.'

Rory looked at her as if she were mad. 'Do you work for him?'

'No. I know a little about the Borders . . . '

'She's being modest,' Jamie said. 'She's an authority on Sir Walter Scott. She thinks I could use him to promote Reidfern. She has some amazing ideas.'

'I see.' Rory looked at Tess and then at Jamie. 'I haven't interrupted a romantic evening, have I?'

'Not at all,' Jamie said. 'We are both thrilled beyond words to have your company.'

'In that case,' Rory said, 'I'll finish off the lasagne.'

15

Everything had gone wrong. With every smutty story Rory told, Tess was freshly aware of her own humourless, sexless self. She tried to smile politely but her facial muscles were frozen. She was like one of those actresses who overdose on Botox. How had she possibly imagined she might have a proper relationship with Jamie? As soon as she could, she made her excuses and left.

The horrors did not let up. The next day she got back from work and her mother rang with some weird story about Jamie's father who had apparently heard all about her and wanted Tess and her parents to come to some party in London which her mother thought would be fun. Tess said she was expecting a call and rang off. And then, as if to punish her for that lie, the phone *did* ring and it was Jamie who asked if she'd like to meet up that night. He and Rory were off to see their mother in Oban the following day and would be away for most of the week. He did not seem surprised when she made an excuse and he made no effort to suggest a future date.

In Tess's less rational moments she wondered if Fate hadn't led Rory to his brother's door at that particular moment, thus preventing her from leaping into the void. But she was bereft without Jamie's company. In the last few weeks they had seen so much of each other. Without

Rory, their friendship might possibly have ended abruptly. Now it seemed to have ended anyway. As the days went by, she knew Jamie had spoilt Scotland for her. In the evenings she played backgammon with Dr Knox, and Scrabble with Grandma and Sheila, her ears alert to the sound of the telephone. Whenever it did ring and turned out not to be Jamie she was torn between relief and disappointment.

And then at last she had a rather formal call from him. Could he take her out to dinner on Thursday? He knew she'd be going home on Saturday and it would be nice to say goodbye. She said primly that that would be fine.

She was ready and waiting by seven. Jamie was twenty minutes late and full of apologies. There'd been a crisis at the castle, something had short-circuited; she wasn't sure what. She barely listened to his explanation, she was simply glad to be in his car with him again.

He had chosen Burt's Hotel in the centre of Melrose. It was an elegant place that was gloriously old-fashioned. Its walls were full of gilt-framed paintings, patterned carpets, impeccably starched white tablecloths and napkins, and staff who were unfailingly courteous.

They were led to a table for two and after Jamie had ordered wine and water, he stared at her in that disconcertingly blank way of his. 'I wasn't sure you'd agree to come.'

His candour and his shrewd understanding of her character shocked her. She could feel her face blush red. 'I wanted to say goodbye.'

'How was your last day in Gasterlethen?'

She was grateful for the change of subject. 'I think Mrs Talbot's quite happy to see me go. She's discovered she definitely doesn't want to spend more time with her husband. She can't wait to have the shop to herself again.'

'Are you glad to be going home?'

She swallowed. 'No.'

'I'm pleased to hear it. Tess?'

He had put his hands on the table. She noticed a plaster round his index finger. She raised her eyes. 'Yes?'

'I think ... ' He looked away and then reached for the menus. 'I think we should decide what we want to order.'

They both studied their menus with careful deliberation. Tess chose the chicken; Jamie went for the venison. The waitress arrived with their drinks. Jamie gave their choices. When the waitress left them, he poured out the wine. 'I have some news,' he said. 'Next Sunday evening, I have a Very Important Person coming to inspect the castle. If she likes it — and it will be a very big If — it will be the focus point for a documentary series on England and Scotland. The provisional title is *Intimate Enemies*. Thanks to the referendum, it's a hot topic.'

'Jamie, that's amazing!'

'It *will* be if I can sell it to her. I'll be working flat out till I see her. It's a pity you can't be there. You could impress her with the Walter Scott angle.'

'I wish I could be. To think I'll be back in London and ... ' she stopped. 'In fact I'm supposed to be at your father's anniversary party next Saturday. He contacted my mother. I hear you told him all about me.'

'I actually told him about your mother. I said he should use her services to research our ancestors. He's invited you all, has he? He does things like that.'

'My mother is determined we go. I think she's making a point to Dad. It's *their* wedding anniversary and he'll be abroad on business.'

'You should go. I'm sorry I can't be there. You'll like my father. People always do. His wife's a nice woman.'

She gave a little shrug. 'Well, if we do go, I'll let you know what it's like.'

He raised his eyebrows. 'Are we to keep in touch then?'

He seemed determined to wrong foot her. 'Don't you want to?'

He sighed. 'I have a confession to make. It's an embarrassing one. You may well decide as a result that you don't wish to see me again. The trouble is, if I *don't* tell you, I don't think I'll want to see *you*. It would be too difficult.'

Tess had the weirdest sensation that her brain had been taken over by two voices. One cheered Jamie on, the other advised her to shut him up now before he got any further. 'In that case,' she said slowly, 'you'd better tell me.'

'Right.' He glanced round at the other guests as if seeking their approval. Then he put his elbows on the table and stared at her. 'The first evening we met, you came into the room surrounded by your three elderly companions and . . . I was transfixed. That doesn't happen

162

very often. I told myself, Jamie, you do not walk up to a strange woman and assure her she should spend the rest of her life with you. I was cool. I refrained from going over to you for at least thirty minutes and when I *did* . . . ' He smiled slightly. 'You have a beautiful voice, you know. It's quite husky and every now and then you sound as if you're going to cough but you don't. It sounds like it's wrapped in caramel and sometimes you get near the nut in the middle . . . I'm sorry, this must be very boring for you.'

'How can it be boring to hear I have a nice voice?'

'Well. I chatted away and you were charming and gave no indication that you had any idea of the momentous event that had taken place. And then you went back to London and I spent long, bitter hours thinking that being cool was overrated.'

The waitress came back. The venison was off, she said apologetically. Jamie ordered the fish and followed her departure with a slight cough. The voices in Tess's brain had gone silent. For now, all that mattered was to hear the rest of Jamie's confession.

He pressed his palms together. 'The miracle happened and you came back. I'd been given a second chance. Eventually, I invited you to supper to express my feelings and then Rory arrived — and by the way I could cheerfully have killed him in any number of ways. I noticed that you ate very little and left as soon as you could with what I could only observe was almost indecent speed. She doesn't like me, I thought, I will keep away. So I do but then I think: if I tell you what I feel, at least I'll have tried and if I don't try I might spend the rest of my life wondering what might have happened and so . . . '

'Listen, Jamie . . . '

'Please, I have to finish this. If you find it all excruciating and embarrassing, you only have to say so and I'll tell you I understand and we'll have dinner and talk about castle worksheets or something and at the end of the meal I'll take you home and I will thank you for being honest with me.'

When she said nothing, he threw up his hands. 'Actually,' he said. 'I can see I *have* finished. Tell me what you think. Please take as long as you like. I'll just sit here.'

He gazed at the wall on their left and began to study with apparent fascination a painting of a stag on the hillside. Tess drank her wine, aware that her heart was racing. 'This is silly,' she said at last. 'I'm not even sure what you expect me to say. The idea of a . . . a romantic relationship is totally impractical. You live up here and I live in London. You must see that.'

He shook his head. 'It's only impractical if you don't *want* a romantic relationship.'

'What if I were to tell you I *do* find this excruciating and embarrassing?'

'I would ask you very politely to tell me why.'

'That's not what you said before.'

'I know,' Jamie said. 'Sorry.'

She had never felt so helpless. 'Jamie,' she said. 'I like you so much. I'm incredibly fond of you.'

164

Jamie nodded. 'Oh dear,' he said.

'I mean it. You've become a good friend but . . . '

'Thank you,' he said. 'I understand now.' He gave a short, polite smile. 'I'd like to say thank you for all your hard work this month. You've been the best of good company and I . . . I shan't forget you.'

'So this is it?' she asked. 'We say goodbye tonight?'

'I'm sorry.' He shook his head. 'I can't do the friends thing with you. It wouldn't work. I wish it could.'

It wasn't fair and it wasn't right. She was overcome by an acute case of panic. Life without Jamie would be dullness incarnate. She said, 'I think I'm going to have to tell you something. You see you're not the only one who has a confession to make.'

★   ★   ★

Freya supposed she should be feeling aggrieved about the coming weekend. Felix had, after all, chosen to be away for their thirtieth wedding anniversary. But actually, she was looking forward to her own small adventure. She had rung Tess earlier this evening and they'd had a nice chat. Tess said she loathed being back in London and was looking forward to being cheered up by her mother. Which was lovely since Freya often felt uncertain about her daughters' feelings towards her. Pam had a theory that the whole point of children was to bring uncertainty and self-doubt

165

into one's life. Pam maintained this was a good thing since one should guard against complacency as one grew older. As Freya pointed out at the time, she had quite enough self-doubt without her children adding more.

She put her hands on her hips and surveyed the clothes on the spare-room bed. She had selected her black trousers and silk shirt for tomorrow and Sunday and her shirt dress for Saturday. The Glamour Dress would do for Neil Lockhart's party. She had not taken up Felix's offers of a brand new outfit and two nights in a hotel. She had told him they were an unnecessary expense. She wanted him to know she could not be bought off so easily.

She had planned her London trip with care. Tomorrow she would visit the Society of Genealogists and the London Metropolitan Archives. She would arrive at her friend Sylvie's in time for a large gin and tonic. On Saturday she would attack Oxford Street and find a gorgeous dress for Tess who would otherwise, almost certainly, turn up to the party in one of her black sacks. On Sunday she would take the girls out to celebrate her wedding anniversary. They would drink champagne and later, back at home, she would take great delight in calling Felix and telling him what an enjoyable anniversary weekend she'd had.

On the other side of the bed she had set out Felix's clothes: six freshly ironed shirts, the linen suit he had bought two years ago, underwear, pyjama bottoms and a couple of T-shirts. He was catching a plane from Bristol this evening and

166

even as she thought he was cutting it a bit fine she heard his key in the door and she called out, 'I'm upstairs!'

When he joined her in the room, he was already taking off his tie. His eyes registered the neat piles on the bed and he said, 'You've been busy.'

'Do you want me to help you pack?'

'No, no, you've done quite enough. It won't take me long. Give me twenty minutes and then we'll have some tea together.'

'Do you want something to eat?'

'I'll grab a sandwich at the airport.'

There was a febrile energy about him today. He was not a fan of modern air travel and was always stressed before a journey. It was best to leave him alone to sort himself out.

When he came downstairs he had changed into cotton trousers and a polo shirt. He said, 'I'm ready.'

'Passport? Boarding card? Book for the plane? Reading glasses?'

'All present and correct.'

'Come and have some tea then.'

'They sat at the table. She poured him a cup. 'Can you relax for a while? You have almost twenty minutes before you have to go.'

He glanced at the kitchen clock. 'Freya,' he said, 'there's something I have to tell you.'

She smiled. 'You sound very serious.'

'I am. There isn't a good way of saying this. I want us to separate.' His tone was quiet, almost conversational. 'I want to stop living with you. I'm so sorry.'

Freya had the weirdest sensation that the world — the literal world — was crumbling about her. She gripped the table with her hands. Her eyes filled with tears, obscuring her vision. She wanted to say something but she couldn't. Her stomach felt as if it were falling away but in fact her entire body was shocked into a frozen stillness.

'I was going to wait until I came back but I think it's better to tell you now.'

His eyes were sympathetic and he sounded apologetic, as if he'd forgotten to buy some ingredient she needed for a recipe. Still, she couldn't speak. If she simply sat and waited, perhaps he would tell her she had misunderstood what he was trying to say.

'What I suggest,' he said, 'is that when I come back next Wednesday we discuss what to do. I've looked at our finances. You can stay here and I'll rent a flat in Bristol until we sort ourselves out.'

She found her voice at last. 'Why have you stopped loving me? Is there someone else?' Even then, she hoped he would assure her he *did* love her and offer some unimaginable explanation that they could sort out together.

He looked down at his feet. 'No. No, there isn't. I suppose it's been a gradual understanding. We'll talk about this when I come back.'

'Is this why you arranged the Spanish trip?'

'No, but . . . ' He rose to his feet. 'I was happy to go along with it.' He glanced at his watch. 'I'm sorry. I must go now.'

She didn't move. She watched him walk out of the kitchen. She remained in her chair until she heard his car drive away. Then she stood up. He hadn't touched his tea. She took his cup and saucer and threw the warm liquid down the sink. She felt she'd been thrown into some terrible nightmare. Felix, kind, gentle, loving Felix had taken less than a minute to tell her he was leaving her. She held up the cup and, hurling it across the room, watched it splinter into pieces.

16

Anna had chosen obstetrics for the very good reason that it was the one area of medicine where the majority of patients weren't ill. They had interesting conditions which, most of the time, led to euphoric conclusions in which doctors were showered with praise. There were the occasional desperately sad tragedies, just as there were more frequently difficult mothers-to-be and mothers.

Mrs Halligan was one of these. A pale-faced woman with bottle-black hair and intense brown eyes, she had, she told Anna, a low pain-threshold which in her case meant she was a self-indulgent prima donna. This morning she'd cried that there was no way she could be allowed to go home tomorrow. Anna thought she could detect a trace of real fear in Mrs Halligan's eyes and agreed that perhaps she could stay at St Peter's for a further two days.

And now Miss Diamond stood at Mrs Halligan's bed, surrounded by her usual tribe of medical students and fellow trainees. When Mrs Halligan announced that Doctor Cameron had said she could stay on, Miss Diamond sighed. She then launched into a clear, concise and extremely graphic account of the Caesarean procedure. 'You see, Mrs Halligan,' she concluded, 'it would be very odd if you did *not* feel sore after an operation like this. Indeed, if you weren't sore, I would be extremely worried about you. It is far better for you to leave us this afternoon and begin your convalescence in your own home where you can relax and be comfortable. You are a lucky woman. You have a beautiful baby boy. Go home and enjoy him.'

In the face of her consultant's comprehensive display of professional expertise, Mrs Halligan was silenced. Anna's admiration lasted up until the moment Miss Diamond gathered her acolytes round the nurses' station. In a light, clear voice that Anna knew could be heard by the nurses behind them, she said, 'I have tried for some time to work out what is the point of Doctor Cameron. I think she must exist in order to show the rest of you what *not* to do. The NHS has very little money and we cannot afford to fill our beds with nervous hypochondriacs. Mrs Halligan is easily frightened and ready to tumble into hysterics at any moment. By concurring with her entirely unnecessary demand to stay here, Doctor Cameron simply proved to Mrs Halligan that she was right to want to do so. If we all behaved like Doctor Cameron, the NHS would be bankrupt within the year.'

Anna did not try to defend herself. Miss Diamond was right to rebuke her but wrong to take such pleasure in doing so. When she finally got away, she wished she had William here to do his usual brilliant magic of transforming a demoralising experience into an interesting one. Well, she thought, she was not going to give up on medicine, however much Miss Diamond might want her to. She was not going to give up on William either. She had maintained a lofty silence for over two weeks now and it had got her nowhere. For a moment, as she walked down the corridor, she thought she saw William coming towards her but it was just a man with curly dark hair. Anna came to a stop. She pulled out her phone and looked at it. Then she sent William a text: PLEASE CAN WE TALK?

★　★　★

Freya woke late the next morning after a troubled night. She limped downstairs at midday and put the empty bottle of Merlot in the recycling bin. She was glad she hadn't cancelled Sylvie. She couldn't bear to stay in a house full of happy family photos on the walls. If she didn't leave soon, she would pull them all down and destroy the lot of them. She would tell Sylvie everything. Sylvie would be furious. They would spend the whole evening assassinating Felix's character. And then, on Saturday, she would see Tess and would tell her *nothing*. She would leave to Felix the pleasure of telling his daughters what he had done. She and Tess would go to the party in the evening and have *fun*.

It took three cups of coffee, a long bath and strong painkillers to repair the excesses of the night before. She took her case through to the spare room and slowly packed the clothes she'd put out on the bed.

When Freya boarded the train, she fell asleep almost at once and only woke when it reached its final destination. As she walked towards the Tube she glanced around her and wondered how many jettisoned wives there were on the concourse. She felt a new, strange rage well up in her. If Felix were to come up to her now, she would hit him. She had been a good wife, especially in the last few years. She had responded to his moods with sympathy and understanding and where had it got her? Didn't Jesus say that the meek would inherit the earth? Boy, did he get that wrong! Meek people just got trampled on! Freya felt better already. She wanted to embrace her rage. It was better than self-pity any day.

She arrived in Putney at six and was greeted with a hug by Sylvie who said it had been far too long, they must have a drink at once and how *was* she? Freya was about to tell her but was distracted by a book on the coffee table — *How to Make your Life (and your Garden) Happy.* The cover showed Xander sitting serenely on a bench, his long legs stretched out in front of him. On either side of him there were wide herbaceous borders full of lupins, delphiniums, Michaelmas daisies and gypsophila. Xander, dressed in jeans and a grey T-shirt, appeared to be the embodiment of masculine perfection: a strong man at peace with his spiritual side.

Sylvie noticed her interest and smiled. 'It was an impulse buy. He looks so gorgeous, don't you think?'

'I happen to know he *is* gorgeous,' Freya said. 'Xander Bullen was our gardener in Wimbledon!'

'No! Really? You lucky woman! What was he like?'

'Well, actually,' Freya said, 'he had quite a crush on me.'

'Men always have crushes on you,' Sylvie said. 'It's very boring for the rest of us.'

'Oh Sylvie,' Freya sighed, 'you have no idea . . .'

But Sylvie's phone had started ringing and it was clear within seconds that something was very wrong. When she came off the phone, she stared anxiously at Freya. 'We have a family crisis, I'm afraid. Candy and Amelia are on their way. Candy's in a terrible state.'

Candy was in a terrible state. The last time Freya had seen Candy was two years ago. Freya had gone to Putney for lunch and Candy and her daughter arrived. For the rest of Freya's visit, the conversation had been exclusively concerned with the state of Candy's marriage and the all-round brilliance of Amelia who was an unprepossessing two-year-old with a nose that produced unlimited quantities of green slime. Freya had been unsurprised when Sylvie told her a few months later that the marriage had collapsed. Now, according to Sylvie, the husband had suggested a marital resuscitation and Candy was distraught.

This was not the time to confide in Sylvie about her *own* marriage. Freya took on the preparation of the potato salad while Sylvie made a watercress soup and agonised over her daughter's state of mind.

Candy and Amelia arrived at seven. Amelia was half-asleep and Candy took her straight upstairs.

'How do you think Candy looks?' Sylvie asked in a hushed whisper.

'She looks rather good,' Freya said. 'She's lost weight.'

'I know. I'm terrified she'll get anorexia.'

'I'd say she has a long way to go before she looks anorexic.' Already, Freya regretted her decision to come here.

Candy came downstairs and attempted a tremulous smile. 'Magnus says . . . ' She took a deep breath. 'I am trying so hard not to cry . . . '

She wasn't trying that hard, Freya thought, watching Candy burst into tears.

The entire evening was given over to Candy's dilemma: should she take Magnus back? Who would believe that such a simple question could produce four hours of soul-searching? Freya never wanted to hear the name Magnus again. It was a stupid name, designed for a Roman soldier not a chartered surveyor who'd just left a girl called Tamsin. As they sat drinking coffee, she said in a bracing tone that it was really quite simple. Did Candy still love him?

'I don't know,' Candy sniffed. 'He's made me so unhappy, he's had at least two affairs to my certain knowledge and now this one with Tamsin . . . '

'Stop there,' Freya said. 'You've answered the question. He's made you miserable. It's far better to end it now and find someone else while you're still young and attractive. And you *are* attractive. You look so slim.'

Candy gave a mournful nod. 'I can't eat a thing at the moment.'

'Well,' Freya said, 'that's not so bad . . . '

'Freya,' Sylvie protested, 'it really is . . . We don't want Candy to get too thin.'

'I'm sure that won't happen,' Freya said briskly. 'And if you want my advice, you should cut Magnum ('Magnus,' Sylvie murmured.) out of your life. Take control!'

For a moment it seemed that her confident assertion had settled the argument but then Candy's eyes started watering again and Sylvie protested that it wasn't that simple. 'Amelia misses her daddy,' she said.

Freya made her excuses and went to bed. She was awestruck by Candy's monumental self-absorption. Not once in the evening had she asked Freya how *she* was or how her girls were doing. To be fair, they had never had much time for Candy but even so she might have managed at least one polite query.

The next morning was even worse since Freya had to share the breakfast table with Amelia who'd been unpleasant enough at two and was even more charmless now she was four. They sat in Sylvie's pleasant little dining room and Amelia complained about the cereals. 'I don't like Rice Crispies, I want granola and blueberries.' She complained about her drink. 'I don't like orange juice, I like apple juice.' She even complained about the sun in her eyes and they all had to move places to accommodate her.

When Sylvie and Candy went off to the kitchen to produce something the child *might* like, Amelia stared at Freya and stuck her tongue out at her.

Freya leant forward. 'Have you ever heard of the Rude Old Woman in the Cave?'

Amelia stuck out her lower lip.

'She loves children like you,' Freya told her. 'Every time you say, 'I want', instead of, 'Please can I have . . . ' the Rude Old Woman jumps with joy. Every time she sees you make that extremely ugly face, she laughs again. She laughs because she knows that once you've been rude one hundred times, you will turn into a Rude Old Woman too and you'll spend the rest of your life in her dark, cold cave.'

Amelia's lower lip wobbled. 'That's not true,' she said.

Freya gave an eloquent shrug of her shoulders.

Amelia stared uncertainly at Freya. 'I don't have my daddy,' she said.

'Neither do I,' Freya said. 'Get used to it.'

Sylvie came back with her latest offering. 'There you are, darling,' she said. 'Scrambled egg on toast with two little tomatoes.'

Amelia pointed an accusing finger at Freya. 'She's been horrible,' she cried and burst into tears.

Freya had behaved appallingly and she knew it. Sylvie and Candy were horrified and had every right to be. Freya apologised before making a speedy exit. There was no question of her staying another night with Sylvie and her ghastly family. How could she be polite to pathetic Candy and awful Amelia when she was consumed by an ever-increasing fury at her husband? She walked with a beating heart down the street, cursing him as she did so.

She found a bench on Putney Heath and sat down with her phone. In a few minutes she had found a hotel in Kensington, a short walk away from the party. She booked a room and then rang Tess to tell her the change of plan. Then, she consulted her *A to Z*. Felix had told her to buy a dress and enjoy the party. She fully intended to do so.

Her energy was failing by the time she found the small shop in Knightsbridge. It reminded her of the one she used to manage in Wimbledon. She stared at the shop window and her heart leapt. Discretion was not a word one would use to describe the dress on the mannequin.

As soon as she went through the door she was approached by a young woman in high heels and a grey dress. 'Hi, there,' she said. 'Can I be of any help?'

'I hope so,' Freya said, 'it's my thirtieth wedding anniversary today. I'm looking for two dresses for tonight, one for me and one for my daughter. We're both the same size and I know what she likes. That pink dress in the window . . . '

'Isn't it heaven?' The girl gave a conspiratorial laugh. 'It just shouts sex appeal! If my mother bought that for me, I'd love her forever!'

'That's a pretty good endorsement,' Freya said. 'Perhaps I'd better try it on.'

When she finally stepped out of the changing room, the girl let out a little cry. 'Isn't it fabulous? You see how the black stripes down the sides emphasise your waist and your hips? And that black zip down the back is so perfect! It's a complete showstopper. Your daughter will love it!'

'I'll take it,' Freya said. She noticed that the girl had a second dress draped over her arm and said hopefully, 'That looks nice.'

The girl held it up. 'It's deceptively simple,' she said. 'It looks great when it's on.'

The girl proved to be right. When she saw Freya in it she clapped her hands. The dress was perfect: sheerest green silk with a black under-slip.

'I'll have that one too,' Freya said. She hadn't enquired the price of either of them and when the nice girl accepted her credit card and handed her the receipt, Freya did feel a momentary sense of guilt. She consoled herself with the thought that if she and Felix had had the anniversary party she had originally assumed they would have, he'd have had to spend far more.

As she picked up her carrier bags, the girl said, 'Have a wonderful party tonight. I know your daughter will love her dress!'

'She will,' Freya assured her. 'Green is her favourite colour.'

She checked into her hotel in the late afternoon. The continuing silence from Felix — she must *stop* checking her phone — had lowered her spirits but it was impossible not to be cheered by her room with its enormous bed, the walk-in shower and the outstanding views of Kensington Gardens.

The shower was heaven. As the water rained down on her she could feel it washing away her anger. Tonight she would refuse to think about Felix and her frightening future. Tonight, she would enjoy the party, flirt outrageously, laugh with Tess and enjoy the luxury of her hotel room.

At six, she eased herself into her dress and performed a twirl in front of the mirror. It was not a dress for the faint-hearted. Shocking pink, with the ostentatious black zip that went all the way down to the base of her spine, it fitted her like a glove. She had at least paid lip-service to her age with her hair, putting it up into a neat roll at the back of her head.

When Tess arrived her reaction was — possibly — reassuring. 'Oh my God, Mum!'

'Is it too much?' Freya asked. 'Do you think it's too obvious?'

'It's very obvious,' Tess said, 'but you can take it.'

'I've bought you one too,' Freya said, picking up one of the bags from the floor.

'No offence, Mum, but . . . '

'It's not like this one. Look.' As Freya had suspected, Tess was dressed in her calf-length black dress that made her look like a girl who's come straight from the convent.

For Freya, the evening began once Tess put on her dress. 'You look like an autumn nymph,' she breathed. 'You should always wear green.'

'I love it,' Tess said. 'It must have cost . . . '

'Never mind that.' Freya picked up her bag. 'There is a very sophisticated bar downstairs. I think we should try it out.'

She ordered margaritas and, while they waited, gave a quick murmured assessment of the clientele. 'The man in the corner is fascinated. He can't stop staring at you, Tess. He's pretending to look for his companion. I suspect, she doesn't exist and that actually he's plucking up courage to come over but of course he won't, and over near the bar there's a romantic couple who have both noticed us . . . '

'You're smiling at him,' Tess protested.

'He smiled first.'

'It doesn't matter. You'll get her coming over to have words if you don't behave.'

'Nonsense, I'm just being friendly. This is such fun and we owe it to your friend, Jamie. Did you have a lovely time in Scotland with him? What did the two of you do together?'

Tess shrugged. 'We visited Scott's home and his graveyard and . . . '

Freya rolled her eyes. 'Poor Jamie. You do remind me of my father, you know. The two of us spent one holiday traipsing round the Elwy Valley in Wales because Gerald Manley Hopkins had written some verses about it. I was ten at the time and far too young to appreciate his poems — to be honest, I still don't — but dear Daddy stomped around, declaiming away and gazing at me with such happy expectation that I had to pretend to enjoy it. I wish he were here now. I do miss him.'

'I know you do,' Tess said. 'I'm not sure you would want him here at the moment. I don't know what he'd make of your dress.'

'He'd rest his head in his hands,' Freya said, 'and he'd say, 'Freya, oh Freya, you will be the death of me!' Oh look, here are our drinks!'

The rims of the cocktail glasses were frosted with salt and the liquid was a pale cloudy green. Mother and daughter took tentative sips and Tess murmured, 'That is *good*!'

'It's the only way to drink tequila,' Freya said. 'If the party is dull we can come back for more.'

'I don't know why we're going,' Tess said. 'I'd be quite happy to celebrate your anniversary here.'

'Oh,' Freya said, 'I'd forgotten that.'

Tess raised her glass. 'I haven't. Here's to you and to Dad. Cheers, Mum!'

'Thank you.' The margarita slipped down Freya's throat like nectar.

'I still don't understand why we've been invited. It seems so random.'

'I told you. Jamie's father hoped to use us as bait to get his son down here.' Already the margarita was giving her confidence. This was no time for tact. Freya was not at all sure that tact was a particularly sensible quality anyway. She said, 'Tess, can you look me in the eye and assure me the young man has no interest in you?'

Tess raised her eyes to meet those of her mother and faltered. 'He *did*,' she conceded at last, 'but I . . . I discouraged him.'

'Poor Jamie. Is he ugly?'

'No! No, of course he isn't.'

Freya gave a sympathetic nod. 'Is he boring?'

'No!' Tess took a reckless gulp of her drink. 'The fact is I . . . I didn't want to have the sort of relationship . . . *that* sort of relationship.'

'Why not? What is wrong with him?'

'There is nothing wrong with him! I just . . . I

don't need a boyfriend in my life right now, especially one who lives in Scotland. I'm sure you think that's very dull but . . . '

'To be honest,' Freya said, 'I think romantic love is a minefield. Perhaps you're right to leave it alone.'

'Really? That doesn't sound like you.'

'Well, perhaps I don't feel like me at the moment . . . '

'Oh my God!' Tess clutched her mother's hand. 'Don't look now but the romantic man has left the room and now the romantic wife is coming over here. I *told* you she'd be cross.' The woman stopped in front of Freya.

'I'm sorry to bother you,' she said, 'but my husband's taking a phone call and I thought I'd ask you . . . He loves your dress, you see, and I wondered . . . Would it be very cheeky to ask you where you bought it?'

17

Their destination was a gleaming white three-storey townhouse, minutes away from the hotel and with views over Kensington Gardens. Tess was taken aback by the grandeur of the place and even Freya was a little apprehensive although, 'I don't see why you're so surprised,' she told Tess. 'If Jamie Lockhart owns a castle, it stands to reason that his father must be wealthy.'

'Yes, but Jamie's castle isn't a grand sort of castle. It's used for business parties and weddings. It's not as if Jamie lives there.' Tess cast a glance at her mother. 'Are we going in?'

'Of course we are. I've spent a small fortune on our party dresses.' Freya mounted the steps and rang the bell.

The door was opened by a young man in a maroon shirt and black trousers. He welcomed them into a high-ceilinged hall with grey walls and a charcoal carpet and took Freya's jacket and Tess's mac, hanging them with great care on the coat rail behind them. Freya's attention was caught by a gilt-framed painting on the left of the staircase. It depicted a wild-haired man in a kilt looking out at the world with a gun in his hand and what looked like a slaughtered stag behind him.

They were directed up the stairs to a large drawing room with elegant windows and a vast ornate chandelier. There was an enormous antique mirror at one end of the room and a huge landscape painting at the other. It had its own little light above it and must therefore be very, very expensive. The deep pile carpet, the vast Chesterfield sofa, the Chinese table lamps by each window all spoke of barely restrained opulence.

Mother and daughter gazed at the group in front of them. 'Look at the women,' Freya murmured. 'They're all dressed in fifty shades of grey. I look like a firework at a funeral.'

'Everyone likes fireworks,' Tess said.

'*You* never did,' Freya reminded her. She beamed at a young waiter who handed them thin flutes of champagne. 'Dutch courage,' Freya murmured and downed a third of it at once. She was aware she was being watched and found herself locking eyes with a slim, dark-haired man in the far corner of the room. He was tieless, with a black suit and white shirt. He was also quite extraordinarily handsome, a rare phenomenon in mid-life men who weren't famous actors. She knew, even as he turned his attention back to his companion, a voluble, pinstripe-suited male with gesticulating hands, that he wanted to come over to her. She rather hoped he would do.

The next moment she thought she was dreaming. An identical man, his eyes fixed on Tess, was walking towards them from another part of the room. As he drew nearer she could see he was considerably younger. She glanced enquiringly at Tess whose face was a portrait of stunned bewilderment.

'Jamie?' Tess sounded almost angry. 'What are you *doing* here? You should be at home. You have a serious meeting tomorrow.'

'I'm getting a plane back later tonight,' he said. 'It's under control.'

'You must be mad. You have to prepare for it, you need to be alert and awake. I can't believe you thought this was a good idea!'

The young man offered his hand to Freya. 'She's not going to introduce us, is she? I'm Jamie Lockhart and you must be Tess's mother.'

'Please call me Freya.' The man was lovely, she thought. His soft Scottish accent could melt an ice-cube. How could Tess not be impressed by him? She really must be a lost cause. Freya gave him an encouraging smile. 'I gather my daughter's been dragging you round graveyards and museums all August.'

'She did me a great favour. I'm revising my entire marketing strategy thanks to Tess.'

And now another gorgeous young man came up to them. He took Freya's hand and kissed it. 'You must be Tess's mother. I'm Jamie's brother, Rory.'

Unlike Jamie, his voice held no trace of a Scottish accent. He had his brother's dark eyes but was otherwise quite unlike him: reddish hair, not black, and an altogether more muscular and rugged type with a great deal of confidence. He had a bottle of champagne in one hand and caught her eyes drifting towards it. 'If you finish your glasses,' he said, 'I'll fill them up now. The waiters here are very slow to do it.'

'Oh, why not?' Tess said. 'The whole world

seems mad tonight.'

If Tess felt it all right to do so, who was she to disagree? Freya swallowed her champagne and held out her glass, murmuring without much conviction, 'I really shouldn't.'

'I'm delighted to meet you,' Rory told her. 'I've been staying with my brother in Scotland. I must tell you from bitter experience that if we stay with these two, they'll talk about nothing but musty castles and dead writers. Let me take you away, Mrs Cameron . . . '

'Please call me Freya.'

'I love that name! Now if we go over to the piano, we can hog the canapés.'

Freya said gaily, 'I do love canapés!' It was quite obvious that Jamie wanted to talk to Tess.

Having emptied the bottle, Rory put it down, took her hand and walked purposefully towards the piano. He told Freya he refused to believe she was old enough to be Tess's mother. His curse, he said, was that he found women of his own age dull. Older women were far more fun. He was an outrageous flirt and Freya was quite disappointed when they were joined by someone else.

'This is my stepmother, Eva,' Rory said. 'Eva, this is Freya Cameron, mother of Jamie's friend, Tess.'

'You're the genealogist,' Eva said. 'I'm so glad you could come tonight. Rory, will you go and talk to my aunt? She's over there in the corner. You know she adores you and she's all on her own.'

'I'd be delighted,' Rory said, making a face of

silent horror at Freya as he went away.

Freya cast a critical, if veiled, eye on her hostess. She would be far more attractive if she weren't so thin and it was a pity she had chosen to wear a low-cut dress. Thin women should never wear low-cut dresses. Despite these handicaps, she was an excellent hostess, asking Freya various questions about her career and seeming genuinely interested in her answers.

A couple came up to greet Eva who introduced them as, 'our very dear friends, Harry and Nicola'. They couldn't be *that* dear since Eva lost no time in slipping away to join another group. Harry, an overweight man with a puce-coloured complexion, seemed pleased to meet Freya, his plump wife Nicola less so. Harry was halfway through a long explanation as to how he had first met their hosts when a hand touched Freya's elbow and a voice said, 'Nicola and Harry, how lovely to see you. May I ask you to do me a favour? We've invited some new friends. They've recently moved to Marylebone and I know they'll get on with you. Would you go and say hello to them? They're over there with Charlie and Charlie is on his seventh glass of champagne so they need rescuing. I'll catch up with you both later.'

It was the man who had smiled at her. It was like looking at Jamie Lockhart twenty years on. The man had the same dark hair, eyebrows and eyes and the same pale skin. But whereas Jamie's face was curiously immobile, this man had an easy laugh and a winning smile with which he was currently seeing off poor Harry and Nicola.

He turned to Freya. 'The trouble with being a host is that too many of your guests want to talk to you. I've been trying to meet you forever. My name's . . . '

'You have to be Neil Lockhart,' Freya said. 'You look very like Jamie. I'm . . . '

'You are Freya Cameron. I recognise you from the picture on your website. It doesn't do you justice.'

'Thank you.' His eyes seemed to bore into her soul, firing every nerve-end in her body. There was an almost tangible electric current between them. This was turning into a very good party. 'You shouldn't stare at me, you know,' she said. 'It's a little off-putting.'

'I'm sorry. I've been trying not to stare at you ever since you arrived.' He nodded towards Tess and Jamie who were listening politely to a man with a beard. 'Look at our children. I suspect my son has lost his heart. Is there any hope for him?'

'To be honest,' Freya said, 'I doubt it. My daughter's only interest is her work.'

'Jamie's a very persistent man. Let's go and help them out. Once Julian starts talking, he never stops.'

He was very impressive, she thought, apologising to his friend Julian but insisting that he needed Jamie and Tess to find Eva. 'I think you'll find her in the study, Jamie. Tell her I need to show Freya the Lord Chancellor and then I'll be back for the speeches. And, Julian, I have a request for you too. Eva's aunt is desperate to talk to you. She's sitting by the fireplace. Can you go and have a word? Thanks so much.'

He led Freya out of the drawing room, one hand lightly resting on the small of her back. She had to fight against the urge to lean into him. As they walked down the stairs, she asked, 'Is Eva's aunt really desperate to talk to him?'

'Eva's aunt is desperate, full stop.'

'And is Eva really in the study?'

'I very much doubt it but Jamie needs some privacy with your daughter. He's come all the way from Scotland to see her.'

Freya sighed. 'She's a funny girl.'

'He's a funny man. They are clearly made for each other. Jamie says you live in Somerset. I occasionally come to Bath on business.'

'We live outside Darrowbridge. Bath is only a half-hour drive.'

'I must come and see you sometime.'

Freya said primly, 'That would be nice.'

Neil opened a door on his right and said, 'Here we are.'

'Oh!' She put her hand to her throat. 'This is a lovely room. It is just what a library should be.'

She could imagine her father in a room like this: book-lined walls, chocolate-brown carpet, sturdy oak desk. There was even a fire in the grate. She noticed a wide, ornate frame above the mantelpiece and asked, 'Is this your Lord Chancellor?'

He nodded. He stood in the middle of the room with his hands in his pockets. She wondered if he knew how attractive he was.

She walked across to the fireplace and studied the pen and ink print of a good-looking man in army uniform, with short curly hair and dark, brooding eyes. The inscription beneath told her that he was Lord High Chancellor of Great Britain to His Royal Highness, George, Prince of Wales. 'It would be fun to find out about him,' she said. 'Do you still want me to research your family?' She turned. 'You're staring at me again, you know.'

'I can't help it. I've wanted to be alone with you from the moment you arrived. To be honest, at the moment, I don't give a damn about my ancestors. If they give me an excuse to see you again, I shall be most grateful to them.'

Freya wondered if the margarita had been a good idea. It was wildly exciting to be alone with this man in this library but she had no idea how to respond to him. Her heart pounded. She should probably tell him to behave himself. She should possibly walk out now and go back to the party. This man was dangerous. She stalled. 'We've only just met.'

'This has been the longest evening of my life. Every moment's been an hour.' He took his hands from his pockets and walked over to her. 'You have no idea how beautiful you are.'

This was crazy. She felt as if she were on fire. She stared up at him and tried to tell him he was being absurd but he stopped her with a kiss and she thought: tomorrow, I will go back to my husbandless home and I shall never forget this moment.

'Freya Cameron,' he said, 'can I see you again?'

And now she took a step back. 'No,' she said. 'You absolutely can't.'

For Tess, the evening was like a dream during which she seemed to be an entirely different person from the Tess she had always known herself to be.

The new Tess appeared briefly when she put on her new dress in her mother's hotel bedroom and saw her reflection in the mirror. Then, when she saw Jamie walking towards her at the party, she felt a rush of such joy that she thought she might faint. And when he looked at her, she could see in his eyes that he thought she was beautiful. That was when the new Tess elbowed the old to one side. She wanted to hug Rory when he offered to take her mother away.

'I hope she'll be all right with him,' Jamie said. 'He's definitely trying it on with her.'

'Mum will love that,' Tess assured him. 'I can't believe you've come all this way for such a short time. You must be mad.'

'I wanted to see you.'

The old Tess would have been tongue-tied, confused, unsure how to proceed. The new Tess looked up at him and said, 'I'm glad you came.'

'I was afraid you might be angry. You did seem so certain our situation was hopeless.'

She said, 'Well, actually . . . '

And that was when the first of a stream of guests came up and said, 'Jamie, I'm so pleased you're here! Are you going to introduce me to your lovely companion?'

It had never occurred to Tess that she might be more than averagely attractive. She had a beautiful mother and a blonde sister with breasts. She was long accustomed to playing third fiddle in the family. But tonight, she *did* feel lovely. Confidence was a new sensation and she enjoyed it, although she would have preferred to enjoy it in Jamie's exclusive company. Jamie's manners were impeccable but she could sense he was as impatient as she was with the fact that they were spending their precious time in party talk with random guests.

And then, while they were listening to probably the most boring man in England telling them exactly why the congestion charge in London was doomed to fail, the cavalry arrived in the unlikely forms of her mother and Jamie's father.

The presence of Jamie's father only added to the dream-like quality of the evening. He looked so very like Jamie: like Jamie with a face whose features had been shaken and stirred. He even wore an identical dark suit and white shirt. He came over with her mother and asked, a little apologetically, if she and Jamie would go and find Eva. Even more apologetically, he asked the boring man to go away and talk to someone else. It was impossible not to like him, even if he did guide her mother away with what seemed to be a rather proprietorial hand on her back.

The boring man said, 'That's so typical of Neil. He wafts up here with the most beautiful woman in the room — apart from you of course, my dear — and tells *me* to go and talk to Eva's hideous aunt. I'll catch up with you two later . . . '

'Not if I can help it,' Jamie murmured, ushering Tess away. 'Another two minutes and I might have had to kill him. Let's go to the study.'

The study was downstairs. It was half the size of the drawing room, with pale green walls and primrose-coloured curtains. There was a small sofa opposite a long table of palest ash on which sat an impressive amount of computer hardware. Behind the table was a tall, elegant chair. Tess thought that if she had a room like this in which to work, she would finish her thesis in no time at all.

'Well,' she said, 'Eva's not here.'

Jamie shut the door behind him. 'I know she's not. I saw her in the sitting room.'

'Jamie! We should go and tell her what your father said.'

'My father knew very well where she was. He also knew I wanted to be alone with you. In a few hours' time I'll be back in Scotland. You and I need to talk. Come and sit down.'

On the wall behind the desk, there was a framed Marc Chagall print of a man in a black suit, holding the hand of his partner who was flying in the air above him. Tess felt as if she were flying too. She walked over to the sofa and sat down.

Jamie remained standing. He put his hands in his pockets and cleared his throat. 'I came here tonight to prove that distance, at least, isn't a problem. I live in Scotland and you live in London but I'm here now and it hasn't been difficult.'

'You won't think that tomorrow,' Tess said.

'You'll be exhausted.'

'I'd rather be exhausted and happy than not exhausted and unhappy. I don't mind waiting till October to see you as long as I know you *will* come up in October. I want to say that, as far as I'm concerned, it's all very simple. I don't want to say goodbye to you. And if you feel the same, then nothing else matters. I appreciate you have a problem with . . . with physical intimacy but I've thought about that. If *you* have a problem, then it's my problem too. We can work it out together . . . There are people we can see for that sort of thing. I'll wait, I'll wait as long as it takes.'

Tess stood up and walked across to Jamie. He had made the most monumentally romantic gesture in coming here and she felt it was time to make an effort of similar magnitude. She took a deep breath and raised her face to his. 'Jamie,' she said, 'will you kiss me?' There was the ticking of a clock from somewhere in the room and for a few moments its sound seemed to get louder and louder.

His response was unexpected. 'To be honest,' he said, 'I'm not sure I want to. Call me old-fashioned, but I don't normally kiss women who have to clench their fists in anticipation of the experience.'

'I'm sorry.' She unclenched her hands. 'I didn't know I was doing it. Please. I want you to kiss me.'

He approached her warily, stared at her unhappily and gave her a brief, fleeting kiss. 'How was that?'

'Well,' Tess said, 'I didn't hate it.'

He gave a polite nod. 'Thank you. That's most encouraging.'

She laughed. 'Actually, it is.'

A head appeared round the door and Jamie said, 'Oh, Eva, we were looking for you. Dad thought you might be in here.'

Eva did not point out, as she was fully entitled to do, that it was fairly obvious she hadn't been. A flicker of amusement did cross her face but she only said, 'I was looking for him. We ought to get on with the speeches.'

'He's gone to the library to show Tess's mother the Lord Chancellor.' Jamie looked purposeful. 'Tess and I will go and get them.'

'I'll come with you,' Eva said. 'It will be nice to get away from the noise for a moment or two.' She smiled at Tess. 'I'm so glad you could come tonight. We don't see enough of Jamie. I'm sure you're the only reason he's here this evening.'

'I don't see enough of you and Dad,' Jamie said, opening the door for the two women. 'I feel quite ashamed. I must make more of an effort to see you both in the future.'

'That would be nice,' Eva said, adding pointedly, 'you live in London, don't you, Tess?'

They walked across the hall. 'I do hope Neil isn't boring your mother,' Eva said. 'He's so proud of his Lord Chancellor.' She opened a door and that was when the dream ended and the nightmare began.

For a split second Tess was conscious of a large, comfortable, brown room but almost immediately her attention was drawn to the entwined couple in the middle of it. It was the outrageous black zip — half undone — that alerted her to the fact that the woman with her arms round Jamie's father's neck was her mother.

18

It was almost comical, though Tess had never felt less like laughing. As Jamie's father registered the fact that he had an audience, he froze and for a few moments his face was devoid of expression. There was a terrible silence while everyone took in what was happening.

Her mother was the first to move. She turned sideways and spoke with commendable control. 'Neil,' she asked, 'would you mind doing up my zip?'

He did so immediately and she walked over to the sofa, picked up her bag and went straight across to Eva.

'I am so very sorry,' she said. 'This is entirely my fault. I'm afraid I drank far too much champagne. I shall go back to my hotel and drink gallons of water.' She glanced at Tess, murmured, 'I'll see you tomorrow, darling,' and walked out of the library, shutting the door behind her.

Neil stirred at last. 'Eva,' he said, 'I'm so sorry you had to see that.'

'I'm sure you are.' Eva's face was deathly pale.

'It was the act of a moment. I was showing her the picture . . . '

'I'm sure you showed her all sorts of things. I think, in the circumstances, we will keep the speeches as short as possible.'

'Eva,' Neil said, 'you have to believe me. It was

nothing but a drunken grope. You know I have no head for alcohol . . . '

'We can talk about it later,' Eva said. 'Right now, we need to return to our tenth wedding-anniversary celebration. Perhaps,' she added, 'you might like to tuck your shirt in.'

She turned on her heel. Neil attended to his clothes, glanced briefly at Tess and Jamie, murmured, 'I'm so sorry,' and then went to the door. 'Jamie,' he said, 'you won't be long, will you? I would appreciate some support up there. Perhaps you could speak instead of me?'

'You want *me* to say something? For God's sake, Dad . . . '

'Please.' Neil said, 'you're good at speeches.' He opened the door. They could hear him calling to Eva in the hall.

'Can you believe them?' Jamie asked. 'They both still want *speeches!*'

'I must go after Mum,' Tess said. 'Ring me tomorrow evening. I'd like to know how the meeting goes.' She hesitated, then gave him an awkward kiss on the cheek before racing across the hall. She only just remembered to collect her mac before going out into the night. She could see her mother in the distance, an elegant figure in her grey jacket, pink dress and heels. Tess couldn't help admiring the way she'd handled her exit. It had been a lot more dignified than that of Jamie's father.

She caught up with her on the corner of the road and said breathlessly, 'Mum, can we stop for a moment?'

Her mother halted. 'Go back to the party,

Tess. I think I need my bed.'

'I wouldn't go back to that party if you paid me a million pounds. Mum, what were you *doing*?'

Freya started walking again. 'You could see what I was doing.'

'You know what I mean. How could . . . ? You'd only just met him!'

'I know.' They were almost at the hotel now. 'I need to go to my room and have a very large glass of water.' She put a hand to her forehead. 'Would you care to join me?'

'Yes,' Tess said. 'Yes, I would. But I don't . . . '

'Tess, I'm sorry but I can't say any more until I get that water. My throat feels like sandpaper.'

A woman in a cocktail dress stood at the reception desk, quizzing the man behind it about a message he'd received from her husband. 'Are you sure he said he'd arrive in the morning? Did he not say what *time* he'd arrive?'

The receptionist said he hadn't and the woman shook her head with impatience before going over to consult her male companion. 'You see, we're all at it,' Freya murmured to Tess, before asking the man behind the desk for her room key.

In the lift, it was Freya who broke the silence. 'What happened when I left?'

Tess made a face. 'Eva was an ice queen and returned to the party. Jamie's father looked like he wanted to die. He asked Jamie to make his speech for him . . . '

'Speech?' Freya murmured.

'It's their tenth wedding-anniversary party.

200

They were all supposed to be making speeches.'

'Of course! Oh God!' Freya hit her forehead with her hand. For a moment her eyes sparkled. 'I'd love to be a fly on the wall when they start.'

'You wouldn't,' Tess said. 'Eva would swat you with one blow.'

Once in her room, Freya kicked off her shoes and made for the water bottles. She poured out a big glass of water and drank long and hard. Tess walked over to the window and looked out towards the big houses on the edge of Kensington Gardens. She wondered if Jamie was making a speech. What would he say? Here's to the happy couple?

Behind her, Freya said, 'Felix has left me.'

Tess turned at once. Her mother sat at the end of the bed, hands round her glass. Tess stared at her in blank incomprehension. 'He's left you? What do you mean?'

Freya shook her head, as if trying to dislodge a fly from her hair. 'He's left me. He wants us to live apart.'

'He loves you!' Tess protested. 'He's always loved you!'

'And now he's stopped,' Freya said. 'He told me before he went to Spain. He hasn't rung, he hasn't made any contact at all. He said he'd find somewhere else to live when he came back.'

'But . . . ' Tess felt she had been hurled into some strange alien landscape. 'It's ridiculous. He must have a reason. Has anything happened lately? Perhaps he's unhappy at work, perhaps he's depressed . . . '

'He does get depressed. I always thought it

201

was a sort of illness but now I wonder if he hasn't felt like this for ages. He should have said something before. It's not fair. He just announced it and then he left for the airport. I don't . . . I don't deserve this.' She finished her water and went over to the dressing table to refill her glass. 'After tonight, you probably think I *do* deserve it but . . . '

'Of course I don't.'

Freya shrugged. 'There's no excuse. I mean I drank too much but then I set out to drink too much. And Neil Lockhart is a very good-looking man and I thought at least there's someone who still finds me attractive . . . ' She took a deep breath. 'I shall write to Eva tomorrow, I shall explain about Felix and tell her I jumped on Neil, which by the way isn't true . . . '

'I didn't think it was, and anyway, none of that matters. What matters is you and Dad. You should ring him. Would you like *me* to ring him?'

'Absolutely not.' The words shot out. 'Felix would hate that. You can talk to him once we've talked to each other. You never know, he might feel quite different when he comes home.'

'I bet he does. I bet he'll come back and you'll find it's all some huge misunderstanding.'

'He as good as told me he'd stopped loving me. It's pretty difficult to misunderstand that.'

'Look,' Tess said, 'you've drunk a lot, you've had a traumatic evening and . . . Perhaps you should go to bed now and we can discuss things in the morning. I'll come over and . . . '

'Tess?' Freya held out a hand. 'This bed is huge. Would you like to stay the night?'

'Would you like me to stay?'
'Yes,' Freya said, 'I'd like that very much.'

★ ★ ★

Anna was meeting Tess and her mother at a place near Embankment. She had decided against cycling. Knowing her mother, there'd be wine and champagne which suited Anna just fine. She was crossing Waterloo Bridge when her phone rang. She pulled it out of her bag and clamped it to her ear. 'William! Thank you for calling!'

He said, 'I don't see the point in . . . '

'William, listen!' She was terrified he'd change his mind and ring off. 'I want you to know, I hate myself for letting you down over Trevor's engagement party. I shouldn't have done it, I don't know why I did, I had some stupid idea I needed to sort out stuff and I truly regret it. You're such a good friend, I can't afford to lose you. Please say you forgive me and let us be friends again. Please?'

'Look,' he said, 'I'm only ringing to explain. I was hurt about the Trevor thing, I admit I was hurt. But when I thought about it, I knew it was because I'd got you wrong, I hadn't understood you . . . '

'You *do* understand me, you understand me better than anyone!'

'No, no I don't, or rather, I didn't. You're not who I thought you were and — I don't know how to say this but the truth is, I don't like you now.'

He might as well have hit her. She felt her eyes sting, and she bit her lip hard.

'I appreciate your apologies.' His voice was careful and deliberate. 'I'm sorry I haven't rung you before. I hoped you'd give up calling me. I'm sorry, Anna, but I don't want to see you again.'

She swallowed hard and took a deep breath. 'Right. I won't bother you again. Goodbye.'

He didn't like her. William didn't like her. She started crying now and stumbled along the bridge, aware of curious glances from those about her. She found a Ladies' at the station and washed her face and put on new make-up. William said he didn't know her. Well, she didn't know *him*. She'd messed up once, just once, and he'd showed himself to be a pious, judgemental prick. She wouldn't be his friend if he paid her. *And* he'd made her late for the anniversary lunch.

When she arrived at the restaurant, she stood on the pavement for a few moments, trying to catch her breath. She caught a glimpse of her mother and sister through the window. They were the only customers and sat at a table in the centre, their heads close together. Tess talked earnestly and Freya listened. Anna stood, unseen, and watched them with rising curiosity. Tess never talked earnestly to Freya and Freya was not a natural listener. She was one of those people who wait with barely suppressed impatience for a brief hiatus in which to interpose her own opinion. Possibly, Anna thought, that was a little unfair, but certainly she could not recall an occasion in which her mother had ever behaved with such apparently mute docility. When Anna walked in, they both sat up straight as if they'd been told off for slouching.

She glanced at their tumblers of mineral water. 'Where's the champagne?' she asked. 'I thought this was supposed to be a celebration.'

Her mother stood up and kissed her cheek. 'Tess and I rather overdid the alcohol last night.' She did indeed look grim, with puffy eyes and a pale complexion.

'That's all very well but while you two were partying I was saving babies . . . '

'Were you, darling?'

'Not exactly, but I'm ready for wine even if you aren't.' Anna took her seat and raised an arm to the waiter who'd been standing listlessly by the aspidistra plant; he seemed grateful to be called.

'Please,' Anna told him, 'I'd like a glass of house white. In fact, bring a bottle. I can always take it home with me.'

'Certainly,' the waiter said. 'Would you like to hear our specials?' Encouraged by Anna's nod, he rattled off a choice of four dishes.

'Have you two already decided?' Anna asked. 'Are we having starters?'

'Do have one if you like but . . . ' Her mother's voice faded into nothing.

'We're not terribly hungry,' Tess said. 'We're having spaghetti Bolognese.'

'Some celebration this is turning out to be,' Anna said. She glanced up at the waiter. 'I'll have the seafood special, please.'

He nodded with apparent satisfaction at the excellence of her judgement and walked through to the kitchen. For a moment as he opened the door, there was a burst of laughter from one of the staff and then the place returned to its quiet, hushed atmosphere.

'So,' Freya said, 'how are you, Anna?'

'I've had a rubbish week, thanks for asking, but at least I don't have a hangover. You both look like zombies. I presume the party last night was a success?' She caught a brief, fleeting glance between the two of them which annoyed her — but then, everything annoyed her at the moment. 'Did your friend come?' she asked Tess.

'Jamie? Yes, he did.'

'That was nice. Did you meet him, Mum?'

'Yes. He was charming.'

'And what was the party like?'

'It was in a very grand house in Kensington.' Freya made a visible effort. 'Tess and I had margaritas before the party. That was probably a bad idea but they were delicious, weren't they, Tess?'

Tess nodded.

The waiter brought Anna's wine, opened the bottle and poured a little into her glass, waiting expectantly for her approval.

'I'm sure it's fine,' she said, and then took a quick sip. 'It's very nice,' she murmured and he nodded his pleasure before going off to greet three newcomers. Anna raised her glass. 'I suppose I should make a toast, Mum. Happy anniversary and here's to the next thirty years!' She caught another of those odd conspiratorial glances. 'Is something wrong?' she asked. 'I mean I was expecting a jolly party and you two act like someone's died.'

'There's something I should tell you.' Freya took a sip of her water and then tried to speak. She opened her mouth, shut it again, and bit her lip.

Tess spoke for her. 'Dad has left Mum,' she said.

It was, literally, an incredible statement. Anna must have misheard it. She stared first at her mother, then her sister. Tess sat biting her fingernails. Freya's face looked tight and taut.

'I don't understand,' Anna said.

Freya gave a small shrug of her shoulders. 'Join the club. He told me on Thursday afternoon.'

'Why?' Anna asked. 'What did you do?'

The words were out before she could stop them. They were gratuitously offensive and she didn't need Tess's furious protest — 'For God's sake, Anna,' — to point that out.

Freya took her hands from the table. She bent down to pick up her bag, took some notes from her wallet and placed them on the table.

'Mum,' Tess said, 'what are you doing?'

'The money should cover your meal. I have to go home now. I don't feel well and I can't face Anna today . . . '

'Mum, please,' Anna said, 'I shouldn't have said that. It just came out. Please sit down.'

'I don't want to sit down. Tess, I'll talk to you soon. Goodbye, Anna.'

'Look, I'm sorry,' Anna said. 'It's all such a

bombshell. I didn't mean . . . '

'Of course you did.' Freya's voice was hard and certain. She walked across to have a word with the waiter before collecting her small suitcase from its place by the coats. Anna watched her mother walk out onto the pavement, head held high and her face carefully devoid of expression.

Tess sat back and folded her arms. 'Well, that was amazing. Even by *your* standards that was amazing.'

'I said it before I could think. I swear I didn't mean to upset her. It was shock, that's all. I can't believe she's just *left* us. Do you think I should go after her?'

'Multiply your shock by ten and you'll have some idea how Mum feels. And no, I think you should leave her alone. You've done quite enough.'

'I know. You don't need to tell me. I feel terrible. I just don't understand. Dad adores Mum. He'd only leave her if she'd done something . . . '

'Right. So it would never be *his* fault . . . '

'That's not what I'm saying. But . . . ' Anna glanced rather warily at her sister. 'Mum loves to be admired. I know she loves Dad but . . . She does have a weakness. We were never given a good reason for the move to Darrowbridge. You know that's true.'

Tess threw up her hands. 'I knew you'd bring that up. Elephants and Anna never forget. In your case, you never forget things you only *think* might have happened.'

'That's not fair. I have every reason to believe that Xander Bullen . . . '

'I don't want to talk about Xander Bullen . . . '

'You never *do* want to talk about him.'

'He has nothing to do with this. I stayed at the hotel with Mum last night. I woke up at three and found her sitting by the window. I don't know how long she'd been crying. She kept asking me why Dad's left her. She's devastated. You must have seen how ill she looks . . . '

'I was wrong to say what I did and I'm sorry I said it. I'll ring Mum later and grovel. Have you spoken to Dad?'

'No. Mum is very keen that we keep out of it for the time being. He hasn't contacted her since he left. He gets back from Spain on Wednesday evening.' Tess stared levelly at her sister. 'He is not behaving well here.'

'I agree,' Anna said. 'Of course I agree!' She felt cross. She resented the fact that she had to play *mea culpa* to Tess's righteous sister act. It was easy for Tess to be reasonable and rational. She'd had a night to get used to the news. 'Did Mum want to go to the party last night? It seems such an odd thing to do in the circumstances. How could she possibly expect to enjoy it?' She watched Tess reach across for the bottle. 'I thought you said you drank too much last night.'

'I didn't drink as much as Mum.'

'So . . . How was the evening?'

Tess poured wine into her glass.

Anna raised her eyebrows. 'Tess? How was it?'

'I don't want to tell you. You wouldn't understand.'

'Now you're being seriously annoying. You have to tell me. What happened?'

'There was an . . . incident. I was with Jamie and his stepmother. We went into the library. We saw Jamie's father kiss Mum.'

'Oh my God! And you tell me Dad's behaved badly!'

'You see? Instant condemnation! You have no idea! She was in a state about Dad. She drank far too much. Jamie's father comes on to her and she lets him kiss her.'

'Oh well, that's all right then. It's quite understandable.'

Tess put down her fork and knife. 'Why are you in such a foul mood?'

'Possibly because I've just learnt that my parents are splitting up.'

'You were in a foul mood when you got here.'

The two of them stared at each other and Anna was the first to speak. 'You're right. I'm sorry. It all seems so unimportant now. William and I have fallen out. I had a horrendous call from him on the way here. That's why I was late. He was quite cruel.'

'That doesn't sound like William.'

Anna waved an impatient hand. 'He was transferred to South Reading Hospital at the beginning of August. He'd asked me to go with him to his brother's engagement party just before he left . . . I said I would but . . . But then I didn't.'

'Why not?'

'It was silly. I'd bumped into Patrick Wainwright in May . . . Do you remember Patrick?'

'Of course I do. How is he?'

'He's married with a daughter. They live a mile or so away from me which is weird.' Anna took a large gulp of her wine. 'Anyway, Patrick invited me over to supper and I suppose I thought William would understand.'

'You went to supper with Patrick and his wife?'

'Well, actually, his wife was away.' She caught Tess's eye and blushed. 'I don't even know why we're talking about this.' She let her eyes wander restlessly round the restaurant. 'Nothing happened. Patrick kissed me and I realised I should leave. So I did.' She finished her wine and stared defiantly at her sister. 'Why are you looking at me like that?'

Tess raised her eyebrows. 'It's interesting, that's all. You're very quick to judge Mum . . . '

'I'm not judging her.'

'It sounded like it to me. And meanwhile . . . '

'All right.' Anna bit her lip and stared up at the ceiling. She said stiffly, 'I do regret going over to see Patrick. And I regret letting William down.'

'I take it he's still upset.'

'I keep saying I'm sorry. And now he says he doesn't want to be my friend. It's so childish.' She glared at her sister. 'So that's why I was a cow to Mum and I know that's no excuse and I'm sorry. Can we talk about our parents now? I've tried to give you *my* theory. Why do *you* think Dad's acted totally out of character?'

Tess put her hands to her face. 'I haven't a clue,' she said.

19

It was Sunday evening and Eliza was still in a state of shock. Yesterday morning she had picked up her copy of *The Times* and, as was her habit, had gone straight to the obituaries page.

And there it was: *WOODWARD Dennis, passed away peacefully on 26ᵗʰ August 2014 after a short illness, aged 87 years. Beloved husband of Vera (deceased) and father of George. A good friend to many, he will be sadly missed.*

She had cut it out and put it on her noticeboard in the kitchen. She sat looking at it now. It seemed absurd that Dennis Woodward had spent eighty-seven years on the planet and now that he was dead his life had been reduced to three lines. He had been a beloved husband to Vera, a father to George and a friend to many. And now he was dead.

What would *she* have written? 'Dennis Woodward, husband to Vera and father to George, was an exceptionally ugly man whose physical shortcomings were utterly irrelevant in the face of his infectious passion for art. He will be greatly missed by his many friends and most particularly by Eliza Sample whose life will not be the same without him.'

That was true. It might be melodramatic but it *was* true. There were times in her life when a cocktail of events led her to view herself and her life in a new and radical manner. There was the day when, still a teenager, she realised that her mother's intemperate rages were motivated by marital unhappiness rather than by Eliza's failings. Years later, there was the night she went downstairs to find the husband she adored asleep on the sofa. Stephen was a complex, fascinating man who worked too hard and cared too much. She had often come downstairs to find him sprawled against the cushions, reeking of whisky, his mouth wide open and a thin line of spittle trailing down his chin. On this particular occasion, she stared at him with a strange, almost detached understanding that her passion and her sacrifices had been wasted on a weak alcoholic whose charisma and charm, still evident in public, had diminished and would continue to diminish at home.

The notice of Dennis's death had triggered another revelation. She was lonely. She saw old friends like June so rarely not because they were dull but because she was jealous, jealous of their husbands if they had them, and jealous of their children and their grandchildren.

Dennis was the first true companion she had made in years. At a stage in her life when friends seemed to die with worrying regularity, a new one was a prize indeed. She had known he would have come to tea if he could. Every Thursday since, she had haunted the National Gallery, drifting through the rooms like a disembodied ghost, unable to settle in any of them, waiting for him to appear so he could tell her he'd lost her address or had been struck down with flu, hoping he would take her arm, ready to show her some new ancient glory.

After each of their mornings together, she had gone home with a renewed sense of purpose to open her laptop and attempt to keep up with him. She had prepared with great care for her choice of the Lady Jane Grey picture. 'Do you know,' she had told him, 'that this is one of the most viewed pictures in the gallery? Do you know that the floor in front of it has to be re-varnished regularly?'

She had expected him to tell her that popular pictures weren't necessarily great pictures. But he had surprised her again. He had looked at it carefully, told her it was historically inaccurate, for poor Jane had been executed outside rather than in a dungeon, and then he had looked at her and said, 'It *does* move me. You were right to bring us here.' She had felt as proud as if she'd won the Turner Prize. And now he was dead.

She was glad at least that his illness had been short. She remembered what he had said about his sister. And he was right: it was selfish to mourn, but since he was dead he couldn't tell her so and she *would* mourn him. She would keep his sad little obituary on her board until she ceased to miss him. She would go back to the gallery, if only because he would have been cross if she didn't.

He would, she thought, be unimpressed by her current decline into self-pity and introspection. He had been a man of joyous enthusiasm. She poured her nightly glass of red wine and stood to attention. 'Dennis Woodward,' she said, holding her glass in front of her, 'I salute you.' She felt a little foolish but that was stupid. There was, after all, no one here to see her.

★ ★ ★

On Monday morning, Freya was cleaning the kitchen floor when the telephone rang. She supposed this was what it would be like for the next three days. The phone would ring and it would be the outside world or Anna or Tess and she had no wish to speak to any of them. Or it would be Felix. She felt a surge of relief as she heard Pam's customary way of announcing herself. She could just about manage to speak to Pam.

'Freya, I'm not interrupting your work, am I?'

'No, of course not.' Freya tiptoed across the wet floor and went out onto the patio.

'I'm at the office so I can't talk for long. It's about Percy. He had a funny turn on Saturday. I checked on him last night and he was fine but . . . If you have a moment today, could you call on him? He shouldn't be living on his own but I suppose I'd feel the same. The idea of an institution terrifies him.'

'Of course it does. I'll go round in an hour or so.'

'Thank you. You and Felix must come over to supper. I want to tell you all about Simon's plans. He and Naomi want a March wedding. What are you doing on Saturday?'

I don't know, Pam. Felix has decided he wants to end our marriage and I'm not sure either of us would be great company at the moment . . .

'I'm pretty sure we're busy,' Freya said. 'I'll

215

ring you later in the week.'

Perhaps if Pam had been at home she might have said something, though in fact she preferred to postpone the predictable sympathy for as long as possible. She could only hold herself together by refusing to think beyond Wednesday evening.

She took round some homemade soup — leek and potato, Percy's favourite — and rang the doorbell. She could hear little Serge barking furiously. She should have rung Percy first. But now he appeared and seemed as pleased to see her as Serge was.

'Can I offer you tea?' he asked. 'Or would you like coffee?'

'I'm all right, thank you.' The coffee would be instant and the tea would taste like dishwater. Normally, Freya accepted either with good grace. Now she felt she was in no state to see anyone, least of all provide comfort and care.

The kitchen was not as spotless as usual. The pine dresser had a patina of dust across its surface. There was a half-empty pack of sliced brown bread on the table and a small carton of milk without its lid.

Freya took a chair by the table and bent down to stroke Serge. 'Pam told me you've been unwell,' she said.

'I blacked out,' Percy told her. 'One moment I was watching the News and the next I felt Serge licking my face. I've promised Pam I'll keep this by me.' He held up the pendant he had round his neck.

'Quite right,' Freya said. 'You have my number on it, don't you?'

'Pam's number one and you're number two. The thing is . . . ' Percy's eyes drifted down to Serge who was now draped across Freya's feet. 'I'm worried about Serge — if something happens to me. Pam said she'd take him but she has to go to work every day and he hates being on his own. He's always loved you and I wondered . . . '

'Of course I'd take him. But Percy, nothing is going to happen. You're tough as old boots.'

'I'm not scared of being dead,' Percy said. 'I feel I'm on borrowed time anyway to tell the truth. I watched Elaine die. One moment she was there and the next she wasn't. Her body was there but Elaine had gone.'

'Oh Percy!' Freya reached for his hand.

'I tried to feel her presence but no, it was just me . . . me and Serge. So I know what to expect and I'm not scared. But I worry about Serge. He's not good on his own.'

'Neither am I,' Freya said. 'I'm with Serge on that. I promise, you don't have to worry about him.'

'Thank you, Freya. You've eased my mind.' He glanced at her hopefully. 'Are you sure you won't have a coffee?'

'Just a quick one then.' She glanced at the carton of milk. 'I think I'll have it black.'

★   ★   ★

In the evening, her phone rang and a voice said, 'Freya?'

It was him! She couldn't believe it. Her hands

217

tightened round the handset. 'Hello, Neil.'

'I hope you don't mind me calling you,' he said, 'I want to apologise for my appalling behaviour the other night.'

'It was my fault, too.' She hesitated. 'You might as well know — I've told your wife about it in a letter. My husband's in Madrid this week on business. Just before he left on Thursday, he told me he wanted to leave me. So I'm afraid I was a bit of a loose cannon at your party.'

'You were a very beautiful loose cannon.'

She smiled. 'Thank you.'

'When does he come back from Madrid?'

She stood by the window, gazing out at the dusky sky. 'Wednesday.'

'Do you want to see him?'

'What do you think? He hasn't been in touch since he left. He knows I'm just sitting here waiting. It's pretty humiliating really.'

'Then don't wait. Come and stay with me.'

That made her laugh. 'That's very kind. I've spent all this morning composing a long and very contrite letter to your wife. I'm not sure I can face the idea of swapping small talk with her.'

'You wouldn't need to,' Neil said. 'I've moved out. I'm staying with Rory in Chelsea.'

'Oh, I'm so sorry! Now *I* feel guilty.'

'It's not your fault. We should never have had the party. Things haven't been right for a long time. So, there you are. Come to London.'

'You *are* joking, aren't you? I've known you for five minutes! Can you imagine what your children would say, what *my* children would say?

218

And Felix would come home and . . . '

'Exactly. He'd come home and find you gone which would serve him right.'

'There is that,' Freya conceded. 'I suppose your son's flat doesn't run to a spare room?'

'It does and I would be delighted to share it. The bed is very comfortable.'

She couldn't help smiling. 'You are a very wicked man.'

'You have only to ring and I'll meet you off the train.'

'Thank you. It's out of the question but you've made me feel better.'

'I could make you feel all sorts of things if only you'd let me.'

'Neil! I'm ringing off now.'

'Can I talk to you again soon?'

She said, 'This is silly! You know nothing about me.'

'I'd like to rectify that. Ring me if you change your mind.'

She wouldn't, of course, but she *did* feel better. As Felix had often said, she was a sucker for flattery. She wondered what Neil would say if she took him up on his offer. She suspected he'd be appalled.

★   ★   ★

Whenever she could, Freya set aside Tuesday mornings for Ivy. Today, Ivy was in an odd mood: fretful, easily distracted. There was no talk of Marilyn. She'd had some phone calls, she said, but she couldn't remember why. At breakfast

219

she'd eaten sausages and they'd disagreed with her. Freya talked brightly about favourite breakfasts: fresh fruit salad, she suggested, with homemade yoghurt and strong black coffee. And then Ivy said quite suddenly, 'Where is Felix? He should be here!'

Freya was surprised into silence and then her eyes began to smart and all she could do was to press Ivy's hand and agree that, 'Yes, he should be!'

On the drive home, she marvelled at Ivy's extraordinary lapse into her old perceptive sanity. But of course it was no such thing. From time to time Ivy's brain flared into life like a brief, beautiful firework, offering a tormenting glimpse of what had been lost.

Freya had planned to stop in Darrowbridge for eggs but Dulcie Makepeace stood on the pavement, chatting to a friend; she was in no mood to make conversation so she drove on. She hadn't seen Dulcie since the balloon-debate fiasco. That had been a terrible evening and Felix hadn't helped afterwards, shutting himself away with the television and going off to work the next morning without saying goodbye. He hadn't been himself ever since. They used to go for an Indian meal fairly regularly. The last time had been a few days before the debate. And their sex life was virtually non-existent. The only times he'd shown any interest was when he'd had a few drinks.

Freya turned into her drive and stopped the car. She sat, frowning at the windscreen. The memory was sharp as ice. She was on the platform, accepting with faked confidence the half-hearted applause for her Bovary speech. Her eyes scanned the audience and there was Felix — Felix who regularly decried the use of mobiles in inappropriate occasions — staring down at his screen while his wife was dying onstage.

Everything fell into place. How had she been so blind to all the signs? There was no mystery. Felix was a walking cliché. He had met someone else.

In the kitchen, the answerphone flashed and she hit the button. *'Freya, it's Felix. I'm sorry I've missed you. I should be home about eight tomorrow evening. I've been in touch with Harry from work and he says I can stay with him until I find a place of my own. Anyway, we'll talk plans tomorrow.'*

She played the message over and over and each time her anger increased. He had had no intention of talking to her. He knew she visited Ivy on Tuesday mornings. And now he had told Harry from work that he'd left her. There was no apology, no explanation, just a brief, curt message. He couldn't wait to get shot of her. Well that was fine. If he expected her to wait at home in order to hear his 'plans' for their future, if he really expected that, he didn't know Freya.

In the evening, she honed the letter she had spent the entire afternoon composing. Finally, she read it through for the last time.

'Felix, I have gone to stay with a friend in London. There is no need for you to move out since I have no wish to stay in this house on my own. Once I've worked out what I wish to do,

I'll let you know. For the time being, I think it's best if we don't communicate. I doubt you would tell me the truth anyway. Freya.'

The letter had originally run to four pages and into it Freya had poured all her bitterness and rage. But actually, brevity was far more effective and dignified. He didn't want her. A four-line farewell was all he deserved.

★   ★   ★

On the train the next day she sat in the Quiet Carriage, only too happy to switch off her phone. She had the sense that her life was spiralling out of control and she had neither the will nor the energy to do anything about it. Felix had pushed her off her planet and now she floated in space with no idea of her destination. She was Anna Karenina setting off to meet Vronsky though Anna Karenina's husband loved her and Freya's husband didn't.

She remembered a silly argument she'd had with her own Anna, who must have been sixteen because it was then that she started going on about her legal right to have sex when she wanted. On this particular night, she hadn't come home till the early hours of the morning and Freya waited up for her. When Anna eventually returned, very much the worse for wear, she did what she always did in these circumstances and plunged into a pre-emptive attack. 'Why did you call us after women who *died*?' she demanded. 'It's like you wanted us to fail or something . . . ' And she had ranted on and on, her pronouncements growing ever more incoherent until Freya lost her patience and told her to go to bed.

The girls would be horrified by her flight to London. She would have to tell them soon. She'd had a number of missed calls from them in the last few days. And what would she do if Neil was not there to greet her? Why had she ever thought this was a good idea? A man who could flirt with such enthusiasm while his marriage fell apart could hardly be expected to be a safe port in a storm. He'd sounded — understandably — taken aback when she rang him. What would she do if he didn't turn up?

There were any number of friends on whom she could call. There was no one to whom she could face telling the truth. The trouble with being part of a couple for such a long time was that one was totally unprepared for life as a soloist. Most of her friends were Felix's friends too. What would they do with a Felix-less Freya? *Their* Freya was a successful woman with a fascinating career, a loving husband and two clever daughters. The truth was that Freya's career provided her with just enough income to buy nice dresses and good haircuts. The truth was that her husband didn't love her and her daughters never talked to her about anything remotely personal. The truth was that Freya was an abject failure. She couldn't even indulge her misery by crying since a young woman with plaits sat opposite her. The woman was reading *Anna Karenina* and was directly responsible for the thoughts in Freya's head. Freya hoped she'd get off soon. She did, at the next station, smiling at Freya as she did so, which made Freya feel bad.

By the time she got off the train she had formulated a plan. If Neil wasn't there — and she was now pretty sure he wouldn't be — she would find a B&B for the night and send a message to Felix. Why *should* she move out of her own home? She'd done nothing wrong. He could go and live with his new woman in some horrid flat in Bristol. She would go home tomorrow and insist that he sit down and tell her the truth.

A kind man helped her get her suitcase out of the train. She wheeled it along the platform and through the ticket barrier. She planted herself near the stationery kiosk and scanned the people on the concourse. She tried to school her expression into one of calm and ease and slight amusement.

And then she saw him. Neil stood, checking his watch, impossibly handsome, his thin raincoat over his suit. His face broke into a beautiful smile when he saw her. He strode straight across to her and put his arms round her. As romantic gestures went, it was up there with *Anna Karenina*.

20

Tess had had a disturbing dream on Sunday night. She was in the library at the party. Her mother was in the arms of Neil Lockhart. As she stepped towards them, the couple raised their faces and they were no longer her mother and Mr Lockhart, they were Tess and Jamie. Tess could feel Jamie's breath on her face and his body pressed against her own.

The memory made her feel awkward when Jamie rang her on Monday evening and their conversation was difficult enough without it. He assumed everything was settled. She'd told him she'd come back to Scotland for her October Reading Week. As far as he was concerned, the week was already set aside. She was beginning to see that life for Jamie was quite clear-cut. He loved *her* and she'd kissed *him*. Ergo, there was nothing to worry about. All was well.

And he seemed almost indifferent to the actions of his father and her mother.

'Did Mum strike you as drunk at the party?' she persisted. 'She didn't seem to be. At the time she seemed far more composed than the rest of us.'

'Different people act in different ways,' Jamie said. 'I have a friend. When he's had a few drinks he speaks with huge passion about the state of the planet. When he's sober he doesn't give a damn. How does your mother usually act in that situation?'

'I don't know. She gets quite merry after a few glasses of wine. What's your father like when *he* gets drunk?'

'I have no idea. I don't see him very often. I expect he goes round kissing strange women.'

She couldn't understand his flippancy. She couldn't understand his family. 'Has he said anything to you about it? He must have said something.'

'He did send me a text. He said he'd been an idiot.'

'What did you do?'

'I sent one back to say I agreed with him.'

Tess sighed. 'And that's it? Has he been in touch since?'

'Rory rang last night. He wants me to invite Dad up to Scotland.'

'Well, that's thoughtful of him.'

'No, it isn't. Dad's moved into Rory's spare room. Rory's worried it might prove permanent.'

'He and Eva have split up? That's terrible!'

Jamie sounded unconcerned. 'I don't blame Eva for throwing Dad out. I don't know why she ever took him *in*. You'd think his marital track record would raise alarm bells. Don't worry about him.'

'*I'm* not worried about him. I'd have thought that you might be. I just keep going back to that night.' Tess hesitated. 'It was very unnerving to see my mother in the arms of a strange man especially when . . . '

'When what?'

She said, almost apologetically, 'He does look so very like you.'

'He's fifty-five!' Jamie was outraged.

'Well, he looks much younger.'

'Right,' Jamie said. 'Is that supposed to make me feel better?'

She smiled. 'I'm not trying to make you feel better.'

'No,' Jamie said wistfully. 'I didn't think you were.'

She almost laughed but she said sternly, 'Jamie, this is important! Do you think your father and Eva will get back together?'

'I have no idea and I don't care.'

'You should do. We're talking about your father. You should ring him.'

'You're right. I will. I have things on my mind at the moment. The TV lady has got back to me. She wants to do it!'

'Oh, Jamie, that's brilliant!'

'It's better than that,' Jamie said. 'I might just have got you a job.'

'What do you mean?'

'I told her I have a beautiful, photogenic castle with a violent, dramatic history and that I also have a beautiful, photogenic girlfriend who is an authority on Sir Walter Scott and the Borders.'

There were various disconcerting assumptions in his response. For now, Tess focused on the last of them. 'I'm not an authority on the Borders! Why did you say that? Why did you even mention me?'

'I wanted to impress her. I *did* impress her. I showed her that photo of you with Sir Walter at

Abbotsford. She likes it. She likes *you*. When I told her you were a natural speaker . . . '

'Jamie, I'm *not* a natural speaker. How can you possibly *know* if I'm a natural speaker?'

'You have a great voice and, to be honest, if you can make *me* interested in Walter Scott, you are clearly a born teacher. I know you'd be brilliant. Don't start worrying yet, though, the whole idea may well fall to dust. She's sending one of her minions to look at the castle. I'll give you a ring afterwards. I think we can afford to be a little excited about this.'

'I'm glad it went well. At least, I think I am.'

'You'd be mad not to be. Imagine if you could go on television and talk about Sir Walter. You'd have publishers queuing up to commission books from you.'

'What would your cousin Susan say if she saw me pontificating on television about Border history?'

'She'd be incandescent. If for no other reason, we must make sure you do it.'

'I can't think about this now. I'm way behind on my marking. I'd better go.'

'All right. I miss you. I'll see you in October.'

I'll see you in October. It was like a mantra. It reminded her of Chekhov's three doomed sisters forever going on about moving to Moscow. She felt almost nostalgic about her life pre-Jamie and pre-party. It seemed so simple and straightforward. Now, her emotions were all over the place and she felt like a rudderless boat, veering first one way, then the other.

Jamie rang again on Thursday evening. 'The

minion is keen,' he told her. 'They want to do a series of documentaries. Thank heavens for the referendum. 'Scotland is hot,' she said. She said that a lot. Your Sir Walter was a great fan of the Union. Did you know that?'

'Well, of course I did. I told you that . . . '

'You see? You're an expert. You'd be on hand to provide the scholarly context. You could wear some floaty dress and sit with your hand caressing that marble bust of Sir Walter in Abbotsford . . . '

'I wouldn't be seen caressing Scott's head for a million pounds. And I certainly wouldn't wear a floaty dress, it would be quite unsuitable.'

'You're right. Perhaps you should wear a suit and have some glasses. You'd look terrific in a suit . . . '

'I don't *have* a suit. Why are you obsessing about my wardrobe?'

'It stops me obsessing about *you*. October seems too far away. Incidentally . . . '

She loved the way he pronounced every syllable. 'Incidentally what?'

There was a new awkward tone in his voice. 'Have you spoken to your mother today?'

'She won't pick up the phone. Why?'

'I tried to ring my father last night. You made me feel guilty. I couldn't get him so I rang Rory. He said Dad met your mother off the train and took her out to dinner. Rory seemed to think she was coming up to stay in the flat.'

'But that's crazy. She knew Dad was coming back. Why would she do that? Why would she want to stay there?'

'I have no idea. Rory treats the place like a dustbin. He might be wrong, of course. Rory often *is* wrong.'

'I'd better make some calls. I don't understand anything. This is all such a *mess!*'

Rory had to be mistaken. She tried ringing her mother again and left a number of questions on voicemail. 'Where are you, Mum? What's going on? Can you ring me?'

She put the phone down and almost immediately it whirred into action. She picked it up and took a deep breath. It was her father.

'Tess,' he said, 'how are you?'

'I'm *well! Hi!*' She sounded like a children's TV presenter, her voice ready to explode with enthusiasm, while she desperately played for time. 'How was Madrid?'

'It's a lovely city. There's so much to see. Unfortunately, I was holed up in conference rooms most of the time. Tess, I'm trying to get hold of your mother. She's not at home and I can't seem to get her on the phone. Do you know where she is?'

'I'm not quite sure.' Tess picked up the pack of spaghetti she'd bought and then put it down again. 'I think she might be in London. She might be staying with . . . She might be with the Lockharts.'

'The Lockharts? They're the couple who had the party on Saturday? So you both went along to it?'

'Yes. Yes, we did.'

'That's nice. And your mother stayed on with them?'

'No. I'm pretty sure she did go back home. But I think she might be with Mr Lockhart now, with him and his son.'

'That would be your friend from the Borders?'

'No. That would be Jamie's younger brother, Rory.'

'I see. So Mrs Lockhart's gone away?'

'Not exactly. Mr Lockhart's moved into Rory's flat.' Tess sat down at the table. She had no idea what to say. 'There was a disagreement at the party. Between Mr and Mrs Lockhart.'

Her father sounded understandably confused. 'I thought it was their wedding anniversary.'

'It was. But they had an argument.'

'That was unfortunate.'

'Yes,' Tess said feebly. 'It was rather.'

'So why would . . . ?'

'Dad, I don't know much more than you. Jamie told me on the phone that he thought Mum might be at Rory's, that's all.'

'I see. Well, it's a great mystery but . . . '

'Dad, I think I should tell you . . . Mum told me what you said to her before you went to Spain.'

'Did she?' There was a brief silence and then, 'I'd better get on, Tess, I have some soup boiling on the cooker. If you hear from your mother, tell her I'd love to know what she's been doing. Goodbye now!'

Tess put the phone down and pushed her fingers through her hair. What was it with her parents? They were both as mad as each other. She prepared her supper and flung saucepans on the hob in a frenzy of frustration. How could

231

either of them get anywhere when they wouldn't talk to her or each other? On the whole, she preferred her mother's silence to her father's jolly conversation.

She was eating her meal when her mother rang.

'I thought I'd left my charger at home,' she said. 'I found it in my case and now I'm listening to my messages. How are you, Tess?'

'Dad rang. He wants to know where you are. He's tried to ring you but . . . '

'He has *not!* You may tell him I'm staying with Neil Lockhart.'

'Can't you tell him yourself? He wants you to ring him . . . '

'I wanted him to ring *me!*'

'But, Mum, what do I tell him? Are you . . . Are you *with* Mr Lockhart?'

'He's collecting a takeaway at present.'

'You know what I mean.'

'I don't think I do, Tess. I know you and your sister hate intrusive personal questions. You may tell Felix I'm happy. If he wishes to know anything else, he can ring me.'

The phone went dead. Tess stared at it in stupefaction. She had never heard her mother talk to her like that before and, actually, she felt she deserved the rebuke. 'One last call,' she said aloud, 'and then that's it.'

Her father picked up almost at once. 'Hi there, Tess.'

'I've spoken to Mum.' Tess spoke with brisk efficiency. 'She says you *haven't* rung her. She *is* staying with Mr Lockhart and Rory. She says

232

she's well. If you want to know more, I suggest you ring her. I can't keep acting as go-between.'

'Of course you can't. I only wanted to know where she was. That's all I needed to know. I won't bother you again.'

'It's not that but . . . Look, why don't I come and see you? I can't make this weekend but I could come down the next.'

'That's very kind but I'm visiting a friend . . . '

'I could come the weekend after.'

'Can I ring you next week? We can sort out something then. I'd better sign off now. I have some soup boiling on the stove. I'll speak to you soon.'

The mixer tap was dripping slightly and Tess walked over to the sink and tightened it. She wondered where he was going and who his friend might be. Surely he couldn't be seeing someone else? It was inconceivable. But then, everything about him at the moment was inconceivable. She took her half-eaten pasta and tipped it into the kitchen bin. She felt in need of caffeine and put the kettle on. How could he sound so normal when he knew that *she* knew what he'd done? Perhaps he *was* normal. And yet, if he hadn't tried to ring her mother why would he pretend he *had*? She spooned coffee into her mug and frowned as she remembered his soup. It had been boiling on the cooker for a long time.

*   *   *

On Friday evening, Tess met Anna for a conference over a pizza. The weather had been

233

beautiful all day and the evening air still retained its warmth. They sat at a pavement table. Anna was at her most business-like. 'Let's lay out the situation. Mum's moved in with her new boyfriend . . . '

'We don't actually *know* he's her boy-friend . . . '

'His wife throws him out because he's all over Mum. Then he invites Mum to stay so she can sleep on the sofa?'

'If you put it like that . . . '

'Good. We agree. And meanwhile Dad is quite happy.'

'Or he wants us to *think* he's happy.'

'I offered to go down this weekend but he's visiting a friend.'

'I offered to go down *next* weekend. He said the same thing.' Tess picked up her glass. 'I think his friend might be a woman.'

Anna shook her head. 'I don't believe it. There's something very odd going on. I think we should both go down tomorrow, whatever he says. I bet you he's there.'

'I can't do that. Rachel is moving out.'

'Is she? Why?'

'She's moving in with her boyfriend and the new flatmate arrives in the afternoon. I have to be there.'

'What's the new one like?'

Tess shrugged. 'I have no idea. We advertised on Gumtree.'

'She might be horrific. Then what would you do?'

'I'd move somewhere else, I suppose.'

'I'm sorry. I'd hate it if Olivia left. How long have you known?'

'About Rachel? It's been on the cards for weeks. I can't say I blame her. Our flat's dark and depressing. Her boyfriend's place is lovely.'

Anna stared at Tess. 'We should see each other more often.'

'I'm all right,' Tess said. She was touched by her sister's comment. 'Will you go down to see Dad on your own? What would you do if he *is* away?'

'I have a key. If the weather continues like this, I'll sit out in the garden all day. It'll be good to get away. I'm fed up with London at the moment.'

A couple walked past them, their arms slung carelessly round each other's waist. 'So I told her,' the man said, 'if that's the way you feel, I couldn't agree more!' Their laughter hung in the air. Tess said, 'Are you still not talking to William?'

'William's still not talking to *me*. I didn't think I'd miss him so much. Isn't that pathetic?'

'No, not at all.' Tess raised her glass and smiled at her sister. 'Here's to *us*,' she said. 'We *should* see each other more often.'

21

It was quite something to be a sex-goddess at fifty-three, especially when one's husband had gone elsewhere for physical satisfaction. On her first night with Neil, they made love three times. *Three times!* She and Felix had always prided themselves on their thriving sex life. They would usually manage it twice a week, though in the last few months . . . Don't go there, she told herself, don't even think of going there.

Neil said he could not get enough of her. On Thursday, she was in Cromwell Road, outside the Society of Genealogists, when he rang. 'Freya,' he told her, 'you've bewitched me. I had a client this morning. We discussed a complex land search and all I could see was my head between your silky white thighs . . .'

'Neil, stop it!' she laughed. 'How can I concentrate on anything when you talk like that? I hope none of your colleagues can hear you.'

'I'm out on the pavement,' he assured her. 'And I ache for you. Don't imagine you'll sleep tonight.'

That suited Freya. It had been a week since Felix dropped his bombshell and bombshells were not conducive to nocturnal tranquillity. Sex with Neil was the perfect antidote. When they'd finally fallen apart, spent and exhausted, she had slept like a child. In the morning, she woke at dawn and was consumed by panic. Why was she here? Why hadn't she waited to hear what Felix would have to say? What would become of her? And then there was Neil, his hand tracing her breasts and then moving down, his fingers touching, probing, stroking. He was like a magician, deleting her fears with each caress until all that mattered was this moment, this ecstasy.

She barely needed his wicked midday phone call. Every time she thought of Felix she had only to recall Neil's love-making to recover his magic. Felix had torn apart her sanity and now Neil kept it together.

On Friday evening, he drove her to a small country hotel just outside Oxford. Rory was hosting a party on Saturday and escape, Neil said, was imperative. The next morning, they missed breakfast. They walked along the river and stopped for lunch at a pub with wooden floors and pine tables. The weather was perfect — it was more like summer than autumn — and they sat outside, their eyes squinting in the sun.

'I can't believe I'm here,' she said. 'This time last week, I was walking in London, an abandoned, angry wife and now I'm . . . '

'You're here with your red-hot lover,' he said. 'Feel free to agree with me.'

'I do. But it's so odd. We know nothing about each other.'

'Ask me anything you like,' Neil said. 'I lay my life before you.'

She gazed at the river. Two ducks bobbed primly along the surface, occasionally dipping their beaks in the water. She said, 'Tell me the worst moment of your life.'

'Oh Lord,' he said, 'I've had a fair share of those. The very worst would be a long time ago. I was fifteen. You know what it's like when you're that age. The whole world revolves around *you*. My mother had been ill for months and that made me cross. She'd always wanted more children and it just never happened so she spoilt me rotten. And then she got ill and was too tired to humour me and I didn't understand. And then she died.'

'Oh Neil!' Her eyes pricked with tears. So many things made her cry at the moment.

'Are *your* parents still alive?'

'My father died two years ago. I adored him. He was a professor of English Literature at Oxford and the cleverest man I've ever known. Most people were terrified of him. I sometimes think I'm the only person who *wasn't* terrified of him. He always made me feel important. I miss him very much.'

'And what about your mother?'

'I have no idea whether she's alive or dead. I'm an only child like you. My mother left Daddy and me when I was seven. I can hardly remember her. She had blonde hair. I remember her scent: she smelt of rose petals.'

'So it was just you and your father?'

'He married again six years later. She was lovely. She's still alive but she's away with the fairies now.' Her eyes drifted back to the river. She must go down to Darrowbridge soon and see Ivy. She shivered. She didn't want to think of Darrowbridge.

Neil reached for her hand. 'It's my turn to ask a question. I want you to confess something. Give me a confession, the juicier the better.'

'I don't know you well enough for that,' she said. 'I can give you one but you'll think it silly. When you met me at the station, I didn't think you'd be there. You took me out to dinner. And I drank too much. I have to confess that that was deliberate. I was nervous as hell. I could barely remember the last time I slept with a man who wasn't my husband.'

'May I say, Mrs Cameron, that when I finally got you into bed that night, you gave no indication of any nerves whatsoever?'

'It was all that wine. It made me forget.' She lowered her voice. 'And actually, Mr Lockhart, you gave me no time to remember.'

'You bet I didn't. I'd been thinking of nothing else for days.'

'You weren't apprehensive? You didn't feel even a little uncomfortable at the restaurant?'

'Oh God, yes. It was the most uncomfortable evening of my life. I was in an almost permanent state of arousal. Thank heaven for the very large napkin on my lap.'

'You are quite outrageous,' she murmured, casting a furtive glance towards the elderly couple two tables away. Either they were deaf or they were very broad-minded. 'Now *you* have to confess something. And keep it clean.'

He sat back and folded his arms. 'This is a big one. When Jamie told me about your website, I was curious. I am genuinely interested in finding out about my ancestors but actually I was more interested in *you*. Jamie was obviously smitten by your daughter and I thought I'd better find out about her mother.'

'I'm afraid,' Freya said, 'Jamie doesn't have a chance. Tess is very single-minded about her career. She's not interested in romantic complications.'

'You don't know Jamie,' Neil said. 'He's like my father. When he wants something, he won't be deflected until he gets it. If he wants her, *she* won't stand a chance.'

'That's all very well,' Freya said, 'but *you* don't know Tess. Anyway, I interrupted you. You were looking at my website . . . '

'That's right. I saw your photo and I'm afraid I forgot all about ancestors and Jamie and your daughter. You seemed to smile straight at me and I knew I had to meet you. Hence the invitation.'

It took a moment to grasp what he'd said. 'You asked me to the party because you fancied me?' She was genuinely shocked. 'It was your *anniversary* party!'

'I told you it was a big confession. It was bad. I do feel bad.'

'I should think so. Neil, that is terrible!'

'I know, I know. Can we please move on before you decide I'm beyond redemption? Ask me another question.'

'I can't think of one. I'm too shocked by your confession.'

'All right. Here's one for free. Shall I tell you about the best moment of my life?'

She felt she should ask about Eva — at least find out if his marriage was bad enough to justify

240

his invitation to a strange woman. But if she did, he might ask about Felix and she didn't want to bring him into this setting and this occasion. She had the company of Neil — so much better-looking than her husband — she had the sun on her back and she had the Oxfordshire countryside. 'Yes,' she said, 'I'd like to hear that.'

'The memory's quite clear. I was at a party. A friend was telling me about his plans to build a conservatory. He's a very dear friend but I'm afraid my attention was wandering. I've never quite understood the point of conservatories. As far as I can see, you either want to be outside or in. And then a woman walked into the room. She wore a tight pink dress with the most suggestive zip I have ever seen and I knew straight away that I'd met the woman of my dreams.'

Freya smiled. 'That's so romantic. I don't believe it for a minute.'

'What about you? What has been the best moment of your life?'

'Oh,' Freya said, 'that's easy.' She raised her glass and smiled at him. 'That's now.' When she looked into his rich, dark eyes, she could almost believe it.

★ ★ ★

Anna had planned to get a taxi from the station but it was such a beautiful morning that she decided to walk. She stopped off at the supermarket to buy rations: eggs, pasta, tomatoes and bread. As she made her way up the lane she tried to work out a plan. She had not rung her

241

father to say she was coming. He had, after all, told her he'd be away. If he *was*, she supposed she'd have to consider the possibility that he had indeed met some new woman, though she wouldn't believe it until she'd seen it with her own eyes. If he was at home, she could then, legitimately, confront him. 'Dad,' she'd say, 'I insist that you tell me what is going on.'

She could no more imagine herself insisting than she could see him responding. He had always been a private man where his emotions were concerned. He was like his mother. Grandpa Philip's funeral had been a perfect example of their self-control. The family were out in force and everyone was crying. Only her father and Grandma were dry-eyed, their faces still as stone. Afterwards at the wake, the two of them were assiduous hosts, passing round sandwiches, consoling lachrymose relatives, maintaining a constant flow of conversation. And yet, Anna knew, they'd both adored Grandpa Philip.

She turned into the drive and came to an abrupt stop. Her father's car was there. For the first time, Anna had qualms about her presence here. It was quite possible — it was very likely — that her father had made up an excuse because he wanted to be alone. Worse, he might want to be alone with some woman. Why hadn't that occurred to her before? He might regard her visit as a colossal invasion of his privacy. She was almost tempted to turn round and go back to the station. On the other hand, she had a right to want to know how he was and why he wanted to split the family. She went up to the front door and her fingers hovered over the bell before pressing it. She heard it ringing inside the house. She waited and then rang again. She opened the letter flap and peered through it into the hall. She could see a vase of dead roses on the table. There were crimson petals on the flagstones. There wasn't a sound from anywhere.

She took out her key and pushed at the reluctant door. The obstacle proved to be a small collection of bills, circulars and letters. She picked them up and put them on the hall table. The house smelt airless, empty, abandoned. 'Dad, where the hell are you?' she murmured.

She froze. She could swear she heard a slight cough from the spare bedroom. She quelled the urge to turn tail and run and tiptoed into the sitting room. Her eyes fell on the poker in the fireplace. She picked it up and went back to the hall. The house was silent again. If there was an intruder up there, he was a very *still* intruder. She took off her shoes and left them in the hall before creeping upstairs and along the landing to the spare room. The door was ajar. She took a deep breath, tightened her grasp on the poker and sidled into the room.

There was someone in the bed and he must have sensed her presence since he turned to look at her. She would never forget the expression on his face. For just a moment there was a glimmer of hope in his eyes. Then he saw it was her and the light dulled and he said, 'Anna? What are you doing here?'

She hardly recognised him. He had a rough

growth of beard on his chin, his eyelids were red and puffy and his hair was a mess.

'I nearly brained you with this,' she said, waving her poker above her head. 'It's just as well you showed your face to me!' He made no attempt to pretend to be entertained by her feeble attempt at levity. She put the poker on the chest of drawers and went round to his side of the bed. 'Dad? What's going on? And why are you in the spare room?'

He hauled himself up by his elbows and sat back against his pillow. His pyjama buttons were in the wrong holes, giving his chest an oddly misshapen appearance. There was a sour smell of alcohol mixed with sweat in the room.

'I'm a little out of sorts,' he said. 'I'm not very well.' He reached for the glass of water by his bedside table and drank deeply from it. He put it back and stared up at her as if he hardly knew her. 'I thought I told you not to come this weekend.'

'I was worried about you. With good reasons as it turns out. Tell Dr Cameron. What are the symptoms?'

'I . . . ' He looked out of the window as if trying to remember. 'I'm not exactly sure.'

She frowned. 'I'm not surprised you feel ill. There's no air in here.' In a few quick movements she opened the curtains and then the windows. 'It's a lovely day out there,' she said.

'Anna,' he protested, 'this is very kind but . . . '

' . . . You wish I was back in London? I'm sorry, Dad, but this isn't good enough. I tell you what we're going to do. You are going to have a shower, wash your hair and have a shave. And I am going to make some lunch for us. Is that clear?'

'I'm really not hungry . . . '

'See how you feel after your shower.' She picked up the poker and then stopped by the door. 'Promise me you'll wash your hair.'

'Nag, nag . . . ' he murmured. For a moment a smile hovered. 'I promise,' he said.

★   ★   ★

Freya and Neil returned to London in the early hours of Sunday evening and almost immediately wished they hadn't. As they opened the door of Rory's flat they were greeted by the stale smells of smoke and alcohol. In their room, the bed was a mess and on the floor around it there were empty beer cans, a black lace bra and one high-heeled black shoe.

'For God's sake . . . ' Neil murmured.

They heard the sound of flushing water from the bathroom and went out to see Rory emerge with a white face and red eyes. He wore pyjama bottoms and a dirty white T-shirt and looked like death would be welcome.

'Hi there,' he said weakly. 'I've been trying to clear up but I don't feel too well.'

'Rory,' Neil said, 'there've been people in our bedroom. You could have spared our bedroom.'

'I'm sorry.' Rory put a hand to his stomach. 'I thought I'd do the kitchen first . . . '

'Neil,' Freya said, 'the poor boy's *ill* . . . '

'The poor boy,' Neil said, 'has had the whole

245

day to sort this out.'

'I was celebrating,' Rory said. 'I have a recall in the morning. It could be a breakthrough.'

'I very much doubt it,' Neil said. 'If you look like you do now, they'll . . . '

'He'll be fine,' Freya said. 'What time is the audition?'

Rory frowned. 'I think . . . It's half past ten.'

'Good,' Freya said. 'Go to bed. I'll bring you water and you must try to drink it. In the morning I'll give you a big breakfast. I'll sort out the flat tomorrow. Do you have clean sheets?'

Rory nodded. 'In your room. In the cupboard.'

'Excellent. Off you go now.'

'Freya,' Rory said, 'you are a total angel. Please never leave.' He turned and walked with great care to his bedroom.

Neil shook his head. 'I don't believe this.'

'At least he's done the kitchen,' Freya said.

It was difficult to see what it was that Rory had done. The vinyl floor was sticky and damp. Every available surface was covered with glasses, ashtrays, pieces of baguette, bottles and cans. On the cooker, a big saucepan had the remains of a noxious-looking curry. Another pan had congealed wads of rice.

'I'll tell you what we'll do,' Freya said. 'If you change the sheets in our room, I'll make a start in here. I'll tackle the rest of the place tomorrow.'

Neil went across to her and took her hands in his. 'I don't deserve you,' he said. 'And Rory *certainly* doesn't.'

22

'So what exactly is wrong with him?' Tess sounded bemused.

A woman and her child wanted the lavatory and Anna moved away towards the door of the train. 'He *says* it's flu but it didn't look like that to me. I think it's a case of acute depression. I made him promise he'd call the doctor first thing tomorrow'

'Anyone would think it was Mum who left *him*,' Tess said. 'Did he talk about it?'

'Only to say it was his decision. He seems exhausted. He got up this morning but had to go back to bed. I took a taxi to the station. Oh and, by the way, I called in on Pam today. I told her what's happened.'

'Oh, Anna . . . '

'I felt I had to. There's Dad on his own and he's in no state to go to work at the moment. Someone needs to keep an eye on him.'

'That's all very well but if Dad won't even talk to *us* . . . '

'I told him Pam would drop by on Wednesday evening and he wasn't very happy. So I said it was Pam or Grandma, and on balance he preferred Pam. I had to promise we wouldn't tell Grandma.'

'I have no intention of telling Grandma. She left a message the other day and I daren't call her back. It's all so difficult . . . '

'I know. And, by the way, I asked him if he'd like you to come down next weekend and he said he wouldn't. He wasn't exactly thrilled to see me. Have you spoken to Mum yet?'

'I've tried. I'm not going to keep hounding her.'

'All right. Let me know if you *do* hear from her. How's your new flatmate?'

'Oh, fine . . . In fact . . . ' Anna could hear a voice in the background. 'I'd better go. Emily wants us to rearrange the fridge.' Tess spoke in a voice of faded resignation.

'Good luck,' Anna said. She went back to her seat. Poor Tess, she thought. Emily was obviously going to be a disaster. There was one point in her favour. She'd saved Anna from having to relay the lowest point of the weekend. She liked to think she *would* have told Tess.

It had happened on Saturday night. She'd made a risotto for supper and her father had barely touched it, although he'd assured her it was very good.

'So good you only managed two mouthfuls.' She couldn't bear it any longer. 'What's happened to you, Dad? What has Mum done to make you like this? Was she seeing someone else?'

She knew at once she'd gone too far. It was actually quite frightening. He took his plate to the sink and then stood with his back to her. Finally, he turned and stared at her with blazing eyes. 'Let me tell you something,' he said. 'At some stage your mother and I will have a talk. And when we *do*, I have no intention of

248

confessing to her that I chose to indulge your taste for *gossip* and *tittle-tattle*.'

'That is totally unfair.' She tried to keep her voice steady. 'I'm trying to help you. How can I help if you won't say what's wrong?'

'I don't *know* what is wrong. If I find I need help I'll seek it from a professional therapist not from my *very* junior doctor daughter. I didn't ask you to come here. I didn't want you to come here. And now I'm going to bed.'

She felt like she'd been attacked by a thunderstorm. She'd been wrong to push him. On balance, she thought as she made her way back to her train seat, she was glad she hadn't told Tess.

When she got home, Olivia was sitting with her laptop on the sofa. She looked up at Anna and put it to one side. 'How was your dad? Was it as bad as you thought it would be?'

'Worse. He didn't want to talk to me. He didn't want me there. I shouldn't have gone down without telling him. He's always hated surprises. I felt . . . I felt like an intruder.'

'Have you had any supper? There's some ham in the fridge.'

'I had a sandwich on the train.'

'I'm sorry you're having such a rotten time.' Olivia put her laptop to one side. 'I'm about to make it worse, I'm afraid.'

'Why? Has something happened?'

Olivia sighed. 'I had Jason round last night. You know he works for Corkscrew Productions? They're planning a short series on holistic gardening and they've found a very hot presenter.'

Anna put her hands to her aching head. 'It's not who I think it is?'

Olivia nodded. 'Xander Bullen. Apparently he has a huge, perfect garden and a telegenic family. Jason says he'll be a star.'

★   ★   ★

Rory came back on Monday evening, bearing gifts: flowers, wine and chocolates.

'Rory!' Freya said. 'This is too much!'

'It's not enough but I want you to know how much I appreciate you. You gave me a five-star breakfast this morning and I bet it took you all day to clear up the place. I feel abjectly humble.'

'I was happy to do it. I like to be busy.' This was true. Pam had rung this morning. She'd been quite wonderful really. She'd been short and to the point. 'Freya, Anna came to see me yesterday. She told me about you and Felix. If at any time you need to talk or want my help, you have only to call. I'm going now but don't forget.' And that had been that. She'd been kind and tactful and Freya had almost fallen apart. And then she'd looked at the sitting room with its crumbs and its glasses and its mess and she'd got to work.

'I have to tell you,' Rory said, 'this flat has never looked this good. You are a miracle worker. Can I have a hug?'

Freya smiled. 'You can!'

Rory put his arms round her and embraced her tightly. 'You even smell perfect,' he said.

A voice came from the doorway behind them.

'Get your hands off my woman, you libidinous toad. I can't leave you alone for a minute.'

Rory grinned and released Freya. 'I'm showing my appreciation. Do you even know what libidinous means?'

'It means over-sexed and as far as you're concerned that's an understatement.'

'It takes one to know one. If . . . *when* Freya sees that you're way past your sell-by date, I'll be waiting in the wings.' He sniffed suddenly. 'Is that chicken in the oven?'

'Yes. I didn't know if you'd be in but . . . '

'Of course I will be! I *adore* chicken. I shall never go out while you're here! Shall we open the wine?'

Neil cast a despairing look at Freya. 'Do you see what you've done? We'll have him round our necks forever!'

Freya laughed. She felt she was in some Noël Coward play with two gorgeous men on hand to amuse her. Who needed Felix when there were Neil and Rory?

★ ★ ★

Lunch with Flora was always very civilised. There were crisp white napkins on the polished table, cut-glass tumblers of water — with a thimbleful of sherry beforehand. Flora's house-keeper was an excellent cook. For first course there was tomato soup, followed by fish pie and then trifle.

The conversation focused on the referendum. Katherine and Maggie — for once in agreement

— both supported the Union while Flora backed independence. 'It's a leap of faith,' she conceded, 'but sometimes one needs to be brave. A vote for Union is a vote for England and the Tories.'

'You've been talking to Susan,' Katherine said.

Flora acknowledged the truth with a sheepish smile. 'She is indefatigable. She's out every night, pounding the streets. If the vote goes against us, I don't know what she'll do.'

'I wouldn't worry about Susan,' Katherine said. 'She's a very strong woman. Are all of your family with the two of you on this?'

'Of course. Jamie's hoisted the Scottish flag on his castle. And down in London, poor Archie is beside himself because he can't vote. It doesn't help that Susan rings him up to berate him for leaving his homeland in its hour of need, even though he left eight years ago and would have lost his job if he hadn't. Poor Archie feels quite marooned. At least he has his cousin down there, though he has *not* been behaving well.'

Katherine's shoulders rippled with anticipation. 'Are we talking about Neil Lockhart?'

Flora nodded. 'He and Eva threw a party to celebrate their tenth wedding anniversary. Eva's only been up here once which doesn't surprise me. She was so cold all the time. Eventually she bought a thick cardigan. She was a nice young woman. I told her to get her circulation checked.'

'But Flora,' Katherine urged, 'what happened at the party?'

'Archie said it was all very odd. There was a woman at the party, very glamorous, Archie said, but quite *obvious* if you take my meaning. He said Neil couldn't keep his eyes off her and then the two of them disappeared for a *considerable* period of time.'

'On his wedding anniversary?' Katherine's eyes sparkled. 'Can you believe it?'

'Knowing my nephew,' Flora said, 'I can believe it too well.'

'So did they come back?' Katherine asked. 'Did Eva notice?'

'Neil came back. Eva and the woman were conspicuous by their absence. Neil made a short speech in which he thanked everyone for coming. Then Jamie stepped forward and announced that his stepmother had been taken ill and that in the circumstances it might be better if everyone left.'

'Perhaps she *was* ill,' Maggie said.

'Archie rang her a few days later. He told me she sounded very strange.'

'Well!' Katherine said. 'Well!'

On the drive back to the Commune, Katherine talked knowingly about the Lockhart bad blood. Aware that her strictures were received without comment, she said a little tetchily, 'You're very quiet.'

'I've been trying to remember something,' Maggie confessed, 'and now I have. When Tess was with us she told me she and Freya had been invited to the party. Jamie's father wanted to pick Freya's brains about family research. I don't know if they went but . . . '

'You must find out,' Katherine said. 'They would have seen it all. Maggie, you must ring them.'

'I don't believe any of it,' Maggie said. 'It sounds very far-fetched.'

'Where the Lockharts are concerned, nothing is beyond belief.' Katherine nodded wisely. 'I did warn you about them.'

That settled it, Maggie thought. She would ring Freya who would tell her what had really happened, which Maggie would, with great satisfaction, relay to her sister-in-law.

⋆ ⋆ ⋆

The washing-machine had stopped mid-cycle. The only clue was the red light that kept blinking the letter D at him.

Freya kept her household file in her desk. Felix took it out and rifled through the various documents until he found the instructions he wanted.

It proved to be quite simple but Felix felt childishly pleased that he'd sorted it out. The D stood for drain and the relevant compartment was blocked by a hard knot of tissue. Well, he thought, he was not completely useless.

He took the file back to the study and opened the drawer. It was then that he saw the folder. Written across its cover was 'Anniversary Stuff'. He was tempted to leave it alone. He knew he could not.

The first page had a title, 'Speech', and then below it a few paragraphs and notes, all of which had been covered with Freya's thick black felt-tip. The second page contained a list of guests — fifty all told — and a sample invitation:

Felix and Freya want you to join them in a celebration of their thirtieth wedding anniversary. Dress informal. Food provided!

Finally, Felix found a few cuttings kept together with a paper clip. There were adverts for weekends in Rome and Venice, membership to an exclusive wine society, a trip 'of a lifetime' to the Arctic, a place Felix had always hoped to visit one day.

He'd had no idea she'd planned any of this. When he dismissed the idea of a party, she'd seemed unconcerned. Why hadn't she said anything? He knew the answer to that one. Felix didn't want a party. Therefore, there would be no party. He felt unbearably selfish. He didn't deserve her. He had never deserved her.

The phone on Freya's desk rang and, without thinking, Felix picked it up and said, 'Hello?'

'Felix? I thought you'd be Freya. Why aren't you at your office?'

It was his mother. Felix stood up and walked to the window. 'Hi, Ma. I'm working from home today. I'm afraid Freya's not here. Can I help?'

'Well, you might. I'm ringing out of rampant curiosity. Katherine and I had lunch with a friend today. Flora Macdonald. She told us a strange story about a party in London. Her nephew, Neil Lockhart, and his wife were hosting it and I remembered that Tess said she and Freya might go to it. Do you know if they did?'

'Yes,' Felix said. 'Yes, they both went.'

'What did Freya say about it afterwards? On second thoughts, get Freya to ring me. You were always hopeless at relaying good gossip. I've tried to ring Tess but I suppose she's working. In fact, I rang her last week — Robert's grandson is thinking of applying to her university — and she never got back to me. She hasn't changed her number, has she?'

'I don't think so.' Felix swallowed. 'Tell me about the party. It might jog my memory.'

'Well, all this is courtesy of Flora's son, Archie, who I suspect is blessed with a vivid imagination. According to him, a sensational lady appeared at the party and entranced the host. The host and the lady disappeared for a while. Then the host returned — without the woman — and announced that the party must finish since his wife had been taken ill. According to Archie, it's all very sinister . . . '

Felix cleared his throat. 'I wish I could enlighten you but . . . '

'I knew you'd be useless. Your father was just the same. I remember when . . . '

'Ma, I'm sorry, I have a client calling me on my mobile. I'd better take it. I'll talk to you soon . . . '

Felix turned off the phone and put it down on the desk. Tess had told him Freya was staying with Neil Lockhart. Her vagueness as to the reason was now explained. Freya wasn't staying with the man. She was living with him.

He sat at Freya's desk, staring at all the clutter she kept there: the calendar notepad, frozen on the day she'd left, the jar of pens and pencils, her dictionary and thesaurus, the photo of Tess and Anna on their tenth birthday . . . And then he saw it: a pink envelope propped up against the picture frame, labelled 'FELIX'. Inside, he found a voucher for a balloon ride over Bath. There was a small sheet of paper inside the envelope and Felix took it out. '*Felix, I bought this for you for your anniversary present. It seemed mean not to give it to you. I'm sorry you've stopped loving me.*'

This was a different Freya from the woman who had left the short, bitter farewell note. '*I'm sorry you've stopped loving me.*' Felix could imagine her sitting at her desk as she wrote it.

He sat and stared through the window at the drive and front garden. But what he saw was a different garden, the one they'd had in Wimbledon, and Xander Bullen in his red hat, pulling up weeds and then smiling as Felix approached him.

'Xander,' Felix said, 'I have something I need to say. It isn't easy. I know how fond Tess is of you and . . . '

'It's all right.' Xander sprang to his feet. His face was white as a sheet. 'I know what you're going to say. I admit it. I'm in love with your wife. I've made a fool of myself. Freya's been very kind and generous but . . . You want me to go.'

'Yes,' Felix said. 'But not because of that. I had no idea . . . ' Felix was out of his depth and knew it. He could think of no suitable response. Xander looked utterly miserable. Felix actually felt sorry for him. 'We're moving in a couple of months and there's no need to keep a gardener. I'll give your details to our successors here. I have to say though — given what you've told me — I do feel it's best if you leave us today.'

'Right. Of course. I'll get my things together.'

Felix handed him an envelope. 'There's a bonus in there along with your wages. Goodbye, Xander. I hope things go well for you.'

And then, as Felix left, Xander called after him, 'It only happened the once.'

Felix nodded and walked back into the house. He assumed Xander meant that he'd only once revealed his feelings to Freya.

But then as the days went by, the words took on a new and scarcely credible significance. At odd times, Xander's words would break into his thoughts: *It only happened the once.*

23

Tess wondered if she might be getting Emily out of proportion. Certainly, the labels were an irritant. The fridge was now full of them. Emily had even labelled her soya milk though Tess assured her she had no desire to use it. Yesterday, Emily brought home four apples, put them into Tess's papier-mâché bowl and labelled *each* of them. Tess had been very inclined to label the bowl, 'Tess's property'.

On both Monday *and* Tuesday evening Emily had colonised the kitchen. She sat at the table, pouring over Facebook like it was the Holy Grail, and chatting on her phone to her mother or her sister or her boyfriend. Worse, she would look quite affronted whenever Tess came in to make a sandwich or a coffee.

When her father rang on Wednesday to ask if she'd come down after all, Tess's first reaction was one of heartfelt gratitude at escaping from Emily. Her second was to question why he'd changed his mind. 'Are you sure you want me to come?' she asked. 'I'm not offended if you don't. Anna said you needed time on your own.'

'Well . . . ' There was a long pause. 'I'm afraid I was very unfair to poor Anna. I was out of sorts but that's no excuse. I'll try to do better this time. Let me know when your train gets in . . . '

And then, just a few minutes later, her mother rang, which Tess found a little bit spooky. Freya, like Felix, was anxious to tell her she was very well and would love to see her. 'Are you free tomorrow evening? Come over after work and we'll have a drink on our own before the boys get back.'

Presumably the 'boys' were Neil and Rory. Tess accepted at once and prepared to cancel Rachel who'd invited her over to see her new love-nest. Tess felt no compunction about doing this. If it weren't for Rachel, there'd be no Emily.

She arrived the next evening at a smart red-brick building in Chelsea, opposite the Thames. The intercom had five names with corresponding buzzers. Tess was trying to identify Rory's name when a woman with stiff hair and a shiny handbag came up behind her. 'Are you looking for Rory?' she asked. 'He's on the first floor in Flat Two.'

She unlocked the door and Tess, following her in, asked, 'How did you know I wanted Rory's flat?'

The woman smiled. 'It's always pretty young women who want to see Rory,' she said.

'I see.' Tess laughed, though she rather resented being seen as one of his groupies. She climbed the first flight of stairs and stood on the landing, admiring the tasteful wallpaper and the grey carpet. Rory, she thought, was a very lucky young man. She knocked on the door and within moments it was flung open.

'Wow,' she said.

Her mother wore an apron — now, Tess could see it was an apron — with the imprint of a woman's naked torso. Freya laughed and took it off at once. 'Isn't it dreadful? It's Rory's, of course!'

Tess stepped into the narrow hallway. She caught a glimpse of the room on her left. Her mother's silk nightdress lay on the double bed. She turned away quickly and followed her mother into the sitting room. There were signs of a bachelor owner: a poster of Marilyn Monroe pouting at the camera, a vast television, a framed collage of photos of glamorous blondes and inebriated males draped over each other, a big, squashy, leather foot-cushion. But there were also signs of her mother's influence: a jug of roses stood on the mantelpiece, the three cushions were positioned neatly on the sofa and the coffee-coloured carpet bore signs of a recent vacuum.

'It's very nice,' Tess said. She walked across to the window and stared out at the river. 'It's a great location.'

'It *is* nice, isn't it? Let's have a glass of bubbly. It's only cheap but still . . . '

The kitchen was in need of re-decorating. The vinyl, patterned floor was worn and the laminated covering on the beige units was curling in corners, exposing the cheap plywood beneath. A colander full of washed spinach stood on the draining board, a jug of rice was ready for action and there were rich smells from the oven. 'I can see you've been busy,' Tess said. Last time she'd asked about Neil, her mother had bitten her head off. Tess watched Freya open the bottle and said cautiously, 'So, how's it all going?'

'Well, of course, it's rather odd.' Freya gave a

smile that went on a little too long. 'I'm staying with two men I hardly know for a start! But I think it's good for me. I was in a very cosy rut down in Darrowbridge. And the boys are such fun. They insult each other all the time but they do make me laugh. You'd think it might be difficult but Rory seems quite happy to have us here.'

'You're in no hurry to leave then?'

Freya poured out the drinks and led the way back to the sitting room. 'To be honest,' she said, 'I don't know what I want. I mean obviously, soon, I must talk to Felix, and Neil must talk to Eva and we'll have to sort things out. For now, I'm quite happy to take one day at a time. But how are you, Tess? Tell me about *you*.'

'I have a new flatmate. I don't like her much. Mum . . . Anna went down to see Dad on Saturday. She's worried about him. He looks really ill. Anna thinks he's seriously depressed.'

Her mother flicked her hair back with her hand. 'That's nothing to do with me. He said he wanted *out* and so I *moved* out. It's a little late for him to have second thoughts. Do you know he hasn't rung me once since he came back from Spain?'

'Have you rung *him*?'

'It's not my place to do so. I wasn't the one who wanted to change everything. If I think about Felix, it makes me miserable, and I am trying . . . ' Freya moved towards the window and brushed her eyes with her hand. 'I'm trying very hard not to be.'

'I'm going down to see him on Friday. Can I

give him a message?'

'I can't think of anything. You could be an angel and bring back my black mac. It's hanging in the hall.'

'Of course.' Tess took a sip from her glass. 'I thought I'd go and see Ivy.'

'Oh darling, would you? I've been in touch with the home and I plan to go down in a week or two . . . ' They heard the sound of men's voices and then the key turning in the door. Freya brightened at once. 'That will be them,' she said. 'This is such *fun*!'

Neil was charming and showed no sign of awkwardness while Rory greeted Tess like an old friend. She did her best to be responsive but it was difficult to be comfortable with them. She felt disloyal to her father just by being there. It was painful to watch her mother lapping up compliments, laughing at every not terribly funny joke, gazing up at Neil as if he were the answer to every woman's prayer. And Rory's florid praise of her mother's culinary and cleaning achievements soon began to grate. Tess wondered how long she'd be content to be the perfect housewife.

Rory went out after supper, apologising profusely for breaking up the party. After he'd gone, Neil asked Tess about Jamie. 'Have you heard from him recently? I seem to remember he said something about a TV show?'

'The signs seem to be good,' Tess said. 'You should ring him.'

'I know.' Neil smiled and took her mother's hand. 'I've been a little . . . preoccupied lately.'

263

That was it. Tess couldn't take any more. She rose to her feet and said, 'I'm afraid I shall have to leave the party too. I have a lecture to prepare.'

'May I say something?' Neil's eyes stared straight at her. 'I know this evening can't have been easy for you. It's not easy for any of us. It was good of you to come and it's meant a lot to your mother.'

'Well . . . ' Tess said feebly, 'I'm glad.'

'All this must seem so crazy.' He flashed Tess a smile. 'I met your mother and . . . I adore her. I'm a lucky man, I know that. But we've done nothing wrong. Your father no longer wants your mother and I do. I want her very much.'

'Oh Neil!' Her mother leant against his shoulder and put her hand to his chest.

No question. It was definitely time to go. Only later did it occur to Tess that Neil's poor wife had been airbrushed out of the equation. The party had happened less than a fortnight ago and already he'd forgotten his wife of ten years. He wasn't the only one to be behaving strangely. Freya Eliza Cameron had always been proud of her feminist credentials and yet now she simpered and smiled every time her 'boys' praised her housework and cooking abilities. Tess's father's behaviour was incomprehensible and *she* was having sex dreams. Nothing and nobody made sense.

⋆ ⋆ ⋆

On Friday, Tess was half-asleep throughout the day, the result of a long night spent following the course of the Scottish Referendum. She only just made the train to Darrowbridge and it was standing room only. She was forced to stand in between the carriages, her rucksack between her feet, her body swaying gently against a sharp-suited young man who seemed to think she was touching him up.

'What's your name then?' he asked.

She sighed. 'Tess.'

'I'm Gideon. It's a crap name, don't you think?'

'No. I like it.' She shouldn't have said that.

'You have beautiful hair.'

'Thank you.'

'Some people hate red hair. I don't.'

'My hair's auburn not red but . . . '

'Don't take offence. Didn't I say I liked it?'

'Well, thanks again.' Her phone rang and she had to lean against Gideon in order to dig it out of her pocket. 'Jamie,' she said with exaggerated enthusiasm. 'Hi!'

He sounded downcast. 'Have you heard the news from Scotland?'

'I'd have to be blind and deaf not to. I'm so sorry.'

'Well, I'll keep the flag flying.'

'Look at it this way. Now the Union's safe, you'll keep attracting English visitors. And it might be good for the programme.'

'That's why I rang. You're on your way to see your father?'

'Yes. The train's packed.'

'I won't keep you long. I thought I'd better warn you that you'll get an email this evening.

It'll offer you a provisional plan of what you might want to talk about . . . '

'But I haven't a clue . . . '

'I know. Don't worry. Don't answer it. We'll talk about it Sunday evening. I've got a big wedding on tomorrow.'

'All right. I'll speak to you then. Bye now.'

She managed to put her phone away without bumping into Gideon.

'Is that your boyfriend?' he asked.

She nodded. 'We get married next month.'

'Oh.' Gideon shifted slightly.

'He likes my hair too,' Tess said.

'Good,' Gideon said. 'I'm very happy for you.' He said nothing for the rest of the journey.

When Tess arrived at the station there was no sign of Felix. Instead, Geoff, the local taxi driver, stood by his cab waving to her.

'Geoff,' she said, 'is there something wrong with Dad?'

'He sounded fine two hours ago. He asked me to collect you. He probably fancied a beer or two.'

Her father was a past master at sounding fine when he wasn't. As they drove through Darrowbridge, she half-listened to Geoff while he aired his extremely suspect views on the Scots and their referendum. When he finally stopped the car, he told her that Felix had sorted out the bill.

'I'll see you on Sunday,' he said. 'Can you remember the train you're getting?'

'It's the four thirty but . . . '

'Good, I'll pick you up at four ten. It's always better to be early.'

He drove off before she could question him further. She picked up her rucksack and waved as she saw Felix in the doorway. Anna had led her to believe he'd resemble a tramp. He looked thinner and pale but his clothes were respectable and his hair was clean. He was touchingly keen to show how well he was managing. 'I went online today and learnt how to make pastry and so tonight we have ham and mushroom pie made with my own fair hands. I was about to start work on the beans.'

'I can help with them,' Tess said. The house was aired — 'It's like the Black Hole of Calcutta,' Anna had warned — and in the kitchen the beans were ready and waiting.

The house phone rang and Tess could have sworn that Felix flinched. She picked it up and rather quickly wished she had not.

Grandma was in no mood for small talk. 'I presume you're with your father,' she said. 'At least I have the chance to speak to you at last.'

'Grandma, I'm so sorry. I have meant to ring you . . . ' She threw a glance at her father who reacted by shaking his head vehemently and pulling a bottle of wine from the fridge. 'The thing is we're about to eat supper.'

Grandma was implacable. 'It can wait. This afternoon, Katherine spoke to Archie's wife, Sally.'

'Who's Archie?' Tess asked. 'And who's Sally?'

'They are relatives of Neil Lockhart and they were guests at his anniversary party . . . Are you still there?'

'Yes, Grandma.'

'Sally told Katherine that Neil has left his wife to go off with a woman called Freya Cameron. Now I hope I'm wrong, but am I right to assume she was talking about your mother?'

'Well yes, I suppose she was . . . '

'But I don't understand. I thought she'd never met him before the party.'

'That's right. You see . . . She was in a bit of a state . . . '

'*Why?*'

Tess gave up. 'I have Dad right here. I think you'd better ask *him*.'

Felix had just poured two very large glasses of wine and he looked at Tess in horror. She didn't care. She handed him the phone and picked up her glass.

'Ma,' Felix said, 'how nice to talk to you again . . . ' He stood up and began pacing the kitchen, pushing his hands through his hair. 'No, of course I mean it . . . I didn't want to worry you . . . No, I'm fine. I told Freya before the party that I wanted us to separate . . . Of course I'm telling you the truth . . . I really can't explain it now . . . No, absolutely not, I'm deluged with work which I'm trying to do, so I can get up to Scotland to see you in a few weeks' time . . . Yes of course I still want to come. I'm very much looking forward to it. We can talk about things then . . . You mustn't be cross with Tess. I asked her not to tell you. I wanted . . . I wanted to tell you in my own time and to be perfectly honest this isn't it. Tess has just come down from London, dinner's getting cold and I'd rather talk to you about this, face to face . . . I'm sure you're concerned and I appreciate that but both Tess and I know very little about Freya's movements at present and . . . Ma, I do *not* want to talk at the moment, I'll see you soon.'

Tess had begun preparing the beans. When her father finished his call, she put down her knife for a few moments before taking it up again and continuing with her job.

Felix picked up a saucepan and then slammed it down on the hob. He said, 'I can't cope with my mother at the moment.'

Tess raised her eyebrows. 'You made that pretty obvious.'

'The rumour-mills are working overtime up there.' Felix pulled up a chair beside Tess. 'Can you leave the beans for a moment? I would be grateful if you could tell me exactly what *did* happen at the party?'

Tess put down her knife. She wondered if her father had asked her down here in order to ask her that question. 'Mr Lockhart wanted to show Mum a picture of his ancestor in his library. Mrs Lockhart asked Jamie and me to tell them to come back to the party and then she came with us, which was a pity because we found Mr Lockhart kissing Mum.'

'I see.' Felix gave a rough laugh. 'Your mother is amazing. A week after she despatches her husband, she moves in with another man.'

'Mum didn't despatch you. *You* despatched *her*. I had supper with her and Mr Lockhart on Wednesday. Mr Lockhart said that you didn't want Mum and he did. He has a point.'

Felix pushed his hands in the pockets of his

trousers. 'What's he like? Tall, dark and handsome?'

'Yes to all three,' Tess said. She was in no mood to be gentle with him. He was being quite irrational and she hated upsetting Grandma.

'Is your mother happy?'

'What do *you* think, Dad?'

'I mean, do you think she's happy with *him*?'

'She says she is.'

'Well.' Felix stood up and walked across to the window.

'Dad, you can hardly blame her for . . . '

'I don't.'

'Good.' Tess picked up her knife and began again to cut the beans. 'I thought I'd go and see Ivy in the morning. Will you drive me over there?'

'You can take your mother's car. I'm not in the right mood to see Ivy.'

'It's supposed to be sunny tomorrow. We could go for a walk in the afternoon.'

'No.' Still he had his back to her.

'Why not? It'll do you good to get out. Anna said you wouldn't leave the house last weekend.' She stared at his back. 'Why did you ask Geoff to come and get me? And why is Geoff driving me to the station on Sunday?'

And now at last, Felix did turn. 'I can't leave the house. That's why I'm on sick leave.'

Tess frowned. 'I don't understand.'

'That makes two of us.'

'You mean you literally cannot walk out of the house?'

'Correct. Don't look so worried. It's a

symptom of stress or something. The doctor came over on Tuesday. He says it will pass.'

'But, Dad, that's terrible. How do you manage for food and stuff?'

'Believe it or not, Tess, I do know how to order groceries online.'

'But . . . '

'I'm dealing with it, Tess. Tell me about Lockhart's son. The one you met up in Scotland. What's his name . . . ?'

'He's called Jamie.'

'Are you and he just friends or . . . ?'

'We're just friends.'

'Thank God for that.' For the first time that evening, Felix gave a genuine smile. 'One Lockhart in the family is more than enough.'

24

Maggie had been deeply upset by her call to Felix. Tess sounded unhappy and uncomfortable while Felix sounded positively unhinged. Maggie had a restless night. This afternoon she had taken herself off to the cinema and watched — if that was the word — a film called *Guardians of the Galaxy* that she had completely failed to follow.

This evening, she and Katherine were washing up after dinner. Katherine had cleared away the plates and Maggie had loaded them into the dishwasher. Now Katherine had donned her yellow gloves and was washing the remaining pans while Maggie dried.

'Maggie!' Katherine said, and then again with more volume, 'Maggie!'

Maggie blinked, 'Yes?'

'You've spent the last five minutes drying up that one Pyrex bowl. I know you're upset by all the rumours but . . . '

'I'm a silly old woman,' Maggie said. She put the bowl down on the table with an air of heavy finality. 'You were right and I was wrong.'

'Well, that's a first! What was I right about?'

'The Lockharts.' Henry the Second had ordered monks to whip him after the murder of Thomas à Becket. In the same way it seemed only right to Maggie that it should be Katherine to whom she should break the latest news.

'Oh dear,' Katherine said. 'Are we talking about Jamie or Neil?'

'Why would I talk about Jamie?' Maggie strove to subdue her irritation and recall her impulse towards humility. 'I rang Felix last night. The rumours are true. Freya's moved up to London to be with Neil Lockhart.'

'Oh!' Katherine's hands stood suspended above the frothy bubbles. This was another first. Katherine had no idea what to say.

'Felix pretends he's all right,' Maggie said. 'He even told me he'd asked Freya for a divorce before the party. I don't believe that for a second. He's always adored Freya.'

'Of course he has. Do you remember their wedding? Freya was the most beautiful bride I've ever seen. When she walked up the aisle with her father, Felix turned round and he looked . . . ' Katherine dropped her hands at last and began to wash the casserole lid. 'I shall never forget how he looked.'

Maggie shook her head. 'The first time I met her I thought she'd be trouble. She was far too beautiful. I couldn't understand what a glamorous model would do with Felix.'

'I don't see that at all. Everyone likes Felix.'

'I know but he's no Cary Grant. She could have had her pick of any number of beautiful young men.'

'But she wanted *him*,' Katherine said. 'And they've always seemed so happy. Why would she leave her marriage to go off with a stranger? It doesn't make sense. Perhaps Felix *did* say something to her beforehand. It's not like him to tell lies.'

'You didn't hear him on the phone. He was absolutely fine. He was very happy. He was busy with work. He did promise he'd come up here soon but I'm not even sure he meant *that*. I feel so guilty. If I hadn't pressed Tess to come with us to Flora's party in May, she'd not have met Jamie, and Freya wouldn't have met his father.'

'That's ridiculous,' Katherine said. 'No one could predict this would happen.'

'You did.'

'I did no such thing. If Freya ran off with Neil Lockhart, she must have had some compelling reason to do so. A woman in her fifties does not walk out of a happy marriage in order to follow a stranger to London.'

'She might if he were very . . . desirable.'

'Nonsense. Can you imagine either of us doing that?'

'No,' Maggie said, 'but then we weren't deluged with offers by gorgeous admirers.'

Katherine sniffed. 'Speak for yourself,' she said.

★　★　★

Tess would never forget saying goodbye to her father. He stood impotently in the doorway while she climbed into Geoff's taxi. He gave a buoyant wave that was utterly at odds with the frustration in his eyes. She was going back to London while he was literally imprisoned in his house.

On the train, she sat trying to digest everything that had happened. She still didn't know why he'd created this mess. She wasn't

274

even sure that *he* knew. None of it made sense. If he wanted to leave his wife, why would he care so deeply — and he obviously *did* — about the fact that she had moved in with someone else? And, meanwhile, here was she, stuck in a no-man's land, aware that she was deeply attached to Jamie, which was in itself an impossible state of affairs and now made more so by the undeniable fact that her father hated all men called Lockhart.

She began to flick through her emails and found the one Jamie had told her about. A woman called Geraldine wanted — '*asap please!*' — a five-hundred-word analysis of Scott's influence on Scotland. She also wanted to meet Tess in person, presumably to see if she was as perfect as Jamie had told her. There was an email from Jamie to say he'd met a local historian who Tess would like. He ended with a cheery *See you soon!*

Her phone went. She pulled it from her bag and answered it without checking the caller, which was a big mistake since of all the people in the world she least wanted to talk to right now, Richard the Lunger was probably top of her list.

'Thank you for not hanging up.' His voice was stiff and formal.

'Hi, Richard, how are you?'

And now the words came out in a torrent. 'I want to talk to you. Actually, I want to talk *at* you, if that's all right with you. You see I've been thinking about you for quite a long time and I feel — I do feel quite sincerely — that you need to know a few things. You and I saw each other for over a year. We went out together, we rang each other, you were pleased to see me, I was pleased to see you and then, when I eventually do the obvious next step, which any other man would have done long before by the way, you treat me like I'm some sort of pervert and I am *not a pervert . . .*'

'I never thought you were . . .'

'Yes, you did, or if you didn't you looked as if you did and I honestly think you're quite fucked up or else you have no idea how a man might feel when a woman he cares for can't bear him to show even the slightest display of affection. You hit me! I mean, you really hit me! The point is, Tess, if you don't like men you should stay away from them because it's not fair to make them feel guilty when they've done nothing wrong and . . . That's all I wanted to say. I just wanted you to know.'

'Can I speak now?' Tess glanced round the carriage. The only other occupants were an elderly couple in the aisle opposite her and they were both absorbed by their magazines. 'One: we saw each other a lot because I thought we were friends. Two: I never knew that friendship between a man and a woman had to include sex as well. Three: if you thought it did, you should have told me long before you lunged at me. Four: next time you meet a girl you like, don't blame her if she doesn't want to have sex with you. It isn't obligatory. I'm sorry you're so angry but I refuse to let you make *me* feel guilty because I don't happen to want to go to bed with you.'

There was a long silence and then Richard said, 'All right. I'm going now.'

Tess put the phone down. Her eyes were drawn across the aisle. The woman smiled at Tess, gave her a thumbs-up sign and continued to read her magazine. Tess gazed out of the window. She meant what she'd said to Richard. She had never given him any indication that she'd wanted more than a platonic relationship. And that pious comment — if you don't like men you should stay away from them — was just pathetic. As the train continued on its way, the words *stay away* seemed to merge with the rhythmic sound of the engine and continued to beat inside her head like a gentle hammer against her skull.

⋆   ⋆   ⋆

Freya and Neil sat finishing their bottle of wine while watching the first episode of the new *Downton Abbey* series. This was Freya's choice and one that Neil found incomprehensible; he kept pointing out anachronisms of speech and the excessive use of pauses. When they heard voices in the hall, he sat up immediately, his eyes bright with curiosity. Rory had not returned home from a party last night.

Now, he came into the sitting room, radiating smells of beer and tobacco. 'Hello, lovebirds. Can I introduce you to Hayley? Hayley, this is Neil, my dad, and this is his beautiful lady, Freya, who looks after us both.'

Hayley raised a hand and waved it without

much enthusiasm. 'Hi, Neil. Hi, Freya.' Hayley had long black hair and a spiky fringe which finished just above her kohllined eyes. She had a small nose, an enormous mouth and, Freya thought, a rather weak chin. She wore a small black leather mini-skirt and a long-sleeved close-fitting black top under which a pair of generous-sized breasts strove to escape.

Rory said carelessly, 'We're tired so we're going straight to bed. Goodnight.' As they went out of the room, his hand caressed Hayley's backside.

Neil's eyes followed Hayley out of the room. 'I have to say,' he murmured, 'I have never seen Rory look *less* tired. I can't say I blame him.'

Freya thought about pointing out the girl's weak chin but decided that Neil might misconstrue what was simply an interested observation. Instead, she agreed a little stiffly that Hayley was very striking and then suggested that, since *Downton Abbey* had just this moment ended, Neil might like to help her wash up the dinner things.

Neil downed the rest of his wine, put the glass down on the table and took Freya's face in his hands. 'Hayley doesn't have what you have.'

'That's true,' Freya said. 'She doesn't have my years.' She felt quite sad: sad and old.

'If I were a wine expert, I'd say she's like a young, transparent little Riesling. Personally, I prefer a mature red Rioja anytime.'

Freya finished the last of her wine. 'You're a smooth-talking bastard, Mr Lockhart.'

'I mean it.' Neil took her glass from her hand and put it down beside his own. 'Personally, I

278

feel like a taste of my mature, red Rioja right away. The washing-up can wait.'

★　★　★

Over breakfast the next morning, Freya asked if she should make scrambled eggs for Hayley, but Rory said she was still asleep. 'She's doing an audition at two,' he said, 'so she'll probably spend the morning in bed. You just carry on as usual. She can let herself out.' He finished his coffee, stood up and kissed Freya's cheek. 'How do you always look so lovely at this time of the morning?'

'Because she *is* lovely,' Neil said. He kissed Freya's other cheek. 'Thank you for a fabulous breakfast, have a great day and remember I love you.'

'I love you too,' Freya said, her good humour thoroughly restored after last night's temporary blip. It had been silly to feel so discomfited by Hayley's presence. She was just a girl, after all, who would go the way of all the pretty girls in Rory's life. It had been ridiculous to expect Neil *not* to notice Hayley's breasts. He had given delightfully satisfying evidence last night that she, rather than Hayley, was the object of his love and his lust.

She spent longer than usual clearing up after breakfast and the night before, and it was some time before she settled down to write an article she had been commissioned to write for a Sunday magazine supplement. Her subject was the difficulties thrown up by discovering new relatives when researching one's ancestors, and she wanted to create something punchy as well as informative.

She had finally thought of a good opening sentence when Hayley entered the sitting room, dressed in one of Rory's T-shirts, and raised a hand to give the same sort of vague wave she'd given the night before. 'Is it all right if I have a shower?'

'Of course,' Freya said. 'You'll find towels in the cupboard in the hall. Did you sleep well?'

'When you share a bed with Rory,' Hayley said, 'you don't do a lot of sleeping.'

Freya wasn't sure whether to give a knowing laugh or a sympathetic smile. She didn't feel like giving either. Fortunately, Hayley didn't seem to expect a response since she drifted out of the room as lifelessly as she'd drifted into it and a few minutes later, Freya heard the sound of the shower. She turned her attention back to her laptop and realised she had now forgotten the brilliant first sentence she'd been about to put down. After deleting at least eight alternatives, she finally thought of one that was a little pedestrian but would have to do: 'All relationships should be handled with care, new ones as much as old.' She glanced at her watch. Hayley had been in the shower for ages. At this rate there would be no hot water left. Only when she heard the shower stop and the consequent opening of the bathroom door did she return to her article.

There was something about Hayley's presence in the flat that made concentration difficult. She had only written a couple of paragraphs when she heard Hayley banging around in the kitchen, presumably preparing herself either a late breakfast or an early lunch. Freya felt very strongly that she should not intervene. It wasn't as if Hayley had asked for help. Eventually the noise in the kitchen stopped and then some time later, Hayley emerged in her clothes from the night before and said, 'I'm off now. See you soon,' and left without waiting for a response, almost as if she had already forgotten her.

As soon as the door closed behind her, Freya went through to the bathroom and pursed her lips. There were little pools of water on the floor and the wet towel had been thrown in a heap in the corner. The kitchen was even worse. It was clear that, in Hayley's eyes at least, Freya was just a housekeeper. There was a dirty frying pan on the hob and a sink full of dirty plates, cups and cutlery. A half-empty bag of mushrooms sat on the chopping board along with the innards of the green pepper Freya had been reserving for the evening supper. On close examination of the fridge, she noted that the last of her fruit yoghurts had gone. It was too bad and Freya very much hoped she'd never see her again.

Her hope was dashed later that evening when Rory turned up with Hayley while she and Neil were watching a film. Rory disappeared into the kitchen and came into the sitting room a few minutes later with a couple of generous-sized bacon sandwiches. He yelled to Hayley who came in, wearing Rory's T-shirt. Hayley sat next to Neil and put her long bare legs up on the coffee table while she ate.

Later, in bed with Neil, Freya told him that Rory and Hayley had left a big mess in the kitchen. Neil sighed and said Rory was hopeless. She should leave him to do his own clearing up. The trouble was, as Neil knew very well, Freya cared far more about a clean kitchen than Rory did.

The next morning, over breakfast, she did say a little playfully to Rory that he and Hayley had forgotten to wash their things up the night before and that if he washed up as he went along, he would find that it only took half the time to do.

'You sound like my mother,' Rory told her good-naturedly. 'I know I'm a slob. So is Hayley. I'll tell her we have to do better in future.'

Freya didn't know which part of Rory's response was the more annoying, the comment that she was like his mother or the implication that Hayley was going to be around for a while. She and Neil went out for dinner that night and the main subject of conversation was a result of the unwelcome discovery Freya had made before they left the flat. She had spent some time getting changed and had emerged from the bedroom to find Neil, Hayley and Rory on the sofa, watching television. Rory and Hayley were eating a fry-up on trays. Slipping into the kitchen for a quick glass of water, she had taken one look at the sink and blanched.

As they ate their meal, she tried to make Neil see the delicacy of her situation. 'I am living in Rory's flat,' she said. 'I can't nag him about cleaning his kitchen when it *is* his kitchen. I'm not even paying any rent. I was happy to clear up after him when he was on his own because I felt it was my contribution. But it's different if I'm going to be cleaning up after him *and* Hayley. It doesn't seem fair.'

'I'll have a talk with him,' Neil said. 'Not that he listens to anything I say.'

Freya sighed. 'It's been fun to stay here, but it can't go on. I have to start thinking about my future. Felix said I could keep the house in Darrowbridge and . . . '

'Freya,' Neil said, 'I don't want you to go back to Darrowbridge. I want us to be together.'

'That's very sweet but not terribly practical.'

'Why not? We'll rent a small little love-nest of our own.'

'Well, if you're serious, perhaps it's time you talked to Eva. I mean, there she is, on her own in that great big house while you and I are tucked into your son's spare room. It's crazy. She can't be happy there. Perhaps it's time for you to consider selling the place.'

Neil looked startled. 'That house belongs to Eva. Her father left it to her years ago. I could never afford a house like that.'

'Oh!'

'But you're right about Rory's flat. We ought to find a place of our own. Perhaps you should start doing some research.' Neil reached across for her hand. 'Let's face it: as long as we have each other, it doesn't matter where we live. I'd be happy in a shoebox in Whitechapel if I was with you.'

It was on the tip of her tongue to remind him

that she hadn't left behind a lovely old house and garden in order to live in some poky little flat. Then she remembered that Neil had given up a beautiful mansion in Kensington in order to be with her. It was a shock to find that Neil's wife, rather than Neil, seemed to be the owner of the beautiful mansion, but after all, Neil was a solicitor and must therefore be fairly affluent in his own right. Besides, Neil was right. They had each other. She would be happy with him anywhere. And at least in a shoebox in Whitechapel, she wouldn't have to clear up after Hayley.

25

Tess's new flatmate had gone home for the night in order to attend her grandmother's funeral. This was a sad occasion for Emily and her family but great for Tess who had the flat to herself for an entire evening. She poured herself a large glass of water and placed her phone on the kitchen table. She took a deep breath, picked it up and rang Jamie.

He sounded tired. 'Hi, Tess. How was your father?'

'That's why I'm ringing.' Tess straightened her back and curled one hand round her glass. 'He's bad. He gets panic attacks if he tries to leave the house. The doctor's signed him off for a couple of months. And then . . . he found out about the party. I had to tell him about Mum and your father. I don't understand him. He seems so angry with them both. It's like he's totally forgotten what he said to Mum the last time he saw her.'

'I see.' She could hear him sigh down the phone. 'I don't pretend to understand your father's thought processes but I can see why he might feel hostile towards my family . . . '

He understood. She knew he would. 'It's awful to see him like that. And I realise . . . ' She took a deep breath. 'I realise I can't see you again.'

'All right . . . ?'

His voice dropped and then rose, waiting for

her to explain her decision and she wasn't sure she could. She felt she held a tangled ball of wool in her hands and when she tried to extract a strand, the knot simply tightened. She said, 'It's all hopeless, I mean, if things were different, to be honest, I'm not even sure if they *were* different . . . but anyway, everything's such a mess and I can't deal with you and me and . . . I'm sorry, Jamie, but I feel, I really do feel, it's better just to say goodbye.'

There was silence and then he said again, 'All right,' but this time there was no question mark, just a weary sort of acceptance.

She said, 'As far as the TV series is concerned, I'll email Geraldine and tell her I can't . . . '

'You'll do no such thing. It's a great opportunity for you and probably for the castle, too.'

'It seems wrong, that's all, when . . . '

'Why? Just because we're no longer going to see each other? You'll do a brilliant job.'

'I wish I had your confidence. I wish things could be different.'

'Well. Perhaps it's my fault. Perhaps, I let myself get carried away. Look . . . if there's nothing else, I'd better get on. I have Martha coming round and . . . '

'Martha?'

'I think I mentioned her. She's our local historian. We have a lot to discuss, so . . . '

'Of course. I'll let you go. I suppose there's nothing else to say.'

'I don't think there is. I can't bully you into wanting to see me. Goodbye, Tess.'

She put the phone down. She had expected to feel relief but she felt a sort of dead numbness. She was grateful to him for not trying to push her further. She bit her lip and knew that most of this had nothing to do with her parents' troubles. For weeks she had sensed she was wandering into a strange new country for which she was totally unprepared. Like all normal people, Jamie wanted sex. She supposed that a very small part of her — the sleeping, subconscious, sex-obsessed part — wanted it too. The trouble was that the having-sex-with-Jamie thoughts cast ever-darker shadows over the lovely Jamie thoughts. However patient he promised he would be, there would come a time when he'd tire of his fucked-up, or rather *not* wanting-to-be-fucked-up girlfriend. She was frightened of failing him but far more scared of the alternative. It was easier to take the simplest path of action: run away.

★ ★ ★

There were times when the sheer randomness of her memory startled Anna. Months ago, William had asked her to give Tess a message, a simple task she had signally failed to carry out. If it weren't for the Riddlers, it would have remained buried in the back of her mind, along with goodness knew how many urgent but neglected requests.

John and Amy Riddler had arrived at St Peter's in the early hours of the morning. When Anna saw them in the afternoon, Amy was distraught and exhausted. She'd had strong contractions all day but the cervix was still hardly dilated. Her husband was barely holding together his supportive, grimly positive demeanour. When Anna examined her, she discovered the baby was stuck behind the cervix. 'I'm going to try to dislodge him,' she said.

'Her,' Amy breathed. 'She's a girl. We're going to call her Marnie — if she ever comes out.'

Two hours later, Anna was with them when Marnie decided to enter the world: a girl with dramatic eyebrows, a full head of black hair and a pugnacious little face. While Amy, weary but happy, smiled down at her daughter, her husband embraced first the midwife then Anna, fervently singing their praises and that of the hospital.

As Anna cycled home, the name of Marnie ran like a river through her mind, prompting a memory that remained frustratingly out of reach. This was not surprising, since her brain was simultaneously conducting a non-stop interrogation into the possible reasons for her father's extraordinary behaviour. It was Tuesday night and she still hadn't heard from Tess, which could either mean that the weekend in Darrowbridge had been a disaster or that it was utterly uneventful which actually, Anna thought, would in the current circumstances be a positive piece of news. Back at the flat, she made a mug of tea and picked up her phone.

'Tess? How was the weekend? You said you'd ring me.'

'Oh yes . . . ' Tess's voice trailed away as if she'd already forgotten about it.

'Did you manage to get Dad to talk?'

'A little. He can't leave the house at the moment. He says it's agoraphobia.'

'Oh God, poor Dad!'

'He didn't seem too upset about it. His doctor assures him it'll go soon.'

'That explains a lot about last weekend. Why didn't he tell me when I was with him?'

'Perhaps he didn't know. Perhaps he came home from Madrid and stayed in bed till you surprised him. I only found out because he'd hired a taxi to collect me even though he was up and about. It was obvious something was wrong.'

'He needs to get help. I'll ring him and . . . '

'I think you should leave it for the present. He's on antidepressants and he's got two months' sick leave. He doesn't want us to fuss.'

'Did he talk about Mum?'

'A little. He asked about the party. He still makes no sense. The way he talks about Neil Lockhart, you'd think Mum had left *him*. He hates Neil Lockhart.' Tess gave a little laugh. 'He hates all Lockharts.'

'That can't be easy for you. He must know you're friends with Jamie.'

'Well, I can't be. Not now.'

'Can't you? Would you mind a lot if you didn't see him again?'

'It's sad to lose a friend. You know how you miss William.'

To retrieve a wayward memory was like a long-awaited sneeze. Anna felt all the better for it. 'I've just remembered something,' she said, 'and I must tell you before I forget it again.

289

William asked me to give you a message ages ago and I've only just remembered. He said you were nice to his cousin, Marnie. He said she wanted to say hello. Hello and thank you. He obviously felt it was important to pass it on, but it wasn't exactly riveting and I forgot.'

'I remember her. I liked her a lot.'

'I'm so glad I remembered. It was really bugging me . . . ' Anna went on to explain about the Riddlers and baby Marnie and it became obvious that Tess was paying no attention because she suddenly broke in in mid-sentence.

'Could you do something for me? I don't think I have William's number. Could you ask him to give me Marnie's?'

'I suppose so. Given his glacial silence, I can't promise he'll talk to me but . . . '

'If you prefer I can call William myself.'

'No, I'll do it. It's a good excuse to try again with him.'

'You won't forget?'

'Of course not. Tess, are you all right?'

There was a long silence before her sister responded, and the silence was a revelation to Anna. Tess was on the verge of telling her something deeply important. That fact alone showed how far they had come in the last few weeks. The fact that Tess decided not to tell Anna showed how far they still had to go.

'I'm fine,' she said at last. 'I have marking to do. I'd better . . . '

'Tess, I'm on my own here next week. Olivia's going away on Tuesday. Come over to supper and stay the night. In fact, you could take a long break from your delightful flatmate and stay three nights if you like. What do you think?'

'I'm not sure. I have . . . '

'Oh, do say yes. I hate being on my own and we could come up with a concerted plan for Mum and Dad . . . '

'Well . . . All right. Thank you.'

Anna felt quite energised by her conversation with Tess. She would get in some wine and plan a few good meals for next week. She'd enjoy that. She heated a can of baked beans and put bread in the toaster. All she had to do now was to work out how best to help her increasingly mad parents, persuade William to like her again, and be a better sister to her twin. No problem.

She spread the hot beans over her toast and sat down at the kitchen bar. She wondered what it was that Tess had almost told her. She wondered when they'd stopped talking to each other and why. It was probably her fault. She'd been a horrible teenager, she knew, angry with her mother and angry with Tess for not sharing that anger. She'd hung out with bad boys and despised Tess for not doing the same. And then they'd left home and they'd both been busy, living in different parts of the country. Even when Anna came to London, it was difficult to meet up. Or rather, it was difficult to make an effort. They were like two juggernauts steaming purposefully away in different directions.

And now their parents had their meltdown and she and Tess had talked more in the last few weeks than they had done in years. She wasn't sure why it was now so important to get through to Tess. She supposed that amid the shipwreck of their parents' marriage, she was anxious to find some part of the family to which she could still cling. Whatever the reason, it was a weird discovery to make: more than anything in the world, right now, she wanted to turn her vast juggernaut around and find her sister again.

★   ★   ★

Felix had been on his own for three weeks. He still found it impossible to step out of his front door. He could, however, venture into the garden at the back. On good days, he dug up weeds, looked at emails, cleaned the house and watched TV. He had begun to take an interest in cooking, if only to confound his daughters who asked him regularly what he was eating. Tonight he had made a casserole with diced pork and olives. It had been rather good. Felix put what was left of it into a small bowl and covered it with cling-film. Freya would have been impressed. She loved anything with olives.

He was about to wash up the casserole dish but he made a quick diversion to the radio and turned it on, pushing up the volume. Two men talked earnestly about workplace *issues* and *best practice* and the *bottom line*. Felix found them both irritating but at least they drowned out thoughts of Freya.

He could hear what sounded like a steady thumping on the front door and switched off the radio. He couldn't imagine who would call at ten to ten on a cold autumn evening. He went through to the hall and flung open the door. Pam, dressed in her voluminous grey mac, held a bulging bin bag in one hand and a lead in the other. Percy's little pug, Serge, was at the end of the lead and looked unhappily up at Felix.

'I'm sorry to bother you,' Pam spoke in little gasps. 'I rang your doorbell but you didn't hear me.'

'Come on in. Would you like coffee, or something stronger? You look as if you need it.'

Pam gave a long shuddering sigh and set the bin bag down on the floor. 'A glass of wine would be very nice.'

Felix settled them in the sitting room. Serge and Pam both seemed to be as tense as each other. Serge sat on his haunches, his face raised towards the ceiling as if waiting for a starting gun. Pam perched herself on the edge of her armchair, her back straight, her hands cupped round her glass.

'Percy's not been well,' she told Felix. 'I called round as soon as I got back from work. I went upstairs and could hear Serge whimpering. I went into Percy's bedroom and he . . . ' She took a quick gulp from her glass. 'He was dead. I could see right away he was dead. Serge lay beside him. It was so sad . . . '

'Pam, I'm so sorry. What about Percy? Is he . . . ?'

'I made some calls. They've taken him away. The thing is . . . I can't take Serge with me to the office tomorrow. My job's on a knife-edge as it is. People keep talking about voluntary redundancies. Would you mind looking after him until

Friday evening? I can't leave him on his own during the day. He's used to being with Percy. I'll try to sort something out. I might be able to take him to my aunt in Cardiff at the weekend. He's a good little dog, he's housetrained and everything. I've brought his dog food and his basket and . . . '

'Pam, of course, I'll look after him. Finish your wine and go home to bed. You look white as a sheet. Don't worry about Serge.'

'Thank you.' Pam swallowed hard. 'You're very kind.'

When Pam had gone, Felix picked up the bin bag and went through to the kitchen. He took out the dog cushion, the food and the two dog bowls. He filled one with water and set it down near the fridge. Serge padded over to the French windows and whimpered.

'Right,' Felix said in an overly cheerful voice, 'let's take you outside, shall we, Serge?'

In the garden, Serge sniffed around the lawn before finding a place in the flower bed. He looked up at Felix and then, with some reluctance, lowered his backside.

'Well done, Serge!' Felix said. 'Who's a clever boy?'

Serge looked as pleased as a dog with a squashed-in, wrinkled face *could* look, and gave an expectant, breathy pant. He followed Felix back into the kitchen and sat staring at him as he finished the washing-up. When Felix had finished he said cheerfully, 'Bed time now, Serge! Come to bed!' He bent down and patted Serge's cushion.

'Good boy!' Felix said. 'See you in the morning!' He shut the door and went up to bed. He thought of poor Percy taking his last-ever breaths with only Serge for company. Felix wished he'd been a better neighbour.

The howling started almost as soon as he switched off his bedroom light. He went down to the kitchen and opened the door. Serge stood, one ear up, the other down, his unblinking eyes fixed hopefully on Felix.

'Poor old boy,' Felix said. 'Do you miss Percy?'

Serge looked up at him as if he knew Felix would make everything all right. Felix couldn't resist those enormous, sad, trusting eyes. He picked up the dog cushion and said, 'Just for tonight, you can sleep in my room.' He went back upstairs with a delighted Serge breathing heavily behind him. He placed the cushion on the floor, watched Serge climb onto it and went to bed.

As was usual at the moment, Felix slept fitfully. In the morning he reached out for Freya. Each morning he woke surprised to find he was alone. Today was different. This time, he touched her soft, smooth hair. He thought he was at last going mad. When he opened his eyes, he found himself staring into the bulbous eyes and nasally challenged features of Percy's dog. Felix heard a strange sound in the bedroom and realised that for the first time in three weeks he was laughing.

26

Eliza approached the gallery like a bullfighter sizing up his opponent. There were to be no more listless meanderings round the place. Today, she was determined, would be different. Today, she would recover her enthusiasm for beautiful paintings. Something would catch her eye if she had the right attitude. She ascended the big staircase slowly.

Twenty minutes later, she found it, or rather she found *him*. The portrait was so big that she had to crane her head back to take it all in. She took a few steps back. The painting was called *Lord Ribblesdale* and the artist was John Singer Sargent.

She was sure she would have loved Lord Ribblesdale. He was tall and slender and very elegant in his Edwardian hunting clothes. They were far more fetching than the present-day uniform of red coat and white breeches. One hand held his riding crop and the other was in the pocket of his buff-coloured trousers, pushing back the calf-length coat to expose his smart cream waistcoat. His top hat was worn at a jaunty angle and he exuded confidence and humour. She stood and imagined the conversations she could have had with him.

Before she left the gallery, Eliza went to the shop and bought a postcard of her gentleman. Could he have imagined that over a century later he would still be arousing the imagination of visitors? She suspected he could have.

At home, after lunch, she sat down at her laptop and investigated her lord. He had been a Liberal politician and a trustee of the National Gallery. Years after his portrait was painted, Virginia Woolf met him and wrote to a friend that he was very like his portrait, 'only obviously seedy and dissolute'. Eliza brushed that aside. Virginia Woolf was not renowned for her appreciation of men.

She went onto another website and discovered with pleasure that he was generally well liked. It appeared that he was one of those Edwardian aristocrats who were bright and intelligent and knew how to enjoy life.

And then she scrolled on down and read that his father had killed himself, his two sons had been killed in action and his first wife had died of consumption.

Eliza began to cry. It was only after she stopped crying that she understood she was crying for herself rather than for poor Lord Ribblesdale. She made a cup of tea and sat sipping it in the kitchen, trying to quell the small insistent voice inside her head. But still it continued. *I want to see my daughter*, it said. *I want to see Freya.*

★ ★ ★

On Friday morning, the postman asked Felix to sign for a parcel. Felix liked the postman; he always had interesting ailments — the current one was a dodgy knee that necessitated a snail-like walking pace — and invariably made Felix feel young and healthy.

Felix had just finished signing his name when Serge slipped between his legs and made a dash for freedom. At the same time, Felix could hear the sound of a car and he knew — he had no idea why he knew — that that car was destined to flatten Serge. And then he heard a voice — which of course he knew later was his imagination or his subconscious or just possibly the postman — and it said, 'Save him.' And that was what Felix did.

He flew down the path and grabbed hold of Serge just before he was about to career onto the road and just before the green Vauxhall drove past, going faster than it had any right to in a lane with a thirty mile per hour speed limit. Felix stood by the gate, clutching Serge to his heaving chest and murmuring, 'It's all right, boy, it's all right,' though whether he was speaking to Serge or to himself he wasn't sure.

The postman walked up to him and said, 'That was a close shave. You look quite pale. You should go and have a cup of sweet tea. Add a bit of brandy if you have any.'

'I'm well.' Felix nodded. 'I'm well. Thank you.' He wanted to ask the postman if he had told him to save Serge but if he *hadn't*, the postman would think he was insane and he would probably be right.

'Bloody motorists,' said the postman. 'If I were Prime Minister, I'd ban anyone under thirty-five from driving. That'd sort them out.' He gave

Serge a pat, hauled his sack onto his shoulder and walked on down the road.

Felix turned and looked at his door. He put his left foot forward and then his right. Then he turned again and stood, still clutching Serge, smiling out at the world.

★   ★   ★

On Monday evening, Anna had a call from her mother. It was the first time they'd spoken since the abortive anniversary lunch. 'Anna?' she said. 'I can't get hold of Tess. How are you?'

'I'm fine,' Anna said. Adding pointedly, 'It's nice to hear you.'

'I thought I could take you both out to dinner on Wednesday if you're free. I have something to tell you and . . . Have you spoken to your father lately?'

'I rang him yesterday. He's looking after Percy's dog. Did you hear that Percy had died?'

'Yes. Pam told me. I'm going down to Darrowbridge to stay the night with her on Thursday. Felix suggested I call in on him. Anyway . . . Talk to Tess and get back to me. It would be nice to see you both.'

'*It would be nice to see you both.*' Had she even noticed that she'd failed to answer any of Anna's calls? Tess said that Freya was on a permanent adrenalin rush and yet just now she sounded abstracted, distracted, almost as if she didn't know who or where she was. It was impossible to keep up with the vagaries of her parents. Yesterday, Anna had rung her father and could hardly get a word in edgeways while he told her about the long walk he'd forced poor Serge to do that morning. She hadn't dared mention the word agoraphobia.

Her phone went again and she blinked at the sight of Patrick's name on the screen. Her hand hovered over the phone. *They* hadn't spoken since the evening she'd had supper with him. She picked it up and said briskly, 'Hi, Patrick!'

'I'm outside your flat,' he said. 'Can I see you?'

It seemed silly to say no. She told him to come on up and then rushed over to the mirror above the mantelpiece, hating herself for the instant need to check her appearance. When she opened the door, he held out a bottle of red wine. 'Please,' he said, 'accept this as a peace offering.'

She smiled. 'There's really no need. Come on in. Do you fancy a glass?'

'Yeah, all right.' He looked tired. His T-shirt and denim jeans smelt of paint. His black jacket was worn, with slivers of lining appearing round his cuffs. He still looked like a film star. 'Can we talk? I need a friend at the moment.' His face twisted a little. '*Are* we still friends?'

'Of course we are.' While she opened the wine and found glasses, Patrick roamed round the room, picking up things and putting them down. He went across to the window on the far side of the sitting room and picked at the broken blind. 'How can you bear this? It would be easy to fix it.'

'I've tried, twice,' Anna said, opening his bottle. 'It's not as if it hides a beautiful view.'

'I could do it for you. It might take a bit of time.'

'That's very kind but it can wait.' Anna set the glasses down on the tea chest and sat down on the sofa. 'So what's wrong? I take it something *is* wrong?'

Patrick collected his glass and stood, staring at the unfortunate blind. 'It's Fizz,' he said. 'She's been having an affair.'

'Fizz?' Anna's voice exploded with disbelief. 'That's ridiculous. Who told you?'

'She did. Do you remember coming round to supper with all our 'friends'? Do you remember Matthew?'

'He worked with her. He had a sister who was a dentist.'

'She's been sleeping with him.'

'I don't believe it.' She was shocked. How could lovely Fizz, who spoke so warmly about her husband, even contemplate having an affair? 'You must be mistaken,' she said but even as she said it she thought back to that jolly evening they'd all spent together and saw it through new eyes. Matthew was an attractive man and apparently single and yet it had never once occurred to her to flirt with him, probably because it was quite obvious that he had no interest in flirting with *her*. Matthew's sexual antennae, she thought, were waving furiously in another direction.

Patrick finished his wine. 'She's been going out every Wednesday evening for months now. She *said* she was going to yoga classes with her friend, Abbie Spencer. So on Wednesday she goes off to work as usual and I take Lola to work with me as usual, though I'm a little late because

I can't find my phone and then in the evening I put Lola to bed and I find my phone in her room and I take it downstairs and then the phone rings and I pick up and it's Abbie Spencer expecting to speak to Fizz and I realise I've got her phone and Fizz has probably got mine — it's happened before — and Abbie asks me to tell Fizz she can't make lunch the next day and I ask her why she's not at yoga with Fizz and she says she's never done yoga in her life and I must be confusing her with another Abbie, and I say that's probably what it is and then I sit down and wait for Fizz to come home and while I'm waiting I look at some of her messages . . . '

Patrick took a gulp of his wine and then set the glass on the mantelpiece before digging his hands in his pockets. 'So Fizz comes home at half past ten and at first she tries to pretend it's all been a misunderstanding but she knows it's no good, so then she starts crying and says I don't know how difficult it is for her to come home and see Lola wanting me rather than her. She says she can't help resenting me because she's the one who's earning all the money but I'm the one who gets to be with Lola and she says she thinks that's why she started an affair with Matthew and I tell you, Anna, I am standing there listening to all this self-righteous, self-pitying crap and then I tell her what it's really like to be a house-husband. I tell her how hard it is to take Lola to nursery and have the other parents — who are all mothers by the way apart from one sad man in his fifties — and they all look at me in a way that is virtually shouting out: why can't you get a proper job, you loser? And then I tell her there are some days I'm so bored I want to scream, days when Lola and I do the old Postman Pat jigsaw for at least the twentieth time or when I'm walking in Greenwich Park with her and she won't go in the buggy so we're walking at the speed of a tortoise. I remind her I gave up my acting career so that she could pursue all her high-flying legal ambitions, I remind her that she *wanted* me to look after Lola and if she resents me for doing that then she has no one to blame but herself. And finally I tell her that if she ever again tries to make me feel I'm responsible for her squalid little affair then I'll see to it that she never spends another day with her daughter. Can you beat the sheer hypocrisy of the woman? She tells anyone who listens that she's so lucky to have a husband who's prepared to look after the baby and then the moment I find out what's been going on, she uses it to excuse what she's done. I mean, can you believe it?'

There was something terrible about watching Patrick unravel in front of her. It was as if he were tearing at his skin, revealing his raw, naked heart and she was sure he would later regret it. 'Patrick,' she said, 'I'm so sorry. Does she want to leave you? Does she want to go off with Matthew?'

Patrick gave a laugh. 'No. She knows I'd get Lola. She's terrified of losing her.'

'Then in that case you can work things out. I totally understand why you're angry but . . . '

'You don't understand. I don't *want* Fizz to

stay. She's like some alien being. I don't know who she is. I don't recognise her. She revolts me. And that means I'm free. *Now* do you understand?'

'No,' Anna said. 'I'm not sure I do.'

'Way back in May, when you came up to me in that maternity ward, you introduced yourself and it felt like I'd got my oldest friend back. And then you were so good with Lola and *she* liked *you*, which means a lot with Lola. What I'm saying is: you and I are meant to be together. I really believe that. And now we can be. I want you to help me start again. We'd be so good. You know we would. Can't you see us together?'

For almost a moment, Anna *could* see. She could see her and Patrick playing with Lola in the playground, smiling at each other over Lola's head. They'd all live together in that nice clean mansion block and on Sundays they'd go to lunch with Patrick's parents who had always liked her apart from that one last time when his mother had treated her like Delilah about to cut Samson's hair off. And in the evenings she'd come back from a hard day at hospital and Patrick would be waiting with a tomato and basil tart and afterwards they'd sit hand in hand watching a bit of television before going to bed.

Patrick's phone went. He glanced at it and said, 'I'd better take this,' and his voice was hard as steel. 'What is it? . . . I'm with Anna . . . because right now I need to see a sympathetic face and Anna is sympathetic . . . I have no idea . . . You must see you've forfeited any rights to ask a question like that and I'm sure as hell not going to answer it.' He switched off his phone and put it in his pocket. He came over to the sofa and sat down beside Anna. 'Do you know what I want to do now?'

'I have a pretty good idea.'

He leant forward and kissed her and when she pulled away, he gave her a quizzical glance. 'Don't you want me?'

Anna took hold of his hands and held them hard. 'Patrick, why did you answer Fizz's call just now? You could easily have left it.'

'I knew she'd be worried. She wanted to know where I was. I stormed out of the flat in rather a hurry.'

'But you more or less told me you don't care about her any more so why should you worry if *she's* worried? You answered her call because you wanted her to know you were here. You wanted her to know you were here with me. You don't want to have sex with me because you love me or even because you fancy me, you want to have sex so you can get back at *her*.'

'You've got it all wrong. I told you I've been crazy about you for months.'

'Oh Patrick!' Anna released his hands. 'You fancied me. And you knew I fancied you. You're angry and bitter and at the moment you hate your wife. I'd probably be the same. Except, I'm not sure if you can afford to be very angry. You invited me to supper and we both know what would have happened if Lola hadn't woken up. Neither of us is in a position to cast stones at Fizz.'

'That's totally different. Fizz has been lying to

305

me for months. You and I got carried away on one single evening . . . '

'Patrick, you know that's not true. You didn't invite me over to discuss Felicity Eggins' second marriage. You wanted to have sex. So did I.'

'But that's what I'm saying. This time there's no Lola and there's no guilt . . . '

'It doesn't work like that though. I wanted you *then* and afterwards I felt guilty. Patrick, I *hate* feeling guilty. You and Fizz produced Lola who's confident and happy and has single-handedly converted me to the idea of having children sometime in the future. The two of you have made her what she is. I'm not sure you have the right to indulge your very natural wish for revenge by . . . by wilfully dismantling your family. At the very least, you need to count to ten, or maybe one million, before you decide to cast Fizz into the wilderness.'

Patrick had been sitting forward with his hands gripped together. Now he sprang to his feet and started pacing round the room again, like a lion in a cage. 'She put herself there! She wants to be with Matthew!'

'It doesn't sound like that to me. There may be all sorts of reasons why Fizz had an affair with Matthew but I bet you love isn't one of them. If she loved Matthew she wouldn't be so desperate to stay with you, however much she adores Lola. Perhaps she was flattered — he's a partner in her firm, isn't he? Perhaps she *did* resent the fact that you are the primary parent and I know that's not fair but I've noticed that fairness doesn't seem to count for a lot in these cases. So go home, rage at Fizz — but do it quietly in case you wake Lola — and talk to her and go on talking until you fix things.'

'How can I trust her after this?'

'If she knew about you and me she'd probably say the same. Go home and talk to your wife. You're a brilliant father. Do you want to undo all the great work you've done and break up Lola's world? Fizz has been an idiot but at least it sounds like she *knows* she's been an idiot.' Anna stood up and went across to him. 'You need your family.' She kissed his cheek. 'Go home.'

Patrick pushed his fingers through his hair. 'I don't want to go home.'

'Well, tough.' Anna strove to keep her rising impatience out of her voice. 'We all have to do things we don't want to do.'

'All right. I'll go.' Patrick threw up his hands in a gesture of surrender. 'Thank you for your diagnosis, Doctor Cameron.'

'It's a pleasure.' She gave him a push towards the door. 'Go on, Patrick. Go back to your wife.'

'What about you and me? Are we still friends?'

'Of course we are. But perhaps we won't see each other for a while.'

'Perhaps we won't. I'll see myself out.'

After he'd gone, Anna went over to the offending blind. Patrick was right, she thought, it was very unsightly, she really must mend it. She would like to believe she had been very noble in renouncing Patrick. In fact, it was easy to turn down a man who only wanted to sleep with her in order to get back at his wife. It helped that she no longer found him so desperately attractive.

She'd realised that as soon as he started talking about the sacrifices he'd made. She didn't blame him of course, but there was something very unattractive about self-pity.

There was also the William factor. She'd left a message last week on his phone: 'Hi, William, Tess asked me to ask you for the phone number of your friend Marnie, so here I am. Get back to me. I'd love to see you. Any time ... ' She wouldn't ring again. He'd responded with a text comprising a phone number and nothing else.

It was neither fair nor rational to blame Patrick for the end of her friendship with William but she couldn't help herself. Irrational feelings were invariably more powerful than rational ones.

27

It was touching to see how much trouble Anna had taken. There were clean sheets on Olivia's bed and flowers on the dressing table. There were fillets of salmon and a splendid salad for supper along with a bottle of cold white wine. As they sat talking about Anna's morning set-to with her terrifying consultant, Tess felt her own dramas of the afternoon loosen their hold on her and when Anna asked her what *she'd* done today, she was surprised to discover that she actually wanted to tell her.

'I had a Skype audition,' she said. 'It's all down to Jamie. He'd told them I was a natural in front of the camera so of course I was terrified.'

'Of course you were. What did you talk about?'

'Who else but Sir Walter? I spent a few minutes describing the traditional view of him as a committed old Tory Unionist and then I brought out my copy of *Waverley* — I have it in my bag, I'll lend it to you. Waverley's a hero who keeps changing sides. He can't decide whether he's a Hanoverian or a Jacobite. It's almost as if Scott can't make up his *own* mind. Anyway, that's what I talked about.'

'And how did it go? Did you get any feedback?'

'That's why I was late coming over. Geraldine rang me back at six.'

'And you've let me rabbit on about Miss

Diamond! What did she say?'

'She liked me.'

'Tess, that's brilliant! We should be drinking champagne.'

'Yes,' Tess said. 'Yes, it's good. She thinks Martha and I would make a good team. We both have the same hair apparently. I don't know why that's so important.'

'Have you told me about Martha? Who is she?'

'Well,' Tess said, 'she's an expert on Borders history.' She hesitated. 'She's a friend of Jamie.'

'This is all quite brilliant. Why do you look so very unexcited?'

'I suppose . . . I suppose I'm a little jealous of Martha.'

It was only now she said it she knew it was true. Anna looked as surprised as she was.

'When you were thirteen,' Anna said, 'you had a crush on Xander Bullen. Since then . . . I've always assumed you didn't really care for men.'

'So did I. I miss Jamie, that's all. I'll get over it.'

'Why *should* you? If you want to see him again, you should do so. You don't need to tell Dad.'

'I couldn't do that.' Already, Tess regretted her admission. She tried to smile. 'I do feel sorry for Mum sometimes. She named her daughters after the most romantic heroines she could find and look how we've turned out!'

'Speak for yourself! I've always found Mum's choice of names for us rather sinister. She once tried to convince me there was some sound feminist reason, but look at the facts! She called her daughters after Anna Karenina and Tess of the D'Urbervilles: two women who comprehensively messed up their lives. A psychoanalyst would have a field day with that one.'

'You've always been hard on her.'

'She's taking us out to supper tomorrow. I said we'd meet her at half six.'

'Oh Anna, I can't. I'm meeting someone. I can't get out of it.'

'That's all right. I'd like to have Mum to myself for a bit. I have a lot to say to her.'

'Do you?' Tess eyed her warily.

'I think I know why Dad left her. Do you remember the week before we moved to Darrowbridge? Dad came back late with a black eye. He *said* he'd been mugged and had put up a fight. I think he'd confronted Xander Bullen.'

Xander Bullen. Tess reached for the bottle and filled her glass. 'Do you want some?'

'Oh, go on then,' Anna said. 'Can you finish the salad?'

'No, that was lovely.'

'The thing is,' Anna said, 'I know you always liked Xander but . . . I've never told you this before . . . Xander told me once that . . . He didn't actually tell me but he *implied* that he and Mum were very close. I think that's why Dad moved us all to Somerset. He knew they were having an affair.'

It was too much to take in. The full enormity of Anna's conclusions hit Tess like a tidal wave. She sat, aware some response was expected. All she could manage was to mutter feebly that she thought Anna was wrong. She reached for her wine and hoped it would dull her sensibilities before the tidal wave submerged her.

* * *

Anna was the first to arrive which pleased Freya. It was ridiculous to sulk about ill-timed remarks she'd made nearly a month ago. Ill-timed remarks were part of Anna, and a good mother should embrace the bad along with the good. Far better to forget past unpleasantness and concentrate on the here and now. She couldn't wait to tell the girls her news.

'Anna,' she said, 'how lovely to see you. I've ordered wine and olives.'

'Great,' Anna said, taking off her leather jacket to reveal a low-cut black top that Freya would have coveted even five years ago. 'It's good to be here.'

'Rory promised me we'd love this place. To be exact, his words were, 'cheap but good'. I told him that was my sort of restaurant!'

The waiter arrived with her order and invited Freya to try the wine which she assured him was unnecessary. Now Anna was here, she couldn't wait for Tess to arrive. What would they say? What would they think?

Anna reached for an olive. 'Do you remember Xander Bullen?'

'Of course I do! He's got a gardening book out. Did you know that?'

'A friend of Olivia works for a TV production company. He and his boss are going to see him on Friday. They want to give him his own

312

gardening programme.'

'Do they? How extraordinary. But of course he'll be perfect for television. He's so good-looking and he has such charm. I'm glad he's doing well.'

Anna reached for her glass and took a gulp. 'You were very mysterious on the phone. You said you had some news.'

'I do but I'll tell you when Tess comes.'

'I'm sorry. I meant to tell you. She sends her love. She can't make it. She's meeting someone.'

'Really? Do you know who the someone is?'

Anna gave Freya one of those appraising glances that had accompanied most of her teenage years. 'Mum,' she said, 'you do know she's in love with Jamie Lockhart?'

Freya shook her head. 'No,' she said, 'she isn't. I asked Tess most particularly about him. She assured me she had no feelings for him.'

'I can see why you'd want to believe that.'

This was what always happened when she and Anna were alone together. Why had she thought it would be different this time? Anna would make some gnomic utterance designed to make her feel smaller than an atom and so on it would go. Freya pressed her hands tightly together. 'I think that's a little unfair. You weren't at the party in Kensington. Tess had no idea Jamie would be there. I could see he was keen on her but she looked rather irritated to see *him*.'

'I imagine she felt a little uncomfortable given that you were standing next to her. She spent the whole summer getting to know him. Then you meet his father and in a matter of minutes you fall into his arms. Last week Tess told Jamie she couldn't see him again. She said it wasn't fair on Dad.'

'I don't see what your father has to do with any of this.'

'Well, funnily enough, he's not too keen on the Lockhart family.'

'I see.' Freya took a sip of her wine and then folded her arms. 'And of course this is my fault. Can I just remind you that it's your father who wants a divorce? Felix has no right to have any thoughts about the Lockharts. He made it very clear he didn't give a damn what I did with my life as long as he wasn't involved in it.'

'Dad's always loved you. I'm pretty sure he still does. I think he's spent fourteen years trying to cope with what happened and in the end he just couldn't.'

'Anna,' Freya said, 'I have no idea what you're talking about.'

'Xander Bullen,' Anna said. 'I'm talking about Xander Bullen.'

Freya stared at her daughter. 'What does Xander have to do with this?'

'Mum,' Anna said, 'Xander told me.'

'Xander told you? Xander told you *what*?'

'He told me you loved each other. And I think he told Dad. I think that's why Dad came home with a black eye the week before we moved. I've always known that Xander was the reason we moved to Darrowbridge. Dad wanted to get you away from him. So we had to leave Wimbledon.'

For a few moments Freya sat staring blankly at Anna, trying to work out what she was saying. It was crazy, it was incomprehensible, but what was important was that Anna was convinced of its truth and in fact there was a horrible twisted logic to it. Freya shook her head, too stunned to refute any of it. Even if she tried, Anna wouldn't believe her. 'So I'm the villain in all this,' she said. 'How you must hate me.'

'Mum, of course I don't hate you. I'm simply trying to work out why Dad, of all people, would want to break up his marriage.'

'If you knew how hard I have tried, year in, year out, to be calm and understanding and make excuses for your moods and your nasty little barbs and your cold, polite phone calls and all the time you felt these things and you never said. Why *didn't* you say anything?'

'I don't know . . . I should have done . . . I wasn't sure and . . . '

'I'll tell you what I think. I think you didn't *want* to find out you might be wrong. I think it suited you very well to make *me* responsible for everything wrong in your life. You're a very good hater, Anna. You know that phrase 'passive aggression'? It could have been made for you.'

'That's not fair . . . '

'You know that it is. I can see it in your face. I am so fed up with being patient and careful with you and with Felix. I've had enough, Anna. I don't care any more. I give up on you both.' She bit her bottom lip hard and reached down for her bag.

'Mum, what are you doing? You wanted me to talk to you and now when I *do* talk, you won't listen. You can't just walk away every time we disagree.'

315

'Watch me.' Freya threw a note down on the table. 'That's for the wine. I won't pay for your meal this time. It's impossible for the two of us to be alone together. I can't stay here. I don't know you, I don't know my husband, I don't know anyone.' She pushed her chair back, stood up and then glared at Anna as she tried to do the same. 'Sit down! Don't you dare try to follow me! I have *nothing* to say to you.'

She went out into the dusk, almost tripping over her heels. Oh it was terrible, terrible. She had been so proud of her family, she had loved and nurtured and cared for them and this was the result. It had all been false, it had all been one huge messy failure. She would never see any of them again. And was it true about Tess? Did she really love Jamie? She must talk to Neil, they must talk to Jamie, she must talk to Felix. Felix! She was so sure he'd met someone else. But if he hadn't, if Anna was right, it was even worse. She could never, she would never forgive him. A sob escaped her throat and she shook her head hard. She would not cry. She would go home and talk to Neil.

She was almost at the flat when she heard her name being called and turned to see Rory running towards her. He was carrying a large bouquet of red roses. She stopped and waited for him to catch up with her. She said, 'What beautiful roses!'

'They're for Hayley.' He kissed her cheek. 'We had a little argument the other night. She caught me fooling around with someone. And then this evening we were supposed to be going out with friends. And I got to the pub and she sent me a text to say she was tired and I thought: Rory, you must take action. One, buy flowers. Two, return home. Three, grovel. What are *you* doing here? I thought you were taking your daughters out to dinner.'

'There was a change of plan.'

'We could have a takeaway,' Rory said, 'unless you feel like cooking something.'

'I don't, I'm afraid. I shall make your father take me out.'

'That might be a good idea. I'll rustle up something for Hayley and tell her I love her.'

'I'm sure that will impress her.'

He took his door keys from his pocket. 'Now we must creep into the flat and surprise her. I want to overwhelm her with my romantic gesture.'

In the event, it was Rory and Freya who were surprised. At first they thought the flat was empty, but then they heard a sound. The door into the sitting room was wide open. For at least a moment — or at least until Rory cried, 'Hayley, what the fuck are you doing?' — Freya didn't understand what was happening. For at least a moment she thought that Hayley might be kneeling in front of Neil because she was trying to find a contact lens or something.

Then Neil said, 'Oh fuck!' and Rory said, 'Fuck you!' and Hayley got to her feet, adjusted the shirt that as usual seemed to be her only item of clothing, pushed back her hair and turned to face Rory. 'I was only doing what your friend did to you on Saturday.'

Rory gave an extravagant grimace. 'That is *so* gross. You were doing it to my *father*. He's my father and he's *old*.'

'Freya's old too. That doesn't stop you flirting with her.'

'I always flirt with older women. It's polite and it cheers them up. I can't believe you would do this.'

'I couldn't believe what you did on Saturday. So there you are. We're quits. Now I'm going to pack.' She walked out of the room, brushing Freya's arm in the process.

Neil sat with his hands held in front of his crotch. 'Rory,' he said. 'I'm so sorry.'

Rory didn't even look at him. He thrust his roses into Freya's arms and went off after Hayley.

'Freya,' Neil pleaded. 'Freya . . . '

'Do you have any idea how ridiculous you look?' She threw the flowers onto his lap, turned on her heel and stormed into their bedroom, flinging open drawers and pulling out her clothes.

Neil came in and looked at the suitcase on the bed. 'Freya, will you at least let me try to explain?'

That stopped her. She straightened her back and put her hands on her hips. 'I would *love* to hear your explanation, Neil, I really would. Explain away!'

'I came home from work. Hayley was here. She said Rory was out and I knew you were too so I offered to cook and she offered to help and we couldn't find anything so we had a drink and then we had another and she started to . . . It was a moment of madness, it meant nothing. You mean everything to me . . . '

'If I mean everything to you, why did you let that girl even touch you?'

'I was a little bit drunk and she's young and she's beautiful and she was very persuasive. It's like . . . ' He scratched his head and narrowed his eyes. 'Imagine you're on a diet and someone offers you a chocolate truffle . . . '

'Are you saying that being with me is like being on a *diet*?'

'No, no, of course not, you're perfect, you're utterly perfect. It's only that Hayley's so young and she seemed so eager and . . . '

'And you are disgusting and pathetic and amoral and I never want to see you again because you make me feel quite sick, so feel free to go and eat as many chocolate truffles as you like, though perhaps in future you should stay away from those belonging to your son. Now get out and let me pack.'

'Freya,' Neil said, 'this hasn't been easy for me, you know. I fell in love with you and almost at once we were living together in a cramped flat with Rory . . . '

'You said you wanted me to live with you!'

'I know and I don't regret it for a moment but it all happened so quickly and tonight, I suppose, was just me letting off steam and . . . '

Freya put her hands on her hips. 'Let me tell you something. I am giving you the benefit of the doubt here and assuming you *are* drunk because if you aren't you are even worse than I think you are. Let me tell you something else. From now on, you won't have to let off steam because I won't be here.'

'That's not what I meant. I love you!'

'Well, all I can say is that your idea of love is very different from mine. Now get out of this room before I start to scream.'

Neil looked at her for a moment before displaying, if belatedly, some prudence, and left the room.

She marched round the bed and slammed the door shut. It didn't take her very long to finish her packing. She shut her case and wheeled it across to the door. She found Neil waiting for her on the other side. From Rory's room came the unmistakable sound of lovemaking.

Neil tried a weak smile. 'Rory's obviously forgiven Hayley,' he said. 'Can't you forgive me?'

Freya raised her chin. 'I think the three of you are made for each other. I want to forget I ever met any of you. Goodbye, Neil.'

'I can't let you walk out like this. Where will you go?'

'That is not your concern. Step aside.' She hesitated and then turned and went to the bathroom to retrieve her toothbrush. When she came out, Neil said, 'Freya, please . . . '

She ignored him. In the lift down to the ground floor, she stared at her reflection in the mirror and saw a mad woman with thin streaks of mascara running down her cheeks. She struggled out of the lift and then struggled again down the steps of the building. Finally, she reached the pavement and began to walk, pulling her case behind her. She stopped after about ten minutes, aware she was on the Embankment.

She stared down at the Thames. What a fool she had been! Neil was not Prince Charming, he never had been. He was a man who was ruled by his penis. He had wanted to have sex with her and *she* had wanted to erase the appalling fact that the husband she loved did not love *her*. She had wilfully disregarded Neil's obvious flaws, she had run into his arms to get back at Felix, she had, in short, made a monumental fool of herself. What was it Rory had said? '*I always flirt with older women. It's polite and it cheers them up.*' Oh God, Freya thought, how she hated herself. She was selfish and silly and worthless.

The water was as black as the night sky above it. It would not be difficult to tip herself over the edge and let the water cover her. If she were Emma Bovary or Anna Karenina she wouldn't hesitate to throw herself in. But she was Freya Eliza Cameron and she would hate Neil to think she had killed herself on his account and there was no pleasure in envisaging her husband and her daughters crying at her funeral as she wasn't at all sure they'd bother to come. For now, she had to think practicalities. There was only one option. She saw a taxi coming her way and she hailed it.

28

Anna had continued to sit at the table, occasionally sipping her wine. When she caught sight of the waiter staring at her, he looked embarrassed. He came over at once and asked if she was ready to order.

'My mother's been called away,' Anna said. 'Will you bring me the bill for the wine? And a cork so I may take the bottle away with me?'

It was ironic that her mother, such a stickler for appearances, should be the one to erupt from the restaurant while she stayed stubbornly here, resolutely ignoring the whispered asides of other clients, determined to act as if all was well. Once she paid her bill, she walked out with her head held high.

As she unlocked the padlock of her bicycle, she was aware she'd drunk a little too much. She cycled back with extra care, concentrating on the traffic around her. It was a relief to impose an embargo, if only temporarily, on all thoughts about the evening.

Tess was still out when Anna got home. For once, she was glad to be on her own. She sat on her bed, her arms hugging her knees. There was no point in trying to defend herself. She had been clumsy, tactless and unfair tonight. And as for the rest, she thought bleakly, her mother's brutal assessment of her character was spot on. When Anna thought back to her teenage self, she saw only resentment, bitterness and bile. As she grew up, she had assumed she'd taken on a new maturity, taking care to ring home with punctilious regularity. Who was she kidding? Her *grown-up* behaviour had been worse than her earlier sulks and tantrums. How could she blame Freya for lashing out at her this evening? She certainly hadn't acted like a mother found out in a fourteen-year-old affair.

Anna's eyes focused on the chest of drawers opposite her but what she saw was the road outside their old house in Wimbledon, and Xander walking towards her along the pavement. He'd waved and asked her where she was going.

'I'm meeting a friend in town,' she said. 'Where are *you* going?'

'I have a fossilised stone for Tess. Is she in?'

'You do know we finished our fossil project weeks ago?'

'Yes, but Tess likes collecting them.'

'Xander,' Anna said, 'you come over a lot, and Tess . . . Tess really likes you.'

'The feeling's mutual. It's impossible *not* to like Tess.'

'Yes,' Anna said. She wished she hadn't started this now. She was aware that her motives for doing so were mixed. It was true she was concerned that Xander might just enjoy being the focus of one girl's adoration, but it had always irked her that he was so much more interested in Tess than he was in *her*. Doggedly, she stumbled on. 'You know what I mean. And she's thirteen and you're nearly thirty.'

He'd stared at her for a few unsettling

moments and then he laughed. 'I'm not sure what you're getting at,' he said. 'It's not just Tess I come to see.'

'Yes, but you don't garden for us now.'

'No. That's true.' He gave her a speculative sort of smile. 'You have a very beautiful mother, you know. Has it never occurred to you to wonder why your dad's so keen to carry her away from Wimbledon?' He laughed again and then patted her arm before walking on and calling out, 'See you, Anna. Take care now.'

★   ★   ★

Freya paid off the taxi and stared up at the grand old mansion block. There were five steps up to the entrance. She pushed down the detachable handle of her case and struggled up to the big black door with it. She took a few deep breaths and then pressed the button next to the word 'SAMPLE'. A clear voice answered almost immediately. 'Come on in, Freya.'

She went through to the hall and pushed up the handle. A door on the right opened and a small, thin woman stood silhouetted against the light. Her white hair was cut in a short, elegant bob. She wore grey slacks, a green ribbed jersey and a pendant. Her face, despite its network of thin wrinkles, was still beautiful. Her eyes were Freya's eyes but she was a stranger. Freya had hoped she might experience a waterfall of memories and recollections but there was nothing. She felt embarrassed to be here, in this state, with this elegant old lady.

324

'I'm sorry,' Freya said. 'I had nowhere else to go. It's only for one night.'

Her hostess stepped aside to let her into the flat. 'I'm glad you rang me. I've made up your bed. Would you like a glass of wine? I have only red, I'm afraid.'

'That would be nice.' Freya moved her case to one side of the door. 'Do you mind if I use your bathroom first?'

As soon as she had shut the door behind her, she pressed her back against it and raised her eyes to the ceiling. It was just one night. She would leave first thing in the morning. She glanced round at the white floor tiles and white walls. She went to the basin and stared at her reflection in the mirror. She saw a wild-looking woman with dishevelled hair, swollen eyes and a face streaked like a zebra. There was a glass jar full of cotton wool balls on the small wicker chest of drawers. She took one of them out and began to clean her face.

When she finally emerged from the bathroom, Eliza came out of the kitchen with a silver tray containing two long-stemmed glasses generously filled with red wine, and a bowl of cashew nuts.

Freya took a seat on the sofa. 'You're very kind. I do apologise for my dramatic intrusion. I think I owe you an explanation.'

Eliza settled into the armchair and picked up her glass. 'You don't owe me anything.'

'I'll keep it short. I had a disagreeable encounter with one of my daughters and returned home early. I found my partner in a compromising position with his son's girlfriend, so I packed and left. I'm going down to Somerset to stay with a friend tomorrow.'

Eliza nodded as if Freya's explanation was quite normal. 'I'm sorry about your daughter and your unsatisfactory lover but I'm glad you came to me.'

The word 'lover' issued from her mouth with no trace of affectation or awkwardness. This was not a woman who would be easily shocked. Freya took a sip of her wine and then attempted a smile. 'I couldn't believe it when I got your email. I'm sure you must regret sending it.'

'I don't regret it for a moment. I'm pleased you're here. I wasn't sure you'd want to reply. I spent a great deal of time composing it.'

Freya reached for the nuts. She was, she realised, hungry. 'It seemed so odd to hear from you after all this time. I meant to tell my girls tonight. What made you do it?'

'Very selfish motives, I'm afraid. I'm old and discovered I was lonely.' She regarded Freya with unblinking blue eyes. 'I suppose you've had no supper. I can offer you an omelette.'

'That would be marvellous. Can I help?'

'No. I won't be long.' Eliza looked almost amused. 'Finish the nuts.'

Freya had already emptied half the bowl. Once Eliza had gone, she took another gulp of wine. It seemed surreal to be sitting in this stranger's flat but at least she had found the one place in the world that could distract her from the horrors of the last few hours. She had not seen her mother for forty-six years and now she could hear her in the kitchen making an omelette.

Already, the wine was relaxing her. She glanced around at her surroundings, admiring the soft grey carpet and long rose-coloured curtains. There was a small desk in the corner on which sat a laptop and a brass lamp. On one side of the mantelpiece, a modest-sized television sat on an antique chest of drawers. The only lighting came from the standard lamp behind the sofa. The whole effect was one of calm tranquillity.

Freya's eyes wandered over to the mantelpiece above the gas fire. She put down her glass and walked across the room, feeling suddenly giddy as she took in the collection of framed photographs. There was a toddler sitting on the lap of a laughing young woman with long blonde hair falling over one eye. The next showed a small child with plaits and a steady, serious expression. She recognised the third: it was a professional photo in which she modelled a black cocktail dress with her usual Lauren Bacall expression. And now she and Felix came down the aisle together, both of them beaming as if they'd just discovered the Holy Grail. Another had the two of them sitting together. Felix held Anna and she had Tess. And finally there was one taken by her father only a few years ago. It had been Christmas. She and Felix stood with the girls and all of them stood behind Ivy who sat holding a cracker. It was incredible to see her life played out in this sitting room.

Eventually, Freya went through to the kitchen, another pristine room with a cork floor, shiny black surfaces and a bright pink fridge.

'Do sit down,' Eliza said. She served up the

omelette and refilled Freya's glass.

'Won't you join me?' Freya asked.

'I've already had two this evening and at my age that's one too many. Do you want any salt?'

'No, this is perfect.' Freya watched the old lady squirt washing-up liquid into the sink. 'When you left home,' she said, 'I thought it was because I'd been horrid to you.'

Eliza put on a pair of plastic yellow gloves and dropped her frying pan into the water. 'I'm afraid your father and I handled it all very badly.' She cleaned the pan and put it on the draining board. 'I fell in love with Stephen. He was your father's best friend and a diplomat. He'd been posted to Argentina. I decided to go with him.'

'And you left me behind.'

'Yes.' Eliza began work on a small Pyrex bowl. 'Your father wanted to keep you with him. I felt, in the circumstances, it was unfair to take you.'

'He would never talk about you. He removed all the photos. I have none of you.'

'Well,' Eliza said, 'I can see why he would do that.'

'Were you happy with Stephen?'

'We had our moments. It's difficult to be happy when you both feel guilty. He missed his old friend and I missed you.'

'I don't understand,' Freya said. 'I don't understand the photos on the mantelpiece.'

'Your father promised to keep me informed of your progress. For a long time, I kept the pictures in a folder and then, a short time ago, I bought frames for them.' She took off her gloves and took a seat opposite Freya. 'I don't expect

— or deserve — anything from you. I do want you to know that not a day has gone by in the last forty-six years when I haven't thought of you. I have a friend — Stephen's sister — I visit in Bath. Every time I stay with her, I'm aware you live nearby. I'm an avid reader of your blog on your website. It's very good.'

'Thank you.' Freya had wolfed the omelette in seconds and now she put her knife and fork together.

Eliza fixed her eyes on those of Freya. 'May I ask you something? On your website you call yourself Freya *Eliza* Cameron. Why did you do that?'

'I suppose . . . ' Freya hesitated. 'I wanted to remember I once had a mother.'

Eliza tried to speak and failed. She took out a tissue and blew her nose. Freya watched her try to recover her composure. She reached out for her mother's hand. 'Eliza?' She smiled. 'It's *very* nice to meet you.'

★ ★ ★

At midday, the next morning, Freya sat on the train to Darrowbridge, gazing out of the window and thinking about Eliza Sample. Eliza was elegant and sophisticated. She'd abandoned her seven-year-old daughter to live a glamorous life with a man she loved. Yet when she told Freya she'd never once stopped thinking about her, Freya believed her.

Freya could still remember the strong conviction that had sustained her throughout her own pregnancy: the belief that motherhood would be her crowning achievement. And when the twins were born, she was exalted, giddy with the knowledge that these tiny girls were why she was here.

They were supposed to be boys. Sylvie, a self-styled foetal diviner, had assured her they were boys. Their names were already chosen. They were going to be Peter, after Freya's father, and Philip, after Felix's, though as Freya told Felix, she had never cared for the name of Philip and liked the idea of shortening it to Pip. Pip and Peter. They would grow up to be gorgeous young men with the twinkling eyes of their father and the intellectual brilliance of their paternal grandfather.

She had never forgotten the moment when the doctor — who seemed to delight in telling Freya *not* to push — finally told her to push now this minute. Freya, duly obliging despite the fact she felt she was giving birth to an elephant, released into the world the first of her babies and asked faintly, 'Is Peter all right?'

She barely had time to register Felix's odd response, 'I'm not sure about Peter, but the baby is beautiful,' before the officious doctor told her to push for England and, four minutes later, Pip followed Peter into the world.

Only they weren't Peter and Pip. Sylvie had made a big mistake and Freya didn't mind at all. She sat cradling her baby daughters while Felix talked to the midwife. She gazed down at their little heads and imagined talking to them about life and love.

They had been such sweet little girls. Anna

had been far sturdier and more confident, organising endless games in which Tess, always so pliant, was happy to join. And then, about the time they left Wimbledon, adolescence kicked in and Freya felt quite at sea with them. Tess took to spending long periods in her room, while Anna spent most of her free time with her terrifyingly confident new friend, Olivia. Sometimes Anna would return from meals with Olivia's family and talk admiringly of the heated discussions that took place round their kitchen table, ignoring the fact that it was difficult to have heated discussions with daughters who were so very unforthcoming.

It went without saying that she was proud of them. Freya was the first to admit that it had taken her a long time to work out what she wanted to do with her life, apart from being a wife and mother, of course. She had already tired of modelling by the time she met Felix and, despite her protestations, found it remarkably easy to leave the clothes shop in Wimbledon. She was delighted that the girls were so focused on their chosen careers. It was possible that they were quite contented with their lives. She didn't *know* because she never had those sorts of conversations with them.

But she should have done. She should have tried harder. It was the same with Felix. All these months, she'd known something was wrong and she'd just paddled along, waiting for things to get better. It was too late for her and Felix. It wouldn't be, it mustn't be, for her and her daughters.

* * *

Felix spent the afternoon cleaning the house. Freya rang at three. Her voice on the phone sounded cold and clear. She was running late, she said. She intended to go straight to Ivy's home before checking in with Pam. She thought she would be with him a little after six.

The last time he'd seen Freya, he told her he wanted a divorce before scurrying off like a frightened rabbit. He had no idea what he would say to her.

The doorbell rang at six twenty-five and there she was in her jeans and long black jumper.

'Freya,' he said, 'come into the sitting room.'

'This isn't a social call. The kitchen will be fine.'

And then her face changed as Serge, huffing and puffing, pushed his way through Felix's legs to get to her. She knelt down to greet him. 'Hello there, little Serge! How are *you?* Let's go into the kitchen, shall we?'

Serge was happy to go wherever Freya wanted. In the kitchen, he stood up on his hind legs, waiting to be lifted onto her lap. She said gently, 'Not now,' and brought her chair right up to the table, clasping her hands together, her face cold and pale.

'Would you like a glass of wine?' Felix asked

'I'd prefer water.'

'Well, I shall have wine.' He attended to their drinks, hating the silence, unable to speak. He joined her at the table and cleared his throat. 'Freya,' he said, 'before we get down to business,

I wanted to say, I am fully aware . . . I have behaved . . . '

'I stayed with my mother last night,' she said.

'Your *mother*?'

'Yes. She got in touch with me at last. She's rather good fun. I always thought she didn't love me but she did. You'd like her. She said something that made me think. She said she and Dad had never been good at talking to each other. It seems that you and I are the same. So I'm talking to you now, Felix, and I want you to listen very carefully and then talk back to me. Do you understand?'

Felix nodded. 'Yes.'

'I saw Anna yesterday. She thinks — and she thinks *you* think — that fourteen years ago I had an affair with Xander Bullen. Is that true?'

He was shocked to his core. He took a swig of his wine and then nodded.

'So all this time — *all this time* — you believed I was unfaithful and you kept it to yourself. You know, I look back at our married life and I wonder if there was anything real about it at all. All these years you've thought these things about me and you never felt I deserved to hear them? You believe Xander and I had an affair. Why? Where's your evidence? Tell me. Tell me *now*.'

Felix's mouth was dry as dust. He took his glass to his lips again, had a sip and put it down again. 'It was after we put the house on the market. I went out to the garden to tell Xander we no longer needed him. I think he must have thought . . . Well, I don't know what he thought

333

but he told me he was in love with you. He said he'd told you and you'd been kind to him.'

'Why didn't you tell me this at the time?'

'I rather hoped that *you'd* tell *me*.'

'I thought you'd be cross with him. He needed the work and . . . ' She frowned. 'You said you believed him. So what's this about? He had a crush on me. I told him not to be silly. He got over it. So why . . . ?'

'He told me it only happened once.'

'It did. He never brought the subject up again.'

'Freya,' Felix said, 'I *heard* you.'

'I don't understand. What did you hear?'

'You remember that night I came home with a black eye? I'd been home before that. I came back at six. Xander's red hat was lying on the hall table. I stood in the hall and I heard the two of you making love in our bedroom.'

Freya sat and stared at him. 'I don't believe . . . Felix, this is rubbish!'

'I know what I heard. It was unmistakable.'

'I don't know what you heard but it wasn't *me*. I wasn't there. At six o'clock, I was at the shop. They'd thrown a surprise farewell party for me. What with all the excitement over your mugging I forgot to tell you. Do you understand, Felix? I wasn't *there*.' She pushed her hands through her hair and he noticed for the first time how tired she looked. 'I'd like that wine now.'

'Right,' he said. 'Right.' He rose and went to the fridge. He heard Freya's voice, sharp and worried, behind him.

'The question is: who exactly *was* upstairs?'

334

Felix gave Freya her wine and sat down beside her. 'What time did you get back from your party at the shop?'

'About seven, I suppose.'

'And were the girls there?'

'I think Tess was out, or she might have been in her room, I can't remember. Anna was in the kitchen making a sandwich. She said she didn't want dinner. She wouldn't talk to me. I don't know why . . . '

Felix swallowed hard. 'There must have been something she said to you. Did she look upset? What did she say?'

'I've told you, she wouldn't say anything to me. I do remember her eyes were very red. I wanted to tell her about my party but she took off with her sandwich and I . . . ' She put a hand to her mouth and rubbed her index finger along her lower lip. 'You should have seen her last night. She was so angry with me. She actually brought up Xander. She accused me of sleeping with him and . . . Why would she do that? Unless . . . ' She pushed her chair back. 'I can't believe it. She was a child. It doesn't make sense.' She stood up and pushed her hair back from her face.

Felix felt a little sick. 'The alternative,' he said, 'is that Xander brought a girl to our house, took her upstairs, made love in our bedroom, while Anna made tea in the kitchen.' He reached across for his tablet and opened the cover.

'Felix?' Freya came back to the table. 'What are you doing?'

'I'm going to try to talk to Anna,' Felix said.

He pressed the Skype button. His eyes remained fixed on the screen as a photo of Anna's face came up along with the word 'connecting'. Freya moved her chair away from Felix.

And now at last Anna herself appeared, sitting on her sofa, smiling and waving. 'Hi, Dad. I've got Tess here with me. She's in the shower. She'll be out soon.'

'Anna,' Felix said. 'I want to ask you something. I won't be angry or shocked but I need you to tell me the truth.'

'Are you all right, Dad? You sound very serious.' She leant forward, concerned, and then her face changed. 'Is Mum with you?'

Freya moved closer to Felix. 'Yes,' she said, 'I'm here.'

'Mum, if this is . . . '

'Do you remember the evening I got mugged?' Felix asked. 'That afternoon, when you finished at school, what did you do?'

They both watched her eyes veer away from the screen. Guilt was written all over her face. Felix couldn't bear it. She folded her arms and asked warily, 'Why?'

'Anna, Xander Bullen told me he had an affair with your mother. One reason why I believed him was because on that particular evening I came home at six and heard two people making love in our bedroom.'

There was a strange expression on Anna's face: half relief and half straightforward bewilderment. 'Dad, I went back with Patrick after school. His mother gave me a lift back. I got home a few minutes before Mum. I don't know what you're talking about. If you did hear a noise upstairs, it wasn't anything to do with *me*.'

Felix could see Tess in the background, draped in a towel with her hair hanging wet around her shoulders. He wondered how long she'd been there. She came forward now and sat down beside her sister.

'It wasn't Anna,' she said. 'And it wasn't Mum. It was me.'

Freya stifled a cry and Felix gripped the edge of the table with his hands. He forced himself to sound calm and measured. 'Tess . . . just tell us what happened.'

'I've been meaning to tell you . . . I just didn't know how to . . . I hadn't realised you thought . . . Xander came over to say goodbye. I was on my own in the house. He said he loved me. I was so happy he loved me. He took me upstairs and we kissed on the landing. He wanted me to show him I loved him. He took me into your room and he kissed me again and then he sort of lost control and I got scared and tried to get him to stop but he didn't seem to hear me and we made love and it hurt and I hated it.' She stared out at them with great haunted eyes.

Felix felt physically sick. He had been in the house when his daughter was being raped in his bedroom. He could have raced up the stairs and saved her. Instead, he had assumed his wife was making love and he'd been too much of a coward to confront her. He could have pulled the bastard off Tess but he had walked away and got drunk. He could scarcely take in the full extent of his culpability. He felt a hand on his arm and moved aside to let Freya speak.

'Tess,' she said, 'of course you hated it. That wasn't making love. That was rape.'

They saw Anna's face crumple and then Tess cried out, 'I'm so sorry. This is all my fault. I never thought . . . I never meant . . . I'm so sorry . . . I've ruined everything!'

'Darling Tess.' Freya's voice was soft and urgent. 'Darling sweetheart, this is *not* your fault, this is not your fault at all. You were thirteen, you were a child. That man was twenty-nine! He was *sixteen* years older than you. If I had him here now, I would kill him for what he did to you. Nothing matters but you. You are *not* to blame yourself. I *forbid* you to blame yourself! Do you understand? I forbid you!'

Tess was half-smiling, half-crying, but she nodded and then she nodded again.

'That's my good Tess. Now I tell you what I want you to do. Go and get dressed and dry your hair before you catch pneumonia. Go now. I want to have a few words with your sister but I'll talk to you tomorrow evening. Do you know that we love you? Do you know we love you very much?'

'Yes. I know. I love you too. And I'm so sorry, Mum, I'm . . . '

'I know you are. I'm sorry too. Now go and get some clothes on and dry your hair. Go now!'

They watched her turn and disappear from the screen. They waited a few moments and then Anna whispered, 'She's gone.'

'Good.' Freya's voice was brisk now. 'Listen

carefully. I want Xander Bullen's address. You told me yesterday that Olivia's friend was going to visit him. I need his address and I need you to find it out this evening and text me the details. I don't mind how late it is but I want the address tonight. Will you do that?'

'Yes, all right. Mum, those things I said . . . '

'There's no time for that now. Get me that information and look after your sister.' Freya reached for the tablet and switched off the connection.

Felix slammed the table with his hand. 'Oh God,' he said. 'That fucking bastard!'

'She was thirteen,' Freya whispered. 'She was thirteen and I never realised.'

'You were brilliant with her. You did everything right. I couldn't speak. I wanted to but I couldn't.'

He walked over to the wall and kicked it.

'That won't help,' Freya said.

'It helps *me*. I should have seen what sort of man he was. Tess was always hanging around him. She idolised him. I remember thinking he was very kind to her. You see what he did? I went out to tell him I had something serious to say and he . . . '

'He used me as his smokescreen. I was just as bad. When he professed his love for me, it seemed very sweet and rather flattering. I remember telling him he should look for younger women.' She took a tissue from her bag and blew her nose. 'It makes my flesh creep to think about it.'

'Do you realise I was *there*? I stood there in the hall, listening to those sounds, hating myself and hating you and all the time I could have stopped it. I could have stopped it.'

'We're both to blame. I should have told you what Xander said to *me*. You should have told me what Xander said to *you*. If we'd had a halfway healthy marriage, none of this would have happened. I enjoyed his attention. I should have seen that he was only fully engaged when he was with Tess.'

Felix kicked the wall again.

'Felix!'

'I'm sorry. I don't care if he lives in the Outer Hebrides. I'll drive off tomorrow and find him.'

'We'll both find him.'

'I'll kill him.'

'That wouldn't help Tess. Feel free to beat him up. I'll beat him up too.' Freya bent down to pick up her bag and stood up. 'I need some fresh air. I'll walk down to Pam's. I told her I wouldn't be long.'

Felix put a hand to his forehead. 'I'll come with you.'

'No. I need to be on my own. I need to think. I'll ring you as soon as I hear from Anna.'

Felix thrust his hands through his hair. 'I could have saved her . . . '

'We can talk about that later. Don't dwell on it now. We'll sort out Xander tomorrow and then we'll sort out Tess.'

He nodded and followed her through to the front door. There were huge questions to ask and huge decisions to make but they would wait. As he opened the door, he said, 'Freya, I'm sorry I doubted you.'

She stared at him without expression. 'You

should be,' she said. 'I take responsibility for lots of things, but it was you who killed our marriage. Goodnight, Felix.'

29

They were lucky and, realising this, set out with an odd sense of exhilaration. Xander Bullen did not live in the Outer Hebrides, he lived in Hampshire, an easy journey along the motorway and down the A34. Freya had brought her case with her. Felix would drop her off in Andover later and she would go back to London and see Tess. For now, all that mattered was the meeting with Xander.

In the car, Felix and Freya discussed strategy. Felix, they agreed, would do most of the talking. Once they'd worked out their tactics they lapsed into a silence occasionally broken by Serge who lay at Freya's feet.

As they turned off the motorway, Felix asked, 'Did you tell Pam what we were doing today?'

'No.' Freya stared out at the green fields on either side of the dual carriageway. 'Mostly, we talked about my future.'

'I see.' Felix hesitated. 'Did you reach any conclusions?'

'I think so. Did you know that Percy left Pam his house?'

'No. I'm glad. She was always so good to him.'

'I suggested I could rent it from her.'

Felix threw her a startled glance. 'You'd move there with Lockhart?'

'Oh . . . I didn't tell you. I left him.' She sounded unconcerned, almost as if it meant nothing at all.

Felix struggled to equate her calm, careless tone with the enormity of what she was saying. He threw a fleeting glance at her. He could see she had no idea what that casual, small statement meant to him. In his mind's eye, he watched tall, dark, handsome Neil Lockhart fall into the quicksand and disappear slowly from view.

'I see,' he said at last in a deliberately neutral sort of tone. 'As far as Percy's house is concerned, I think it's an excellent idea. But it makes more sense if I'm the one to live there. You're the one who works from home. Serge should stay with you. It would only confuse him, being in Percy's house without Percy. And if you really imagine I would let you stay down the road while I swan about in comfort in our home, then you don't know me very well.'

'I don't think I do know you,' Freya said, in that same detached manner. 'I don't think I ever did.' She glanced at the satnav. 'We turn off soon. I feel nervous now.'

'We're not the ones who should be nervous,' Felix said, but he didn't talk again. He came off the dual carriageway and negotiated his way through a series of ever-narrowing country lanes on either side of which were large country houses with big gardens and paddocks. Twice, Felix had to slow down for ladies on horseback.

'Of course we're in *Downton Abbey* country,' Freya murmured. 'The big house they use is in this area.' Her fingers drummed on the window. Serge, sensing her discomfort, tried without success to climb on her lap.

And now, finally, the satnav's perky little flag

appeared and they arrived at their destination. They sat and stared at the old wooden gate and the drive that led to a Hampshire cottage: red-brick walls, tiled roof, wisteria trailing across the front. Traversing the front of the house was a big stone patio with garden chairs and a table. On the right of the drive, there was a square lawn with silver birches in the far corner and a variety of shrubs and flowers along the borders.

Felix said at last, 'He's done well for himself.'

They walked down the drive without talking. Freya held Serge's lead. Felix rang the doorbell.

'Do you realise we're both dressed in black?' Freya murmured. 'We look like Jehovah's Witnesses.'

A voice called, 'I'm coming!' and the door was flung open. A pretty girl in red trousers and a cream top said, 'Hi, there! You're early! Do come in and . . . Oh, isn't your dog beautiful?'

'He's called Serge,' Freya said, 'after Serge Gainsbourg.'

'Right.' They could see she'd never heard of him but was too polite to say so. 'I'll let Xander know you're here. He's just changing. I won't be a moment.'

They watched her run upstairs and heard a brief murmured exchange. Then down she came and invited them into the kitchen. They followed her through the corridor into a big airy room with wooden floors, white-painted furniture and red gingham curtains. A quiche and a bowl of coleslaw covered in cling-film sat on one of the work surfaces. On the middle of the pine table stood a small vase with four white roses. There was a mint-green high chair in the corner and on the wall there was a big noticeboard plastered with photos of a plump smiling baby and various adoring helpers, the most frequent of whom was Xander.

The girl smiled. 'I'm Poppy,' she said, 'but I guess you worked that out!'

'It's nice to meet you, Poppy,' Freya said. 'You have a lovely home.'

'I know. We're very lucky. My gran left it to me.' Her voice trembled for a moment. 'She died three years ago.'

Freya walked over to the photo collection. 'And that's your baby?'

'Yes, that's our little Georgie. She'll wake up soon and then you can meet her. We called her after my gran.'

Freya smiled. 'You look too young to be a mother.'

'I'm twenty-three! Most days I feel very old. Georgie doesn't sleep too well.'

'I remember that feeling! Have you known Xander long?'

'We've been together forever! My parents live in the village. Xander's looked after their garden for years and he used to help out Gran. In fact, he's been amazing . . . ' They heard his footsteps in the corridor and his voice ringing out, 'Hi, there, I'm sorry I wasn't . . . ' He stopped in the doorway and looked blankly at his visitors. His clean hair gleamed as did his crisp white shirt, his sleeves rolled up to the elbows. 'Poppy,' he said, 'I thought you said they were Nina and Jason . . . '

'Oh.' Poppy was embarrassed. 'I assumed they *were* Nina and Jason.'

'No,' Felix said, 'we're Felix and Freya.'

Poppy gazed a little uncertainly at Xander.

'Well,' Xander began, 'it's fantastic to see you both.' He smiled at Poppy. 'A long, long time ago I used to work for these people. They were very good to me.' He scratched his head. 'This is rotten timing, I'm afraid. I'd so love to catch up on all your news, but we're expecting guests. They're rather important. They want to talk about a TV series. Can you believe it? And they'll be here any minute so . . . '

'That's all right.' Felix folded his arms. 'We won't take much of your time. I needed to ask you something.' His eyes rested briefly on Poppy. 'I can say it right now if you like.'

Xander hesitated. 'I think I heard Georgie stirring. Poppy will want to get lunch ready before she wakes. We'd better get out of her hair. Come and look at our pond before you leave. We're rather proud of it.' He strode across to the back door. 'Come this way then.'

It was a beautiful garden. They stepped out onto a stone path, lined on either side with lavender bushes, beyond which were raised vegetable beds. 'We suffer from rabbits,' Xander said. Further on to the left, was a large old garden shed, its roof and walls covered in a cascade of small, starry white flowers — '*Clematis flammula*,' Xander said. 'It begins to bloom in August.' He sounded like a tourist guide anxious to herd his clients through the exhibits as quickly as possible. And now, finally, they reached

346

Xander's pond, an oasis of calm tranquillity. Beyond it a wooden fence separated the garden from a large meadow.

'I do love water in a garden,' Freya said.

Xander put a hand to the back of his neck. 'I'm afraid I'm rather an evangelist where ponds are concerned. I could go on forever about them.'

'We mustn't let you do that,' Felix said. 'We know how busy you are.'

'That's true.' Xander glanced briefly at his watch. 'This is very frustrating. As I said, I would love to chat but . . . '

'I'll be brief,' Felix assured him. His voice sounded friendly and relaxed but his eyes never left Xander's face. 'You see, Freya and I are getting a divorce.'

'Oh.' Xander's expression was one of bewildered concern. 'I'm so sorry to hear that. Is that what you came to tell me? I don't quite see why . . . '

'It was my decision,' Felix said. 'I told her I knew she had an affair with you in Wimbledon.'

'Oh.' Xander's eyes drifted back to the house as if seeking help. 'I'm sure you must be very upset but . . . '

'Freya refuses to admit her guilt. So I suggested we came together to see you.'

Xander gave an incredulous smile. 'I assure you, Felix, there was nothing to . . . '

'The thing is,' Felix said, 'a couple of days before we moved, I came home early from work. I saw your hat in the hall and I thought I heard the two of you making love in our bedroom.'

'Oh dear.' Xander stared out at the meadow. A

thin patina of sweat glistened on his forehead. He put his hands on his hips, stared down at the ground and then fixed his eyes on Felix. 'This is all rather embarrassing. It was a long time ago. I was young. I admit I had a . . . a crush on your wife. I do remember telling you that and, on that one occasion, we did get carried away. I felt very bad about it. I still do. It was never meant to happen. I regretted it almost at once. I know Freya did too . . . '

'Which is odd,' Felix persisted, 'since Freya wasn't there at the time. Tess was. She was the one in our room with you.'

Xander wiped his forehead with his hand and began rubbing his chin. 'Look,' he said, 'I didn't want to tell you the truth but I'm going to have to tell you now. The thing is . . . Tess had been pestering me for months. To be honest, I was embarrassed by her persistence. I came round that afternoon to ask Freya for a reference. Tess was there on her own. She . . . she told me there was an intruder in your bedroom. I went upstairs to investigate and then she shut the door and started to undress. I told her to stop. She said if I didn't make love to her she'd pretend I'd assaulted her. I was scared. I didn't know what to do. I suppose I panicked.'

'And so you felt obliged to have sex with her?'

'Look, it was the last thing I wanted to do. I was terrified. She was getting hysterical . . . '

'Liar!' Felix leapt forward and punched Xander in the face. Xander lost his footing and fell into the water and Felix waded in after him.

Xander struggled to his feet, shouted, 'You

fucking lunatic,' and lashed out at Felix, directing a stinging blow at his face. Felix stumbled, rose again like a deranged leviathan and then lost his footing as Xander hit him again. Felix tried to get up. Xander raised a clenched fist and Freya shouted, 'Don't you dare!'

She'd released her hold on Serge's lead and made straight for Xander, plunging into the pond, throwing back her shoulder bag and hitting him hard on the side of his head with it.

'*That*'s for hurting my family,' she yelled. She hit him again. '*That*'s for raping my Tess,' and then again, 'And *that*'s for raping her too!'

Xander, his arms flailing in a desperate attempt to defend himself, yelled, 'All right, I had sex with her. I didn't mean to hurt her! I thought she wanted it!'

'She was thirteen!' Freya cried. 'She was only thirteen!'

Xander lunged at Freya and now she too fell into the water. Xander pushed his way out onto dry land and was set upon by a frenzied Serge, barking in a high-pitched fury and pushing his teeth into Xander's ankles. Xander shouted, 'Get off, you fucking animal . . . Get off . . . '

'Xander?' Poppy's voice stunned them all, even Serge. Freya ploughed across to Felix who was trying with obvious difficulty to get up on his feet. She helped him out of the pond, picked up the lead and called out, 'Serge, come here.' Serge issued an impressive growl at Xander but did as he was told and allowed Freya to fix his lead to his collar.

Xander seemed to be rooted to the spot. Felix

pushed the wet hair back from his face and limped up to the group of onlookers. Poppy stood clutching baby Georgie. Beside her stood a young couple. They both wore sunglasses and they both held mobiles. The young man appeared to be videoing Xander.

Felix wiped blood from his lip and nodded at Poppy. 'We were just leaving,' he said. 'We can see ourselves out.'

'Come along, Serge,' Freya murmured. She took Felix's arm and they made a slow progress up the path and through the house, their shoes squelching as they did so, a thin trail of water marking their progress.

'I think,' Felix gasped, as they shut the front door behind them, 'I've done something to my ankle.' He winced with pain. 'Would you be able to drive?'

'Of course. Lean on me.' Freya's black shirt clung to her skin like glue. 'We could stop somewhere if you like. We could go into Andover.'

'I am not walking through Andover looking like this.'

They stood by the car, doing their best to shake off the excess water. 'Thank God I have my case in the boot,' Freya said. 'I'll find some dry clothes. We'd better get your trousers off before your ankle starts swelling.'

It took time to pull them off. Freya helped him exchange his wet shirt for her black polo-neck jersey and it stretched with visible protest over his chest. At least Freya could change into her own clothes. She found clean underwear and her blue shirt dress and sandals. Finally, she helped

Felix into the car and Serge leapt in after him. She went round to the driver's seat, looked at Felix and smiled. 'I shall never be able to wear that jumper again. How do you feel?'

He nodded. 'I'm all right.'

'You've split your lip,' she said. 'It's bleeding.'

'There was a big stone in the pond. If I hadn't tripped over it, I'd . . . '

'I'm glad you did. I got to join in the fight. He'd have hit you when you were down. I did enjoy hitting him. He did look scared.'

'So he should be. I know how much stuff you keep in your bag.'

She turned on the ignition and cast another quick glance at him. 'You look like you've been hit by a steamroller.'

'I *feel* like I've been hit by a steamroller.'

Freya put a hand to his mouth and brushed away the thin streak of blood. 'Are you sure you don't want to stop for . . . '

'I don't want to stop for anything.' Felix tried to shift his position and then winced with pain. 'I'd just like to go home.' He put a hand to his mouth. 'I know you wanted to get to London today. If we can . . . '

'I can go back to London tomorrow. I'll make up a bed in the spare room.'

'That won't be necessary.' Felix shifted his stricken ankle with difficulty. 'You can have your own room. I've been in the spare room since you left me.'

Freya put her foot on the accelerator. 'You mean, since you told me *you* wanted to leave *me*.'

351

Felix shut his eyes. 'I don't know what I mean,' he said.

★ ★ ★

Olivia came home at ten and stopped dead at the sight of Anna. 'Oh my God,' she said, 'what have you done?'

Anna was making a mug of tea. She put the kettle down. 'Are you referring to my hair?'

'It's auburn. You've dyed it. Why've you dyed it?'

'Solidarity with my sister,' Anna said. 'She's left you some chocolates on your bed.'

'She didn't have to do that.'

'I know. I told her. I don't suppose you've been able to talk to Jason yet?'

'No, I haven't had a moment.'

'Oh but . . . '

Olivia grinned. 'Of course I've talked to him. He says as long as he lives he will never forget this afternoon.'

'Oh my God, what happened? I've been thinking about it all day. Did Jason get my text? I know my parents wanted to confront Xander. I wanted Jason to know they weren't mad. I wanted Jason to know Xander raped Tess.'

'He got your text when they drove back to London. He couldn't get back to you because he had a call from his boss. He'd sent him the film and . . . '

'Jason sent him a film? What film? Tell me. Tell me what happened.'

'I can *show* you.' Olivia pulled her phone from

her bag. 'Jason managed to get most of the fight on his mobile. You know you said you'd like to beat the crap out of Xander Bullen? Well, your parents got there first.'

'Jason won't make it public, will he? The last thing Tess needs is . . . '

'Of course he won't. He knew I'd want to see it, that's all.' Olivia leant over the kitchen bar, her hands holding her mobile. 'Watch this and see Xander's hopes of TV stardom die a very, very watery death.'

★ ★ ★

There was no question of going back to London. Felix was not well. He made a brave but unsuccessful attempt to eat the supper Freya made and she insisted he go to bed. She took him up a hot drink at ten. He was in his pyjamas but was hobbling about, laying out clothes on the floor.

'Felix,' she said, 'what on earth are you doing?'

'I'm packing. If I can get to Percy's house in the morning . . . '

'You're crazy,' she told him. 'You have a fever. Your left eye is almost completely closed. Your face looks like someone's thrown a paint-box over it. You're not going anywhere. I'll stay on for a bit . . . '

His voice was unexpectedly fierce. 'That's not fair on you. I can't ask you to do that.'

'No,' she agreed, 'you can't. This is my decision. I will stay here until your fever's gone and your face looks halfway normal. Now get

353

into bed.' She stood and watched him struggle onto the mattress. She put down the mug and helped to lift his injured ankle up and under the duvet. 'Good. Now have your drink and try to sleep. Did you take the painkillers I gave you?'

'Yes. Thank you. Freya, I need to say . . . '

'No. You don't need to say anything. Not tonight. Go to sleep.'

She went downstairs and accompanied Serge into the garden, watching him make a fastidious study of the flower bed until he found the right place in which to lower his haunches. She took him back to the kitchen, said goodnight and went upstairs with a glass of water.

In bed, she lay looking out at the stars, revelling in the silence of the countryside. She could hear Felix sneeze and, a few moments later, she sneezed too. She had thought she would find it difficult to sleep tonight but it was easy. All she had to do was to close her eyes.

30

Anna had suggested to Tess that they meet for a brunch on Saturday, a fortuitous idea since she'd stayed up late with Olivia on Friday night and needed a lie-in. She arrived at the café in Fulham at ten thirty and ordered strong black coffee.

She was sipping it with deep appreciation when she saw her sister walk straight past her. She called out after her and grinned at her reaction.

'Your lovely blonde hair . . . ' Tess said. She took a chair opposite Anna. 'I can't believe it.'

'Oh.' Anna waved a careless hand. 'I fancied a change.'

'You've succeeded. You look totally different.'

'I want to look different. I want to be different.'

Tess rolled her eyes and took a seat opposite Anna. 'This guilt trip you have is ridiculous and . . . This is typical of you. It's so extreme . . . ' She stopped as the waitress came towards them and asked for coffee. Anna ordered scrambled eggs, smoked salmon and toast for them both.

Tess leant forward. 'Just so you know, brunch is not on you. I'm not sure I can cope with you being so nice to me all the time. It's a little unnerving.'

'I'd take advantage of it while you can. You know what I'm like. Normal service will soon resume. How did you get on at work yesterday? I was lucky not to kill any patients. I kept falling asleep.'

'Me too.' Tess rested her elbows on the table. 'I've some news. Mum rang me on the way here.'

Anna had a brief vision of her mother wading into the water and laying into Xander Bullen. 'How is she?'

'She's still at home. Dad has flu and she's looking after him. She sounds pretty ill herself but she says it's just a cold. She plans to come back to London later this week. I'm not sure where she'll stay.'

'Won't Neil be waiting for her?'

'No. He's off the scene. Mum broke up with him on Wednesday evening.'

'But . . . ' Anna stared at Tess. 'I saw her Wednesday evening.' She could remember everything she'd said. She'd been, even by her own standards, spectacularly unpleasant. And her mother had run off, in order presumably to break up with the man who might have made her happy. There is no way, Anna thought, I can begin to make things up with her.

'It must have happened after she saw you,' Tess mused. 'Did she say anything about him to you?'

'No,' Anna said. 'Not a thing.'

'It's all very odd. I asked her if there was any chance of her and Dad getting back together . . . '

'Well?' Anna prompted. 'What did she say?'

Tess shook her head. 'The way she sees it, Dad chose to believe in Xander rather than in her . . . Oh, Anna, don't look like that, it's different for you.'

'No,' Anna said, 'it really isn't.' She clasped her hands round her hot mug. 'So what will happen when Dad's better?'

'Mum's moving back to Darrowbridge. Dad plans to rent Percy's house. She said she'll tell us all about it on Thursday evening.'

'I'll be on duty then.' She was almost relieved.

The waitress arrived with Tess's coffee. 'You two sisters?' she asked.

Anna nodded. 'How can you tell?'

'The hair, of course. You don't see hair like that very often. Your breakfast won't be long.'

Anna caught Tess's eye and grinned. She put her mug to one side and leant forward. 'So Mum sounded all right then?'

'She was great,' Tess said. 'She wants to pay for me to have counselling. I told her I've organised it.'

'Have you?'

Tess nodded. 'Marnie's put me onto her lady. She says she's great.'

'Marnie?'

'William's cousin. That's why I couldn't come with you on Wednesday. I rang her as soon as you gave me her number. When she visited Durham, she'd just finished her A-levels and was unsure about her university choices. William had invited me to supper and then had to dash off to his hospital. So Marnie and I spent most of the evening together and we got talking . . . '

'About university choices?'

'We dealt with them quite quickly. And then she told me something terrible. She'd been raped by one of her school-friends a few months earlier. She said he didn't seem to think he'd done anything wrong. She said that sometimes she wondered if he *had*. When William eventually got back he found two very emotional women. He was great actually but . . . the next morning I felt so embarrassed. Apart from Rachel, I'd never talked to anyone about Xander. I couldn't face seeing him after that.'

'So William knew . . . '

'He promised he wouldn't tell you. I felt so ashamed.'

'But you could see what Marnie went through. Why couldn't you . . . ?'

'It's quite easy to give advice to other people. It's taken me a while to believe I could be different if I wanted to be. Anyway, at least I'm going to try. Marnie was very encouraging.'

Their meal arrived and, as they tucked into their eggs, Tess had more good news to impart. 'I had supper with Rachel last night. I was so tired I nearly cancelled but I'm so glad that I didn't. Her brother was there. He's landed another great part in some Hollywood blockbuster. In six weeks' time he's off to the States for at least seven months. He wants me to look after his house again. Same rent as before but with two extra responsibilities. Besides the cats, he's now acquired some goldfish and a Bonsai tree. I'll be back in London Fields. I can't wait.'

Her sister, Anna thought, had acquired a whole new energy. Tess had a meeting with Geraldine in a couple of weeks and more work to be done on Sir Walter. Anna felt she did a good job of hiding her own feelings but it obviously wasn't *that* good. When they said goodbye, Tess hugged her and murmured, 'Don't worry too much about Mum. You'll sort it out.'

Anna had no such confidence. It wasn't just her mother. It was William too. His past tentative attempts to get her to spend more time with Tess now took on a whole new meaning. She had, she felt, let down all those she loved.

And then on Sunday she had an email from him.

'*Here's a photo of one our hospital admin staff. Wife of Miss Diamond's ex. See the resemblance?*' Attached was a photo of a woman with blonde hair in a smart grey suit. She was older and slimmer than Anna but she had the same short haircut and blue eyes. Anna couldn't believe that Miss Diamond's dislike of her was fuelled by a vague similarity with her ex-husband's partner. Even so, she felt warmed that William had cared enough to suggest it.

On Tuesday, Anna carried out a Caesarean section. This was only her second and she took care to arrive in good time. At least there were no complications to worry about. This was Harriet Arnold's first baby; it had proved to be breech and a Caesarean had been advised. Harriet's husband, Ed, a giant of a man, stood clutching his wife's hand while Anna and the rest of the team worked. His features only relaxed when Anna pulled out the baby and he said, 'Oh Harry, you lovely lady, we have a son and he's beautiful. Oh Harry, he's beautiful!'

And that was when everything went wrong. Harriet began to haemorrhage. The baby was placed with the neonatologist. As the red and seemingly endless flow of blood oozed out, the anaesthetist said sharply that he'd have to put Harriet to sleep for a while. Harriet's husband stared desperately at Anna who told him gently he'd have to leave. The anaesthetist moved in, the husband was moved out and Anna tried to ignore the scared faces around her.

She began to massage Harriet's womb but still the blood flowed. She asked for a drip to firm up the uterus and help reduce the bleeding and then, trying to keep her voice firm, asked the anaesthetist to help with more drugs. Nothing was working. Anna's brow was drenched with sweat and she called out desperately, 'Can someone find Miss Diamond?'

After what seemed an eternity, Miss Diamond arrived. She pushed Anna to one side and barked orders for instruments, blood and further doses of drugs. Then she placed a B-Lynch suture round the womb. Anna held her breath and watched as the womb at last fell into line and began to contract; slowly, but surely, the blood settled.

There was an awestruck silence, broken only by the sound of Miss Diamond's heels on the hard floor as she left the theatre.

The anaesthetist looked across at Anna. He said slowly, 'The last woman I saw in this situation had to have a hysterectomy.'

Anna nodded. 'I think Miss Diamond might just be a genius.'

An hour later she went to see her. She knocked on the door of her office and went in. Miss Diamond sat behind her desk, sipping her coffee, cool as a cucumber, just as if she performed life-transforming surgery every day of her life. Perhaps she *did* perform life-transforming surgery every day of her life.

'Miss Diamond,' Anna said, 'I wanted to thank you. What you did for Mrs Arnold was magnificent. I felt so useless. I tried everything I could; I didn't know what to do next.'

Miss Diamond put down her cup. 'Of course you didn't. You're a junior doctor. You're here to learn from people like me. For the record, you did everything correctly.'

'Thank you,' Anna said. She turned and went to the door.

'Doctor Cameron?'

Anna waited for the inevitable killer comment. 'Yes?'

'I like the hair,' Miss Diamond said. 'It suits you.'

★ ★ ★

Freya rang Tess on Wednesday night and said she'd be staying in Darrowbridge for the time being. Felix's flu had turned into bronchitis. She suggested Tess came down to them for the weekend.

Stepping down from the train on Friday night, she could see her mother waving and was attacked by nerves. She wasn't sure what she dreaded most — the thought that Freya might want to talk about Xander or, the more likely scenario, a weekend of careful, tactful avoidance.

It appeared that Freya had no time for tact. As she drove them away from the station, she said briskly, 'Let's deal with Xander Bullen right

361

away, shall we? I should tell you that Felix and I called on him the day after we Skyped you.'

'What? How did you . . . ?'

'He lives in Hampshire,' Freya said as if this explained everything. 'The journey was easy. We confronted him and he more or less admitted he'd pretended to be interested in *me* in order to conceal the fact that he was targeting *you*.'

'Oh.' Tess swallowed. 'What's he like now?'

'He's a creep,' Freya said. 'His wife is young enough to be his daughter so, as the French would say, *plus ça change*. You were the victim of a very nasty man and Felix and I will never forgive ourselves for failing to keep you safe.'

'Mum, if Dad hadn't believed you were having an affair with him, he'd never have left you.'

'That's something else I need to deal with. If your father and I had had a healthy relationship, he would never have fallen for Xander's lies and he certainly wouldn't have kept them to himself for so many years. Your father and I broke up because our relationship was wrong. None of this is your fault.'

'I can't believe you went to see Xander. He must have been terrified.'

Freya gave a small, tight smile. 'I don't think it was the best day of his life.'

'Right.' Tess lapsed into a brief silence. 'How is Dad?'

'He's a little better. The doctor's put him on antibiotics and he's bored stiff with being an invalid. I left him getting dressed. He's determined to join us for supper. I should tell you his face looks a little battered. He fell and

362

hurt himself last weekend. He's so looking forward to seeing you.'

'Me too.' She glanced at her mother. 'Anna sends her love.'

'That's nice.' Freya turned into the drive and stopped the car. 'Here we are,' she said.

Tess gave a long sigh. 'It's good to be home.'

Any diffidence Tess felt as she entered the house was soon overturned by the eruption of Serge, who barked furiously at her for a good three minutes until deciding she might be a friend. She had thought it would be difficult to be together with her parents but they made it very easy. There was a slight formality between them, a new diffidence in her father's tone whenever he addressed her mother. But, almost, one could believe things were as they should be.

Freya had excelled herself with roast chicken and all the trimmings, followed by apple crumble. Over supper, Felix put a hand on Tess's arm and said gravely, 'I have something to say.'

Tess reddened. 'If it's about Xander Bullen . . . '

'It isn't. I wouldn't dream of blighting this evening by mentioning him. It's Scotland. I believe you start your Reading Week in a fortnight?'

'Yes, but . . . '

'Hear me out, Tess. You and I did at one point talk about travelling up to Scotland together. Now in fact . . . What is it, Serge?'

Serge's paw was scratching at the French windows and he uttered urgent little whining noises.

'I expect he can smell a fox,' Freya said. 'I'll let him out.'

Felix watched Freya rise from the table. 'I've promised Ma I'll go up to the Commune for a few days. She'll never forgive me if I don't go. You can come down here on the Thursday evening and then we can drive off together in the morning.'

Freya returned to her seat. 'You can get the night train down from Edinburgh on the following Saturday and be back in London on the Sunday.'

'It's my treat,' Felix said. 'Your mother has gone online and done the sums. I want you to go and I want you to see your friend, Jamie.'

'I would love to go with you,' Tess said, 'but I don't even know if Jamie *wants* to see me.'

'Then you'd better go and find out. Do you like him?'

'Yes. Very much. But . . . '

'In that case, go, Tess. I rarely give you advice but I know of what I speak. If you're lucky enough to find someone who can make you happy, don't mess it up. Do your best to make it work or you'll always regret it.'

In the silence that followed they could all hear Serge barking somewhere in the garden. Freya pushed her chair back. 'I'd better go and see what he's doing.' She went across to the French windows and disappeared into the darkness.

'Dad?' Tess reached for his hand. 'If you really believe all that, why are you planning to move into Percy's house? Why aren't you doing your best to get Mum back?'

Felix gazed out after his wife. 'Believe me,' he said, 'I'm working on it.'

By the end of the following week, Felix was better. He was determined to go back to work after Scotland. He would spend the next week organising Percy's house, he said. When he came back from his holiday he'd spend one last night at home and then move in the next day.

He assured Freya he could sort out Percy's house on his own. Freya announced they would do it together. In fact, it was a relief to them both to spend the days sorting out cupboards, packing up boxes and cleaning floors. In the evenings, they collapsed in front of the television.

When Tess arrived on the Thursday night, she seemed to be alight with anticipation. The next morning, Freya stood in the doorway with Serge and waved goodbye to the travellers. Tess gave one last dazzling smile before the car disappeared round the corner. Freya hoped they'd been right to encourage a meeting with Jamie. It was ironic to think that it was only now when she and Felix were splitting up that Tess was at last confiding in them.

She went back into the house and put Serge down. She felt dispirited about the weekend ahead of her. She'd planned something special for Saturday and on Sunday morning there'd be a visit to Ivy. It still left the evenings to get through. She squared her shoulders and went to the kitchen to find her shopping list. Serge followed her and sat down on his back legs, his head to one side, his protuberant eyes gravely regarding her.

'I know,' she told him, 'I try to be positive. I'm off to the supermarket. The weekend will be fun.'

Serge regarded her with a sceptical expression.

She got back at eleven to find the postman had visited. She put the letters on the hall table and then brought in the food bags, flowers and wine carrier. Serge barked ecstatically at her return. Already she couldn't imagine life without him. She put the kettle on for coffee and went through to the hall to collect her post. There was a handwritten envelope addressed to Freya Cameron, c/o Felix Cameron. She opened it, raised her eyebrows and took it through to the kitchen.

'Dearest Freya, I am writing to let you know that Eva has been most gracious and taken me back. I want to apologise for my extraordinary behaviour the last time I saw you. As I said at the time, I was thoroughly inebriated but that is no excuse. I hope you will find it in your heart to forgive me. I shall always remember you with love and affection. I hope that one day we can meet for a meal and laugh about all this. I think about you every day and shall always treasure our time together. Neil.'

Freya found matches in the kitchen drawer. She dropped the letter in the sink and set fire to it. It made a bright, brief flame but left a black mark on the sink that took some time to eradicate.

She spent the rest of the day making up beds, cleaning the house and preparing the evening meal, stopping only to take Serge for a walk in the woods. At seven, she realised she had no idea which train to meet. She was about to make a call when the doorbell rang.

'All right, Serge,' she said. 'Keep calm.'

Anna stood in the doorway, clutching a huge bouquet of red roses. She looked as nervous as Freya felt.

'Hello, Mum,' Anna said, and then her voice broke. 'Please . . . can we start again, please?'

31

All three of them were nervous. In the front of the car her father and grandmother maintained a dogged conversation about the weather while Tess sat in the back, twiddling her hair with her little finger and telling herself that she hadn't *asked* Jamie to have her over today.

They dropped her off by the Abbey ruins. 'I'll keep my phone on,' Felix told her. 'If you decide you want to join us, we'll be at Burt's Hotel for at least the next hour or so. And then after that, we'll be enjoying the delights of the Autumn Fair so . . .'

'I'll let you know what I'm doing. Don't worry. Have a good lunch.' Tess got out of the car, gave a cheerful wave and crossed the road. She walked up the lane and stopped outside Jamie's house. Once again, she was struck by its familiarity. Almost, she felt, it expected her to be here. It gave her courage. She knocked firmly on the front door.

She waited for what was probably less than a minute but seemed like a lifetime. Then he opened the door and stood aside to let her in. She smiled but he didn't smile back. He wore black jeans and a black jersey. She wondered if his choice of colour was a subconscious statement.

'Thank you for inviting me to lunch,' she said. 'Thank you for getting in touch with me.' His tone was unnervingly formal. He closed the door and moved towards the fireplace.

'I was coming up to Scotland to see Grandma. It seemed wrong not to contact you, especially now . . . ' She stumbled but she had to mention it for why else was she here? ' . . . Especially now my mother and your father are no longer together.'

'You must be pleased by that.'

'Of course I am. I still hope she and Dad might get back together.' She had forgotten the way in which his face could remain so resolutely unreadable. But his eyes, dark, wary, possibly hostile, never left her face. She attempted a smile. 'I did think you might ring me once you heard. But you didn't. I thought perhaps you'd transferred your affections to your local historian.'

'*Martha?*'

'Then I googled her and discovered she's a sixty-five-year-old grandmother.'

'She has your auburn hair,' Jamie conceded. 'In her case, I'm not sure it's natural. She's an extraordinary woman. You would like her.'

'I hope I get the chance to meet her.'

'I'm forgetting my manners,' he said. 'Let's go to the kitchen. I have wine in the fridge.'

She followed him through. His politeness lowered her spirits. She sat at the table while he attended to their drinks. The kitchen was as neat as it had been the last time she was here.

He took a seat beside her and considered her gravely. 'I'm confused,' he said at last.

There was to be no small talk then. 'I can't say

I blame you,' she said.

'Why would you expect me to ring you? You said you didn't want to see me again.'

'I said I felt I *couldn't* see you again.'

'I really can't see the difference. I can't force you to care about me. If you *had* cared, you'd have made a small effort to make it work. Our parents' affair was a convenient excuse for you.'

His perception was impressive and also off-putting. 'Jamie, I don't blame you for giving up. I'm hard work, I know that. Most men would run a mile. I'm seeing a counsellor now, by the way, but . . . I don't blame you for giving up.'

'That's very gracious of you.' There was a slight glint in his eye. 'At least . . . I'm not sure if it *is* gracious. Are you suggesting I *shouldn't* give up?'

'I'm not saying one thing or the other.'

'Tess,' he said, 'I find it very difficult to know what you want me to do.'

'I can see you're a little angry and I sort of understand but . . . ' This was proving impossible. It was like wading through mud. 'Can I just say that it's very difficult sitting here trying to tell you how I feel when you look at me like I'm some crazy alien? It's not easy to admit I'm in love with you. You can ask me to go or say you don't want me . . . '

'Wait a moment.' Jamie frowned. 'Did you say you were in love with me?'

'Isn't it obvious?'

'Where you're concerned, nothing is obvious.'

She looked at him steadily. 'Well, I do. I love you. Now do you want me to go or stay?'

Jamie put his glass to one side. 'I don't want to be rude,' he said, 'but that is possibly the stupidest question you've ever asked.'

She let out a sigh of exquisite relief. 'I thought you might have lost patience.'

'You should have known better. I was attempting to conduct a strategic retreat.'

'Was that what it was?' She smiled. 'It was very effective.'

They sat looking at each other. 'Just so you know,' he said, 'if the doorbell rings I intend to ignore it.'

'Good,' she said gravely, 'so will I.'

He looked at her again. Then, slowly, tentatively, he kissed her. It was longer than last time. Tess had the oddest feeling that Jamie's house was holding its breath.

His eyes went down to her hands and he broke into one of his rare, sudden smiles. 'Hey, Tess,' he cried, 'you weren't clenching your fists!'

★   ★   ★

Felix and his mother sat opposite each other on a table by the window at Burt's Hotel. Their fish and chips had arrived at last and Felix commented on the unusual number of guests in the restaurant.

'It *is* busy,' Maggie agreed. 'Perhaps they're all coming to the fair this afternoon.'

'Perhaps they are. Do you hope to buy some Christmas presents there?'

'I may do. We'll have to see.' She poured out a glass of water from the jug on the table. 'Now,

371

what were we talking about before the food arrived? We've covered Tess and the little dog you've been looking after and you gave me a detailed description of your journey up here.'

Felix nodded. 'I thought you'd be interested to hear about the pub we found in Lancashire. The lunch was excellent.'

'It sounds delightful. But I would like to change the subject now, just in case Tess comes back earlier than expected. I think I should tell you that Neil Lockhart has gone back to his wife.'

Felix put down his knife and fork. 'Has he? That was quick. Freya only left him a few weeks ago.'

'So you know that.' Maggie took a sip of her wine. 'Felix, I don't want to pry . . . '

'That's what I love about you, Ma,' Felix said. 'Other mothers would be desperate to interfere. You understand that it's not your place.' He raised his glass. 'I salute your dignity and . . . your reticence. It's wholly admirable.'

Maggie gave him a withering stare. 'I presume you are *trying* to annoy me? Of course I want to pry. I'm your mother. Are you taking Freya back?'

'I'd take her back tomorrow. Unfortunately, she shows no wish to be taken.'

'I don't understand any of this. I thought you loved her.'

'I did. I do.'

'So why did you tell her to leave you?'

'It's very simple. I thought she'd been unfaithful. I was wrong.'

372

'That doesn't sound simple at all.'

'Those are the facts. I gave her no chance to explain her side of things. I told her very brutally that I wanted to leave her. And then I found out she was blameless. Why would she want to come back to me?'

'I wouldn't say Freya is *blameless* . . . Let's not forget Neil Lockhart.'

'He'd never have happened if I hadn't done what I did. The fault is all mine. I won't have you condemn her.'

Maggie threw up her hands. 'I don't. I feel sorry for her. Felix, I'm your mother. I know you. You must be intolerable to live with. You never say what you mean. Look at you now here with me! I don't believe for one moment you'll accept defeat. You know you'd be miserable without her. You can tell me, you know. Stoicism is a very overrated virtue.'

Felix laughed. 'Ma, you are such a hypocrite. Twelve years ago you had breast cancer and cancelled a visit without saying why. We only discovered the reason six months later. If I'm a stoic, I learnt from an expert.' His phone rang and he picked it up at once. 'It's Tess,' he murmured, his eyes stiff with anxiety.

Maggie watched him sit back and assume a calm, easy manner. 'Hi, Tess, how's it going? . . . Good . . . No, that's fine . . . Tell him to call in. Tell him I'd like to say hello.'

He put the phone down and took a gulp of his wine. Maggie watched him bite his lip and saw his face contort in an effort to control himself. She cut a piece of her fish and ate it with great concentration. Finally, she said lightly, 'Is Tess all right?'

He nodded. 'She's exceptionally all right. They're going out to the castle later this afternoon. There's some function going on and she wants to help. She won't be in for supper. He'll bring her back at ten. He'll call and say hello before he goes home ... She sounds happy. She sounds so very happy.'

★   ★   ★

They all waited up for them. Katherine and Robert sat playing backgammon. Maggie knitted. Sheila and Derek argued amiably about the referendum. Felix chatted to Linda. At a quarter past ten, they all heard the car pull up outside. Katherine went over to the window.

'They'll see you pulling the curtains back,' Maggie protested. 'What are they doing?'

'They're talking,' Katherine said. She moved away from the window. 'Now they're coming in.' Katherine returned hastily to her chair. 'I think we should all try to look natural.'

Maggie raised her eyebrows but resumed her knitting. Katherine and Robert stared intently at the backgammon board. They heard voices in the hall and now Tess came into the sitting room with Jamie who, understandably, looked a little taken aback by the reception awaiting him.

Felix was the first to move. He sprang from his chair and strode over to Tess's young man. 'Good evening, Jamie,' he said. 'I'm Felix. It's so very nice to meet you.'

374

*   ⋆   *

On Tuesday afternoon, Anna sat in the impressive glass foyer of South Reading Hospital, flicking through the messages on her phone. William had been told she was here. He was working. He'd be with her as soon as he could. That was twenty minutes ago. All right, she thought. As long as it takes.

Another fifteen minutes went by and then there he was. She hadn't seen him for three months and he looked pretty much the same except that there was no welcoming warmth in his eyes, and that hurt. 'Anna,' he said, 'your hair.'

She smiled. 'Hi, William.'

'Is this because of the photo I sent you?'

'I'd already done it. I must say Miss Diamond seems to like the new me.'

He sat down beside her. He seemed to be at a loss as to what to say. 'So . . . How are you?'

'I'm well. I spent last weekend with my mum. On Saturday we went to Bath and I met my grandma for the first time.'

'Really? How did *that* go?'

'I didn't think I'd like her. She walked out on her family when Mum was a child. The two of them met up again a few weeks ago. This weekend, she was staying in Bath with her sister-in-law. She took Mum and me to the Pump Rooms for lunch. She greeted me by asking if I was the clever academic daughter or the one who was horrible to her daughter. I told her I was the horrible one and after that we got on well.'

Briefly, William's face relaxed. 'She sounds

fun,' he said. '*Have* you been horrible to your mother?'

'Yes. It's something I'm trying to change. It's one of many things I'm trying to change.'

'Look . . . ' William seemed to be at a loss as to how to reply. 'Why are you here, Anna? I can't stay long and . . . '

'I wanted to see you. I wanted to tell you, to your face, that I know I let you down and I'm sorry. But I think — I really do think — you're being unfair. Can you look me in the eye and swear you've never done something you wish you hadn't? Can you sit there and promise you've never been ashamed of your behaviour?'

William sighed. 'No,' he said, 'of course I can't.'

'So how come I get the cast-out-of Eden treatment? I miss you.'

'I miss you too. But . . . '

'You said you didn't want to see me again. Ever. That's quite harsh, William. I apologised. I transgressed. Am I not to be forgiven? You said you didn't like me now. Is that true?'

'Look,' William said, 'you don't . . . The main reason I said that was to stop you calling me again.'

'Why? If you really don't like me, then I understand. But if you don't, why did you take the trouble to send me that photo?'

He murmured, 'I don't know how to put this. I was upset when you rang that evening to cancel me but . . . ' He stopped and gave a half-smile. 'The thing is, I wasn't just upset. I was jealous. I was properly jealous and that made me see

. . . When I joined St Peter's, I enjoyed spending time with you. I enjoyed it too much. I liked you too much, which meant my love life was rubbish. I don't want to be on my own for the rest of my life. I'm going on dates now. I am getting over you and . . . '

'That's the problem. William, look at me. I don't want you to get over me.'

'I'm sure you don't but . . . '

'William, are you being deliberately obtuse? Do you really want to make me spell it out?'

The left corner of his mouth lifted slightly. 'I think you're going to have to.'

'Oh William!' She squared her shoulders. 'I like you. I like you a lot. I want to be with you. In the biblical sense. In every sense.'

'Anna,' William said, 'I know what you're like. I walk out of your life and suddenly you miss me. How do I know that if I walk back in, you won't . . . ?'

'You don't know. Neither do I. I do know I've never missed anyone like I miss you. When do you finish today?'

'I'm off at six.'

'I can be here at six. If you want me to. I can go and look at the high life of Reading for a couple of hours. Or I can go home and agree that I'll never bother you again. It's up to you.'

'I don't know what to say. It's a lot to take in.' William glanced at his watch and stood up. 'I have to go.' He glanced down at her doubtfully. 'I suppose we could have a pizza together.'

'Great.' Anna nodded. 'I'd like that. I'll see you here at six.' She sat and watched him walk back across the concourse. Her hands were trembling and she gripped them tightly. He was about to go through the swing doors when he turned and smiled at her. A moment later, he disappeared.

Anna relaxed her hands. He smiled, she thought, he smiled. She rose to her feet. It was time to go and explore Reading. Whatever it was like, she knew she would love it.

★   ★   ★

On Saturday afternoon, for the first time since her return to Darrowbridge, Freya sat down at her desk, able at last to concentrate on her November column. She had lit the wood-burning stove. Serge lay at her feet. All was calm. Tomorrow evening, Felix would come back and on Monday, her new life would begin.

She sat staring at the screen, waiting for inspiration to arrive. It didn't. She opened her left-hand drawer in order to find her IDEAS FOLDER, a name that promised far more than it tended to deliver.

Her Anniversary folder sat at the top which was odd since it had lain at the bottom of the drawer for months now. She picked it up. 'Anniversary Stuff', it said, and then, underneath, in Felix's writing, was the word, 'Amended'.

She opened it up and took out the guest list. Felix had made various comments in the margin, alongside certain names: '*Really? . . . Must we? . . . No!!!! . . . Oh God!*'

When had he done this? *Why* had he done this? She was about to put the list back when she found a new sheet of paper. There was a heading: *FELIX'S SPEECH — heavy editing required.* At her feet, Serge began to snore. Freya began to read.

'We are here to celebrate my huge good fortune in having Freya for my wife. The first time I met her was at a wedding. I can tell you nothing about the bride since I had eyes only for Freya. I was sitting in a church pew when this vision came up and asked if she could sit next to me. Imagine an ornithologist exploring some remote part of the country. Imagine his reaction when the rarest bird in the world flies up to him and lands on his wrist. Imagine that and you will understand how I felt when Freya asked if she could share my seat.

She was — and continues to be — the most beautiful woman I have ever encountered. As I grew to know her I found that her personality was as fascinating as her appearance. She was energetic, enthusiastic, funny and bright and endlessly curious about the world. Somehow, I persuaded her to marry me.

Three years later, we became parents to twin girls. Freya had read Anna Karenina and Tess of the d'Urbervilles while she was pregnant. She burned with indignation at their tragic ends. She wanted to call the children Anna and Tess in order to remind herself what was important. She wanted them to grow up to be confident, clever and independent, to be answerable to no one but themselves. They've turned out pretty well.

379

Inevitably, with a mother like Freya, they have beauty as well. I should warn any men foolish enough to try to hurt them that they will have Freya to deal with.

We lived in Wimbledon throughout the girls' childhood and we were happy. Freya had given up modelling when the girls came along and she used her savings to start up a clothes shop which she ran with great success. As time went on her enthusiasm became a little muted. She seemed restless. In retrospect, I think she was bored with the shop and needed new mountains to climb. Her mood was infectious. At work, I'd been offered the chance to head a new office in Bristol. I decided to take up the challenge.

And now we come to my downfall. We had a gardener who was everything I wasn't: young, strong and exceptionally good-looking. He adored Freya but then most people did. Once we'd decided to move, I told him we'd have to let him go. His response was unexpected. He told me he loved Freya and implied they were having an affair.

Now, you're all sensible people and you're presumably making two obvious suppositions: one, that I would of course assume there was something odd about the young man's wish to give me such explosive information and, secondly, that I would naturally tell Freya about it. Let me try to explain why I didn't show such natural common sense myself.

The young man seemed open and honest and genuinely apologetic. I wanted to talk to Freya about him. I refrained. When apparent new evidence came my way I was terrified. If I confronted her, she might admit she loved him? Suppose she left me? That was unthinkable. We were moving away. She'd forget him. It was too dangerous to rock the boat.

And so we came to Darrowbridge. The girls settled down. Freya found a new and lasting interest in genealogy. I tried to forget the gardener and some of the time I succeeded.

A few months ago, Freya took part in a balloon debate. If you ask her about it she will tell you it wasn't her finest hour. She took on the role of Madame Bovary. At the beginning of her speech she proclaimed to the audience that she was an unfaithful wife. It was like a shotgun going off in my brain.

We have since discovered that the gardener was a twisted individual who told me a pack of lies. Since you are sensible people, this won't surprise you, and, in a way, that's not important. What mattered was that I believed him. In the months after the balloon debate I decided I could no longer live with what I assumed was Freya's infidelity. I arranged to go on a work trip to Spain on the weekend of our thirtieth wedding anniversary. The night I left, I told Freya I no longer wanted to live with her. I gave no explanation. I went off to Spain. Freya being Freya went off to London and found a new admirer almost at once. I came home to an empty house and knew I had ruined my life.

By this time you will all say I deserved everything I got. I agree. Why would Freya ever take me back? Well, I have to tell you this is my speech and my fantasy. So yes, Freya has forgiven me and this is why:

She knows I love her. She knows I will always love her. She knows I will devote the rest of my life to making her happy. She knows I will never forgive myself for my past behaviour. I am far too high-minded to resort to emotional black-mail so I have restrained from pointing out to her that our girls would like nothing better than for us to be together again. What I have told her — and since this is my fantasy, she instantly agreed — is that I firmly believe that our best years are yet to come. On our fortieth anniversary, I look forward to telling you all that we have a strong marriage based on honesty, respect, affection, tolerance on her part and boundless love on mine.'

Freya raised her eyes from the document and gazed at her screensaver: a photo of the family at the wedding of Felix's nephew in Cardiff in March. There was Felix in his best suit surrounded by Freya and their daughters, all of them smiling at the camera, blissfully unaware of the dramas waiting to engulf them.

★ ★ ★

Felix arrived home at six on Sunday evening. He turned off the ignition and climbed slowly out of the car. His muscles ached. He stared at his home. All the lights were on and smoke was rising from the chimney which meant that Freya had lit the fire. This was his last evening with her and he was determined to be positive. He would talk about Tess. He would not dwell on his imminent exile. He would refrain for the time being from trying to persuade her to take him back.

He took his hold-all from the boot and let himself into the house. He could hear Freya in the kitchen and called, 'I'm back! I'll just take my case upstairs.'

When he got to his room, he stopped and then slowly put his bag down on the floor. His bed had been stripped. His clothes lay on neat piles on the mattress. He couldn't believe it.

When he went downstairs, he took his bag back down with him. In the hall, he took out the present he'd bought and went through to the kitchen. Freya was at the sink. He could smell chicken cooking in the Aga, so presumably he'd be given dinner. It was easier to attend to Serge who gave him a rapturous welcome. At last, he looked at his wife.

'Hello, there,' he said. 'I've bought something for you.'

She took it without speaking, opened the paper and pulled out the jersey.

'It's cashmere,' he said. 'Tess took me to her shop in Gasterlethen. We chose it together.'

'It's lovely,' she said. 'Thank you.'

He said, 'I saw the bed. Do I take it I am leaving tonight?'

Freya pulled off her plastic gloves. 'I have something to show you. Won't you sit down?'

'I've been sitting in the car all day. I'd rather stand.'

She went across to the dresser and held up the

383

anniversary folder. 'I found this.'

He put his hands in his pockets. 'Ah.'

'Did you mean me to see it?'

'I hoped you might.'

'Well, I did. And it made me angry. Even now, after everything that's happened, you still couldn't bring yourself to look me in the eye and explain it all to me. You had to write it down.' She threw the folder on the table.

'I wanted to . . . '

'I know what you wanted to do. Why couldn't you just *tell* me? If there's to be any hope for us, you have to start talking. If you get depressed, you tell me. No more painful silences. No more long, lonely cycle rides into the darkness. I can't take that now. I love you, Felix, but I *will* walk if you shut me out. I don't deserve that. I'm better than that. It's taken me a long time to see it but I *do* deserve better.'

'Freya . . . '

'How can I trust you if you don't change? How do I know that in another fourteen years you won't tell me you're leaving because I slept with Neil Lockhart? We haven't talked about him. I've been here for weeks and we still haven't talked about him.'

'I didn't feel it was my place to bring him up. I quite understand why you went with him. I've lost any right to be jealous.' He took his car keys from his pocket and put them on the table. 'I did ask Tess about him.'

'What did she say?'

'He told me he was tall, dark and handsome. I think she was quite cross with me at the time.'

'He was all those. He was also an idiot. I think I've told you that already.'

'It's great to hear it again though.' Their eyes met for a second and then she looked away.

'I'll tell you about him sometime. Felix, we've spent fourteen years living a lie. Secrets in a family are . . . they're like moths in cashmere. They dig themselves in and eat their way out. Our family has been torn to shreds because of secrecy. In future, if you have anything . . . anything at all on your mind . . . then you tell me. Do you understand?'

'Yes.' He nodded. He didn't understand anything except for the extraordinary possibility that she might take him back.

'And there's something else. If we are to get back together, we *will* have an anniversary party and I want the speech. You'd have to edit it, in fact you'd have to rewrite nearly all of it, but I want the speech and I want champagne and I want some fun. But most of all, Felix, I refuse to go back to how we were. If you can't accept that, I'll give you supper and then I'll drive you down to Percy's.' She unfolded her arms and went over to the fridge. 'Although, actually, *you'll* have to drive, because I need a large drink.'

He watched her take out a half-empty bottle of wine. He walked across to the cupboard and took out two glasses. 'Fill them up,' he said.

She stared at him. Then, very deliberately, she filled them to the brim.

Later, he would tell Freya — and he *would* tell her — that this had a profound effect on him, that — and he would struggle to describe it — he felt as if his heart shook off the last embers of doubt and jealousy and self-flagellation But, now, at the moment, all he could do was to smile and smile. He was where he should be. He felt as he *should* feel. He was home.